WHITE LAUNDRY

KATE RICHMOND

published by

RANSOM / PUBLISHING

The characters and events in this book are fictitious.
Any similarity to real persons, living or dead, is coincidental and not intended by the author.

Ransom / Publishing
244 Bath Street, Glasgow, G2 4JW

First published 2005

ISBN 0-9550382-0-0

Design and Layout by Mandy Antliff Design
www.mad-about-design.co.uk

Printed and bound in Great Britain by Bell and Bain, Glasgow

Kate Richmond was born in Newhouse, Lanarkshire. After leaving school she studied accountancy, later setting up her own acountancy business. In 2000 she took time out to write this book. She now spends most of her time on a farm in Spain.

for
Fearn, Ciara, William, Eilie & Duncan

CHAPTER 1

Passengers in the departure lounge at Glasgow Airport shot to their feet in shocked silence as the 757 left the runway and skidded along the grass. It slithered and twisted as its wheels ploughed into the turf; careering to the right, just missing the hanger, before it veered to the left, heading straight for the Bishopton slip road. Emma Findlay, like the rest of the passengers, held her breath for all of the sixty seconds until the plane finally came to a halt at the barrier.

Emma was waiting for the announcement of her flight to Amsterdam where she had arranged to meet Julian, her fiancè. Was this a bad omen? The emergency landing had unnerved her, and she wondered if she were doing the right thing. Was it too late to change her mind?

During the last two years, she had been investigated three times by the Inland Revenue; or rather, her clients had been, and each time they had found nothing of importance. However, the last one, which had ended two weeks ago, had been the toughest yet, lasting seven months. The Inland Revenue had gone back over six years of her client's records, which, normally, would have been very much routine. But knowing, as she did, certain manufactured discrepancies within the records, she and her client had endured gruelling weeks of official inquisition. The strain had been mentally exhausting. In the end, they found nothing; however, the lengthy inquiry had taken its toll, and Emma had to get away for a while.

Her accountancy practice, Forbes and Allan, although successful enough, never made large fortunes; and, from time to time, for substantial increases in fees, she and some of her clients had worked together to 'cook the books', altering figures regarding the suppression of sales. She had suffered no qualms about her questionable conduct, and it was only after the Inland Revenue had started the most recent and intensive examination that she began to have misgivings; and those misgivings weren't so much for ethical reasons but more for her own self-preservation.

She was only too aware that the Inland Revenue had her name tucked away in a computer, ready to be tapped at any time, and any further investigation on their part would result in serious consequences. They would certainly nail her the next time.

The compact disc was playing Engelbert Humperdink, 'A Serenade to You'. A parrot was repeating, hello, hello, in time with the music. Hats from every conceivable country, varied in use and style, from the desert to the oilrigs, from a sombrero to a safety helmet, hung from the rafters. Paper currency from the same varied collection of countries was pinned around the bar.

The barmaid interrupted Julian's daydreaming. "Another beer, meneer?"

"Yes, only this time make it a cool schlitz," Julian said. He was waiting for Emma, his fiancè. She's late, he was thinking. He found it odd because she was always on time and he hoped she would be able to find her way. This was the first time

Emma had driven in Rotterdam and it would be quite easy to miss her turning, especially with the articulated trucks thundering behind. Julian had given her directions ten days ago, over a radiotelephone from the middle of the North Sea, and the entire conversation had been plagued with interference and crackling, reducing communication to monosyllables.

Julian had endured a bad day. The barge, which should have been ready to move out two days previously, was still causing headaches, not just for him as chief engineer, but also for those in the higher echelons, the financial 'lurgies', who plagued his life with a catalogue of costs that were rising by the minute and, for which, no budget or provision had been made. His uneasiness was probably unfounded.

Eighteen hour shifts and tiredness over the last week were beginning to take their toll. The ghosts from the past were starting to worm their way back into his normally sane and positive way of thinking. Julian thought he had buried the past, but even his inner and outer strength failed him at times; and could not keep the gremlins from crowding in. At first, the nightmares had occurred with frequent torment, which was a result of the Aster offshore platform disaster. In spite of his training and the emergency procedures, Julian's survival instincts had led him to the spider deck forty feet above the water, and with no way back, he had been forced to jump. On surfacing, he found himself surrounded by a sea of blazing oil. There was no escaping the inferno. It was all around him. The agonising and haunting screams for help from the drowning and burning men would remain with him forever. The typical North Sea night of strong winds and high waves had made rescue attempts difficult. He was one of the lucky ones and, eventually, had been airlifted to safety from the blazing hell. Even now, the memory and the smell of burning flesh was embedded in his mind, and, as long as he lived, he would never forget that night when so many of his friends and work mates had perished.

The clink of the glass on the bar and "Your schlitz, meneer," from the barmaid brought Julian Burton back to the present. He was reassuring himself that, although this bar was tucked away behind all sorts of port authority buildings and depots, not to mention the heavy, overhanging gantries and cranes, Emma would find it eventually, when she appeared out of the sunlight, almost transparent, and walked with an ethereal bearing through the door into the gloominess of the Curzon Bar.

As Emma passed from dazzling sunshine to gloomy haze, she was at first unable to see Julian.

Nothing took shape or form. On removing her sunglasses, outlines of contours began to develop. Now the bar came into her visual range and she knew only too well where Julian would be sitting. Yes, there he was and how pleased she was to see him. She manoeuvred her way through the customers and before she reached him he was already on his feet, arms wide open to engulf her in his love. He lifted her high and whirled her around. He was larger than life. His spontaneous actions made her so happy.

After their initial greetings, complimenting each other on how well they looked, Julian ordered a soda and ice for Emma.

"Now, tell me," he said, "what is this all about and why the urgent visit to Cuba? Our last conversation was so incoherent that I made little sense of what you were saying."

Emma hesitated for a few moments as she sipped her soda; then she told him everything. How, over a period of a couple of years, she had helped a few of her clients to alter their financial records; and more recently, another client had been investigated. This, she told him, was the third time in two years, the strain of which was becoming too much. She had to get away for a few months; take a break.

"They found nothing untoward, but I know my luck won't last forever," she concluded.

"Why Cuba?" Julian asked, after she had finished.

Emma was a bit surprised at his indifferent reaction, but replied, "No particular reason. I haven't been there and I just thought it would be a good move; sort of, well away from everything."

She waited to see if he was going to make any further comment, and then asked, "Have you nothing else to say?" She really thought he would blow his top. Not that what she had done was really bad. That sort of thing happened quite a lot in the financial world and, compared to insider dealing, embezzlement of funds, and such like, her unprofessional conduct was a grain in a sandstorm.

"I was just thinking. What you've done isn't such a bad crime when you consider the petty pilfering that goes on everywhere. People are at the fiddle all the time. Take office staff, for example, they nick things left, right and centre. They nick pens, pencils, erasers and stationery. Bricks, cement and tools go missing from building sites; bandages, plasters and ointments, from hospitals; and so it goes on. It's not as if it's armed robbery."

"You don't seem to be too concerned, then?" Emma, queried.

"No, not at all. You see, I've a little confession to make myself."

Emma sat up and began to take note, wondering what was coming. Julian wondered how best to begin; or even, should he begin at all? But it was a bit late to backtrack.

"Some time ago, about three years, I was in Colombia," Julian began, "and while I was there a piece of machinery had to be returned to Holland; it was faulty. Well, I got an idea how to make a little extra cash. I obtained a small quantity of emeralds and diamonds, placed them in with the faulty machine and I'm sure you can guess the rest. When I got to Amsterdam, the machine had arrived. It was just a matter of collecting the crate and retrieving the stones."

"What did you do with the stones?"

"Sold them, of course."

"I can hardly believe you. All this time you've been smuggling emeralds and diamonds and didn't let on to me. Mind you, that explains why you always appeared to have endless cash. I often wondered about that. And do you still do it?" Emma queried, after some thought.

"No, I haven't had the opportunity recently and, in any case, I did it more for the kicks than anything else. It was a kind of game, Emma. You see; I wanted to find out if committing that kind of felony would make me feel any differently, act differently, or change me at all."

"And did it?" Emma asked.

"No, not that I noticed."

"Were you not afraid you'd be caught?"

"A little, I suppose, but the risk wasn't all that great. You see, the shipment was always addressed to the company and I was not responsible for the packaging. Any one of a number of people would have had the opportunity to conceal the stones."

"Well, I must say, I'm quite stunned by all this. I suggest we get out of the confessional box. It's depressing me somewhat," and Emma immediately began to think about her forthcoming trip to Cuba and the months of endless sunshine that lay ahead.

She was pleased she had told Julian about herself; she felt lighter already and a heavy weight was lifted from her shoulders. She was unable to suppress her own enthusiasm about her forthcoming trip and now gave vent to her natural effervescent self, allowing her normal frivolous and bubbly personality to prevail over the draconic and severe attitude she adopted for business. She leapt from the bar stool and gave him a whopping, big kiss.

"However," she continued, "enough of my current activities. What's been happening in the oil business?"

Julian emitted a carefree laugh. "The same old story. My contract here finishes as soon as that barge is in the North Sea and on its way. It's already two days overdue, but all the repairs should be completed by the day after tomorrow when she will then be towed to Norway. I'll be sailing with her for three days and, on a satisfactory finished audit report, a Sikorsky helicopter will fly me to Stavanger at which time I'll be on the road again."

"And your next assignment?" Emma questioned.

"That, my dear, will suit you right down to your little panties. It is in Venezuela of all places, Lake Maracaibo in fact. So we could be seeing a bit more of one another, just for a change."

Emma picked up at this. Their relationship was healthy

enough, but the prospect of seeing him more was a welcoming thought. Due to the type of work that took him all over the world, wherever a problem arose, they could be out of contact for months.

"This time it's onshore Lake Maracaibo," he continued. "And an apartment thrown in."

"That beats living in a cardboard box, hands down," Emma sarcastically replied.

"Now, now, Emma, I know we've had some unusual halls of residence in the past, but things will change, you'll see."

Emma reflected - unusual halls of residence? She couldn't believe the state of the places they had been. She recalled, staying at a site compound somewhere in Equatorial New Guinea where, when the rains came, she was up to her knees in mud, and a flea ridden shack in Jakarta; but she did concede one thing, it was always great fun and full of adventure.

"How long this time?"

"Oh, somewhere between six and eight weeks. But you know as well as I do that anything can happen in the oil business and things can change over night. When I get to Maracaibo you can join me, OK, is that settled?" Julian said, making an effort to make up for all those lost months.

"Great, but why the sadness, Julian?"

"I'm getting a bit long in the tooth. This is a career for a younger man. I should like to settle somewhere in the Caribbean, with you of course," he hastily added.

"What, the old bulwark weakening?" was Emma's rhetorical answer.

"Not that so much. But just imagine, Emma, buy a beach

home, the ultimate escape fantasy evoking dreams of lazy summer days whiled away on sandy beaches next to a crystal blue sea. It's the perfect place to drift away; and a room with the ultimate view - a living area open to the sea. Then, from time to time, take the odd contract to keep the cash flowing. That wouldn't be a bad deal."

"You paint a desirable picture. But, Julian, all those years you've been in the oil business, you must be worth millions. You could retire tomorrow," continued Emma.

"That may be the case, but I've travelled so much during the last number of years that I would need to do something. Anyway, we'll see what transpires after Venezuela."

"Yes, you have always been a bit of a globe-trotter and your nomadic life will be a difficult one to change," Emma concluded.

Their conversation was never ending with so much to tell and so much to give. They chatted on with animated enthusiasm; their laughter ringing out, changing the dimly lit bar to light tones.

"That's 5.30 now. Let's say, half an hour to the hotel, an hour or so for ablutions, which takes us to dinner at 8.00 o'clock. Will that give you enough time to get yourself ready, Emma?" Julian enquired.

"Why yes, more than enough."

"I've taken the liberty of reserving a table at Vor Donk's for 8.00," went on Julian.

"Good, then let's hit the road," was Emma's reply.

They drove, in silence, along mile after mile of shipyards, rail yards, petroleum storage terminals, refineries as big as townships, chemical plants, storage plants, thousands of wharfs, and along the streets of the Europort, where the sun, producing a different hue at that hour, danced over the hanging gantries and cranes to the surrounding buildings, giving the sleeping steel structures a dull beauty.

On reaching the hotel they made their way to Julian's room, where, to their delight, a bottle of chilled wine awaited their arrival. Emma made straight for the bathroom.

"Nice touch," she voiced as she began to strip off, having no reservations about her nudity. On the contrary, she was proud of her shapely figure and slim, athletic legs that, whenever possible, were put through the motions, under the heading, of "keeping fit". She was on the verge of stepping into the foamy froth, when Julian appeared at the door with two glasses of the wine.

"One for you, sexy," he said as he handed her a glass. Julian exuded romantic fun and frivolity when around Emma. He grappled with her in a joking and lurching manner. Pulling her close with his free hand, he whirled her around. Drops of wine trickled down her back forcing her to wriggle against him. He felt the softness of her full breasts against him and he felt aroused.

"Enough of that," he jokingly teased. "You incorrigible nymph. But I like it."

She wriggled free and they stood for a moment looking at one another with controlled passion, but their eyes expressed everything. I could give her one right now, he thought, but the moment passed as he turned away. She soaked herself in the bubbles as she sipped. She felt good. She was elated by the female passion, which is awakened by man's sexuality. This feeling in her was very natural, but not often had she experienced it; only Julian brought out her true instincts.

The restaurant was situated on the river; one of those small private bistros where the chef and the proprietor was one and the same person, and who took paramount time and pleasure in the preparation of his cuisine. His dishes and sauces were all freshly made; nothing was pre-cooked, and, when the seasons were right, he gathered, from his own garden, the herbs that he skillfully used to produce the mouth watering flavours for which he was famous. They settled at the table by the window, which had a full view of the river and the small boats, going back and forth in their deliberate business. Some of them were carrying light cargo while others were carrying tourists who, as the sun coloured the evening sky from coral to grey, were imbibing in light refreshments and animated conversation.

A small ferryboat putt, putted its way towards the wharf at Vor Donk's, and, while the boat continued to bob up and down in the water, the boatman, with the practised balance of an acrobat, off loaded supplies on to the side walk, in effortless, rhythmic skill.

"Mr. Julian, it's good to see you again," Jan emitted, through his full moustache as he presented himself in front of them.

It never surprised Emma that, no matter where they were, Julian was always known and recognised.

"Remember your last visit," Jan Vor Donk continued; "when you requested Nuit St. George, well, I have twelve bottles, just for you. How many do you want chilled, meneer?" he asked Julian, knowingly, handing out the menus.

"Tonight, duty calls, Jan. I have many problems. What do you say, Emma, two bottles?"

Emma smiled her affirmative as Jan hobbled away muttering his disapproval.

"I'm sorry, Emma, but due to the delay with the pipe-lay barge, I must go back to the Europort and kick ass. We've overrun the deadline by two days and I'm getting hassled from those above."

Emma had been here before and this was part of their life; romantic greetings, brief stays and sad farewells. She had accepted it long ago.

"You know things will change after Venezuela."

"Yes, I suppose so." Emma could do nothing about it. But in any case she had lots to think about, too. She was so looking forward to Cuba and she would meet up with Julian in Maracaibo.

They enjoyed a full meal of battered Dublin Bay prawns, followed by suckling pig trimmed with roasted prunes and apricots in white wine sauce, washed down with an elegant sufficiency of Nuit St. George; and to sweeten their palate a helping of baked pears soaked in Van der Hum liqueur. They held hands, laughed and were happy, and the evening, all too soon, spent itself in the relaxed company of two people very much in love.

Reluctantly, Julian had to leave and they picked their way along the narrow, cobbled street, filled with tables, umbrellas, and happy smiling faces, postponing the sweet sorrow of parting as long as possible. Eventually, they reached the end by the bridge, where they held on to each other, tightly. His unwillingness to say goodbye, again, was more obvious than usual, as if he had some sort of premonition. They held close for sometime and there was a deeper sadness.

"It won't be long this time, seven days or so," Julian whispered into her sweet, smelling hair as they stood on the bridge over the river.

CHAPTER 2

Julian flagged down a cab for Emma before hailing one for himself, and, as much as he was saddened at leaving her, his thoughts immediately reverted back to the current problem with the pipe-lay barge, the LB10.

She had been purchased, ten years before, by McRoberts, and, at that time, required extensive repairs, which had been duly carried out. However, through time, although the yearly maintenance program had been activated, it had been McRoberts's practise, for financial reasons, to patch and repair parts, as opposed to renewals and replacements. Now, the dividend was due. Julian had inherited the problem.

McRoberts had insisted that the LB10 should be in working order by the 12th, spending minimum resources and expecting maximum performance. Julian knew only too well that continued short cuts and cut backs would eventually result in loss of time and money. The ferryman must be paid.

This year, to nobody's amazement except McRoberts, the hydraulic system operating the pipe moving equipment had been such, that it failed to attain the required standard of operability under the HSE regulations. The pipe handling equipment on the barge had last been used to lay 48-inch diameter concrete coated steel pipes. As each section of pipe is 12 metres long and weighs approximately 10 tonnes and a section of pipe is moved every minute of a twenty-four hour day, it was not surprising that the equipment took a lot of punishment.

This had surely been the case during the last job, which had taken six months. Yes, there had been problems during that six-month period, and, on every occasion, instead of shutting down the equipment and making proper repairs, quick remedies had been the order of the day in an effort to keep loss of production time down to a minimum. There was now no way that the equipment could be brought to its required standard of operability without considerable renewal of parts, and, in particular, the hydraulic equipment. Julian's initial audit report had pointed this out.

The audit report also stressed the fact that, as the barge was scheduled to work in UK waters for its next contract, the HSE would be keeping a very close watch on their operations, especially in light of the relatively newly published Cullen Report in the wake of the Aster Offshore Platform disaster, not to mention the myriad of new legislation which had come into being as a result of that report.

McRoberts had procrastinated for three weeks, deliberating between repairs or renewals, between risk and safety, between £50,000 and £1,500,000. Julian had also reminded Jean le Roux, the chairman at McRoberts, that, should there be a major accident, the Health and Safety Executive would throw the book at them.

"God damn it, man," Julian had stormed at le Roux. "You have no choice here. You authorise the 1.5 million or the HSE will close you down for good."

He eventually got the green light, the piece of paper, the go ahead, six weeks ago, to complete all necessary replacements, leaving him with an impossible deadline.

Apart from the defective hydraulics, there were a number of other general recommendations. The fire detection system was inadequate and subsequently a more modern system had been refitted with a central unit for the loops, a display showing the location of the fire and a printer giving a hard copy of any messages and alarms. The accommodation was found to be archaic and the cabins were now redesigned to sleep two with adjoining wash areas.

Julian was mulling all this over, when the cab pulled up at the security gate.

"Harry Ferguson has left a message for you. He wants you to go over to dock 3 as soon as you arrive," the security guard announced as Julian was checking in.

"Did he say what it was about?"

"No, just that," replied the semi comatose guard, who, at this hour, had no wish to become involved in any kind of lengthy conversation.

"All right, should he call again, let him know I'm on my way," Julian concluded as he was leaving the office.

It was a ten-minute walk to dock 3 and on his way he wondered why Harry was still on duty at this hour. He should have checked out at 10.00 o'clock. However, he reflected, Harry most probably stayed on to run some tests. The LB10 now lay in the water and had been running trials for the past two days, failing every one. The problem had occurred when the replacement part had been fitted. It had put such a stress on the remaining parts, that they in turn needed replacing. It had become a never-ending story.

Julian, still wearing his dinner suit, climbed the gangplank to find Harry at the top anxiously pacing the deck.

"Evening Harry," Julian greeted. "Got it fixed, then?"

He had only to look at Harry's face to see that all was not well.

"I think we had better go below where we can talk," replied Harry gravely.

They made their way in silence down the hatch, down the steep stairway, into the confines of the steel enclosed corridor, to arrive at the office of the chief engineer.

"Right, Harry, what's this all about?"

"We've had a fatality onboard."

"What happened?" enquired Julian, "someone had too much to drink and suffered a heart attack or fell down a hatchway?"

"No, nothing like that," responded Harry, "we were carrying out trials on the pipe moving equipment and there was an accident."

"What the fuck were you doing carrying out trials? You know full well we are still waiting for a new accumulator and manifold before we can commission that equipment."

Harry replied, somewhat sheepishly, that he was trying to hurry things along since he knew they were working to a tight deadline. Julian saw the deceit in his statement straight away. He knew that the sycophantic Harry had been trying to score points over him and creep around the bosses again. But he was also aware that this was no time to start a slanging-match between the two of them, and, instead, set about to limit the damage.

"Who was killed?" he asked, "and how the hell did it happen?

Harry, looking decidedly uncomfortable, replied that it was one of the new Croatian men, whose name he could not pronounce. He had been crushed when a section of pipe had jumped its carrier, and, at the same time, a part of the pipe carrying equipment had slammed into its stop position instead of being brought to a halt in a controlled manner.

Julian fired question after question at Harry in a machine-gun like way. Had the police and the ambulance service been informed? Had the scene of the accident been disturbed? How old was the victim and had his next of kin been informed? There were many more in a similar vein, such as, had the head office and in particular public relations been informed, and, perhaps more important, had Harry remembered to cut off the crew's ship to shore telephone links? The last thing that Julian needed, at this moment, was an army of Dutch newspaper reporters descending on him and screwing things up. He had enough on his plate without that. To each question Harry responded in a hurt tone as if he was the innocent bystander in all the mayhem that had been unleashed as a result of his actions.

Yes, the police and ambulance had been notified. No, the scene of the accident had not been disturbed. The victim was a 21-year-old youngster, who had managed to escape the war and genocide in the former Yugoslavia, only to end up as a corpse in one of the most tolerant nations of the world. He was still in the position where he died, pinned by ten tons of pipe, trapping both his crushed legs to a bulkhead.

Julian could imagine the poor bastard, perfect from the thighs up and with all his vital organs intact. His heart would obviously be still now, either due to loss of blood from his crushed legs or died more quickly and mercifully as a result of shock.

What he did not say, but what Julian was painfully aware of, was that an experienced hand would never have got himself into such a potentially hazardous position. But he did not dwell on this, knowing that a large percentage of the newly hired crew had absolutely no experience of working in this sort of environment. McRoberts had managed to hire people from the four corners of the globe and still attain a measure of uniformity. Without a doubt, they were all cheap; they were all inexperienced, and each and every one of them had no understanding of the English language or any common tongue. A veritable tower of Babel was this workplace.

Julian and Harry sat in silence for a while deep in their own thoughts, and after some time Harry was the first to interrupt the stillness.

"Julian, those parts that we've been waiting for have now reached Cherbourg. But if they are sent by freight, they won't reach here until the day after tomorrow."

"That's no good. We must have them in place by then. We are running out of time. Due to this delay, the Norwegians are threatening to pull out of the contract and they will use any excuse to re-negotiate at a lower rate. And should that come to fruition, Old Cocker, you and I will be looking for another job."

Julian thought for a moment and went on.

"It's simple, Harry, get one of the lads to drive down tonight, and stress that he must be back tomorrow morning, midday at the latest. So, let's move it. The LB10 could still be in the water and on her way in two days."

"What about the Croatian lad?" Harry went on.

"Look Harry, you attend to the Cherbourg problem and

let me worry about this mess. I'll speak with the police and the paramedics," Julian impatiently retorted.

"Now, on your way man."

Harry eventually stormed off while Julian busied himself with the accident report, which would take days to complete, but a start had to be made. His reluctance to proceed to the scene of the accident was apparent. He had witnessed so many accidents and dead bodies in his time that by this time he should have become indifferent, but this was not the case. He never became indifferent.

The corridor leading to the double joint area was deserted and exuded a deathly chill. On approaching, he thankfully saw that the police and the ambulance service had already arrived. Thankfully, because of the detached and clinical manner in which the services crew handled this sort of thing, allowing him no time at all to dwell in the past. His equanimity was paramount. He could not allow the Aster disaster, any longer, to interrupt his mental composure.

They went through the normal procedures, spending hours questioning him and some of the crew who were in the area, during which time the paramedics had certified the lad dead, zipped the body in a body bag and removed the corpse from the barge.

"We'll be back tomorrow to continue our investigation," said one of the policemen.

Now that there was a possibility of being in the water, in time, Julian did not relish the thought of being delayed yet again, and informed them of his intended departure.

"Hopefully our enquiries will be completed by then, but until we give you the OK, you will stay in the harbour," the second policeman informed Julian, in no uncertain terms.

The two policemen, finishing for the time being, bid Julian a good morning and strolled off. Julian watched them for a while as they made their way along the side of the LB10, up the plank, passing the overhanging gantries and behind the office until they were out of sight. Exhaustion and frustration had completely depleted his energy and he collapsed into a fitful sleep; and long forgotten was the wonderful evening he had spent with Emma.

Harry, the following morning, had been the first to rouse Julian from his cabin. He had spent most of the morning running general tests on the generators, main engines, tensioners and winches, while he sent Harry off to do runs on cranes and check evacuation drills, life boats and life saving appliances. This, together with paper work, kept them busy and well out of one another's way. By midday, Harry's man had returned from Cherbourg with the long awaited replacement parts.

The engineers had been set to work immediately and had been hard at it for eight hours before Julian went below to check on their progress.

"How long now?" he had asked one of them.

"All is going well, Boss. Another two hours. We're just about ready to do the runs."

"Great, make that one and a half and we'll just make the tide."

Turning to Harry he asked if he had been in touch with the shore.

"No, not yet."

"Well, you know the procedure, bad news first and be as brief as you can. Tell them you'll be handing in the accident reports before we sail with the tide."

The police investigation being concluded, they had made the tide and the LB10 had been duly towed out. During the three days that followed, Julian ran his tests. The hydraulics worked like a Swiss watch and the trial runs at sea were completed together with all operability reports.

Julian was standing by the helicopter deck, now, as the Sikorsky approached to lift him to Stavanger. He was beginning to feel good about himself again. Another job well done against all odds. The last five days had been a nightmare but in the end they all pulled through, each man giving two hundred percent of himself. He climbed into the helicopter and as she turned and banked away from the barge, he looked down at the grey water of the North Sea, cold and uninviting. His thoughts, for the first time in days, returned to Emma and he imagined warm, welcoming arms holding him close.

CHAPTER 3

She supposed she would return to Havana and pay this intriguing city another visit, the next time, hopefully, for pleasure, and not to chase her suit case from one end of Cuba to the other. Emma would liked to have spent time savouring the atmosphere of the Calle Obispo, once the heart of the entertainment district, awakening the memory of a past era in the cafes, bars and corner restaurants, bathed in the aroma of rum. She would get great pleasure in visiting the historic 18th Century, Baroque Palacio de los Capitanes Generales, the seat of colonial power until the end of the 19th Century; or to visit the former presidential palace, now the Museo de la Revolucion, tracing Cuba's struggle for independence from the Spanish. She could imagine enjoying an evening at the world famous Tropicana nightclub, once frequented by gangsters and the elite, where scantily dressed dancers twirled and swayed under the stars to passionate Caribbean and Latin American rhythms of mambo, pachanga and salsa; or even to wander the slopes of the Sierra Maestras and the mountain villages, that harboured Che Guevara and his guerrillas, their mountain hideout during the 1950's revolution led by Fidel Castro. But alas, not this time.

It had been a gruelling journey and, to Emma's frustration, arriving at her destination, Varadero, two hours previously, only to board the plane again and chase her suitcase all the way to Havana.

"Why had the tour operators not informed her that she had a choice of airports?" she fumed as she stood outside the airport building. She was the only passenger travelling back to Varadero, and had been waiting for a taxi, now, for one and a half hours.

Her transport eventually arrived, and back on her journey again she began to relax. Tomorrow would be the real start to her holiday and she was looking forward to it very much. But in the meantime she would concentrate on getting to the Bella Costa Hotel.

They drove in silence through the narrow arteries of suburban Havana, passing tall apartment blocks, whose facades still sported the markings of the revolution and Che Guevara graffiti of bygone times; small modest dwellings with their doors open to the evening, revealing the poverty inside, and, on the outside of which, the red clay yards accommodated the squatting men folks, who, with serious faces, were in deep discussion about some current topic or other.

As the orange sun descended into the red horizon, they left the city behind. The road from Havana to Varadero wound its way along the coast, visiting sleepy villages and, from time to time, turned inland towards soft forests and lower slopes of rolling hills.

They had been travelling now for one and a half hours when the driver interrupted Emma's thoughts.

"We stop shortly for some refreshments."

Emma felt that the statement required a reply and said, "That would be just fine."

The car began to decelerate and gently it slipped off the main highway onto the gravelled entrance of a roadside cafe, and as it came to a scrunching halt the driver reassuringly said, "You can get out now, Senora, for 10 minutes."

Emma made her way to the almost deserted bar, where two customers stood at the far end and another two stood by a parked Mercedes. She ordered a black coffee, and as she lit a cigarette, she had time to reflect that there was something surreal about all this. Instead of feeling apprehensive in this situation, the middle of nowhere, accompanied by a driver she did not know, she felt strangely at ease. However, the thought had hardly crystallised, when she became aware again of the men standing by the stationary Mercedes.

Was it her imagination, or were they watching her a little too closely? She dismissed it for the moment and assumed that their visible interest was on account of her sex, but it left her feeling slightly uneasy. Her driver, who had been hired by the tour operators and presumably trustworthy, appeared to notice nothing unusual. But, as she was about to step into the taxi, Emma surreptitiously glanced back at the two men who seemed to be stealthily preparing for their own departure.

Five minutes had passed, and when Emma looked out the back window she could not help but notice that the car travelling behind was the same Mercedes that had been parked at the roadside cafe. However, she wasn't too perturbed, because all she wanted now was to reach the hotel as quickly as possible and get her head down.

The terrain levelled and flattened out and the neon lit names of hotels sprung up and flashed in the distance.

"Are we in Varadero?" she asked the driver.

"Yes, Senora," was the welcomed reply.

With relief the Bella Costa neon light shone out like a beacon beckoning her approach. It took her a few minutes to check-in, and on arriving at her suite, she threw open the door, dumped her cases and flung herself on top of the bed. All thoughts of the two men and the Mercedes had faded to pale.

Well rested, Emma rose early the following morning, full of enthusiasm for the day's prospects. She enjoyed her usual breakfast of fresh orange juice, fresh tropical fruits and two cups of black coffee, after which she went off for a stroll in the hotel grounds, which, at this time of the year, were ablaze with vibrant colours of the Caribbean.

Somewhat later that morning, lying on her sun lounger under a parasol, Emma had time to savour the tranquillity and the contrast between the stretch of the long white sandy beach and the turquoise blue sea. To all and sundry she was a bona fide, happy-go-lucky tourist, not someone who was keeping a low profile. She decided to spend the day mingling and chatting to those around her.

A little sun would hit the spot. As a younger woman she had been a sun worshipper, but with all the scares about skin cancer she now took her vitamin C in small doses. Her body at the age of forty-two was still in good shape, her breasts firm and her legs shapely, but a little muscle toning in the shape of a swim would not go amiss.

Her thoughts were miles away. She found herself thinking about David whom she had divorced five years ago. But he had remained a good friend, advising her on financial matters and backing her whenever she required his help. She knew he had truly regretted what had happened, and the consequences of which had lead to their separation and finally divorce. She was still reminiscing when the Cuban lifeguard came up to her.

"Excuse me, Senora, my name is Lemay and I am on duty at this part of the beach. I was wondering if you would care to try parasailing from the speedboat?"

"I think not, Lemay," Emma replied, noting that his English was fairly good.

"You will enjoy it. It is great fun, and you'll be in safe hands with my friends."

She thought about it for a moment. Her life in Glasgow had been somewhat humdrum of late, dedicating too much of her time to work, and she could benefit from a bit of fun and excitement.

"Yes, on second thoughts, OK I'm game," she voiced.

She went to the edge of the water and splashed the salt water all over to cool her body. This, she thought would definitely take her mind away from her business affairs. She was just about to make her way towards the parasailing when she was approached by a man who appeared to be a guest at the hotel. He was dressed for the beach; a pair of swimming trunks and a beach towel slung over his right shoulder.

"Pardon, Senora, for the intrusion, but I couldn't help overhearing your conversation with the lifeguard," he opened, in hesitant English.

Emma turned towards him, wearing a questioning smile.

"Yes?" she said.

"Please, let me introduce myself. My name is Carlos Lopez," he said as he extended his hand.

"And you are?"

"Emma Findlay," she replied, offering her hand in return, assuming he was about to give her some advice about the water sport upon which she was just about to embark.

However he continued on another vain.

"Are you American?"

"No, I'm Scottish," she replied, and had the distinct feeling he already knew the answer to that question.

"Ah, yes, I couldn't quite place your accent. Come, let us get out of the sun and join me in a fresh orange juice," he said.

"I'd love to, but I've just arranged to go up in the parachute," Emma replied, politely.

"That can wait until later. Come, come, over there in the shade," and she felt herself being guided towards the palm-thatched parasol. She skipped across the burning sand that stung the tender soles of her feet; and, when they reached the sanctuary of the parasol, she was introduced to another by the name of Eduardo Jimenez.

They made room for her on one of the sun loungers and offered her an orange juice, which she thankfully accepted.

"Are you on holiday, Senora?" Carlos Lopez asked.

"I am indeed. I'm taking extended leave and hope to travel and visit some of the interesting places, not only here in Cuba, but the Caribbean and Venezuela. What about both of you?" Emma asked, her curiosity getting the better of her.

"Yes, we are on vacation also," replied Eduardo Jimenez, struggling with the English language.

"And where are you from?" Emma asked.

"We are from Colombia, from Cartagena."

“Oh, I’ve heard about that city. Isn’t that the one that’s surrounded by walls and dates back to the early 16th Century?” Emma enthused, now becoming interested.

“Yes, the Spaniards built impregnable walls to protect the city from ‘pirate attacks’, and, at one time, it was the Spanish main port in the Caribbean,” Lopez informed her.

“It sounds like an interesting place to visit,” Emma replied.

“If you were to go, the charm of the city; the ‘Palacio de la Inquisicion’; the ‘Casa del Marques de Valdehoyos’, and many other places of interest, would keep you there for days.”

“Well, I’m sure I’ll be able to fit it in. You see, I’ll be in this part of the globe for a few months,” Emma concluded.

They chattered on in this way for some considerable time. She learnt that they were businessmen, taking a few days rest in Cuba, and both of them had wives and families back in Colombia. She, in turn, told them she was an accountant and was also taking a bit of a rest from her office in Glasgow. She was also happy to tell them about her fiancé, Julian, and that she would be joining him in Maracaibo in a few days time. She was enjoying their light-hearted exchange that she almost forgot about her prearranged parasailing.

“You must excuse me, now. I must be off. It’s been a pleasure meeting you,” and Emma hurriedly took her leave, thinking, at the same time, that her holiday in Cuba was starting to look good.

Her spirits were high as she walked across the sand to the speedboat, where two Cubans were gathering the parachute together after the last hire. One jumped into the boat and the other picked up the harness, which was put round her back and shoulders. She was quite happy to let him do up the straps and fasteners, and, when he had completed and checked the safety clips over again, he announced that she was all set and ready for the air.

He positioned her in the shallows and explained briefly the procedure which, at that point, appeared to be simple and safe enough, then jumped into the boat and waved ' good luck and enjoy.'

The boat went slowly at first and then began to gather speed. She felt herself being lifted above the waves. Yes, she signalled, everything was fine. Gradually, as the boat increased in velocity, higher and higher she soared until the parachute reached its zenith.

It was exhilarating being up so high and looking down at the now small boats, water skiers and bathers. Varadero beached stretch ahead like an ecru ribbon, bordered with the azure blue of the sea and speckled with multicoloured dots of the beach umbrellas and bathers. She was locked in another world, soaring high and enjoying the vivifying freshness of the gentle breeze, taking her away from all sense of reality. It was a feeling of utter freedom and abandonment as if she was taken out of her own body and was transformed into the archangel herself.

She gradually became aware that the boat was heading farther out and rounding the point, but she was still savouring the euphoric sensation. The white beach below her stretched on forever; and breaking on a blue sea, white-capped rollers agitated the water. Looking far ahead towards the horizon she was unable to discern sky from sea; they melted into one. There was nobody on this section of the beach; no hotels to disturb the vista; it was deserted; it was beautiful; it was the way nature had planned it. Goodness, it was so long ago since she had felt this daring and completely immersed herself in this fancy.

'The sky is so blue,' she thought, 'no wonder the young fall in love in the sun, or is it falling into love with life?'

Suddenly, she was aware that they were bringing her down now, well out of sight from the beach. 'Why should they be bringing me down here? Perhaps this is part of the adventure; a quick dip then back up again,' she reflected. She had seen this sort of practice before. The boat had reduced speed and Emma felt herself being lowered into the water. The tips of her toes, first, brushed the surface of the water, and then her legs. The sensation of the water pummelling through her legs was invigorating to start with, but she was now up to her waist and sinking deeper. She was now hoping like mad he would increase speed, otherwise she would be totally submerged; a position she surely wouldn't relish.

"Open up the throttle, you stupid bastards," she called out, but her voice was carried away by the sound of the waves.

They're dragging me, the shits. I'm not that confident in water to withstand much more of this, Emma's brain screamed, at which point the boat began to gather velocity and up she went. Now, well above the waves and thankful to be in the air, once more, she began to relax, but not for long. Once again she was lowered into the water, then up again, now down again, and now in the water.

"What the hell is he playing at? This isn't fun any longer."

Emma was beginning to panic. She knew that if the parachute became submerged it was curtains for her. This was not fun; this was for real. They hoisted her out of the water once more, only to cut the engine dead again. She landed in the sea with a mouth full of salt water, encapsulated in the parachute and enclosing her in an air bubble. She began kicking and lashing out, but she was still strapped into the harness, which restricted her movements. She kicked now to keep her head above the water. Still engulfed in the parachute, she felt her body being dragged through the water. Oh God! They're crazy!

She was sure she was just about to end her days, drowning, at the hands of two ass-holes. Is this the way it's supposed to be? She was frightened; and, although she had enough air to breathe, she knew she had to escape from the harness, somehow, in order to stand a chance of getting out of this mess alive. Why the hell had she not paid more attention to the way the harness had been fastened in the first place? She was feeling around with her hands, her eyes smarting from the salty water, legs aching and painful. The release catch must be somewhere. She fumbled with something she thought could be the device. She struggled with the clasp for what seemed ages, then, miraculously, the parachute went up and over the top. Now, clear of the parachute she was able to see the boat a short distance ahead. The leering faces of the two Cubans on board, laughing and jeering as if this was the greatest joke of all times, said it all; normal Cuban humour? Was she paranoid and imagining all this?

They fished her out, dumped her into the speedboat and, when they reached the Bella Costa beach, literally threw her out at the edge of the water. Still wearing their smug faces, they called out, "Hope you enjoyed your trip, Senora," and sped off.

She crawled up the beach to her towel, exhausted, and collapsed on to the sun lounger.

"I have been dreaming, haven't I," she said aloud to no one in particular.

When she had regained a more normal state and her breathing under control, Emma had time to reflect and wondered if Lemay was involved in any way. Had he actually put them up to this practical joke? She made a mental note to quiz him later.

Not a 'drinker', but Emma was in need of a stiff vodka after her awful ordeal. She chose a stool at the rear of the Mirador bar, overlooking the beach, where she had a full view of the rest of bar and the entrance. She had quickly visited the powder room where she freshened up; and was glad that she had done so, because, when she looked into the mirror, the face that was staring back at her was that of a stranger. It was expressionless and it had a ghostly glow. She applied 'teint dore', 'flawless finish' and blusher, to give her face life; pinched her cheeks and applied 'rouge pur' lipstick; and finally stuck a false smile on her face.

Juan and Jesus were feeling very pleased with themselves. They had had a good day so far. The Senora had paid 30 dollars for the trip, 300 dollars from the stranger who had wanted Emma scared a little but not harmed and another four trips, to the last of which they were now on their way. They had enjoyed the bit of fun with Senora Findlay; it had added some excitement to an otherwise ordinary day. Four hundred and fifty dollars for the day, and extra from the last trip, because the hire wished to be collected from Cortes Bay which was round the point at Cardenas.

Jesus and Juan had known one another since school days when they had tinkered around the marinas, doing odd jobs and mending engines. They had worked on the boats that the Americans had left behind in the sixties, after Castro had nationalised his country's industries. With no replacement parts available, the engines had been repaired, again and again, with a variety of spare parts from an assortment of different boats, to the extent, that none of them resembled or had any bearing on their original specifications, and, after thirty-five years, were still going strong due to the dexterity of the Cubans.

"Good day today," Juan shouted to the other over the noise of the engine.

"Yes, we could do with more days like this," the other agreed.

Four hundred and fifty dollars was a lot of money for a Cuban to earn in one day and they knew it.

"I wonder why the stranger was so interested in Senora Findlay," Jesus reflected aloud.

"It's none of our business, so don't be going around asking questions," retorted Juan.

They were on a high and anxious to finish the day to get back to their families with the good news about the day's windfall, and perhaps give them a special treat. Yes, life was good again.

They were now rounding the point at Cardenas and Cortes Bay was in sight. It didn't take them any length of time and, as they neared, they could see that the beach was deserted but for a few seagulls. Their decision to beach the boat at the far side and wait for their hire seemed the sensible thing to do. They sat down by the edge of the water, still laughing, joking and in high spirits, and discussing how they would spend the good earnings when they spotted two men walking towards them from the other side.

"That'll be them," Jesus announced excitedly, indicating towards the advancing figures.

"I can't think what anyone would be doing this far out," Juan contemplated, "but I suppose it's no concern of ours, as long as they pay up."

They waved in recognition and the approaching men returned their acknowledgement. Juan and Jesus waited a few minutes before standing up and then began walking slowly towards the men. There were only 10 metres separating the two groups when Juan sensed that something was not quite right and, like a trapped animal, felt he had to run and escape, but to where? The boat was now some distance behind and there was not enough time to run back and start the engine. All he could do was to stand there transfixed as the two men came up to Jesus and himself. The last thing that Juan and Jesus felt was the flash of pain from the nine millimetre as they fell to ground and were no more.

She was mulling over the boating incident while sipping her vodka, trying to get some feeling about the whole affair, when Lemay, the Cuban lifeguard, hurriedly approached her table and sat down.

"Lemay, what's wrong? You look ghastly."

"You remember the two Cubans, Juan and Jesus, who took you parasailing...oh it's awful...well, their boat, it has been found off Cardenas. It is wrecked; it is in pieces. Some sort of accident," Lemay spluttered.

"What about the two Cubans?" Emma stuttered.

"Only parts of them have been found, the bits that the barracuda didn't eat, they're dead!"

"Oh my God, how awful. Are you sure that it's them?"

"There was enough remaining to identify the two of them and bits of the boat."

"What could have happened?" Emma asked, her voice quivering.

"There are rocks over there. Perhaps they were fooling around, ran the boat into the rocks by accident and it exploded. Nobody knows for sure. The police are over there now," Lemay concluded.

Emma remained silent trying to absorb Lemay's tragic news. Although the Cubans had given her a bit of a fright, earlier that day, she felt no resentment towards them and certainly didn't wish this dreadful ending for them. She did not believe, as a rule, in coincidences; but the incidents of the past two days, the two men in the Mercedes, the unexpected dip in the sea and now this, had, at first, seemed too extraordinarily unrelated to cause her any concern. Now, she began to wonder if there was something in all this that could be linked together. She had obviously been so deep in thought to notice Lemay's departure, and when she looked around to question him further, he was nowhere in sight.

Dismissing everything as having no causal connection, all thoughts now turned to Julian and wished he were with her at this very moment. She needed to talk to him, but he was out of contact. She hated this part of the relationship; when she needed him, he was never around.

CHAPTER 4

From where Carlos Lopez was sitting, he could see Emma as she made her way from the dining room towards the cocktail bar. She was a striking woman, Carlos noted; carried herself with dignity; a woman of mettle, and he wondered what was going through her mind at this moment. Eduardo and Carlos had discussed her earlier about the possibility of recruiting her into their business. They were sure she possessed the hallmarks for a likely candidate. So, after dinner, Eduardo went off to contact the top man, their boss, Roberto Garcia.

He waited for a few minutes and then followed her into the cocktail bar, which, at this time of the evening, was milling with guests. After a glance or two around, he spotted her at a corner table by the fountain. Casually he made his way over, and showed surprise at seeing her.

"Ah, Senora, we meet again. May I join you?"

"Why of course," Emma replied, pleased to have some company in the midst of the prattling, throngs of people.

Like many of the top 'narcos', the cocaine traffickers, Lopez and Jimenez had to flee Colombia in light of the extradition treaty with the United States, which had been revoked a number of years earlier, being reinstated due to an increase in cocaine hitting the streets of America. The treaty recognized the shipment of illegal drugs to be a crime against the US. As such, it called for suspected drug traffickers to be extradited for trial to the United States and, if convicted, imprisoned. This struck fear into the hearts of men like Roberto Garcia, Carlos Lopez, Eduardo Jimenez and many others.

Lopez and Jimenez had two objectives. The first one was to keep a low profile until the Constitutional Assembly in Colombia voted on extradition; and secondly, to recruit carriers while they were in hiding. They saw in Emma a strong possibility. She was a worldly person, knew her way around and, in their opinion, she recognized the importance of money. But they also recognized that a wrong approach, at this point in time, would be disastrous and ruin any chances of success.

With this in mind, Lopez set about befriending Emma and adopting a softly, softly manner. Lopez's soft-spoken, educated voice worked well for him, and he used it to his greatest advantage. He charmed her with such skill that was flirtatious without being sexual. He made her feel completely at ease and she responded with warm conversation and a wealth of information about herself, in particular, the reason behind her taking a break from business.

While they were exchanging personal snippets, Jimenez returned and sat down across from Lopez. Emma didn't see the nod of approval that passed between the two men. Unlike Lopez, who had handsome, aristocratic features, Jimenez was swarthy with a rough, weathered face. He was of peasant class, a 'campesino' and spoke with a thick uneducated accent.

"Senora, my English is not good. Please forgive me," Jimenez struggled.

"On the contrary. I understand you very well," Emma replied, trying to make allowances. "I speak a little Spanish, so I'm sure we'll get along just fine."

Carlos Lopez wanted to get straight to the point. He felt he had seduced her enough with his soft talk and charming ways, although he was anything but charming; he, in fact, was a ruthless and dangerous gangster, more dangerous than his counterpart, Eduardo Jimenez, who was a rough type but possessed a softer side to his nature.

"Emma, we would like to make a business proposal and, as you have no pressing business at the moment, we believe it will be to the advantage of all of us," Carlos began.

Emma couldn't wait to hear what was coming next.

Carlos Lopez came right to the point. He realised that Emma was an intelligent woman and any attempt at whitewashing, would, all too soon, become apparent. At first, every hair on Emma's body bristled with an energy that she couldn't explain; even months later when she tried to put the pieces together, she still couldn't explain it. But, as Lopez continued his well-planned recital, that feeling of energy was replaced by a stupor, enervating her reactions. He misconstrued her deadpan face as strength of character. In actual fact, it was of unadulterated fear as his words formed a terrifying picture.

As the soporiferous state lifted, Emma's mind became clear. She knew what she heard was real, and that she hadn't imagined it, but she couldn't believe that, sitting across from her in this very normal setting, there were two drug traffickers.

"Well, what do you think," Jimenez eagerly asked, half in English and half in Spanish.

"No, you don't need to give an answer just now. Take your time and think about it," Lopez quickly interjected, so as not to put any pressure on Emma.

"It's quite all right," She began, when she found her voice. "To be completely frank with you, I could never become involved with narcotics, drugs, cocaine trade or whatever you call your dealings."

"But you're not being asked to become involved in drugs. We are asking you to pick up a parcel containing money and to deliver it to a bank in the Dominican Republic."

"Yes, but it's from the illegal cocaine trade and, as I see it, that's the same thing," Emma replied indignantly. "You are asking me to launder drug money."

For Emma, anything connected to the illegal use of narcotics was taboo. She had never taken drugs, and the very mention of the word cocaine sent her into a tirade of denunciations.

"There's no need to make a decision, now. Sleep on it for a few days."

"I'll be in Maracaibo, then", replied Emma, hoping that this would be an obstacle.

"We'll contact you, there."

And before Emma could make any further comments, Carlos Lopez and Eduardo Jimenez bade her a good night and left.

Emma sat on at the table for a while, mulling over what had been said. At first she was shocked. She had never even known anyone that had taken drugs, and was confused as to why, of all people, she was being singled out to launder money.

But the longer she sat and thought about their proposition; the idea didn't seem so outrageous. She could never resist a challenge, especially one where money was involved; and the undertaking to carry a bundle of money to the Dominican Republic now seemed a feasible enterprise

CHAPTER 5

David Findlay arrived at Varadero Airport somewhat tired and exhausted. Just before leaving for Cuba, he had attended a last minute meeting in London, at which there had been a few raised voices of disagreement and discontent on a delicate matter concerning a further injection of capital into one of his client's companies. He managed to calm everyone's tempers and a cool-headed and controlled discussion had continued, but it had then left him, at the last minute, with the onerous task of negotiating terms with the banks involved and that had consumed all his physical and mental energy. He had scurried all over London to three different banks, through the unbelievable traffic jams, in a short space of time, but it had all been worth it, he had secured the necessary loans.

He was looking forward to seeing Emma again and was intrigued by her urgent summons. It had been a few weeks since last he had seen her and he always made the effort to meet her demands whenever the need occurred. Well he knew that it was only in an advisory and business capacity for her, but that didn't make any difference to him. He still felt upset and guilty about what had happened to their marriage. It had been his fault entirely, he had blown it, he had been a fool and had realised it only too late.

He had had a few relationships since then. It had been 5 years since his separation and he hadn't met anyone who could light a candle to Emma. Yes, he had been in love with another woman during the course of his marriage or so he thought at the time, and, what he now referred to as 'a fling', had been a costly one. But he had always loved Emma.

He had fallen into the trap that many had done before him and had allowed himself to be seduced. Normally, not a man who would have been flattered by a Spanish beauty's attention, but she had known how to turn a man's head with all her endearments, promises and her undying love. He had never seen her again since the day that Emma had found out about their affair. He, if it were in his power, would like to turn back the clock and have Emma with him again. All that was history now, well in the past, and nothing could be done about it; but he still had deep feelings for her and in a way loved her still.

He had collected his luggage, and since Emma had indicated that the negotiations would only take a few days, he had decided to travel light, bringing only a few clothes. Outside, in the bright sunlight, he got a taxi and was now on his way to The Bella Costa Hotel.

"This will be a pleasant change," he chuckled to himself. The prospect of a few days in the sun made him feel good again.

The journey from the airport to the hotel had taken twenty minutes, just enough time for him to shake off all thoughts of regret and adopt a happier frame of mind for Emma, who could never tolerate the down at heel.

To Emma, life was a full wind and had to be filled to its

limits, and so it was for all those that surrounded her. Every day she woke up, she looked forward to the challenges. There was nothing pessimistic about her and even if she had doubts and regrets she never showed them.

He was just about to cross the main foyer when he saw her by the elevator.

"Emma," he called out. And at that she turned around.

"Oh David, it is good to see you," she said as they embraced one another

"Well, I must say, you're looking as stunning as ever."

"You're just an old flatterer. You'll never change," Emma replied. "And you're not looking so bad yourself."

"First," David went on, "let me dump my luggage and have a quick splash. It'll only take me ten minutes; then, after that, I'll meet you here to go over everything that's happened. Does that seem like a good idea?"

"Great," Emma replied. "I'll see you over by the fountain in ten minutes," her voice ringing out with eagerness.

As David hurried off, Emma went to the fountain bar, where she ordered a large club soda with ice, sat down and went over in her mind the best approach with David. She also wanted Julian to be here, but he was somewhere between The North Sea and his next contract in Venezuela.

As she sat there her mind drifted back to that last night with David, all those years ago, when the ringing of the telephone in the bedroom had aroused her from a quiet nap and as David had been in the shower Emma lifted the receiver.

"Yes," she had said, "Can I help you?"

"David," the female voice on the other side of the line had replied.

"He's having a shower."

The line had gone dead. Emma had then called out to David and told him that she thought reception had been on the phone.

"Should it ring again, leave it, and I'll answer the phone in here," he had said, a trice more assertive than usual.

A few seconds later the telephone had rang out again, and she had heard David lift the receiver. For a moment she had thought nothing of it, not until she had overheard his placatory voice.

"Look," she had heard him say in a soft voice, "everything is all right, I'll call you back," he had whispered.

Immediately, she had sensed that something was not quite right; had opened the bathroom door to find David in a state of panic and, by this time, his voice was slightly raised.

"Look, I said I will call you back."

"Who is that on the phone?" she attacked. She had felt fear and panic as if she were totally losing control of something she didn't quite understand yet.

"It's nothing, no concern of yours," David had replied, holding his hand over the mouth piece.

This was not the reaction she had expected. He was always one for interrupting others to put her in the picture. As she recalled, she had then darted back to the telephone in the bedroom and, on lifting it, had informed the person on the line that, she, Emma, was Senora Findlay.

"I don't believe you," the female voice on the line whispered, incredulously.

"I am Senora Findlay," she had firmly stated, "and if you still don't believe me, call reception."

David, overcome by an attack of self- preservation, had followed her from the bathroom and standing behind her at that moment, pressed the receiver down and the line went dead.

"Well, I think we can start by assuming that she is not the receptionist. Who exactly is that?" she attacked.

"It's no concern of yours."

"It most certainly is a concern of mine. Who is that?" Emma had demanded, her voice having risen an octave or two. She had begun to shake with nerves.

"Well, if you must know, it's nobody, nobody of any importance, just someone who has been chasing after me," had been David's weak explanation.

"A woman of no importance, so unimportant, that she has knowledge of your movements and whereabouts, even the hotel that you're in!" she challenged

"We're on holiday, for God's sake," she had screeched, "I don't wear it, you're lying and I know it, even if you don't admit to it," she had finally declared.

A scene had ensued and the outcome was he had been having an affair and a commitment to some Spanish woman. Emma had been stunned, and although their marriage had drifted a bit over the last two years, she still had felt that he was her best friend and that he loved her. She had not given their relationship much thought, because she, herself, had also been under pressure at her office. But this! This! She had been devastated. Emma had never felt so hurt in her life. Had a knife ripped through her body from end to end she would have felt less pain. David, she had always thought, was solid, trustworthy, honest, and had constantly confessed that he had no interest in other women and was devoted to her. It had been obvious from the woman's voice she had known nothing about Emma, or even that David had been married. She had felt no sympathy for her at all. She, Emma, had given David eight good years of her life and the betrayal had been devastating.

That night she had wept a lot with the painful cry of a wounded animal. David had tried to console her and help her, but it hadn't worked. He had tried to justify his actions, by implying that their marriage had been over. Meanwhile, Emma had no idea of what had been going on and assumed everything was fine, just the way they had always been.

The following morning David had left early for a prearranged appointment and they had looked at one another in disbelief at the pain and suffering this was causing both of them. He had looked at her in a way he hadn't looked at her for a long time, and held her, and without saying anything, for there was no more to say, he had left.

"In another year the pain may disappear," she had mumbled and had said, "just go David, you have a plane to catch. I'll be fine, but she had not been fine, not from that night until some time much later, when it had been finally over for her, too; the day she had heard the fat lady sing.

As far as she could ascertain, David and the woman had never got back together and what a waste; to have hurt her for nothing and she had allowed it to change her and her life. Today, she still recalled the emotions she held within. To her friends she had said that it was just one of those things, and had explained that they had drifted apart due to their separate and diverse businesses. But she knew she had not stopped loving him and never would, but she hated him at the same time for the deceit and breaking the unconditional trust that she had bestowed on him She had never told him she still cared and had not contacted or spoken to him for a long time. She had directed her attorney to settle everything.

The telephone at the Fountain bar rang out, releasing her from the reflections of a painful past, just as David was approaching.

"Now, update me about this great deal," David said, as he sat down.

Emma remained silent for a few moments, knowing that, initially, David would be as shocked as she had been, and to choose her words carefully would be sagacious. She reiterated what Lopez had proposed, even naming the big boss, Roberto Garcia; and she was right, David looked stunned.

"No, Emma, no! Have you lost your marbles?"

"All I want you to do is think it over; don't make your mind up now," Emma replied, not too surprised at his first reaction.

"I won't change my mind. You're talking drugs here. You know I would do anything for you, but not this."

"We wouldn't be involved in drugs. We would be picking up the money in Bogota, carrying it to the Dominican Republic, taking our cut and depositing the remainder in a bank account," Emma said, trying hard to play down the drugs aspect.

"No matter how you try to justify this, the fact remains that you are becoming involved. No, wait a moment, Emma, I haven't finished. All right, you're not growing the coca leaf; you're not involved in the process of turning the leaf into the white substance, cocaine; you're not selling it to the addicts; and you're not involved in extortion and killings, but you are aiding these thugs to continue their trafficking, by helping them to launder money."

"I thought the same way as you. But then it came to me that if we don't do it somebody else will, so, why not us? We'll never get a chance again to make this amount of money. Think about it David; a few runs and we'll all be well set up, and that includes Julian."

"So, Julian already knows about this?" David queried.

"No, not yet. I've arranged to meet him in Maracaibo in a couple of days. I'll speak to him about it then."

"Let's change the subject," David suggested, becoming irritable about the entire business.

The following morning and to Emma's surprise, David informed her that he could be interested in the 'laundering business', with the proviso that Julian was in agreement. This was music to Emma's ears; he was a cautious kind of a creature, typical accountant, and every move he made was with a mindful deliberation. After what Julian had told her about the emeralds, she knew that he would go along with the set up, not so much for the money but for the thrill of the game. On the other hand, Emma's sights were completely focused on the dollar bills; the last chance to make that nest egg for herself.

In the meantime, while they were waiting for Julian's arrival in Venezuela, David suggested he would fly to Bogota and familiarise himself with the city. He then made a call to an old friend who, at the present time, was working with the international banking company Barrie and Jones, in Bogota, and told him of his travel arrangements.

For Emma, everything was going like clockwork, and the only thing she had to do was to inform Lopez and Jimenez that she was now seriously considering their proposal

CHAPTER 6

Charles Forsyth, known to his friends as Chas, was head of investments with Barrie and Jones and had been transferred from the London office some two years before. He enjoyed the casual and carefree Latin American way of life and had met a young Colombian woman, uncomplicated and fun loving, who, to some degree, gave him a certain amount of protection from local drug related street crimes, not to mention the more serious, kidnapping.

The draconian existence that he had led in London had begun to eat away at him and with each wasted day he had become more despondent and bored with his lot. The British weather hadn't helped either, and when he finally decided to take up the position in Bogota, the change had been immediate.

David and Chas went back a long way - not that they had seen much of one another in recent years - to a time when both of them played rugby and that sense of fraternity and camaraderie, which was prevalent in the team, remained with them to this day.

Chas had arranged to meet David at Eldorado Airport and had been waiting only a short time when he appeared through the international arrivals.

'Same old David,' Chas reflected, 'sharp as a pin in his fine Italian cut suit'.

After their usual greeting they made their way out of the airport towards the car park A hazardous journey along the busy Autopista Eldorado left David in no doubt about the chaos in this South American city. Horns blasted out like badly tuned trumpets; screeching of tyres and smell of burning rubber, not to mention petrol fumes that in a short time gave him a bumper of a headache. They eventually arrived at Chas's apartment in the area of the Trade Centre. A light snack, prepared by Pina, Chas's girl friend, awaited them. On finishing, David and Chas excused themselves and casually sauntered to the terrace to reminisce. Their conversation was mainly about finance and the effects it had on world economy, which led Chas to ask the reason for David's visit to Colombia.

David explained that a client who was in the export business was interested in extending his activities to Colombia and he, David, had been sent to obtain information on likely importers; the usual stuff, share capital, trading details, reputation, in other words a company search.

"I believe I can help you there," Chas offered. "I have access to all that information back at the office. I can get you a list of importers and do a search on whichever ones you select."

The last thing David wanted was to involve his friend, but he couldn't backtrack now, and neither could he let him in on the real reason for his visit. 'In any case,' he reflected, 'what harm would a company search do?'

Sometime later, Chas returned from his office armed with a list of the most successful importers together with his laptop. Enthusiastically David went along with the charade and they settled down in front of the screen, but he did feel guilty about having to lie to his old friend.

"Try these two; they're here in Bogota," David said, handing Chas the list with a red marker through two companies.

"Right, first we'll get Romero Importers up on the screen," Chas said, eagerly.

Up came Romero Importers, registered in Bogota 1990, directors José Gaviria and Gustavo Martinez. Then they went into the company's financial report; turnover for the previous year 1.5 billion with a 3.8 million net profit, after tax.

"It appears to be solid enough. Try the other."

Chas hit the keyboard again and after a few moments Santos Pardo Import/Export co., registered in Bogota 1988, directors Luis Sanchez and Roberto Garcia; share capital 1 million dollars, fully subscribed, turnover 2 billion and net profit, after tax, 5.7 million, appeared on the screen.

"Is there anything wrong?" Chas asked.

"No, nothing at all," David lied, recalling the name, Roberto Garcia.

In order that Chas wouldn't notice his changed expression, David stood up and under the pretext of being deep in thought, took a few steps to the back of the room where the sunshine didn't reach. He looked down at his feet and a large brown cockroach startled him as it scurried behind the sofa; a shiver went through his body.

"You should try this one first. Apart from the fact it shows greater profits, it's the nearer," Chas called from his laptop.

"Yes, I could pay them a visit tomorrow," David replied, unable to free himself from this falsity. He was as curious as he was concerned about this drugs boss, Roberto Garcia, and he wondered if Emma's Garcia and this one was the same person.

"Let's see what else we can find out while we're at it," suggested Chas.

Chas entered Roberto Garcia's name and up came directorships of two further companies, Quito Mining and The Cali Coffee Co. The first, Quito Mining owned tin and emerald mines and the second, The Cali Coffee Co. owned coffee plantations, both showing substantial net profits and both had been trading successfully for over ten years.

Roberto Garcia was born in 1949, married in 1969 and had two grown up children. He owned three private homes, a luxury apartment in Bogota, a villa in Medellin and a retreat in the hills south of Armenia. As far as David could tell, at this point, he was an extremely successful business man.

"But just for the record, let's see if we can find some information on the other director, Luis Sanchez," Chas suggested.

"Good idea," David replied.

Sanchez's name appeared as co-director, with Garcia, of the three companies, but after that there was a blank; there was nothing.

"Nothing else on him?" David asked, slightly mystified, "That's strange."

"No, I can't seem to go any further on this," Chas admitted while still trying all sorts of different combinations on his computer.

"Not that it matters very much at this stage, but it would be prudent of us to find out a bit more about Sanchez. Any chance of your doing some detective work and try to get something on him?" David asked Chas.

"Yes, that shouldn't be a problem. I'll get in touch with one of my contacts and get back to you. But I want you to be careful tomorrow; this is a dangerous city and they are all out there, thieves, muggers, druggies and guerrillas, all looking for people like you and me."

He promised he would be careful and after Chas handed him the address of Santos Pardo Import Co. David left for his hotel.

With a street map in hand, David set forth for Santos Pardo Import/Export Co. A twenty minute cab ride took him to the predetermined place and on getting out of the cab he decided to take a look around the area, before entering the building. Heeding Chas's advice, he kept to the main streets, and as he circumnavigated the area, he noticed that the roads were all in a similar state of disrepair, full of holes and craters, large enough to lose a grown man. It was a dilapidated part of the city, like many other industrial areas, only worse.

"They couldn't have heard of Mr. Macadam in this part of the globe," he mused.

The buildings were covered with bill posters of past and present politicians, encouraging the people for their vote, with a fair share of graffiti added to authenticate a run-down area. He had never heard of the names on the posters nor did he care. He had only one purpose in mind and that was to go through the motions for Chas and familiarise himself with the area for any future visit.

He had almost circumnavigated the warehouse building when he came to, what appeared to be, the main entrance. The two large metal doors were obviously the vehicle entrance and the smaller one to the left for trade. He tried the handle of the smaller door and to his surprise found it to be unlocked. Stepping into the gloom, he saw that the main area was filled with wooden crates, which appeared to be nailed down, ready for transport. 'To where?' he asked himself.

He called out announcing to whomever, his presence, and after waiting a short time called out again. On receiving no response he made his way over to the crates which, when examined, were destined for Venezuela, Cuba and The United States. After wandering around for a few moments he came to the rear of the building. Here he found three crates that were still open. He looked inside and saw that they contained bags of coffee beans.

Quite satisfied with that, David began walking to his right, along the rear of the warehouse, with the intention of heading back to the exit, when he came to an archway leading to another section of the building. He headed along a dark corridor at the end of which was a door that, when opened, led to an outside yard. Here he saw that the yard was stacked with coal on one side and iron ore on the other. 'Probably for the home market. Everything here seems to be all right,' he thought.

Pleased with his findings he retraced his steps back along the gloomy corridor, down the dark rows of crates which cast ominous shadows all around, and he was almost half way to the main door when, from nowhere, appeared in front of him, a burly unshaven man, blocking his way.

"What are you doing here?" the man challenged.

David, who was taken by surprise, could only splutter that he indeed was hoping to find Senor Garcia.

"He's not here and you must leave immediately," the man asserted, still blocking his path.

David, quickly recovering from the surprise attack, found his voice.

"Look here, I've come a long way to see him. When will he be here? Can I make an appointment?"

Not that David particularly wanted to meet Garcia; he was simply going through the motions.

The burly man stared back with murder in his eyes.

"You can't see him!!!" he shouted. "Not now!!! Not at any time!!!"

With no alternative and without any further exchange David made his way to the exit, leaving behind the aggressive character.

Outside the warehouse again, he didn't feel too disturbed about the unfriendly encounter; after all, he had been the one intruding and snooping around. In any case, since he wasn't a fighting man, he was quite happy to leave things as they were.

At a villa, remote and secluded, on the lower slopes of the Central Cordilleras of Colombia, two men sat, intent, in deep conversation. They didn't notice the monkeys at childish play; the macaws whose vibrant colourful plumage adorned forest trees like gemstones; nor the hummingbirds, busily extracting the nectar from the orchids. Neither were they aware of the three men watching them from their hide-out, concealed by the dense foliage of the jungle.

"You say that someone has been asking questions about Santos Pardo Import/Export Co. and also snooping around the Bogota Warehouse," one man said to the other in a low and toneless voice.

"Yes, that is correct and we have further proof that there is also interest in Quito Mining and The Cali Coffee Co.," the second man revealed.

"This is not good," the first man returned.

"Look, there is nothing to worry about at the moment, however, there is one thing that I feel I must mention," the second man went on. "As soon as my source discovered this interest, he erased everything on Sanchez."

"They're even on to Luis Sanchez?" rasped the first in disbelief, standing up now with his arms flailing. "I don't like the sound of this at all. I want to be informed immediately in the event of further interest. Should they make any connection between Sanchez and any of the companies, we could be heading for trouble."

"Don't worry, we have everything under control," the second man pacified.

"I hope so, for your sake," the first man said, threateningly.

With that the discussion came to an end and the ensuing silence indicated to the second man to take his leave.

The three men were too far out of earshot to hear the conversation, but the remonstrating that they had witnessed, told them that all was not well. As soon as the second man had left the villa, they too faded into the deep foliage of the jungle.

As the plane was making its approach landing, Emma noticed that Caracas was built on many hills. The buildings and houses in the suburbs stretched upwards, clinging to the escarpment and closely knitted together like a colourful patchwork. Not only were the houses built into the rocks but they were set on top of one another, in such a way, that the ceilings of one became the floors of the others. Without any formal planning, the buildings gave the appearance of fine architecture. The colourful houses were interspersed with bougainvillaea and velvet green rubber plants - a Matisse dream. At night the entire hill sides came alive with thousands of dancing and sparkling lights, sending out secret messages across the valleys to the neighbouring hills.

It was a short drive to the Puerto Viejo Hotel and would only take about seven minutes. The driver was going slowly attempting to execute his way around the large holes in the road and, probably more important, to prevent any unnecessary damage to his cab. The area was run down and the houses were small, all in need of facade repair. At this time in the afternoon, there were few people around. Just in front of them, Emma noticed a car blocking the road, and instead of moving to one side as they approached, it remained stationary.

Two men got out and one made his way towards the taxi. Emma thought little of it assuming that it was a breakdown. It wasn't until one of the men wrenched open the cab door and forced his way inside, that Emma became alarmed.

With a gun pointed at the driver's head, he told him to remain still and not to move. Then turning on Emma, he gripped her by the arm, twisting it, until it hurt, and hissed out from his decaying mouth.

"You will live longer if you forget about this entire affair with Garcia. We strongly advise you to leave Venezuela immediately and have no further contact with Santos Pardo Import/Export Co. You are being given only one chance to go and forget everything you have heard or seen, otherwise, you will not live to see your beloved Scotland again. You have been warned. Do you understand?" He then gave Emma's arm another twist, bringing tears to her eyes, and threateningly backed out of the cab.

She sat there dazed and stunned, not having uttered a sound. She felt sick with fear, not to mention the lingering smell from his breath that she almost threw up, there and then. She couldn't imagine anything like this happening to her and for a moment thought she was actually dreaming. Pinching herself to make sure that she was 'compos mentis', and, still in shock, she became aware of her cab moving forward. When she looked out the back window, she saw the car that had just blocked their way, screech off and disappear out of sight in a fog of dust.

"Do you know anything about this?" she demanded of the cab driver.

He was looking straight ahead and made no attempt at an answer.

She repeated herself again. This time the cab came to a grinding halt.

"Get out. Get out now!"

In one movement he threw her suitcase to the ground, with such force, that she was sure it would burst open. Not knowing what to do now or how far it was to the hotel, she remained standing by the side of the road. She was just on the point of setting off when a scruffy urchin with his cupped hands stretched in front of him, came up to her.

"What now?" she voiced.

"Lady, please, a few bolivares for my little brothers. They are starving," he begged. Emma did not hesitate to seize her opportunity.

"OK, I will give you money, but first of all you must take me to the Puerto Viejo Hotel. Is it far from here?"

Without answering, the youth began walking and Emma followed on behind, along the dusty dirt streets. Her suitcase weighed heavy in her grip, but thankfully, as it so transpired, it was not far.

"There," he said as he turned into the next street, pointing to a hotel at the other end.

Grateful for his help, she handed him ten dollars which was a small fortune for the youth, and, with her legs and body still trembling from the ordeal, she took the last few steps to the hotel entrance.

David had just completed his report on Bogota when the receptionist telephoned to say that Mrs. Findlay was on her way up. A few seconds later, the door opened and Emma burst into the room. So relieved to see him, she forgot herself for a moment and threw her arms around him and held on to him. His spontaneous reaction surprised him, because he too held on to her for as long as she needed him.

"Well, well, well, Emma, what's this all about, this show of affection, do I detect a change of heart?"

Emma, quick to recover her composure, brushed the whole thing aside in a brusque fashion.

"Of course not, David, I have just had the most frightening experience," she spluttered, still unable to control the nervousness in her voice.

"You do seem slightly upset. What happened?"

Emma related her ordeal and as she was telling her story, David's flippant expression changed and his face took on a sombre expression.

"Emma, this is unbelievable, it's incredible!" he exclaimed.

"If I didn't know you better, I would think you had been drinking."

"I thought this sort of thing only happened in the movies," Emma said, shaking her head from side to side.

"No, there's more to this. Nobody gets threatened at gun point for no reason. We can forget about an attempted mugging and kidnapping," David challenged.

Emma knew now, that she would need to tell David everything unusual that had happened over the last few days, in fact, since her arrival in Cuba. There had to be a connection.

"I haven't been completely truthful with you."

David gave her a strange look. "Out with it then," he said.

"No, I don't really mean truthful, but I mean, I haven't told you everything, because I thought it wasn't significant at the time."

"What do you mean?" David asked.

Emma began to tell David about the incidents beginning with the two suspicious characters at the roadside cafe in Cuba, her frightening experience in the water and the boating accident off Cardenas.

David sat in silence, trying to find a connection between them.

"I don't get it at all. You went to Cuba for a break, a holiday, and while you were there these unusual happenings took place. And in addition, you were approached by two, so called, drug traffickers and asked to launder money. Then, when you get to Caracas someone holds you up at gun point. Either these incidents are totally unrelated and are indications of an unstable government controlled by criminals or somebody seriously doesn't want you around. I can't see the latter applying because, apart from Lopez and Jimenez, nobody else knows you're here."

"Well, I think it's all very strange, but let's put the whole matter into touch until we see Julian in Maracaibo," Emma suggested, as she watched David pacing back and forth.

"Something else on your mind?" she continued.

"Not really, but I suppose it is worthwhile noting."

David recounted his trip to Bogota, and that after he had told Chas the 'cock and bull' story for his visit, Chas became extremely interested, to the extent, that he made it his business to find out about the more successful of Colombian importers. And he went on to tell her that he got a bit of a shock when the name, Roberto Garcia, appeared as one of the directors of a company called Santos Pardo Import/Export Co., which he found very strange, even more so, now, after Emma's recent revelations.

Emma sat pensively for a moment as David's marble pose waited for her response. Then she began, slowly. She said she agreed with him that the whole thing was a bit odd. However, at this stage, was unwilling to assume anything else than a catalogue of coincidences, to which he replied that she was probably right since neither of them were able to make a reasonable connection.

Emma sat in contemplation for a time, crossing her legs this way and then that, while David continued to pace the floor. They were not aware of their agitated movements as they attempted to solve these seemingly unrelated events. In the end, it was decided to leave everything until they met up with Julian who might be able to shed more light on this dilemma.

CHAPTER 7

Julian's meeting was scheduled for 11 o'clock at Caloil Corporation. He found these meetings all totally boring and unnecessary; just let him get on with the job. Sam Young, clever enough man, he supposed, otherwise he would not be in the position of Vice President South American Operations, but in practical terms he had no idea when it came down to the real job. He had been waiting 20 minutes before a secretary, tall, well groomed, he noticed, hair tied back and attractive long legs, showed him into Young's office. I must keep this one in mind

"Any chance of dinner, later?" he blurted out, the old Julian returning.

She scowled at him, the look answering his question.

"Good to see you again, Julian. How long has it been, nine months?" Young greeted, walking across the room towards him.

"Yes, something like that," Julian replied, recalling that they had not seen eye to eye even then.

Although they had disagreed, Julian knew that Sam Young needed him now to sort out their mess. It was always the same old story, pay peanuts and you'll get monkeys. Caloil had hired a local contractor who had very little experience and, as far as Julian could ascertain, operations were getting well out of control.

"A coffee, Julian?" Sam asked interrupting Julian's thoughts.

"Yes, that'll be fine," but thinking he could really be doing with a double vodka on the rocks.

"Julian, I'll run this by you briefly and anything more you require Senor Antonio Maria is your man."

Julian settled himself down.

"As you know," Sam began, "Caloil has hired you because their offshore development field at Lake Maracaibo has been experiencing many problems. The oil field consists of eight remote wellhead platforms. The original design of the field was based upon these remote platforms being unmanned and being operated by telemetry from the main platform. Ever since commissioning and start up of all the facilities, problems have occurred, which, in turn, have resulted in massive over costs. These over costs are incurred due to the fact that the remote operation has proved impossible and the remote stations have had to be manned 24 hours each day. This also necessitated the hiring of jack-up, accommodation vessels and infield supply boats."

At this point Julian interrupted.

"What about the telemetry equipment. Has that been checked out?"

"Yes," Sam continued, "the vendor specialist who supplied the telemetry equipment has checked and double checked the equipment and has proven it as per the design."

"Well, in that case, it has to be more of a fundamental problem," Julian offered.

"Yes, it would appear that the local controls of the main equipment transfer pumps, instrument and plant air compressors and other ancillary equipment are at fault. And that is where you come into the game; to iron out all these bugs and get the field up and running, back into its designed operating perimeters."

"How many men have you given me?" Julian asked.

"Two engineers."

"Two engineers!" Julian exclaimed in disbelief.

"Yes, but they're good," the sycophant Sam tried to explain.

"Well, I suppose I should be grateful. You could have given me two bad ones," Julian responded sarcastically.

"I've gone over everything to date. You can make a start immediately."

"Fine, I'll begin tomorrow, if that's OK by you."

"Just one last thing," Sam went on as he rummaged in one of the desk drawers, "keys to the company's apartment. It's on the lakeside," and he threw the keys over the desk to Julian.

Later that day, Julian made his way across the city to the apartment block, a prestigious building situated in an up market area with views overlooking Lake Maracaibo. The entrance to the complex, under tight security, was fronted by a large wrought iron gate, which, after identifying himself, was opened by the security man on duty. The gardens inside, he noticed, were immaculately maintained, with flowers and shrubs of a tropical nature. A wide path led to his apartment block, to where he now made his way.

He used his personal key to operate the lift which took him direct to the apartment on the twelfth floor. The elevator door opened into a luxurious reception area leading to the main sitting and dining room, three bedrooms all en suite, a study and a large kitchen with a breakfast area. The floor covering throughout was of Italian marble and the colour scheme of the furnishings which oozed expensive luxury, was cream and gold.

Julian walked over to the window and the panoramic view of the harbour and Lake Maracaibo was breathtaking. He was impressed, but wondered to himself, if he would ever have the time to wallow in this sumptuous extravagance.

After he had taken a shower, Julian decided to make the most of the remainder of the evening before heading for the oil field on Lake Maracaibo the following morning. Because he was familiar with this type of a problem, he knew there would be many tiring hours spent testing and double testing all the plant, equipment and instruments. He knew precisely what was ahead of him. He reckoned he would have two days of non-stop work before Emma's arrival, the thought of which made him restless. She was a remarkable woman and he missed her whenever they were separated from each other. Most of the time he would be living on the accommodation vessel; to be on hand at short notice for any unforeseeable problem. However, he would return to Maracaibo for Emma's arrival.

He was just about to leave the apartment when the telephone unexpectedly rang.

"Yes, Burton here," Julian said.

"It's Greg, Greg Smith," he heard the voice answer.

It took Julian a few seconds to recall who the hell Greg Smith was.

"Good to hear from you," he lied. "How did you know where to find me?"

Greg Smith was in Maracaibo on some oil related business and had been in Sam Young's office some time after Julian had left, and yes, Sam had passed on the number; and where could they meet for dinner? All before Julian had a chance to answer. Greg had heard that El Vaquero was good value and would that suit him - eight o'clock tonight then?

Greg and Julian had met some years previously in India, where they had both been attached to the same company. With Greg everything was at full speed. He worked hard, played hard, drank to excess and chased women. He was vain and sported expensive clothes, one of many indulgences. In the past, they had shared some good times together, but ever since Julian had met Emma, Julian had given the fast lane a body swerve. He supposed that Greg wanted a taste of that fast life tonight.

They met at El Vaquero's, a crowded bar, not too far from the apartment.

"Good to see you. You're looking great, you son of a bitch."

"You're looking great yourself," Julian answered.

They ordered two Schlitz and Greg almost managed to finish his in one. He was larger than life and constantly wore a large grin of vain confidence. Always gyrating and turning around to discover who was watching and eyeing him up.

"How's life treating you these days?" he asked Julian after he had inspected the female talent.

"Living quietly now and working all the hours that God provides," Julian replied, knowing that this was not the answer that Greg wanted to hear.

"You're not serious. Not chasing skirts?" Greg gasped in disbelief.

"I've left the old ways behind."

Then the real question came.

"You and Emma still together?" he asked Julian.

He and Greg had met Emma the same night and Julian knew that it was still a thorn in his flesh that Emma had turned down Greg in preference to him.

"Yes," he answered eventually, but refrained from telling Greg that she would also be in Maracaibo in a couple of days.

After an exchange of banter, in equal doses of humour and sarcasm, they moved into the restaurant, where Greg had already reserved a table in full view of everything.

They ordered fajitas, and the conversation came to a lull while they worked the shredded meat together with celery, chopped tomatoes, and diced vegetables into a tortilla.

"In the mood for some night life?" he asked Julian.

"I'm afraid not. I have an early rise tomorrow."

A couple of chicks now began to respond and take more than a casual interest in Greg, who had been having an eye conversation with them all through the meal.

"Look, there are two beauties by the bar, Julian, how's

about it, old son," Greg trying every device in the book to get Julian interested in the night life. But Julian was equally aware of Greg's ulterior motive and that was to cause domestic trouble between him and Emma. They finally finished eating and Julian, promising to contact Greg in a few days, left Greg to his two beauties and a piece of ass.

The first thing Julian did on arriving at the main platform was to head to the canteen for a bacon and egg sandwich, followed by a cup of tea. He had left the apartment at 6.00 o'clock and after a relatively short journey, first by car and then by boat, he arrived at the oil field at 8.00 o'clock, ready for action.

Next on his list was a meeting with the manager who briefed him in great detail about the problems that they had been suffering since commissioning. He then went over the design and installation plans, familiarising himself with the complete workings and type of controls, equipment and instruments on the platforms.

He then took a boat and made a visit to the eight satellite platforms, each of which was being manned by between six to ten men. His inspection complete for the day, he headed back to the main platform and to his office where he wrote up a detailed report on his findings so far. At this stage, he had no idea where the fault lay or where to make a start. He decided to sleep on it. Tomorrow the real work would begin.

Without any unusual incidents, this time, Emma, accompanied by David, arrived at the Del Lago Hotel, Lake Maracaibo.

The hotel, a superior five star, was situated by the lakeside and was set in expansive grounds, bursting with subtropical plants and flowers. There were three restaurants, a pool bar and a beach bar, all of which were strategically placed around the pool area so as not to cause the guests any inconvenience or exertion in their quest for food and drink.

There was the usual array of shops to the right of the main foyer, where guests idled away their time amid tropical plants, trickling fountains and waterfalls, and sipped exotic cocktails, to the music of a sole pianist playing Beethoven.

Outside by the pool the music was to a different beat. The rhythm of Caribbean and Latin American salsa was for the young at heart. Here, guests of all shapes and sizes, some fat, some thin, some tall and some short, danced and gyrated to their own interpretation of the music. Some danced in a provocative and sensual manner, while others moved stiffly showing signs of their own inhibitions.

They had checked in sometime earlier, and Emma, on making her way to the beach bar where she had arranged to meet David, took a detour past the jewellery boutiques. She could not resist beautiful jewellery; it had always been her greatest indulgence. One piece caught her eye. It was a gold elephant pendant, studded with diamonds, emeralds and rubies. She made a mental note to call again, before leaving, and buy this exquisite piece.

David was already at the beach bar when Emma got there and as she sat down, reminded him, "We're having dinner tonight with Julian."

"No, I hadn't forgotten and it'll be good to see the old trouble shooter again."

Under the circumstances, David and Julian really enjoyed one another's company, although they both liked to show pretence hostility. After all, they both loved Emma in their different ways.

"What time did he say?" David asked.

"He said he would meet us here at eight o'clock."

After they had enjoyed a light snack and a margarita, David left Emma by the pool and went off to make a few phone calls. Emma took the opportunity to have a swim and, on returning to her sun lounger, she became aware of a man watching her. She paid little attention to it to start with. But now, after he had been staring at her for twenty minutes, she was becoming uneasy. It was embarrassing; she was no good at this sort of thing. She ordered a vodka and soda, and he watched her as she poured the soda into the vodka.

She took her first sip. He was still watching her. Then she took a gulp and still he watched. She finished it rather more quickly than she would normally have done. 'What shall I do now?' she thought. Emma didn't wish to leave yet, because she was sure this could be her next contact.

"Yes, I shall have an ensalata mixta," she ordered from a waiter who had approached her.

He continued looking at her as she was eating and didn't take his eyes off her for any length of time. Even if he was her next contact this behaviour was ridiculous, or was this simply another over sexed and under screwed Venezuelan.

She lay back down on her sun lounger to take a little sun and perhaps the man would tire of this game and leave. No such luck! After ten minutes when she opened her eyes he was still there, only, now, he had been joined by another man. Although she understood that the Colombians would contact her sooner or later for her answer, she assumed it would be in a more businesslike manner.

Dear God, he was now standing and making his way towards her. Around the far side of the swimming pool, weaving his way in between the scantily dressed sun bathers, negotiating a path round the sleeping loungers and almost sleeping waiters, finally stopping in front of her.

"Senora, please you come and join me, yes?" she heard him say, in broken English, as she squinted up from her lounger.

She was slightly startled, and even although she had been aware he had been heading in her direction, still, she was somewhat surprised at his non-negotiable invitation. She found it all very unusual and not at all businesslike according to her standards.

The look of apprehension must have shown.

"Do not be alarmed, Senora, you are quite safe here in the Hotel Del Lago."

She hesitatingly confirmed that she would join him in five minutes, allowing enough time to compose herself. But why should he try to reassure her she was safe?

David had gone off to make a few business calls and enquiries, and would meet up with her before dinner. It was important that he found out as much information as possible before a final decision was reached. She had given him all the facts and details, but played down her own feelings about the strange events. "Well, Emma old girl, freshen up a bit and let's see what this man is all about," she muttered to herself.

She donned her sarong, brushed her hair, a little lip gloss and together with the sun kissed colour on her face, she looked good.

Approaching the bar he gestured towards the vacant stool.

"I took the liberty of ordering champagne and I hope Moet Chandon 1988 is to your taste."

"Yes," replied Emma, "that sounds good to me."

"We've been expecting you."

"Who's we?" questioned Emma with some degree of aggression and impatience entering her voice, when she realised that these were, indeed, Garcia's men.

"We'll come to that in a moment, but first let me introduce myself. My name is Pepe Valero and this is Pablo Maria".

"Good health," Pablo voiced as he raised his glass in the familiar salutation.

"And in the meantime enjoy the champagne. I believe 1988 is one of the best."

Emma hadn't a clue. Any year would do her, since her preference was 'vino blanco secco' at 4000 Bolivares a bottle; good value.

"I wish they would make their point," Emma thought, her grit was beginning to kick in at last.

The second man, Pablo, with an outstretched hand, said, "Welcome to Venezuela and Maracaibo. If you are interested in Roberto Garcia's business proposal, you are invited to take a boat trip on the River Limon. A taxi will call for you tomorrow at 12 noon and will take you to Sinamaica, where a boat will be waiting for you. Roberto Garcia will make himself known to you somewhere along the route."

"Why can't he simply meet me here, instead of all this cloak and dagger planning?"

"As you know, Roberto is an extremely busy man and he has dealings in many countries, one of which is here. He has a chalet along the river and would like to take you there. And also, it will be a good opportunity for you to see some of the rural areas and the ethnic people who live there."

Emma could find no fault in seeing part of the countryside, but wasn't too happy about meeting Garcia in the wilderness.

"I don't see why Garcia can't meet me here," she tried again.

"I've already explained that. The meeting will take place at his retreat or not at all," Pablo stated, now beginning to show some impatience.

Emma thought for a moment. She understood the dangers involved in the drugs business, and to become isolated after recent happenings could be a costly move. Her first reaction was to call the whole thing off. On the other hand, she couldn't quite imagine Garcia, who's relying on her for his money laundering, being engaged in any crime against her. And in any case David would be with her.

She reluctantly agreed and after finishing their champagne the two men took their leave, wishing Emma a pleasant journey. She sat for a few moments reflecting on the past day's events, and experienced a new sense of excitement and enthusiasm that had been dormant for a long time.

Julian bounced into the Del Lago in great spirits. Although the last two days at the oil field had seen their fair share of problems, with little progress, tonight, he was putting all that to one side and was ready to enjoy whatever the evening had in store.

As he walked to the elevator he was aware of heads turning in his direction. Not a vain man, but happy in the knowledge that he could still 'cut a fine dash'. At forty-one he still looked very good, with his dark brown hair and sallow complexion. His physique was good and all of his 6ft.3ins was carried erect and proudly. Wherever he went his presence commanded attention. His laughter came easily; he had a great sense of humour and his flamboyance gave the impression that he had no real cares in the world, nor did he give a damn. He enjoyed fun and the good life, but never to the extent of interfering with his work. He was street wise and no matter where he went he took note of what was happening around him; aware at all times of everyone in his proximity. Never did he assume that the innocent looking reveller harboured no ill intentions and was able to discern between the good guy and the bad guy.

Emma had just finished dressing when Julian arrived armed with a dozen red roses.

"For you, sweetheart, with all my love," he said handing her the bouquet.

"What a lovely surprise, the roses are beautiful," Emma enthused as she gave him a hug and pressed herself close to him.

He stood back from her and looked at her, desiring everything that his eyes soaked in.

"You look stunning, tonight. Seeing anybody special?" he asked jokingly.

"As a matter of fact I am. He's my favourite guy, the light of my life and the sunshine of my smile," Emma replied, tilting her head in a coquettish manner and flashing her eyes.

"And you're the fire in my loins, sweetheart," he answered, clutching her close. "Yes, yes, I know, you don't need to tell me. You've done your hair and made up your face. I'll try to keep my hands off until later," he said grabbing her buttocks.

It was well past 10 o'clock before all three of them had finished dinner. The meal was excellent and the conversation flowed in a steady stream. The idle chit-chat and the easy banter was light relief for all. For a moment, Julian forgot the problems on the oil field and David and Emma lost sight of their disturbing incidents.

As coffee was being served Emma struck up first. She told Julian how she had been approached by Carlos Lopez, Roberto Garcia's trusty lieutenant, to launder drugs money for Garcia; her experience with the gunman in Caracas, and the latest contact, Pepe Valero, who had given her instructions for the following day's meeting with Roberto Garcia.

Julian held silent as Emma recounted her story. His first impression was of amusement. Emma was an extremely attractive woman and he thought that these men were simply chancing their luck. But when she came to the part of the gunman things took on a different shade. It was obvious to him that this was indeed drugs business and that was a dangerous game.

Turning to David, he asked, "What do you make of all this?"

David cleared his throat. "I think there's no doubt that this is serious business. While waiting for you to arrive, I made a trip to Bogota, and a friend there, Chas, was able to come up with some interesting information on Garcia and his partner Sanchez. They run a legitimate import/export co. called Santos Pardo. This company shows great profits, very lucrative in fact - 5.7 million dollars. I would say that they're using the company to launder some of the drugs money."

"And, because the DEA, the Drug Enforcement Agency, has made great roads into the traffickers, people like Garcia, Sanchez and the rest of the big drugs barons, they, for the moment, have to lie low. So that's the reason they have approached me," Emma added.

"OK, I'll buy that. But what do you think about their actual proposition?" Julian asked, going straight for the mark.

"We've talked it over, of course, but we want your thoughts before we either dismiss it or otherwise," David quickly replied, indicating to Julian a degree of anxiousness.

"We know that it is drugs money we're being asked to launder. We know it is dangerous; and we know the names of the top men, which makes it even more risky. On the other hand, we're, in effect, carrying a bundle of money to the Dominican Republic, depositing it in a bank account, and getting well paid for our efforts," Julian summarised.

"When you say it like that, it doesn't sound so bad - the drugs money - I mean," Emma chipped in.

"Don't be too sure, Emma. Even if you accept the fact that illegal drugs trafficking is big business and won't ever be eradicated. Are you prepared to subscribe to the drugs trade?"

"Look, somebody will do it, and why not us. It could be

our last chance to make our millions," Emma justified. "And we're really not trading in drugs. We're just trying to make a bit extra money for ourselves."

David thought along the same lines as Emma, but he was only too aware that it could be very dangerous. "Why don't you keep to the meeting with Roberto Garcia? Let's hear what the man has to say, and after that we make up our minds. What do you say, Julian?"

"I'm ready to back you. But be aware of what you're both getting involved in."

David then went on to tell them that Chas had been in contact again and that he had eventually found some information on Sanchez, but would not divulge anything over the phone He wanted David to return to Bogota tomorrow morning.

"How do you feel about that? I mean about being on your own?" David asked Emma.

"I don't have a problem with that. In any case Julian's here now."

"Yes, but are you not staying on the accommodation vessel?" David asked, turning to Julian.

"Well I am and I'm not. I'm staying out there for convenience, but I can just as easily come into Maracaibo each evening."

Julian did not feel comfortable with Emma going on her own to meet Garcia; considering the recent threat to Emma's life. Something that he could not pinpoint was bothering him. The threat could even be a trick sprung by Garcia's enemies. He didn't know. But one thing he was certain about was David and Emma did not fully recognise the dangers in all of this, especially in countries such as Venezuela and Colombia.

"Look, tomorrow I'll go with you. I'll enjoy the ride," he said making up his mind.

"What about the oil field?" Emma asked.

"I can easily get a shift in before we leave," was Julian's casual answer.

And so it was settled. David would leave for Bogota first thing in the morning and Julian would meet up with Emma at Sinamaica.

"Now, watch your back out there in Bogota, David," Julian advised "You're such a typical accountant, you can't see the forest for the trees, and it's not a forest, it's a jungle".

"You're breaking my heart, and you're a great one to talk," said David in defence, "I think I can take care of myself, thank you very much.

"There's no point in arguing with you, David, but all I'm saying is, look out for yourself."

"I will, I will," David answered, impatiently, and, since he had an early call in the morning, he bade them a very good night. With a last parting glance he left them to finish their liqueurs.

Emma and Julian didn't tarry too long after David had taken his leave. They were both anxious to be alone with one another, and yet, didn't want to bring this wonderful evening to an end too soon. They finished the remainder of the wine and slowly made their way out through the foyer to where the doorman summoned a cab.

"I'm glad we decided your place and not mine," Emma voiced. "This is a fabulous apartment, and what views of the city and the lake!!!" she exclaimed, gazing out the windows at the scene in front of her.

"Yes, it's a bit of all right," Julian agreed as he poured them a night cap and came over to where she stood.

They remained by the window for awhile, admiring twinkling city lights below and the riverboats and barges set against the charcoal lake. Then they walked slowly to the master bedroom, taking their drinks with them. The first thing Emma did was to kick off her shoes and start to remove her jewellery.

"No, let me," Julian said coming over to her.

He gently removed her dress, and as it fell to the floor he ran his hands over her well defined body savouring the softness of her skin. He took her breasts in his hands and as he felt her nipples harden, he was aroused. He lifted her and carried her to the bed.

Pressing her against him, he felt the flesh of her soft breasts, and with her back arching, she pressed herself into him. He felt her arching and moving close to him, rubbing herself all over him, kissing him with an overwhelming passion and desire that she had not fully experienced until this moment. His hardness was on her and he reached down and slipped himself into her.

She wanted him now and he her. Her desire was so great that she thought she would explode He was now ready to take her and he pushed himself deep into her. She felt the weakness begin in her limbs and travel up her loins, that tingling sensation, the start of her orgasm. And as his movements became more rapid, they became one in their frenzied passion. They climaxed together; he felt he would go on forever and he cried out her name, over and over again, until he was spent. Finally, with the sensation of fulfilment and contentment, they both came to a wondrous peace.

They lay in one another's arms and she laughed and cried all at the same time. Her emotions and excitement were so aroused, that she was out of control. But slowly the calmness returned.

"God, I love you Emma."

"And I you, all the way back," was her soft reply.

CHAPTER 8

Before leaving, David had made his arrangements to meet Chas in Franc's bistro, Bogota, and he was now sitting at the rear of the cafe where groups of people sat idling away the morning in light-hearted and whimsical chit chat about nothing in particular.

By the entrance, two elderly ladies sat daintily nibbling a cake between sips of coffee and polite conversation, nodding their approval on the current topic of chat. They were wearing the same moulded hair style, in a violet hue, and a similar taste in their apparel. Their cutlery tinkled and chimed against the china ware, and, together with the base murmuring around, produced an almost orchestral movement.

Next to a group of three men, who were obviously discussing some sort of business, one man sat on his own. He, at first glance, appeared to be intent on the contents of his newspaper but, as time went by, every few moments he raised his eyes, and with a cautious slyness looked around before turning his head towards the street outside, and then back to his paper.

David watched him for a short while until his attention came to rest with the couple to his left. They held hands and gazed into one another's eyes, obvious lovers, but there was something familiar and, at the same time, disturbing about the man. It always irritated David when this sort of thing happened to him. He was still racking his brains, trying to replace the man's face into another time and place, when Chas banged down beside him bumping into the table and spilling David's coffee.

"What the hell's got into you? For fuck sake, Chas, get a grip, get a coffee and settle down," David complained, wiping the table with a napkin.

Not normally a clumsy fellow, but Chas seemed to have lost all control of his extremities David noticed that his hands were shaking as he tried to light a cigarette. The waitress brought the coffee, and after a few sips Chas began to calm down.

"David, I don't know how you're going to take this, but things don't look good, not good at all," Chas began, still obviously shaken.

"Right, take it easy and tell me what you couldn't say over the phone."

Chas took a hard gulp of coffee and swallowed with great deliberation.

"Luis Sanchez is the current minister for Education in the Colombian Government. That's the reason why his name was removed. He's in that sort of position where he can just about buy and achieve anything. He has access to influential people in the corridors of power."

"Now, what's so alarming about that? The removal of his name from any business involvement could simply be explained as not politically correct for one who holds a government position, but as long as he declares his income, he's doing nothing illegal," David volunteered, as he sat back and began to relax after Chas's clumsy entrance.

"Yes, I suppose you could make that assumption, but in his case I think not; there's more at stake here. You won't believe this."

"You see," Chas went on, "what I've told you about his government position is factual. But there is more disturbing news, and this is merely hearsay at the moment. Some number of years ago, one of the largest drug cartels, the Cali cartel, was infiltrated by government agents together with the help of the Drug Enforcement Agency and had the support of the present President of Colombia. The cartel was busted and the top drug barons either put in jail or mysteriously killed. Now, my source tells me that, wait for it, this man Sanchez was linked to that Cali Cartel."

David let out a whistle of disbelief, as things were beginning to fall into place. But he didn't want to let Chas in on the full picture; the least he knew the better. For a moment he was sorely tempted to reveal all, but decided against it. So he continued to be greatly surprised at Chas's revelation.

"You've got to be joking!!! What have we got ourselves involved in should this information turn out to be true? Have you found anything else on Garcia?" David exclaimed, incredulously.

"Nothing to our knowledge," Chas answered.

"The DEA deemed Colombia an unsafe country, at that time, because the Government was doing very little about anti-drug enforcement, in other words, not co-operating. The President was consequently forced into doing something positive about his country's drug problem. And hence the Cali Cartel bust."

"Am I thinking what you're thinking?" ventured David.

"Pass it by me," Chas tested.

"Because of his Government connection, Sanchez's involvement with the Cali Cartel was conveniently ignored and he continues trafficking in drugs."

"Yes. And this time, supposedly, under the umbrella of Garcia's Company," Chas concluded.

"And," continued David, "cocaine being one of Colombia's main sources of revenue, and although The President has to appear, to the DEA, to be enforcing and supporting the anti-drugs campaign, he, because of the revenue, allows most of the cartels to continue to operate illegally."

"So, now you've got it," added Chas.

David studied Chas before going on. He wasn't too sure how to handle the next bit. Should he feign total surprise or should he act more casual and indifferent?

Before he could make any contribution Chas continued. "Garcia uses his company, Santos Pardo, as a front for laundering drugs revenue."

"And when things get a bit tough he has his man, Sanchez, on the inside greasing palms, smoothing the way and no questions asked." David interjected, now aware that Chas had no idea regarding the real plan, their involvement with a drugs racket.

"So, I don't think you want to become linked to Santos Pardo Import/Export Co. Should Garcia ever become aware that you have this information or suspect anything, he would go to any lengths to quieten you. You are a dead duck."

They sat in silence for a few moments, each with their own disturbing thoughts.

What was going through Chas's mind, David hadn't the 'foggiest'. But one thing he could be certain of was, although Garcia had Sanchez on the inside, Garcia and his lieutenants were restricted from laundering money in Colombia, and this is why Emma becomes a most sought after asset. However, as David reflected, nothing had really changed for them.

I'll return to Maracaibo today, David decided and he was just about to say so when Chas's mobile phone rang.

"Yes," he heard Chas say.

"They're on to me. Get out of the country," the voice on the other side said, and then the line went dead.

Chas turned to David. "That was my contact and he seems to think that somebody is after him and for me to leave immediately."

"Do you believe that?" David asked Chas who was now looking extremely worried.

"I don't see how they could know about me and in any case there is no link between him and myself."

"Be careful anyway," David cautioned.

Chas and David parted company soon after the call, each warning one another to be cautious, on the assumption that, what was partially conjecture at the moment, could turn out to be true.

As David was making his way past the tables he noticed that the young couple were still holding a head to head romance, but the furtive looking man who had hidden himself behind his newspaper had gone.

Before making arrangements for his return to Venezuela, David committed to writing the detailed conversation that had taken place between himself and Chas, and addressed it to Emma in Maracaibo.

After making a call to Chas Forsyth, a man left a telephone booth, but before he could vanish into the melee of humanity, he was shot through the head at point blank range. His was a life, dedicated to the fight against drugs and opposed to the greed and evil that was omnipresent. He did what he considered worthwhile for the good of his fellow man, but his life was taken by those that had infinite power, the drug barons, and the autocrats.

David's flight was scheduled to depart at 18.00 hours, giving him more than enough time to collect his belongings from the hotel. He hadn't been aware that the young couple, in the bistro, had left seconds after he had and made a phone call. He was confident that nobody noticed his slipping the letter, which was addressed to Emma, across to the hotel reception, together with a handsome tip for safe mailing.

He thanked the receptionist, gathered his baggage and calmly made for the door. It was raining when David stepped out of the hotel. He wasn't surprised at that at all. Since Bogota, located about 8660 ft. on a mountain-rimmed plateau high in the Cordillera Oriental of the Andes Mountains had an annual rainfall of 42 inches.

The day was mild, though, and David would have enjoyed seeing some of the city. But time was of the essence and his return to Maracaibo and Emma was imperative.

Not one of his favourite places, but Bogota held its own kind of fascination in a historical and cultural way, dating back to the mid sixteenth century. And even the violence that it had suffered over the years, from the times before it was captured by Simon Bolivar to the era of violence, the struggle for political power between the governing body and the armed guerrilla bands, not to mention the drugs barons, could not detract from the romance and adventure of the city.

Sometimes called the Athens of South America, it could take its fair share of fame when boasting about the fine museums, the national library, churches and cathedrals constructed in 1565. Oh, all this, David might have seen.

While he had been mulling over Bogota's history, past and present, a cab pulled up.

"To the airport, please," he said to the driver who was of mestizo composition.

"Very good, Sir, will that be the International Airport?"

"Yes, indeed," David responded.

After exchanging with the cab driver the normal pleasantries for one presumed to be a tourist, and when the limited topics were exhausted, David settled back on the well worn seats where in places padding was appearing. He reflected on the events of the day in conjunction with the meeting that would have taken place, by this time, between Julian, Emma and Garcia.

The cab suddenly coming to a breaking and screeching halt, made David sit up and take notice.

"What the hell is going on?" he uttered.

Before the man could respond, the driver's door was wrenched open and one shot was fired through the mestizo's head. The back door at the same time was pulled opened and David, caught off guard, was forced from the cab at gun point and bundled into an awaiting Mercedes which sped off with all rubbers burning. The entire kidnapping took thirty seconds.

He was crushed between two gorillas and driven at mind-boggling speed through the narrow arteries and side streets, coming to a halt in front of the very warehouse he had visited only a few days prior.

He knew there was no point in asking questions; he knew what was coming and would need all his strength for the interrogation that lay ahead. They forced him out of the car, pushed and shoved him along the rows of crates that he had already seen, to the rear of the building, where they sat him down on a chair. Up until this point no words had been exchanged.

After a short while the shorter of the two apes menacingly approached and pushing a gun into David's head, demanded. "What is your business here? Why are you in Bogota?"

David swallowed hard, trying for time as to how best to handle this explosive situation. He was no fighting man; all his battles were won using his head rather than his fists. He was used to outwitting his adversaries in the financial world with the use of his shrewd, judicious skills and dexterity. Here he was powerless and was no physical match against these henchmen. He couldn't win. These men acted on orders, they didn't possess a functioning brain. There was nothing against which he could pit his skills.

"Visiting an old friend," was all he could utter from his dry mouth.

"You lie. You tell us what we want to know. Now!" the dominant man gorilla shouted.

"I've told you, meeting an old friend."

They punched and kicked him to the body at first.

They obviously don't believe me, David thought to himself; neither would I, he mused, as the blows continued to rain down. Perhaps they think I'm a DEA agent.

"What was the information you received from Mr. Forsyth?"

The bastards are on to Chas, David realised.

"I've told you, he's an old friend, and we were exchanging family news and talking about old times."

They kicked and punched until he doubled over and fell off the seat. He curled up into a foetal position to protect himself, but one of the last blows caught him on the head and he blacked out.

"That's enough; the boss wants as much information as possible. We won't get any if he's unconscious."

David didn't know how long he had been out, but when he came too he was still lying on the stone floor, dazed and bewildered, with the taste of blood in his mouth. They sat him back on the seat and began again.

The questions and the beatings continued. David was aware that no matter what he told them, he wouldn't get out of this alive. He had to protect Emma and Julian at all costs. He had to give them time, time for the letter to arrive and get to hell out of the country. He would tell them nothing.

He was now bleeding from the face, his clothes were in shreds and he had no power in his left arm. He wanted them to hit him hard enough to knock him out, into unconsciousness again, where he would be safe. He was in agony. He was afraid he would weaken and at the last moment, talk, giving them the information they wanted. Who were they anyway? His head was throbbing; it felt as if a hammer was pounding inside his skull; he was confused. But he couldn't weaken, not yet. He felt like an animal, hunted down, wounded and trapped, with no place to hide from his killers. His fear was such that the only way he could react was with aggression and rising from the chair, now, he went for them.

"Come on, you mother fucking ass holes of monkeys. Come on, come on and get me," he provoked.

They came at him, the two of them, punching and kicking him on the face and head. He heard something snap as they booted him to the body. The pain was excruciating, he no longer felt human; he was a wounded animal trying to get away from the pain. He fought back as best he could but the blows kept coming until at last he went down and fell into oblivion.

They left him lying there for a while, battered and twisted, and went off to make a phone call. Sometime later, he was taken from the warehouse, still unconscious, to a deserted area in the suburbs, dumped out of the car and shot.

He lay there on the side walk, alone, and bleeding to death as the rain continued to fall on the deserted streets of Bogota. He felt nothing now; he was in no pain any longer, he was where he wanted to be and Emma was safe. It would be recorded as just another drugs related mugging on the infamous and violent streets of Bogota.

CHAPTER 9

Leaving the concrete buildings and the dilapidated dwellings behind, they drove out of the city and headed for Sinamaica on the Gulf of Venezuela. The driver had called for Emma as prearranged and he seemed a congenial enough fellow, giving Emma the benefit of his knowledge along the way.

The journey took about an hour and she felt at one with herself, relaxed and contented, especially after a night of utter ecstasy with Julian. He had made love to her again early that morning before he had left for the oil field. She still tingled at the thought of his hands on her, his warm and caring touch, his unselfish demands, and his wonderful masculinity that had a curiously calming effect.

The driver eventually brought the cab to a stop beside a small makeshift jetty, which boasted of three boats and two modest outdoor cafes. Emma planked herself on a wooden bench which, she noticed, was attached to the table and waited for Julian whom she knew would be arriving at any minute.

One of the loafers, whom she assumed had something to do with the cafes, brought her a bottle of water for which she was most thankful. She felt pleased and quite excited about the forthcoming meeting with Roberto Garcia, and should the deal go ahead there would be a pot of gold at the end of her rainbow, not to mention the stimulation she would get from this unethical and perhaps dangerous mission. Not a particularly dishonest person, in fact, quite fastidious at times, but this business had a fascination that seemed to attract her like 'trout to bait'.

True to form, Julian arrived a short time later, and, after his normal fooling around, she indicated to the boatman that they were now ready to leave.

The River Limon, at the onset, was wide, but as they travelled up stream it began to narrow, going off into little tangents of waterways wherever the levels allowed. On either side of the river grew lush green vegetation of palm trees, nut trees and banana trees with their roots extending into the water making them well equipped to handle the changes in the water level.

This natural vegetation was a wonderful sanctuary for all animal life, Emma reflected, and as they motored on she heard the noise of all the jungle creatures which for her was pure music. Flocks of birds were soaring, diving, and fighting the air with their wings along the shorelines which were a natural feeding stop on the migratory route and a living link between land and sea; between wilderness and paradise.

Further up stream, the vegetation changed to mangroves with their tangled root system pioneering new land. The shallow murky water housed all kinds of sea creatures and a large number of snakes that Emma caught sight of as they motored on. Neither Julian nor Emma spoke very much. Their silence was apple blossom, their eyes and their minds soaking up the natural tranquillity of their surroundings. The 'putt putt' of the engine was the only unnatural sound that interrupted nature's peace.

As they travelled further up stream, the river opened into a lagoon where they came upon a community of people, river people, whose wooden houses were built into the river and on top of wooden stilts and planks of timber. These houses were pieced together in a medley of timber and unequal wood sizes, forming a pattern in design, a patchwork in wood. All around these timber buildings ran a network of jetties that sat in the water like wooden fences. This community of Indians was totally self-sufficient with their quaint little churches, schools, bars and restaurants, all again, standing in the water. As Emma and Julian made their way through these dwellings, a school boat chugged by, ferrying children back to their homes, criss-crossing the river as the boatman went from stop to stop.

Each curve the river took produced yet another and another enclave of rustic wooden buildings, all forming their own little communities. Emma noticed, at this point, that none of the Indian people built their homes very far into the jungle. In fact, all of the colourful dwellings hugged the fringes of the river.

Some of the houses were built half in the water and half on sandy soil at the edge of the jungle whose green vegetation provided a natural backdrop to the scene. Tropical flowers and vegetables were cultivated on the sandy river shorelines by the women, who also found time to run lucrative craft centres of pottery, etchings, carvings of Indian dolls and colourful beadwork.

Emma was entranced by all she saw, and not for one moment did she ever think that there existed groups of people, such as these, who lived their lives, half in one world of cultivated sophistication, pertaining to society, while on the other hand had the freedom of spirit and soul, found only in the wildernesses.

Emma and Julian were so captivated by their surroundings that they didn't realise the river boat was now making its way towards some dwellings which, as they drew nearer, turned out to be a restaurant bar.

"Oh, wouldn't it be great if we could spend some time here," sighed Emma. "I could stay here forever."

"Perhaps for a while, Emma, but you're too attracted to the glitz, glamour and the challenges of the business world, to give it up," Julian reflected, "just like I am."

"Well, you could be right, but it's a nice dream for the future."

The boat was now tied by the side of the restaurant and the boatman, turning to Emma and Julian, informed them that Senor Garcia would join them in half an hour, meanwhile, relax and enjoy a pleasant refreshment.

They scrambled out of the boat, up the 'had seen better days' ladder and along the boardwalk leading to the bar. There were a few people scattered around, some sitting, others standing. They were a mixed bunch; indigenous Indians with flat faces and noses, some more of Spanish decent and at the other side of the room sat three tourist types.

"What would you like?" Julian asked, turning to Emma.

"I'd love a cool beer."

Emma had time to look around and take stock of the situation while Julian went to the bar. There was nothing extraordinary about any of them, but her eyes stopped wandering when they came to rest on a swarthy, unshaven Latin American by the bar. Julian, by this time, had made his way to the very section of the bar where this character was standing and Emma saw that Julian deliberately nudged the fellow.

"Oh, I am sorry, have I spilt your drink? Can I get you another?" Julian said in an apologetic voice to the man, who was so taken off guard and could only splutter a reply in the negative.

After a few moments Julian returned with the drinks.

"I saw what you did. Why?" asked Emma.

"He just looks a bit out of place here and I wanted to see his reaction."

"And?" Emma interrupted.

"It would appear that he is Venezuelan by his accent, with an uneducated voice. Thick Spanish voice."

"Do you think he has anything to do with Garcia?" Emma asked.

"I don't know, yet. Could be."

"Well, in the meantime we could take a stroll by the river," suggested Emma.

"You go; I want to keep an eye on this guy. See if anyone approaches him. Oh, and watch out for the snakes."

Emma drew him a look, not knowing if he was being serious or not, but made her way out of the bar, anyway. She took her beer and wandered out to the rear, along a small platform and onto the grassy riverbank which was covered with low shrubs and vegetation, in some places, very thickly. She turned round and looked back to where she had come from, relieved to see that Julian was still sitting in the same place. She had to admit that, as much as she was someone who wasn't easily frightened, it gave her some comfort to have him with her on this trip and quite at ease on this subtropical riverbank.

She waved to him indicating that everything was fine and he acknowledged her in return. With that, she decided to explore a little further, just a few more steps into the lush vegetation. After all, the Indians who lived here were civilised and Christian like in their ways. They had churches, hadn't they? So she really had nothing to fear from them, whatsoever.

After Emma strolled off, Julian remained seated. The independence of these river people intrigued him, with their craft shops, their schools, churches, community halls and not to mention the grocery shops and rustic bars tucked away in different corridors of the river. They seemed a contented lot. Nothing was done in a hurry. The only disturbing factor that bugged him in this otherwise calm and tranquil place was the presence of the man at the bar. He didn't talk to anyone and appeared to be a stranger to this community. Julian had a feeling that there was something sinister about him.

The local Indians, of course, were well accustomed to visitors and paid little attention to him. So, for the moment, Julian was relaxed, and gazing aimlessly around him, he gave the intended impression of a typical tourist. After a short while, he made his way to the craft shop where he took his time browsing around before selecting four clay Aztec figures. He felt he was doing exactly what any tourist ought to be doing.

When he eventually returned to the bar area, the man was still in the same position and nobody appeared to be taking any notice of him. Perhaps, Julian thought to himself, he is just loafing around and I am being paranoid, making too much out of an otherwise normal situation.

He finished his beer and after looking at his watch, realised that Garcia would be arriving anytime now, so he went in search of Emma. He had no trouble in finding her, she had only taken a few paces further along the riverbank and he spotted her amidst some tropical vegetation, which she was examining.

"Hello, darling, you seem to be enjoying the scenery," Julian greeted, giving her a crushing hug.

"So peaceful and tranquil," she replied, still studying the plants.

"I think it is time we headed back. Garcia should have arrived," Julian went on.

"Yes, you're right, but I hate dragging myself away from this natural environment".

She had no sooner finished speaking when a cracking sound came from the foliage behind her, as if someone or some animal had trod on a fallen branch. As they turned round to see what it was, something whistled past Julian's head and cracked in the branches.

"That's not gunshots, is it?" Emma questioned in astonishment.

The peaceful surroundings had given Julian a false sense of safety and his reactions were slightly delayed. But the realisation slowly dawned as another shot hit the bushes beside them.

"You're darned right it is," Julian called out as he hauled her behind a large palm.

"What the hell's going on?" Emma mouthed, as the scent of fear crossed her face.

They half crouched behind the vegetation and listened. Julian put a finger to his lips, indicating silence. There was some rustling in the bushes further along and to the right. They remained perfectly quiet as they edged their way to a more concealed spot. Manoeuvring themselves into a position of more seclusion and, at the same time, giving them more advantage, they watched in silence to see who was using them for target practice.

The restaurant was now out of sight, but they knew they hadn't gone far. If they called for some assistance they would give their position away to whomsoever lay in wait. They heard a rustling and snapping of undergrowth as if someone or something was making its way towards them.

"Can we make a run for it?" Emma whispered.

"No, it's too risky. The undergrowth will slow us down."

Julian cocked his head to one side.

"They're still out there," Julian whispered, "we'll lie low for a moment. Keep still."

For a while they remained in place and the noise in the bushes eventually stopped. They waited, perfectly still, until they were sure whoever it was, had gone.

"I'm going to take a look around. Now, keep your head down and don't move. Don't worry, Emma, I'll be back," he assured her when he saw the utter panic on her face.

She reluctantly let him go and he wriggled his way through the undergrowth until he was out of sight. She heard his movements for a while; after some time she could hear him no longer. She lay there for how long she didn't know. It was interminable. With her face pressed to the dank, damp greenery, camouflaged by the low growing tropical plants and long grass, she lay there until she could endure it no longer. She had heard nothing for such a long time and made a decision to move towards the riverbank from where she could easily reach the platform to the restaurant. She assessed she had crawled about half way when she heard movement to her right. She lay still and listened. Then a thought occurred to her. Perhaps it's Julian now trying to find her. She called out his name, softly at first, and then a little louder a second time and waited. When she heard nothing, she raised herself up slightly and there, to her horror, five metres away, between her and the platform, stood a man, with, what she thought, a gun in hand.

She ducked down again, as quickly as a thought. What would she do? Where was Julian? She was now in a state of desperation and panic. She couldn't get her brain to function. The dull thud of her heartbeat on the dank soil reminded her of gravediggers and it made her shudder. She was so near the restaurant and safety, and yet so far.

With this thought in mind, she began to calm down and think logically. She would go slightly further back into the jungle, making a semicircle, and come out at the river just a bit downstream from the platform. She began to crawl, making little noise, stopping from time to time to listen. Her progress was slow as she dragged herself through the damp undergrowth, and any recognition to the clothes she was wearing was well past. Her hands were bleeding from lacerations caused by the tough blades of grass and broken branches that she pulled on to ease her way along.

She reckoned she must have been crawling for twenty minutes or so, her hands and face bleeding, when she stopped to take a look at her surroundings. She raised herself up enough to see through the foliage to the river which lay about fifty metres away. Yes, she could easily make a dash for it. Once she was out in the open and in sight of the bar, she would be safer.

Crouching down for a moment to regain her strength and then raising herself up slowly into a sprinting position, she was now set to make a dash towards the river. She was just about to throw herself into full flight when, in front of her, blocking her route, appeared the same man. In her shock and panic she turned around and threw herself back into the tangled greenery and fled through the vegetation, with leaves and branches whipping into her face. Behind her, she could hear her pursuer as he chased her and, at the same time, heard the whistle and the crack of gunshots.

The only advantage she had was the gunman had got just as much of a surprise as her when she had popped up from the undergrowth. He had hesitated for a brief moment, giving her a head start. She ducked and dived, clothes in shreds, hands and face bleeding until she could go on no further. She flung herself under ferns and long grass and lay panting and gasping for air.

How long she lay there she couldn't tell. She must have been semi-conscious from exhaustion for some time. When she finally became aware of her situation, the light was beginning to fade.

"I'm going to die out here. Where was Julian? Why did I not stay put? I should have remained in the place where he had left me," she reprimanded, herself.

All this was going through her mind at the one time. Only the noises of the jungle were audible; the noises of the night. Up until now, she had never wished to be anybody else but, lying on the jungle floor, defenceless, she thought that a good set of muscles would have come in handy. She knew she wouldn't stand a chance against this type of a man who was hand picked for his bulk and combat skills. She was scared. But her thoughts turned to another kind of fear; the fear of the unknown, the solitude and fading light of the jungle.

She had no idea, now, where the river lay; she had zig-zagged so much in and out of the dense palms and mangoes that she had lost all sense of direction. But calmness slowly returned as she looked above the tropical canopy and she saw the brightness in the sky to her left. In that direction she headed.

She had been stealthily making her way towards the steely sunlight, the twigs and the plant life under foot snapping like gunshots with each step she took, and the vegetation thinning every few metres until she came to an area from where she, once again, was able to see the riverbank. She hesitated for only a moment, but before she took that final few steps, something slammed her on her back and brought her to the ground, pinning her down. With her face crushed against the soil and a weight on top of her, she heard a voice utter, "Keep still!" Keep still, she thought, the stupid bastard, she couldn't move. But somehow she managed to free a hand, and picking up a broken branch, jabbed it into what she thought was the person's head. It obviously made its mark as she heard her assailant curse, "You bloody bitch," and at the same time wrench the branch from her hand.

"You're breaking my wrist, you mindless moron," she yelled, spitting dirt from her mouth.

"Look, I'm not going to hurt you, but if you make a wrong move I'll need to quieten you. Do you understand?"

Something in his voice made her stop struggling and she lay quite still hoping for some sort of miracle.

Julian fought his way through the dense undergrowth towards the spot where he had last heard movement. He took a wide circle and lay still, listening. As he got into a crouched position, he saw something move slightly ahead and quietly picked his route between the palms, carefully avoiding the broken twigs and branches. He was right. There was something moving around in the banana plants.

Taking out the gun which he had carefully hidden from Emma, he got to a couple of yards from a man whom he managed to half stun with a blow from the butt. The stranger fell and Julian was able to knock him out cold. He went through the man's pockets and, as he assumed, there was nothing there to identify him. He knew that there would be at least one other and was reluctant to return to Emma straight away. For a while, he looked and listened, and, when he was satisfied that there was no one else in the close proximity, he began to make his way back to Emma.

For ten minutes he had been slowly weaving his way through the vegetation when, to his surprise, he was attacked from behind and a gun was stuck into his back.

"Drop the gun," a voice commanded.

He dropped the gun, and on turning around saw that the man standing in front of him was the same man from the bar, with the gun pointing right at Julian's head. A noise from the bushes distracted the gunman and Julian saw his chance. He hit the gun out of the man's hand, lunged at him and brought him down.

Julian now had him pinned down and managed to retrieve the gun.

"I want some answers, Talk!" demanded Julian.

"Ok, ok. Take it easy," the man said, "I'm Garcia's man and have been ordered to look out for you."

Julian didn't believe him.

"What the hell's going on? First, you attempt to kill us and now you are saying you're protecting us. You can do better than that. I've just taken out one of yours."

"The man you left over there is not one of ours. He is guerrilla. He is one of many, and they are after tourists who isolate themselves just like yourselves and mug or kill for money."

Julian didn't believe this explanation. He knew full well that mugging and kidnapping on the crowded city streets was an every day occurrence, but not here.

"You've no option but to trust me. You and the Senora are still in great danger. There are more of them and we must get back to Senora Emma and get both of you to safety. And also, Garcia is still waiting to speak with you."

"Where is he?" Julian demanded, almost breaking the man's arm.

"I will take you to him. He is not far from here, in a house on the other side of the river."

Julian could do nothing else for the moment but trust this man.

"Any fucking tricks, remember, I'm right behind you," Julian cautioned.

With the man in front and Julian bringing up the rear, they made their way back to where he thought he had left Emma. It was not to his surprise that she was no longer there. He knew her to be an impetuous person and to lie in hiding too long was not her style. But he feared for her safety. He should not have left her, he rebuked himself.

They looked around the area as best they could, trying to keep their presence as inconspicuous as possible from the snipers; and, at the same time, if Emma was still in the area, making it clear who they were by quietly whispering her name.

"I think Senora Emma will attempt to reach the river and the safety of the bar," Julian informed the man.

"That's dangerous; they'll obviously be waiting for both of you there. But I'll have one of my men check out the bar."

Garcia's man located two of his own men concealed in the plantation. He had one stand at an advantage point along the river bank to wait for Emma's appearance; the other he sent to the bar. Then Julian and the man took up a position nearer the platform but hidden by some ferns and tall grass. They sat down to wait.

By this time, Julian had reasonable confidence that the man was telling some truths and he relaxed his vigilance. Julian sat in despair. The thought of anything happening to her was too much to bear. The sun was now lower in the sky and soon the light would give way to dark as the source of brightness slipped below the horizon. If she didn't appear soon, Julian knew he would go back into the jungle to find her.

They had been waiting half an hour and Julian's anxiety was mounting by the minute. He could wait it out no longer. To leave Emma in the jungle, alone and lost, perhaps injured, was now not an option. He had to go out and find her. He was just on the point of setting out in his search, when they noticed the shapes of three figures approaching from along the river bank. The man tapped him on the shoulder.

"Stay perfectly still, it could be the guerrillas."

They remained motionless for a few moments and, as the forms came closer, to Julian's immense relief he saw that it was Emma, escorted by the man from the jungle and one of the lookouts. He ran out to her, she stumbled and fell into his arms.

"Oh, my darling, I'm so sorry, I shouldn't have left you there on your own."

"So you should be, you bloody fool," she attacked from sheer relief, "I could have been killed out there."

After her initial outburst she was so overwhelmed that she couldn't speak for tears of emotion. The ordeal had been unbelievably too much, but she had remained resolute and had miraculously escaped without too much harm to herself.

They were led, in silence, to a quieter part of the river where a small outboard motor boat was moored. On crossing the river, the boat then weaved its way in secretive silence between the houses that stood gallantly in the murky water, until it came to the bank on the other side. They threw the stern line and made her fast. To Emma, all this seemed unreal as she watched the flying insects of the night, mesmerised by the lights from the windows. Mollifying sounds of music pervading the stillness of the river reduced the severity of their plight.

Julian and Emma were asked - but more like told - to alight and to follow. Once more they were escorted through vegetation of palm trees, for a short distance, arriving at a modest wooden dwelling not too far from the river bank. The house was brightly lit up and looked inviting in the twilight.

However, the last few steps Emma took were the longest in her entire life. She wasn't sure if they were heading towards another situation fraught with danger or to a safe haven. She turned her head in Julian's direction and the grim expression on his face revealed the exact same thing was going through his mind. A shudder of trepidation and panic ran through her body. There was no need for them to speak; eye contact said it all. It could be another trap or, on the other hand, a place of refuge and for the moment, safety. They had no choice.

The house at first had appeared small but, up closer, it was larger than the others she had seen on the river, earlier. It was made in a similar design with wooden stilts constructed in marshy water and twisted roots.

They were shown the way along the board walk and up a few slatted steps to a veranda leading to what was obviously the front entrance. The man in front of them pushed open the screen door and allowed them to pass through. Inside, the main reception room greeted them in its warm yellow and red cheeriness, with ornaments of local craftsmanship decorating solid wooden chests; under the circumstances, unnaturally welcoming. From there, they were asked to pass through to a second room which led to the rear veranda.

As they entered, a man stood up from the chaise longue and took a step towards them.

"At last we meet, Senora Findlay and Senor Burton. I am Roberto Garcia."

Emma, relieved at last in finding Garcia and giving her hand in greeting, could only splutter a 'pleased to meet you Senor Garcia'.

"Please, Senora, Roberto. And may I be presumptuous and call you by your Christian names."

Garcia's manner was of relaxed gracefulness and gentlemanly courtesy. Dressed immaculately in a British off the peg suit, he would have graced any high society gathering. His English was perfect, only showing a slight trace of his Latin origins, and Emma, had she not known he was Colombian, would have found it very difficult to place his accent. For the first time in days she began to relax.

"I can see you've had a rough time," Garcia went on, before either of them could speak.

"To say the very least," Julian interrupted with some sort of irritation in his voice.

"Well, so be it, but be thankful you're relatively unharmed. And due to my men you are both alive," Garcia informed them.

Julian and Emma looked at one another and found it hard to believe how, Garcia, so easily, could write off their last few hours in the jungle being chased and shot at by a bunch of gangsters.

"We need answers. You must know who those men were," insisted Julian, who was in no ingratiating mood, even although, it would appear that Garcia had been instrumental in their rescue.

"All in good time. But I suggest that you and Emma take a shower, freshen up and after dinner we can have our talk. And as for those thugs, they are opportunists, who make it their business to stalk tourists in the hope of making an easy buck."

"They almost killed us, an easy buck you say!"

"Senor Julian, this is Venezuela not Scotland. People are shot every day for very little."

Turning to one of his men he said, "Eugene, show the Senor and the Senora the guest rooms." And turning back to Emma and Julian added, "You will find fresh towels and a change of clothes in your room together with any toiletries you may require. Say, 8.00 o'clock for dinner. Eugene will come back and show you the way, later." He then left the veranda, giving neither of them an opportunity for further questions.

All the while he spoke, it was in a quiet, gracious tone and not even when addressing Eugene, did Garcia's voice rise. Tired and exhausted, Emma was in no mood to continue more fruitless enquiries and allowed events to take their own course. Everything would wait until later.

Eugene escorted them back through the main reception room, along a corridor with polished wooden floors, enhanced by oriental rugs, to adjoining bathroom and bedroom en suite.

"I hope you will be comfortable. You will find towels and a change of clothes in the closet."

Julian thanked Eugene and almost felt sorry for the big brute whose arm he had nearly broken some time earlier.

Left on their own, now, they could only look at one another in amazement. He came to her and held her close to him. He comforted her and caressed her. It was hard to believe, that in the heart of this place with its authentic tranquillity and Garcia's reassuring manner, they felt threatened, still.

"Now, don't worry, everything will be fine. I know you've come through a lot today, but for the moment we're safe here. Tonight, final business arrangements will be discussed and if everything is acceptable, you'll be in business."

Emma silently nodded. Her understanding would take longer. But she took some comfort from his words; although there was no explanation as to why they required protection in the first instance.

"But, Julian, my dear, this is not normal. One, the circumstances and the places of these so called meetings are strange; and two, it's not an everyday occurrence to be shot at and chased through a tropical forest in the course of keeping an appointment. I simply don't get it. I do understand that this is a dangerous venture, but we've hardly started yet."

Julian was not about to confirm or disagree. Emma was overwrought and no matter what he said, it would neither help nor hinder her; and merely added.

"Well, for the present, anyway, don't think about it, take a shower and let's see what transpires at dinner. We can't go anywhere tonight, so we may as well make the most of Garcia's hospitality."

"Oh, I suppose you're right, but I'm beginning to get really pissed off. If it weren't for the effort we've made or that fat figure, I'd jack the whole business in now. It's getting too dangerous for my liking."

"Changing the subject, I must make contact with the Oil field and let them know where I am. In that entire fracas, I've lost my mobile, but I'm sure somebody out there has one. You go ahead and take your shower; I'll be back in a few minutes."

Julian went from room to room to establish that they were definitely alone in the guest house. Finding it to be so, he then made his way to the open rear window that led onto an unlit part of the veranda. Silently he climbed out, took a further few steps and conveniently found a gap through which he slipped, unobserved, into the concealment of the greenery.

He sat for a second or two until his eyes became accustomed to the darkness. All around, the jungle orchestra played its eventide tune. Frog taking bass; the shrill, harmonising notes of the crickets, together with the other sounds of the jungle, made a sweet melody.

Taking his time, he moved a little further into the thicker vegetation, and keeping in sight of the pathway, he saw to his right the dark form of an armed guard half concealed by some shrubs. Moving on again and keeping parallel with the wooden track, he discovered that there were a further five armed men dotted along the route, the last one standing guard a few feet from the boat.

Satisfied with his findings, he turned around and edged his way towards the guest house. Hidden behind some tall palms he noticed, for the first time, another boardwalk leading to a second dwelling which was brightly lit up and on whose veranda two guards were pacing back and forth. He took this opportunity to get closer and rising from his position he approached the guards.

"Good evening," he startled them, "I need to borrow someone's mobile," Julian said, as he got nearer, and at the same time thought that they weren't exactly the world's most alert of bodyguards.

Without saying a word one of the men handed him a phone and Julian placed the call to the oil field while looking inside the house. He saw three men, Garcia, Eugene and another, in deep conversation. From his position on the veranda, however, he was unable to hear anything, but he did note that they were deadly serious. So, on finishing his call, he thanked the guard and returned along the wooden boards back to the guest house.

Emma had just finished showering and was in the process of creaming her body when Julian walked into the bedroom. He watched her as she slowly massaged the lotion over her breasts and abdomen, down her pelvis to that part of her inner thigh where it thins. He was aroused, his craving and desire for her was all animal and lustful. He went over to her, and burying his face in her soft breasts, reached down between her legs. She reached out for him, and all the anxiety of the last hours drifted away as they softly made love.

They lay there for a while as the naked desire melted away, and only the creaking of floor boards, somewhere close by, roused them in to activity and they hurriedly dressed for dinner.

"While I was outside, I found an adjoining chalet, where Garcia, Eugene and another man were in deep conversation. It's connected at the rear by a wooden boardwalk."

"Very interesting. Did you discover anything else?" Emma asked.

"No, not much, except that the place is crawling with armed guards.

True to form, Eugene came for them at the appointed hour and led them down the wooden pathway to the adjoining chalet that Julian had discovered earlier. He had decided that, for the present, he would be congenial towards Garcia, so as not to arouse any doubts in Garcia's mind. He was still unsure that the armed guards surrounding the place were there for the reason given, but that uncertainty could wait until later. For the moment, they were in no imminent danger. He would adopt 'the honey pot' method.

On their arrival, they were greeted very heartily and cordially by Garcia - which didn't surprise Julian at all - and who appeared very relaxed and in a jovial mood. He offered them aperitifs and spoke generally about the area and the river people.

The chalet was larger than the guest house and consisted of a large main sitting and dining area, connecting to the kitchen, with three bedrooms to the rear.

They eventually sat down to a wonderful meal of a variety of local fish dishes, followed by main course of beef bourguignon and to finish crème brulee. From his cocktail bar he offered Julian a brandy and Emma took a tequila cocktail.

"It's a bit too late to travel back to Maracaibo, so for tonight please be my guests," Garcia offered. Emma and Julian were in agreement and accepted his hospitality, knowing that it was the most sensible thing to do, under the circumstances

"This is one of my retreats," Garcia went on to explain. "As you can see it's nothing palatial but extremely comfortable and peaceful. When the pressures of work become too much I like to get away and this is one of my favourite places."

"It's so peaceful, so why the armed guards?" Julian questioned, unable to resist the opportunity.

"There's trouble every where these days, even here on the river, and one can't be too careful."

For the time being Julian accepted Garcia's explanation, but really didn't believe him.

"Well, now, let's get down to business," Garcia opened, "have you reached a decision about our proposal?"

As Emma didn't want to call the whole affair off until David returned from Bogota, she decided to play for time.

"In part, yes. We have made up our minds to go ahead with your offer, but only if we have your protection. We know the risks are great and after recent events, which could or could not be connected to you, we need some assurances for our safety.

"That can easily be arranged."

"Carlos Lopez implied that the package would be picked up in Bogota at a point still to be decided," cut in Emma.

Garcia took a strange look at her. "Due to certain circumstances, which really don't involve yourselves, there's been a minor change of plans which, I think, will be more to your benefit. The package and any future packages will be collected here in Venezuela. Everything else that Carlos told you remains exactly the same. You will take the package to The Dominican Republic, where you will deposit the money in an account, the name of which you will be told on your arrival in the country. Each package will contain three million US dollars and your commission is 10%. Do you agree so far?"

"Everything is pretty clear except the commission," Julian answered, knowing full well that Garcia needed them and was probably willing to pay more for their services.

"What? I would say that 10% is an extremely generous offer," replied Garcia.

"I was thinking more in the region of 20%," Julian firmly answered.

Garcia managed a smirk of understanding that also held a mark of impatience.

"Very well, let's consider 17.5%, my last offer and be done with this haggling."

Emma's and Julian's eyes met only briefly, but it was enough for Julian to nod his acceptance.

"Good. In the future you will be notified as to where and when to pick up the package. However, for this first run, the package will be handed over to you sometime tomorrow at the hotel."

This came as a bit of a surprise to Emma but she said nothing. The idea of transporting 3 to 4 million dollars, all of a sudden, didn't appeal to her. The excitement she had felt earlier on in the proceedings now turned into that of fear. As she looked around, she saw that everyone else appeared to be satisfied with the arrangements, and she made herself relax and enjoy the remainder of the evening. Garcia appeared to show more pleasure than anyone else. He had achieved his aims with his beguiling ways and refined mannerisms and was certain that Emma and Julian had also swallowed his explanation about his armed guards.

They bid their host a good night, thanking him for his hospitality and that they would depart the following morning after breakfast. After taking their leave, they strolled slowly back to the guest house. It was a still evening and beyond the canopy of the taller trees they could see the stars, suspended above, bright and twinkling, as they sent their messages all around the hemisphere.

"Look, look, Julian, a shooting star."

"Do you know what the Islamic people say about shooting stars? They say that it's God throwing a star to knock down the devils that are trying to reach Heaven", Julian informed her.

"That's nice. Do you think many devils are trying to reach heaven"? Emma asked in fun.

“I don’t know about that. But there’s one thing I’m sure of, and that is, there are too many of the bastards still here on earth.”

Julian put his arm around her shoulder and they walked the last few steps, in silence, to their home for the night.

CHAPTER 10

Thirty hours after leaving, Emma returned to the Hotel Delago. Julian had already headed for the oil field where he knew his work would be cut out for him. He had only completed one test, so far, to discover where the problem lay. If the tests, scheduled for today, were run, he would go back to Emma later that evening; otherwise he would stay on the accommodation vessel, overnight.

Emma busied herself and sent a long e-mail to her office in Glasgow, giving her secretary instructions regarding certain business and financial matters concerning clients. She was feeling very pleased with herself. The business deal had been successfully agreed and was delighted at the financial arrangements. This was a chance of a life time. She reckoned they would all be better off by more than a million, that is, if she did three or four trips. And she didn't see any problem in that. Things couldn't be better. All this, sent the previous day's strange occurrences into the realms of fantasy; and the understandable initial alarm she felt last night when raw reality hit her at the sums of money she was required to carry, floated away.

Later that previous evening, Julian had eventually conveyed his doubts to her about the explanation Garcia had given regarding their pursuers being isolated muggers simply victimising lonely tourists. But nothing now could dampen the euphoria of her success and all nagging doubts paled into insignificance. She knew deep down that something was not quite right here. She never believed in coincidences and yet, at this moment refused to let her mind dwell on things that might take away her feeling of elation. Garcia was astute and successful; otherwise how could he cover up his drugs trade? The nervous uncertainty she had experienced previously had evaporated.

Her e-mailing complete she took herself to the cocktail bar for a sun downer and on the way the hotel reception handed her a letter.

"This is addressed to you. It arrived with the lunch time mail, Senora."

"Thanks," Emma said, taking the large envelope.

Curious to find out who had sent it, she opened it immediately. 'Ah, from David.' As she read, the colour began to drain from her face. But it wasn't until she reached the last part that she began to feel light headed, and an overwhelming feeling of terror took hold, strangling her breathing. She read it for a second time to make sure she had got it right, and that it wasn't some figment of an overactive imagination.

'If you are reading this,' it read, 'and I haven't returned, they are on to me. Get out of the country, now, fast, you and Julian! Forget about the money and leave immediately.' Oh, my God, what's happened to him? But why should they be on to him? And who are they? It can't be Garcia. He needs us. This can't be true. It's a hoax.

The grey matter crashed. Her brain's mechanism did double loops and backward flips. She looked around to see if anybody could help. They were all too busy. A few minutes to clear her head. 'Julian, I must contact, Julian. He must be told right away.' She got him on the phone.

"You've got to come back to the hotel, right now," she screamed down the line, "It's David."

"What do you mean, it's David, it's David?"

"I don't know, but you must come back, now, please."

"I'm just about finished here. I'll come straight away."

The following afternoon, Roberto Garcia returned to Bogota with only one thing in mind and that was to make sure nothing jeopardised the new made arrangement with Emma Findlay to launder his drugs money, and he would stop at nothing to achieve this. Since the DEA had penetrated the drugs Cartels' activities, he could not use any of his lieutenants, many of whom had been forced into hiding or, worse still, had to flee the country.

His first rendezvous was with Luis Sanchez at the Villa Rosa.

Sanchez had given him a detailed account of events over the last three days.

"It was clear," Sanchez explained, "that Findlay was on to something, because he returned again to Bogota and made contact with Charles Forsyth, who, we know, had been making further enquiries about 'yours truly', Luis Sanchez. We don't know what he was planning, but we can't afford to take any chances."

"How did you get this information?" Garcia asked.

"We had a tail on Forsyth who led us to Findlay. Anyway, we had him taken to the warehouse and put a little pressure on him, but to no avail. I didn't believe him so I had my men take care of him."

"You took his personal documents, I hope?"

"What do you take me for? Of course." Sanchez replied, indignantly.

"Good, in that case he can't be identified, at least, not for sometime. And after Emma Findlay has made her first trip, we'll have no problems from her. Are you certain he made no calls?"

"None at all. We had him followed from the time he left the cafe until we picked him up. We checked with the hotel and he made no calls, so we can assume he didn't contact his ex-wife or Burton."

"What of Charles Forsyth?"

"We got him, too," Sanchez proudly boasted.

They were silent for a moment until Garcia stood up.

"We'll be in contact in a couple of days. Meanwhile I'm going to Cali, to sort out a few pressing matters," Garcia concluded as they were parting company.

He left the Villa Rosa by the same route he had arrived; out by the french windows into the garden, around the swimming pool and across the lawn to the pathway leading through the shrubbery at the rear exit where his mercedes was parked. His two body guards were in attendance, one seated behind the wheel, the other loitering nearby

"Everything all right, Boss?"

"Yes, everything's fine," he replied, getting into the car, "now take me to the airport."

"Where we going, Boss?"

"Cali."

Julian's day had been long, hot and loaded with problems. There had been a small fire on one of the remote wellhead platforms and two of the men had to be airlifted to the local hospital for burns treatment. One of the divers had stayed down too long and was now in the recovery chamber suffering from the bends. Julian had run the five tests, scheduled for that day, none of which had revealed where lay the fault. Tomorrow, he would run the remaining three tests.

It had been a frustrating day and it had taken all of Julian's effort to keep his mind on the job. He was still very much concerned with the nagging at the back of his mind that all was not well in the Garcia camp, and despite the successful meeting they had had the previous evening, he felt something smelt fishy. His mind kept going back to Emma. He couldn't put his finger on it, but he instinctively knew that there was something afoot.

He was just completing the last report for the day when Emma had called in a state of panic. Shaken but not stirred up by her agitated condition, he finished off quickly and called for his transport. It took him an hour and a half to reach the hotel, where he found Emma in the same state.

Throwing herself at him, she exclaimed, "I think something dreadful has happened to David. Read this," handing him the contents of the envelope.

He began reading the detailed account of David's findings and, as he read on, it all became clearer and fit into place. The nagging doubts were now realities. He knew it, his premonition was right, the warning signs had been there. He finally came to the end 'if you haven't heard from me and are reading this, they've got me!'

He looked up at Emma and didn't know what to say. She, on the other hand, could hardly contain herself while he was reading.

"Julian, it's dated 12.30 yesterday, that's more than 26 hours. He's made no contact and left no messages. He was on his way, yesterday to catch the 6.00 o'clock flight. He should have arrived here last night. We should contact the police."

"You're thinking the worst. You know what he's like. He could have gone off somewhere," Julian said, trying to deflate the tension.

"He would have left a message, Julian."

"However, under the circumstances, I think we must assume that something has happened to him; take this letter seriously and do what he says."

"Julian, I can't just leave without knowing what's happened to him, and neither can you leave. There are still tests to run. Let's contact the police."

"Right, but let's start at the beginning. First of all, we can't contact the police. If we do so, we must be ready with an explanation why David went to Bogota - twice. And from what David says in his letter, somebody knows that he has been making further investigations; and that can only be Sanchez and Garcia. They have silenced him, because they don't want anybody to know that Sanchez, as it transpires, is Minister for Education and is mixed up in the drugs scene. Not good. But why would it be Garcia? He's handing the package over sometime today. Except that, if word doesn't get to you about David, they'll assume that you will go ahead, as arranged, and pick up the money."

"Right, and that's why David has been removed- to shut him up. We can't get the police involved when this is drugs and money laundering. Most probably, they have been watching Garcia and Sanchez - who knows what they have in their police files. We're between a rock and a hard place," Emma despaired.

"Yes, you're probably right and for the moment, anyway, we'll sit tight, and if there's no further developments regarding David's whereabouts, we'll get in touch with the authorities."

After some thought Emma asked.

"But who was chasing us back there? It can't be Garcia. He needs us."

"He only needs us up to a point. People like Garcia and Sanchez live under many umbrellas of respectability, and should anyone get too close to them they become a target. Remember, Emma, big fish eat little fish. But I don't think it was Garcia back there in the jungle.

It's some other group, a separatist faction," Julian disclosed, finally voicing what had been on his mind.

"Good God, what have we got ourselves into?"

"Then please leave," Julian pleaded.

"Julian, I'm not leaving until I find out about David and, secondly, I'm not leaving without you. And that's final. But for me, neither of you would be in this tangled mess."

"You're such an obstinate bitch sometimes, Emma, you know that. Let me think. You can't remain here. Pack your things. I'm taking you to the company apartment. You'll be safer there. It's 100 per cent secure with a guard at the gate and a key combination to operate the non-stop lift to the apartment. Come on, let's go," Julian finally ordered, before she was able to show any signs of reluctance.

Emma gave in. She collected her belongings and checked out of the hotel. They were making their way to the car when they were approached by a man who shoved a metal case into her hand. The only words the man spoke were, ' you know who it's from.' She was dumbstruck. She was not expecting the money this quick, but here it was, in her hands; and instead of feeling elated, she was petrified.

Fifteen minutes later saw them arrive at the apartment entrance. Neither of them had said a word during the journey; they were in hell with their own thoughts. Getting out of the car and still clutching the case, Emma could only mutter, "that's that then." There was nothing either of them could say; the cat was among the pigeons and they were at its mercy.

Julian produced his security pass for the guard and the heavy iron gates to the complex opened. Inside he informed the man that Senora Findlay would be staying for a few days.

"Very good Sir, I'll let night security know."

He showed her how to operate the key to start the lift and, when it came to a halt, a further combination to open the lift doors.

"I'll swing past the office in the morning to collect the spare key. Here, you take this," he said, handing her his key.

She sat down, mentally exhausted by the entire affair. A few hours ago, she had been ecstatic with her success, and now she was extremely concerned and worried about David's safety, leaving her deflated, drained and empty. Not to mention the money she now had in her possession and the implications that it entailed. For the first time, it hit her-she was now a criminal-and she didn't like the sound of that word, especially when it was directed at herself. Not only that, but it was she who had encouraged David to become involved and, should anything untoward happen to him, the responsibility stopped at her.

"I'm answerable for all this. If anything happens to David I won't be able to live with myself," Emma voiced her thoughts.

"Don't be absurd, you mustn't talk like that. He's an adult, he knows the risks that have to be taken. Come on, Emma, it was nearly us out there in the jungle and we're still not out of trouble. Now, no more self-recriminations," Julian lectured, trying to lift her morale.

"Until I find out about David, I'm not going to The Dominican Republic, so I suggest we stick that case of money in some security box. Agreed?"

"Agreed," replied Julian.

They showered and after drying she flung herself on top of the bed. Not even the worries over David or the bizarre events could deter Julian's sexual desire for her. She lay, slightly on her side, unaware of her magnetic appeal, with one leg drawn up underneath the other revealing the covetable softness of her inner thigh. He lay down beside her fresh scented body. He felt the softness of her skin under his gentle touch. She turned towards him and giving herself totally to him; he felt the swelling and he gently took her again and again.

CHAPTER 11

Six men squatted on the floor of an old shack, well concealed by the dense forest, on the lower slopes of the Serrania de Perijas, the range of mountains dividing Colombia and Venezuela. They were surrounded by machine guns, propped against the walls and crates of incendiary devices and ammunition, nestling menacingly in the pale, virgin straw. Three of them were from the Revolutionary Armed Forces of Colombia, FARC, and the others from a Venezuelan anti-government faction.

They looked tough; their clothes were badly soiled and in some cases plastered with dried blood. They were angry and hostile. Most of them had been living rough for months and all of them had little to eat in days.

"Our man inside the organisation tells us that Garcia has made a deal with Emma Findlay, to carry drugs money to The Dominican Republic. What we can deduce is that Garcia has now established a new route for money laundering." The big aggressive one with the fat face, who seemed to be the leader, went on, "However, we can't take any chances. It's impossible to cover all airports and flights bound for Dominique and, for that reason, Emma Findlay and her minder must be taken care of before they make a move. Your men," turning to the younger fresher faced man, "were ordered to get rid of them, and failed," he shouted working himself into a tirade.

The younger one interrupted.

"What were we supposed to do? Garcia's men were all over the river Limon like a dose of salts. We couldn't get near them," he challenged.

"That's not good enough, you failed. They must be stopped," he yelled, banging his fists on the hard wooden crates.

A man slouching against the wall slowly stood up.

"This won't get us anywhere, this bickering. We've got to work together," he said, calmly.

"Now, Roberto, what's your plan?"

"Our mission is to bring down the Colombian Government and to achieve that, we must stop the flow of revenue from the drug barons - in this case Garcia - into the Government's hands. The more money Roberto Garcia makes, the greater the Government's cut. With the Government making that kind of revenue, the right wing paramilitary becomes stronger and our job gets harder. The paras are able to purchase hi-tech warfare and our mission becomes more difficult."

"Well, OK, but what's the plan?" the calm one asked, once more.

Roberto, the fat faced one replied.

"We can't let this new route operate. It must be nipped in the bud. And the only way is to take out the Findlay woman and Burton. With them out of the way Garcia can't move his merchandise, that is, not until he finds himself another fool, and we'll deal with that also when the time comes."

"Where do we come in?" the fresh faced one asked.

"You will concentrate on the man Burton. You make your arrangements for that but, this time, don't fail. We, on the other hand will take care of the woman."

The tall calm man spoke again.

"Is everything clear?" Before anybody was able to answer, he went on.

"We'll move out in the morning, before sunrise. Your group first," addressing the fresh faced man. "And Roberto, your lot go half an hour later."

Pointing to one of the crates he continued, "You'll find something to eat and drink over there."

With that he left the shack and sat on the wooden step outside; lit his pipe and gazed straight ahead into the dense mangoes and nut trees of the forest.

The following morning, early, two bands of men left the lonely shack in the lower slopes of the Serrania de Perijas and separately made their way down to the tropical grasslands. Their bodies were heavy with the ammunition and weaponry slung around them. Their progress was slow as they traversed mountain streams glistening in the early morning sun that coloured the water from steel green to a soft aquamarine in the shallows. The terrain was steep in parts and large roots from the Brazil-wood protruded through the bare soil and hung down the escarpment in a tangled formation.

Lower still, they had to fight their way through the dense wall of mangoes, palms and banana trees. There were no tracks and the forest closed its secrets behind them. Only the shrill shriek of the monkeys, high up in the canopy, and the scurrying away of the snakes underfoot, for a moment, took heed of their passing. The air was cool at this time in the morning and the dew weighed heavy on the plant life.

They spoke little as they descended, concentrating on negotiating the mountainous terrain. It wasn't until reaching the grasslands that Roberto, the fat faced leader, split them up and instructed them to make their separate ways to the safe house in the suburbs of Maracaibo. There they would regroup and formulate a plan to take care of the woman.

Roberto was a bad man; he was an angry man. He hadn't always been like that. He had fought with the guerrillas for so long now that he enjoyed killing; any kind of killing. But most of the killing, now, was for the cause, for the revolution, for FARC.

He once had a family, too. He had been a good Father, then, but his murderous ways, his wife had told him, were bad for their children, so she divorced him. He didn't know where they were now, and this made him angrier. And because he liked killing for the cause and was angry, the cause and the anger became the killing.

The other group was given similar instructions, to make their way to their own hide-out, where they would plan, a fatal accident for Burton.

Roberto was happy with the situation, and like himself, the fresh faced Venezuelan had anger and a hatred that would drive him to anything for his Antigovernment movement. Their aims were to disrupt the flow of oil, to destabilise the Government's economic and financial programs and eventually lead to the present Government's downfall.

The aims of both groups were similar; to improve living conditions for the poor and restructure government policies for the benefit of the people. There was great unemployment and poverty in both countries and recent natural disasters had added to the plight of the poor. They were drawn together by their common goals.

CHAPTER 12

She woke, the following morning, to find Julian gone. He had already left for the oil field, leaving her a note saying he would return that evening, if possible, but, because he was scheduled to do a routine audit on one of the remote platforms, he might have to spend the night there; and a further warning to be extremely cautious should she venture out of the apartment, in particular, to pay attention to everything that was going on around her. Meanwhile, her intention for that day was to make enquiries about David.

She started by phoning Chas Forsyth's office in Bogota, only to be informed that Mr. Forsyth had taken a few days leave. And could she have his private telephone number, please. Yes, the telephonist had said and gave it to her. She phoned but there was no reply and she made a point to call again later that day.

Next, she called all hospitals and police stations listed in the vicinity of Bogota. She drew a blank. None of the hospitals had a person answering to his name or description, nor did the police have an accident report on a David Findlay. With no success she realised what her next move would be. She was terrified of the truth. She sat procrastinating, trying to find courage to place the call.

She mustered up strength from somewhere, and, quickly, before she changed her mind, dialled another number. When the voice on the other side answered 'The Mortuary' she thought she was going to pass out with dread. She gave the name and described David, as best she could, together with details of height and approximate weight. They asked her to stay on the line. After five minutes, and to her relief, they returned with a negative answer.

No, there was no corpse fitting that description and she wondered what on earth she could do, now. Then, it came to her: the British Embassy or Consulate: she would go there in person.

She hurriedly left the apartment and had the security man call a cab which, to her surprise, arrived within seconds. She was on a mission now, and all thoughts of the stash of money and the menacing danger disappeared.

She instructed the driver to take her to the British Consulate which was near the city centre, and, after paying the fare, got out and looked around carefully, just like Julian had instructed. Nobody appeared to be watching her. Quickly crossing the pavement, she disappeared through the revolving doors of an office block, noticing as she entered that the Consulate was on the Fifth floor.

The office was located at the far end of the corridor and, on approaching it, she pressed the bell. The door eased open, immediately, to a cheerful, young English woman sitting behind the statutory, well-appointed, reception desk.

Emma asked to speak to the Consul - she was anxious about a missing person. The cheerful secretary told her to take a seat and went off into an adjoining room. On her return, the secretary ushered her into, Mr. Dixon, the Consul's office. He stood up as soon as she entered and invited her to take a seat. Moving towards the percolator he offered her a coffee, which she thankfully accepted. After settling himself behind his desk and shuffling a few papers around, he proceeded.

"Now, Mrs. Findlay, how can I help?"

"I'm extremely concerned about my ex-husband."

She began by explaining the situation, leaving out any reference to the Garcia business, merely stating that Mr. Findlay had gone off to Bogota for a business meeting some three days ago and it was very unusual for him not to be in contact.

"Normally, we don't commence any investigations this soon, but since Colombia is termed 'an unsafe country' anything untoward is checked out immediately." he explained.

He asked her for a full description of David, the clothes he was wearing, birthmarks, colour of hair, height and weight. She gave the Consul every detail about David that she could recall.

"Leave this with me. I'll get somebody from the Embassy in Bogota to handle it and I'll contact you as soon as I receive any news."

His voice was deep and reassuring, which gave her a certain amount of confidence.

"I'm indebted to you," she effused, as she stood to take her leave, thanking him for his time and help.

"I'll be in touch, Mrs. Findlay, as soon as I have any news. Goodbye," he said as she closed the office door behind her.

Outside in the street, once more, she took a quick look around and again noticed nothing unusual. She didn't want to appear paranoid, but her alertness was instinctive, she was on the 'qui vive'.

It was a fairly warm day and as she passed a kiosk grabbed a bottle of ice cold water, took a couple of mouthfuls and walked unhurriedly along the crowded street. On passing a cafe, she decided that she was hungry. Emma went inside. It was cool; thank goodness for air-conditioning. She felt much happier now that something positive was being done about David. She had done everything possible in an effort to find him. There was nothing else she could do, but to leave it in the hands of the Consul.

Sitting in the cafe with her coffee in front of her contemplating her next move, she wondered if Julian would complete the tests soon. That being the case, they could be out of here within the next few days and hopefully the Consul would have something positive on David. But the one thing she was certain of was, she would not leave until they had received word that David was safe and well.

Here in the cafe everything seemed so normal. The preposterous situation in which she found herself was not intrusive. There was no sign of trouble and the people appeared normal, showing no signs of worries or woes. She wondered if they thought that about her, too - just indulging in a little snack between shopping and visiting her hairdresser. Little did they know that only a few hours ago, she had been running for her life, been chased through a forest, lying face down for hours, in fear of unknown pursuers, and, as if that wasn't enough, to have lost David somewhere in Bogota, perhaps even his life, in an attempt to feed her information. According to Julian, they were all still in danger. What more could happen? It was all becoming too much.

Reluctant to return to the apartment, just yet, she felt a need to be with people and her senses told her she would be safer in a crowd. She began wandering along the avenues of the shopping mall to keep her mind busy and from thinking about David. But the normally tempting merchandise in the shops held no interest for her. She anxiously kept looking over her shoulder, constantly worried, suspiciously watching everybody as if they were about to attack her. How much more could she take?

The apartments were only a short ride away and the driver took her right to the gates. She was really happy to be back without getting herself into any kind of trouble. The gates immediately opened up for her and it was not until she was inside that the thought began to manifest. Inside his gate house sat the security guard, whom she did not recognise; he was a stranger. It was neither of the men to whom she had been introduced the previous evening. Her suspicions were immediately alerted 'Why would he open the gates before I showed my identification?'

"Good afternoon," she said, pleasantly smiling, showing no signs of uneasiness.

"Good afternoon, Madam," he replied as she passed.

She walked casually along the path to the entrance and as she walked she realised that, if her suspicions were correct, she would not have enough time to call the elevator and close the doors before he was at her back.

In a split second she made a decision. She ducked behind the hibiscus and bougainvillaea bushes by the front entrance, and waited. She stood perfectly still, waiting like a cat ready to pounce on its victim. Within seconds he appeared, stopped and glanced towards the lobby; a few steps more and stopped again. Puzzled that she was nowhere to be seen, he frantically looked left and right, taking short furtive steps at the same time in an agitated gait.

She knew what she had to do; he had already drawn his gun. She took the bottle of water from her bag, and, thankfully, she hadn't drunk much; it still felt heavy in her hand. She waited until he was in front of her, took a step out of the bushes, coughed and as he swung round, with all the strength she could muster, smashed the glass bottle into the middle of his face. The glass shattered and before she took flight, saw him stagger and reel. She was nauseated at the sight of blood pouring from his nose and eyes as the splintered glass went to work on his flesh. She flew to the elevator, the doors opened immediately and, moving quickly to the rear, shoved the key into the combination lock. Through the closing doors, she saw her assailant, blinded by the blood oozing from his eyes, crawling on all fours.

When the elevator finally stopped at the apartment, she did not activate its return to the ground floor. Too bad for the people on the other floors, nobody was out to kill them. Still shaking, she lifted the receiver and was fortunate to get through to Julian, immediately.

When she had finished her account he told her to keep the elevator on her level.

"I've done that," she answered

"Next," he said, "go to the bottom of the bedroom closet, right corner, and you'll find a gun."

"What are you talking about; a gun?" she gasped.

"Listen, Emma, I've no time to explain. It's already loaded but the safety catch is on. Be careful with it. You'll be safe now inside the apartment. I'll call you when I'm downstairs and then, and only then do you release the lift. Is that understood?"

"Right, I've got all that," Emma replied, but without confidence. The very thought of a gun sent shivers all through her.

"Honey, I'll be with you as soon as I can. Hold on in there for a couple of hours."

"Love you," she said, as the receiver clattered into position.

Straight away, she went in search for the gun, which she found in the exact place that Julian had described. Gingerly she lifted it, as if it would go off without any assistance from her. She released the safety catch, checked how to handle it, then she engaged the catch again. The only time she had any dealings with weapons was as a teenager on her father's farm, where they had messed around with air guns. She was a good enough shot then, so she supposed she could handle this if necessity demanded.

Returning to the sitting room, she placed the gun on the small coffee table and before settling down, she checked that all windows were secure. Why am I doing this? The apartment's on the bloody twelfth floor. I'm going nuts. Well, she thought, I wouldn't be all that surprised if they tried dropping in from a helicopter, just like the Cadbury's milk tray man.

Her adrenaline pumping, now, she could feel her heart thumping, like a crazed rock drummer, but ready for anybody that tried to enter. Still petrified, she sat down beside the table to wait, confident that Julian would arrive soon.

CHAPTER 13

A feeling of well-being permeated through Julian while standing on the deck for a few minutes, before he went down to the control room. He had left early to give himself enough time to complete the tests. The sun was up now, and the rays bounced off the metal structure like steel flashing lances, disappearing into the grey water below. He saw a shark with its dorsal fin cutting through the lake, neither wavering right or left, until it suddenly caught the scent of something in the water, and, in its stupid excitement, frantically lashed about, losing the trail; only to repeat the procedure some seconds later. He enjoyed this time in the morning when nature quietly went to work and the rest of the world slept on.

The first test they carried out, that morning, revealed nothing unusual to suppose that there lay the fault, and by 10 o'clock they were now going through the penultimate one. Then, from the computer screen, in the main control room, Julian saw spurious signals on the instrumentation, causing, for no reason, valve closures and unexplained vessel level trips. The screen showed exactly the valve in question and also the platform - the largest one of the remote platforms - and, at this point in the game, he could neither see the reason for it, nor could he make any logical sense of it.

Turning to the engineer on duty, Julian informed him that he would be going over to the platform in question to carry out further tests on the two instrument air compressors and checking the calibration on the entire instrument air system.

"How long will you be gone?" the engineer asked.

"Until the fault's solved. I'll probably spend the night there and kip down in one of the cabins, should we finish late."

Over on the remote platform, he soon found that the lead and lag timing, of the two instrument air compressors, was not functioning correctly, and this malfunctioning would account for the problems. In this instance, he discovered that the lead instrument air compressor (LIAC), being the one that should supply the air reservoir pressure to the instrument air system, failed to maintain sufficient pressure, and the lag compressor failed its kick in to ensure that sufficient pressure was maintained. He found that incorrect settings of these compressors caused them to act with a will of their own, and not in unison, as they were so designed.

Once he had diagnosed the fault, it was a simple enough matter to correct the settings. Not one to show any great emotion but, under the circumstances, Julian felt rather chuffed with himself; the problem was solved and a sense of self-esteem briefly touched his person.

He was on the point of correcting the settings when he received Emma's call. It immediately took the smugness from his face and his short lived pleasure evaporated.

"Something urgent has cropped up, Willie; I've got to get back onshore."

"You carry on, Boss, I can manage the rest," the chief answered.

"We've found where the fault lies and it's a matter of correcting those settings," Julian went on.

"We should be done here in a couple of hours or so."

Julian didn't have a problem leaving his chief in control. He was a good man and a clever engineer, but Julian felt a bit cheated out of first prize at not finishing the job to the very end.

"Keep me informed about the progress and keep in touch with the main control room," Julian said, as he was leaving. "You'll get me on my mobile. OK, Willie, see you tomorrow."

The sun had travelled three quarters of its daily path by the time Julian got under way. Fearful of the incessant danger encompassing them, and especially Emma's safety, he was more than anxious to return to the apartment, sooner rather than later.

Away from the platform now and time to think, he was sure that, whoever was pursuing Emma, were definitely not Garcia's men. Foremost in his mind, now that the malfunctioning in the telemetry system had been resolved, was to ascertain who was behind the organisation hell-bent in removing them from this green planet. He had his suspicions but had no concrete evidence. Whoever they were and for whatever the reason, they meant business and were ready to kill.

Julian had known the two boat crew who had been standing by, over a period of time, and whenever he was called on to do work for Caloil in South America, Barco and Antonio had been there to ferry him back and forth. Barco he had known longer than the younger one, Antonio. He had been invited to join Barco and his Family for dinner, during his last job with Caloil. It was an honour for Julian. The old Spanish families had their own traditional practices, and for a foreigner to be welcomed into the family was a sign of respect and friendship. Julian wasn't sure if Barco was his real name; probably he was given it years ago because he was always working with boats. It was late enough in the afternoon and shoals of fish were jumping and filling their gills with air from the calm surface of the lake. Their silvery scales glinted in the now weakening sun. There was hardly a ripple as the boat began to distance itself from the platform.

"Not a bad afternoon, Mr. Julian," Barco greeted in difficult English, interrupting Julian's thoughts.

"Yes, indeed, Barco. How's the family?"

"Good, Mr. Julian, good. We have another son. He's big and strong and when he grows up he's going to be a football player. My wife, she say no, but I say, Maria, this is no life working on the boats. For me it's OK, but for him, I no want this life."

Barco continued talking about his family while Julian's mind drifted back to Emma.

'Hope she's all right,' he thought to himself, 'she should be safe enough in the apartment,' he convinced himself.

He took out his mobile phone and dialled her number.

"Baby, I'm on my way, should be with you in an hour and a half. Everything OK?"

"So far everything's quiet. Just get here as soon as you can."

"See you soon," and he switched off.

They had travelled a quarter of the distance between the oil field and the shore, when there was an almighty blast from behind.

"My God, what in hell's name is that?" he said, turning around to look in the direction from whence they came.

There, behind them, the platform they had left minutes before was exploding, throwing up fingers of flames with every violent burst of energy. He couldn't believe what he was seeing. He was in shock. He was motionless. He stared at the blazing eruption. Barco had already cut the engines.

The nightmare had returned. I'm dreaming, he thought. He stood up now and buried his head in his hands. He didn't want to look.

"It's the satellite platform, Mr. Julian, it's exploding," Barco screamed.

Julian didn't answer, he didn't hear. He was recalling a scene from the past. He thought he was back there. He was living the nightmare once again.

"Mr. Julian, are you all right?"

He didn't hear him. Barco came over to where he was standing and shook him.

"It's the platform, it's gone up, look, look," Barco screamed.

Julian slowly removed his hands from his eyes and looked. What he saw, was a burning inferno where the satellite platform should be, throwing up pieces of metal, jettisoned into the sky with each release of energy, hanging, suspended for a moment before they fell back into the blazing platform.

"Christ-sake, man, get the boat around, we're going back, I've left six men on that platform," he yelled, as his brain hit reality. "Get the platform on the radio."

"It's not working," Barco replied.

"Oh shit!"

Approaching the blazing platform, Julian could see that the section nearest to them was the worst hit, and the boat could not get through the burning oil.

"Go round the other side, Barco," Julian ordered, "we can't make our way through that."

The boat sped round the rear, keeping well away from the burning debris. They saw a section where it might be possible to make their way nearer.

"Pull in over there," Julian said.

There were pieces of metal and burning debris all around, but Barco manoeuvred the boat skilfully and they eventually got closer.

"Over there to the metal ladders," Julian pointed.

A few feet away from the landing platform, Julian launched himself into the water and grabbed the metal leg. Hauling himself up, he clambered onto the slippery platform. Once on the metal ladders, he shouted back to the boat.

"Stand by, Barco, and no radio contact, do you hear?"

He dragged himself up the metal treads. His clothes were heavy with water and each step he took became more difficult. At the top, now, he saw that this section was not too badly damaged and he was able to move around. The explosion had been in the section towards the control room. He had to move quickly, because the main platform, sooner or later, would become aware of the explosion and would be sending out a boat to investigate. He wasn't ready yet for their questioning.

The grating treads were buckled by the heat from the explosion. There was no hum from the machinery or pumps; in fact, the main deck was eerily quiet, apart from the hiss of flames emanating from the ruptured oil and gas transfer pipes. It sounded like a giant Bunsen burner.

Julian knew that, on total loss of power, the down hole safety valves of the wells would have failed safe in the closed position, and what was burning was the residual pressure in the pipe lines. There were jet fires all around him.

Julian's first impression was that the seat of the greatest damage was the control room which had almost been completely obliterated. He couldn't understand why this was the case, because the control room was the safest and best protected area on the oil platform. Something registered, but, as his greatest concern was for his men, he didn't belabour the significance.

He started to search the main deck; all around him, there were areas that appeared as normal, while others were twisted shards of metal. In the areas adjacent to the raging fires, the heat was so intense and unbearable that it was impossible to get closer. In spite of repeated calls there was no answer. As best he could, Julian completed a full search of the main deck without finding any of his men. By fighting back flames, he managed to get down to the well deck, which appeared miraculously unscathed, and checking this area thoroughly proved fruitless, once again. There was no sign of the men.

He now made his way back to the main deck and into the carnage that was the control room. There was debris all around, unrecognisable pieces of bent and twisted metal, and it was here that he discovered the evidence of what had happened to his men. Mixed among the debris were the blackened, charred and dismembered remnants of what had once been four human beings. He felt sick to the pit of his stomach. He was not surprised at the scene that confronted him. In all this massacre of metal and human remains, he hadn't expected to find life; but he had somehow hoped that some kind of magical stream had carried the men to safety. No wizardry had flown to their aid and he began to beat the smouldering debris in his grief. Tears of anger and agony poured from him. It took sometime before he was able to function, and when he did, he tried to figure out where the other two were. He guessed that they must have been in and around the cantilever compressor control deck. Making his way there, through the jets of flames, he found that the entire area had completely disappeared, as if it had fallen into the water.

Knowing that there was nothing he could do, he picked his way through fragments of fallen metal, twisted pipes, smouldering debris and avoiding, as best he could, jets of flames, back to the stairway that lead to the well deck, where he knew he would be reasonably safe. Pausing here for a moment to try and work out in his own mind what had gone wrong, but try as he might, he could find no logical reason. In his search for the answers, the reality of what had just happened to his men hadn't penetrated his understanding. But there was something in his memory that he couldn't quite recall. His head became fuzzy as he forced his mind to call back, call back what? He couldn't remember. Then, suddenly and out of nowhere, he remembered similar scenes in Northern Ireland where Semtex explosive had been used to equally devastating effect; and now he understood, intuitively, that this was no accident, this was sabotage.

The incidents and threats that had happened to Emma and him grew clear, and the comprehension they created in his mind became a frightening scenario. His thoughts were not for himself; he feared nothing, he hoped for nothing, he was free. They were for Emma and his men. The unnecessary deaths, not due to an accident or shoddy working procedures, were a result of some faction operating outwith the law of the land, in an anarchic manner. And Emma, how to protect her from the heinous crimes. He saw clearly, now, what he had to do.

Because of the light from the burning flames, Julian didn't realise that darkness had fallen, and that he had spent some considerable time searching the burning satellite. He had to get away before the investigation team arrived from the main platform. Where the flames didn't reach, there was darkness, and as he groped his way back to the metal ladders, he hit hard against overhanging twisted metal and fallen wreckage. He felt no pain. He had arrived at that point, where his welfare and safety was of no importance. He would take his revenge on those who had committed this wicked crime.

Barco and Antonio were still standing by when he came to the bottom of the metal ladders. Briefly he described the scene above and told them, four men dead, two missing.

"Here's what I want you to do. First of all, I want you to drop me on the beach. Then, go straight to the main platform as if you came directly from the burning satellite, and this is what I want you to say. Tell them that you and Antonio were standing off when the explosion occurred. You tried to get close, but couldn't because it was too dangerous and the heat was too intense. You waited for a while, but saw no life or heard any calls for help. You tried to get closer again but it was still impossible. I want you to say nothing about dropping me on the beach. You have not seen me or any of the other men. Do you understand, Barco?"

"Yes, I understand, Mr. Julian. Antonio and me we see nothing; only explosion and flames."

There was question in Barco's voice, but Julian was not about to confide in Barco, and merely added, "You're a good man. Now start her up and keep the lights off; the main platform might have already sent out a boat."

Once on the beach Julian began to formulate his plans. He would need to be extremely careful, even though he would be assumed dead or missing like the others. He watched, silently, as the boat with two crew men sailed off in the direction of the oil field; he turned and headed towards the main road.

He had landed on a deserted and remote area well away from any sign of human life. All around was in complete darkness and only the light of the moon gave him his bearings. He crossed the shingle beach and onward over low lying grass before coming to the main road. Walking quickly, now, he headed to where he had parked his car by the small marina that serviced the oil field. As he suspected, the place was deserted at this time in the evening. There was no sign of people, only the night watchman, who was happily snoring his head off. However, to be on the safe side he took a quick glance around before approaching his car. It appeared to be untouched and exactly in the position he had left it. He went over, lifted the boot and removed his briefcase. Leaving the carport as quickly and quietly as he arrived, he disappeared into the black void, unnoticed.

It had taken him the best part of the night to reach the suburbs of Maracaibo, where he felt it safe enough now to take a cab to the apartments. He had the driver drop him a couple of blocks away and walked the last two hundred metres to the rear of the complex. The sun hadn't risen as yet, and the darkness concealed his movements, allowing him to scale the high wall at the rear, unobserved. Once inside, he crept through the shrubbery to the front entrance, and it was there that he saw some activity towards that end of the grounds nearest the iron gates. This didn't concern him. His main worry was to get to the lift, unseen, before the sun rose. And it wasn't until this moment that he went for his mobile to contact Emma.

She had fought sleep for hours. But sometime during the night, overcome by fatigue, she had fallen into a disturbed and restless sleep. The shrill ringing of the telephone brought her to a startled and confused awakening. But, bewildered as she was, she grabbed the phone.

"Senora Findlay, this is the security company. Are you all right?"

"Yes," she answered trying to focus, "Why do you ask?"

"We're contacting all residents. One of our security guards has been found dead in the grounds."

She let out a gasp as the previous evenings events rattled back to her.

"Are you all right, Senora?" the man asked, once more.

"Yes, yes of course."

Emma remained cautiously silent, wondering what was coming next.

"Did you hear or notice anything unusual?"

"No, I can't say that I did," Emma lied.

"Well, I don't want to alarm you, but until we find a motive, be careful. We've already contacted the police and they should be here soon."

"Yes, yes, I will," she spluttered as she replaced the receiver.

Coming to her senses now, she began to wonder about Julian.

"Where on earth is he?" she thought to herself.

It was six o'clock in the morning and still dark outside. The journey, at the most, should only have taken two hours, and she began to worry all over again about his safety. She went into the kitchen area and began making coffee and some toast when the phone rang out again. She picked up the receiver and this time, to her relief, it was Julian.

"Emma, I'm downstairs, release the lift."

She removed the chair that was keeping the elevator doors ajar and within a few seconds the doors closed, enabling the elevator to leave the apartment, silently. Within a minute she heard it returning, and, when the doors opened, she couldn't believe the apparition that emerged. There was Julian, covered in oil, his clothes ripped, hands and face covered in blood.

"Oh, my God," she exclaimed, "you're like a scarecrow that's been in battle. What happened?"

He wearily dragged himself into the room, exhausted and beaten, after his gruelling trek. She went over to him and gently helped him remove his charred and filthy clothes.

"Julian, what happened?" she asked again.

"I'll explain in a moment, but first, what's all the activity down in the grounds?"

"One of the security guards has been found dead."

"Is it the one that came after you?"

"No, I don't think so. He must have killed the real security man and then taken his place by the gates. I didn't give it a thought last night, but that would appear to be what happened. The company has already phoned the police, and seemingly they will arrive shortly," she informed him.

"They'll be asking questions," Julian added.

"Yes, you're right; they'll be all over the place like an army of ants."

As they were talking, Julian had completely stripped, and his body, in the areas that had been exposed to the intense heat, was covered in cuts and burns.

"We don't have much time, but briefly I'll explain what happened. There was an explosion on the satellite platform, the one on which I had just left shortly after you made the phone call. We weren't far off when it went up; one God Almighty eruption. I got Barco to turn the boat around and went back. Eventually, I found a way up and after a search found four dead and two missing"

"That's horrendous," Emma gasped, "it could have been you, too."

"There's worse to come. It wasn't until I was about to leave that it came to me. You see, I could find no logical reason for the explosion, and then I remembered a report I had read about Northern Ireland where Semtex bombs had been used causing the same devastation. It was not an accident, Emma, it was sabotage. But, I've got to go back to find out for sure, and before Caloil send out their investigators."

"You can't be serious. Who could be responsible for a thing like that?" she asked incredulously.

"I think it was also meant for me. And the only people, who could do it or want to do it, must have some connection to Roberto Garcia," Julian concluded

"So, you're inferring that both of us were supposed to have died last night, you killed in the explosion and I killed here at the apartment."

"Right, Emma, and both incidents would be reported, in your case, as just another street killing, and in my case, as an offshore accident. Big companies such as Caloil don't like unusual happenings leaking out and that's what these gangsters are banking on. In other words, Caloil, whatever their investigators find, will conceal the truth. They, whoever they are, won't be looking for me, because I should still have been on the platform and I'll be presumed dead. But they will come back looking for you. So we must get you to a safe place."

"Why will they assume you're dead?" Emma asked.

"Oh, I forgot. I told the crew not to mention that I wasn't on the platform when it went up. Old Barco owes me one. So, he'll keep his mouth shut."

"Why, Julian?"

"To gain some time."

"All this is happening too fast. First, David is missing, and what would appear to be, second attempts on our lives," Emma exclaimed, showing signs of some irritation now.

"Correct, Emma, you've got the picture. Now, I'm taking you to a good family where you'll be safe. Put a few things together and we'll leave before the police start asking questions."

"Julian, all this is really making me scared. We can't keep on running away from these killers, whoever they are. They're frightening the hell out of me, these petty minded bullies."

"They're anything but petty minded bullies. Hired killers are a more accurate description. And you've every reason to be scared, Emma: this is for real and they've got us in their sights."

Maria was a large, round and jolly woman. She hadn't always been that size, but five children later and a healthy appetite for her own good cuisine had filled her out over the years. Her hair was now turning grey, but you didn't notice that. When she was young Barco had pleaded with her to change her dark hair to blonde and because she would do anything for him - she was his woman and didn't she love him with all her heart - she had bleached her hair a long time ago and had kept it like that ever since. Sometimes, she let it all fall down over her shoulders in a tangled mess and other times she knotted it at the nape of her neck.

It was on this occasion, with her hair tied back and singing happily to herself while she busied herself in the kitchen, preparing a meal for Barco, that Julian and Emma walked in.

"Ah, mia madre," she sang out as they entered, spreading her big hearted arms in welcome.

"Mr. Julian, you come to see your old Maria," she cried out, enveloping him in her arms and, at the same time, transferring the flour from her hands on to his clothing.

"Maria, you old witch," Julian responded.

Noticing the flour marks, she began clapping and smacking her hands together and wiping them on her apron, and then brushing him down in an attempt to undo the damage.

"I want you to meet someone special," he said as he introduced Emma to Maria.

"This your woman?" she asked in her usual jovial and uninhibited fashion.

"Yes, Maria, this is my woman."

"You all come sit outside in the porch and I get you something to drink. You want a beer, Mr. Julian?"

"Yes, please, Maria,"

"And, for Miss Emma, I give her something special. You wait and see," she jollied as she retreated into the kitchen. They heard her muttering away in between short bursts of singing as she happily prepared their drinks. Soon she returned carrying the refreshments and, after handing them out, she sat down and wriggled her fat bottom into a comfortable position.

"You bad man, Mr. Julian. You not come and see old Maria for long time. Where you been?"

"Everywhere, Maria, everywhere."

She prattled on asking him questions about the different countries he had seen since last she saw him, exhaling oohs and aahs and gasps of delight at Julian's knowledge of things she would never see. They sat there talking for a while until Maria, realising the time, jumped up and announced that her Barco would arrive soon for his meal and insisted they stay for some food. Delighted at their acceptance she hurried off to her kitchen, leaving Emma and Julian on the back porch of Barco's modest bungalow, overlooking an unruly garden, where the bare patches were as numerous as the plants that were struggling to survive in spite of the lack of water, and where, in contrast, thrived the lush green herb and vegetable patch that Maria tended and nurtured. It was here that Emma felt completely happy and safe and, for the time being, the dangers that surrounded them evaporated and disappeared.

Just before Julian took his leave, he said to Barco and Maria that he would like to leave Emma in their care for a few days, simply explaining that he would be tied up at work. Maria welcomed the idea and was only too pleased to be of help. To Julian's relief Barco asked no questions, nor did he make any reference to the explosion, in front of Maria. Now that Emma had been removed from any immediate danger he could concentrate fully on finding out the truth.

He had deliberately waited until after dark before making for the apartment so that, should anybody be watching, his movements would go unobserved. He took the same precautions as he had done earlier that morning and entered the complex by the rear wall. Before he had left the apartment with Emma, he had located the fire escape, and it was by that route that he entered his apartment block. He climbed the stairs and, using the second key, entered the flat by the metal fire door leading into the kitchen area. Once inside, he made sure that the fire door was tight and secure; but, unlike the previous evening, did not jam the lift.

He knew he would have a long wait, but was convinced that they would make another attempt on Emma's life, only this time he would be waiting. The element of surprise lay with him. Trying to put himself in their position and think like them, he reckoned that they would attempt to enter by the lift, either using the security man's keys or by tampering with the electronic controls which were housed in the basement.

After checking the two guns, placing one on the table in front of him and the other he stuck into the waistband of his trousers, he went round the apartment removing the light bulbs. He then went to the window. The grounds were well lit up and he could see quite clearly the pathway leading to the front of the building, not that they would walk straight up the path to gain access. But one thing was for sure, they would need to use the elevator to get into the apartment, and he would be waiting for them. The fire escape would prove too difficult; there was no way that they could fight their way through a metal door that was locked and bolted from the inside. He felt fairly confident he hadn't overlooked anything. He was making their entry easy. Assuming there would be two of them - any more than that would have to be worked out as he went along - he had already formulated his plan of attack.

Settling himself down, with the coffee table slightly to his right, he had a full view of the elevator door. He knew exactly how he was going to handle this. He had figured it out, and he would go over everything again and again while sitting there waiting for them.

An old rummy staggered his way along a dark and badly lit street on his nightly scavenging round. He wasn't really old, he just looked that way. His habitual drinking and nomadic life style had taken their toll a long time ago, and what should have been a young man of thirty-five was now a ragged, soiled and tattered tramp, who looked seventy years of age.

He rummaged in the garbage bins for cigarette ends or scraps of stale bread, and, sometimes on a lucky night, he would find a can with a few beans still glued to the inside. On these occasions he would stick his fingers in and scoop the rotting and stale food into his mouth.

This particular night, he was too far gone to notice the bundle that was a human being lying by the roadside, until he stumbled over it. At first, he took it to be a sack and, in his hallucinant state, believed it to be filled with liquor. As he fumbled around looking for his prize of the night, he felt it was rubbery, and, with further prodding, he slowly came to the understanding that it was no secret cache of alcohol, but a human body, still and cold.

Far too confused to know what to do, he gathered his bits together and continued along the street. Slowly he shuffled along in his dreamlike world, dragging his well worn shoes that boasted of better times when they had laces and soles. At the end of the street, he crossed over to the other side where a police car was parked up.

"Hey you, you old drunkard, get off the streets," a voice from the vehicle shouted.

The tramp looked up, and normally would walk the other way disappearing into the night, but on this occasion, for some reason he couldn't explain, he walked up to the stationary car.

"There's a body down that street," he said, not understanding what he was saying or why he knew.

"You're drunk, you old rummy. Get out of here."

They watched him as he shuffled off into the darkness.

"Where to now?" the first policeman asked.

"I suppose we better check out Pepe's. There's always trouble in his bar at this time of the night," the second one replied.

"OK. Do you think there's anything in what that old tramp said?"

"No, his brain is fucked," the other said, "but maybe we'll take a look anyway."

They crossed over the intersection and drove slowly down the street with headlights at full beam.

"What's that over there?"

They slowly brought the vehicle to a halt and, stubbing their cigarettes out on the road, aimlessly walked over to the bundle. By the headlights they could see it was indeed a body.

"Dead?" one asked, as the other bent down to feel for a pulse.

"No, but he soon will be. The pulse is weak and he's pretty cold."

They radioed for an ambulance and, while they waited, searched his clothing for identification, but found none. From the car headlights, they could also see that he had been badly beaten up and had two bullet wounds. The police car escorted the ambulance, at full speed, to the city hospital where he was immediately rushed to the theatre; and where he was stripped of his clothing and cleaned up as best they could.

The surgeon worked on the bullet wounds. The bullet in his head had entered by the right cheek, shattered his jaw and teeth, and had come out the other side. The other bullet had lodged in his pelvis. He had been on the operating table for over four hours before they finally finished, and then he was transferred to the intensive care unit.

All the while, the two policemen kept wait for the surgeon's report for the police department. From his skin colouring and clothing, they judged him to be European, but until he recovered consciousness, they couldn't be hundred percent sure.

"Will he make it?" the one policeman asked the doctor.

"I don't think so. He's in a bad way," the doctor replied, "But one never knows."

"So, we've got on our hands an unconscious, unidentified European who's ready to snuff it at any moment. Get on to missing persons as soon as you get to the station. You never can tell, he may have a doting mother looking for him."

"If this was just another mugging his money would be missing, and he wouldn't have put up such a fight nor taken such a beating for a wallet. No, this sounds like a drugs case to me," one policeman said to the other, as they left the hospital.

"What's new in this city," the other replied, as they headed back to the police station to fill in yet another report on a crime that would never be solved.

CHAPTER 14

The grounds of the complex were deadly quiet now and Julian assumed that the police had finished their investigations for the day. He had been mulling over different scenarios. Satisfied that he had covered all possible angles, there was nothing more to do but wait it out. In the event that he could be here all night and possibly the following day, he had made himself a few sandwiches and a large pot of coffee. But he would remain locked up here until they came. He placed a call to Emma saying that the scene was set and ready for play to begin. She didn't like it one bit that he was there alone to face his adversaries, and continued racking her brains for an alternative solution.

But there wasn't. She wouldn't leave without discovering what had happened to David, and Julian had some unfinished business with the bastards responsible for the death of his men. They were in catch twenty-two; between a rock and a hard place. Before finally ending their conversation he insisted that, under no circumstances, was she to contact him, and he would call her as soon as he could.

Now, glancing out of the window he noticed a few residents coming and going. It was that time in the evening when people went out to be entertained. It was just after midnight and the streets of Maracaibo were still alive with traffic, the restaurants were full of revelry, when he became aware of the dull swish of the elevator approaching his floor. He had heard the lift operating earlier, taking residents to other floors, but this time it was different; none had come to rest at his level. He listened again and was sure it had come to a halt outside his apartment. He felt nervous, frightened and a sense of foreboding overcame him.

He sat there, cat like, waiting in the dark, ready to pounce. He attached the silencer. Steadying the gun in his hand, for what seemed like hours, he released the safety catch, which seemed to resound like canon fire through the still, darkened room He imagined them in the elevator removing the light bulb, ready for the grand entrance, and then taking a few seconds to listen for signs of activity in the apartment.

After what seemed like an interminable time, but could only have been seconds, the doors quietly began to pull back and there, as he had assumed, the outlines of two figures took shape. They hesitated only briefly, and then he saw the one on the left holding a torch begin to move.

'Good,' Julian thought. He aimed upwards and slightly to the right of the torch light and, as the man was about to take his first step into the apartment, Julian fired.

Not waiting to see if the man fell or not, Julian instinctively leapt like an animal towards the lift. Momentarily distracted at seeing his mate fall, the other was easily disarmed, and Julian, with his left fist, smashed him across the face. Being somewhat stunned for a moment, it wasn't too difficult to force the man down. With the gun pointed at the man's head, Julian quickly turned on the table lamp, and, simultaneously, a swift glance towards the man by the elevator door showed that he had indeed hit his target.

"Now, it's your turn," addressing the other, "I want some answers and I want them fast. Who are you and who are you working for?"

"Go to hell, man, I tell you nothing, you piece of shit."

Julian smashed him across the face.

"Now talk," Julian demanded.

"Fuck you, go fuck your mother," the man growled.

Without warning or hesitation Julian shot him on the right foot.

"You bastard, I kill you," the man groaned.

"I don't think so. Have you forgotten? I'm the one with the gun," Julian sneered, "now talk."

The man kept his mouth shut.

"Think you're a tough guy. We'll see if this helps to loosen your tongue," Julian growled, as he shot the man this time on the left foot.

His refusal to talk, under such obvious pain, began to unnerve Julian. However, he had started along this course and he saw nothing else for it but to continue. He took no pleasure in inflicting pain, and now began to feel nauseous. Julian, having no alternative, aimed at his right knee cap and fired. This time there was a flicker of fear on the man's face and Julian was sure he was just about to break.

"You have one other knee, and after that I will shoot you in the stomach, and that's a long and painful death. Now, do you understand me? Talk."

The man was now in unbearable pain and indicated that he was ready to talk.

He told Julian that they were part of the Colombian guerrilla force, The Revolutionary Forces of Colombia, whose aim was to overthrow the Colombian Government, and to do this, had to weaken them. To weaken the economy of the country meant to weaken them financially. So, any revenue that would eventually end up in the government's coffers, either from oil or drugs, had to be stopped.

"We disrupt the flow of oil and in the case of drugs, prevent it from reaching its destination. Our assignment is to get rid of the Findlay woman thus preventing Garcia from laundering his money, and, consequently, Sanchez is then unable to deliver to the government their cut."

"What do you know about the explosion on the oil field at Lake Maracaibo? And don't forget I'll use this gun on your other knee."

"That had nothing to do with us. The antigovernment faction here in Venezuela is responsible for that."

"Where did I come into all this?" Julian asked.

"We also wanted you out of the way, and the antigovernment faction here in Venezuela wants to disrupt their country's economy. It was getting two birds with one stone, you and the oil together."

Julian, satisfied that the man had no further information, indicated that he was leaving the apartment. He surmised that as soon as he turned his back, the Colombian would reach for his gun. Julian walked slowly towards the lift. Then turning around and just as he suspected, the man had gone for the gun which was now pointing in Julian's direction.

"No, I don't think so," Julian said, as he shot the man through the head.

The Colombian's gun fell from his hand and skidded across the marble. Julian waited for a moment before walking over to where he lay. He prodded him with his foot; the man didn't stir, and the dead expression on the Colombian's face told Julian all he wanted to know.

Here he was in an apartment in Maracaibo with two dead men to his credit, and full of remorse and guilt. What he had just done was criminal and premeditated; it was savage and abhorrent. As his distress began to manifest after the killing of two human beings, albeit two dangerous criminals, he realised he had crossed the river to the other side where he would never be the same person again. He was evil. He started to shake and a spasm racked his body. He had to sit down to steady himself. But as he sat there, another thought began to materialise; and he reasoned that the killings were easily justified; it was kill or be killed. With that simple thought he knew he hadn't changed.

Now, once more in control, hardness returned, and neither having time nor inclination to further consider his cold conscience - he would deal with that later - he set about cleaning the apartment and erasing all traces of blood. Under forensic tests there certainly would be traces. However, a thorough clean up job could buy some time; just a few days, until he tracked down the perpetrators.

First, he wrapped the two bodies in polythene bags, stuffing their guns in with them and dragged them one at a time to the fire escape. Going back into the flat he meticulously scrubbed and disinfected the areas where the men had fallen. By the time he was through it was four-thirty and he wanted to be out of the apartment well before sunrise. Checking, for the last time, that everything was in order, he grabbed his few belongings and set them down at the fire escape.

Then he heaved the bodies over the balustrade, removing the polythene before he let them fall to the ground below. He stuffed the polythene into a carrier bag, picked up his belongings, and cautiously made his way down the metal stairs, stopping at the bottom to check that no furtive eyes were watching his movements from behind dimmed lights and half drawn curtains. He darted to the rear wall and threw his baggage over. Taking a few steps back, he then made a run at the wall. With great effort he scaled it, landing on the other side, hopefully, unobserved.

After walking a couple of blocks he found a trash can where he dumped the carrier bag, and, walking on a little further, he stopped and hailed a taxicab.

An extreme weariness overpowered him as he sat in the cab. The adrenalin that had stimulated him earlier now seemed to vanish, leaving him drained and exhausted. He had had no sleep in thirty-six hours and he felt it. Tired as he was, Julian was still alert and careful enough to get out well before he reached Barco's house. After a ten minute walk he reached his destination and found the house in complete darkness. Not wanting to disturb the household, this early in the morning, he went to the back porch where he found a chaise longue. Throwing himself on it, he crashed out immediately.

Emma did not sleep at all that night. How could she? David missing somewhere in Colombia and Julian staked out in that apartment, lying in wait for unknown 'nut cases'. She wanted to help and be actively involved, instead of being a passive bystander; after all, it was by her doing that Julian and David had become enmeshed in this sordid affair. Racking her brains and tossing and turning had curbed all notion of sleep.

Try as she might, nothing rational or realistic came to mind. But, before she went to the kitchen to help herself to coffee, she doggedly decided to find a way to be effective, and, with the light of morning, she knew that providence would show her the course.

With coffee in hand she went to the porch and, with relieved surprise, she found Julian lying on one of the seats, asleep. Standing there just looking at him, she thanked God that he was still alive. All sorts of ominous thoughts had visited her tired mind during the night.

The dawn was breaking when Julian began to stir, slowly moving and stretching himself to ease the body aches and the nightmares that had infested his slumbers like parasites He saw her watching him and, without uttering a sound, held out his arms for her to come. She lay down close to him; they didn't speak; they lay there on the narrow seat, protecting each other from some unknown fate. He raised himself on an elbow, smiled in his flamboyant manner and, as if he had just returned from a day's golfing, kissed her, tenderly.

"I could murder for a strong, black coffee."

She gave him a gentle nudge of endearing familiarity as she left his side, knowing that he would tell her all in good time. When she returned he was sitting up, trying to shake off the drowsiness that comes with very little sleep.

"Well?" she questioned, sitting down.

He gave her a detailed account of his last few hours, missing nothing out. Emma could hardly wait until he had finished.

"You killed two men?" she said.

"That was sort of the idea, kill or be killed," he replied, somewhat sarcastically.

Somehow Julian felt he was on the defensive and didn't know how he should explain it further; and he simply repeated, "Yes, I killed two men."

He did expect some sort of reaction; disapproval, disgust or even a look of fear, but her thoughts seemed to be racing on, perhaps in denial and not willing to accept that anything like this could happen to them. At this moment in time, she was unable to discuss the killings any further.

"You're saying there are two separate groups trying their damnedest to eliminate us. Why?"

"Yes, one's the Colombian guerrillas, FARC, and the other is an antigovernment faction here in Venezuela. Both of them have the same aims; the downfall of their respective, present governments. And to put it simply, their goal is to stop and disrupt, at any cost, the flow of revenue to the government; to financially weaken them and make them less powerful and easier to overthrow. The revenue from oil and drugs, in particular, are targeted, because they are the greatest sources of government income. The guerrilla movement wants the drugs money for its own cause and, together with protection money from other sources, it sees itself as becoming powerful enough to overthrow the government. So, we are standing in the line of fire, and they want us out of the way."

"Why don't they go after Garcia? That would be the obvious solution," Emma queried slightly bewildered.

"Too well guarded. We, and people like us, are unsuspecting soft options. This is their method of making things difficult for the drugs barons, such as Sanchez and Garcia. But don't imagine for one moment, that, if they did get a crack at the Garcias and Sanchezes of this world, they wouldn't take it"

"What a bloody mess, and we've still to find David," Emma stated, shaking her head.

"This is serious, Emma. I want you to go back home. Have you any idea what lengths these people will go to for their cause, and also Garcia to safeguard his drugs empire," Julian cautioned.

"Yes, I do, Julian, but I'm just as dedicated to my cause and I'm not leaving until I find David. But you know, we can't fight all of them; there are too many and we're only two. Be realistic."

"We don't have to fight everyone. I just need a little time to rectify the mess at the oil field and to settle a score."

"Could we not just simply find out what happened to David and then get the hell out of here?" Emma tried, once more.

"Emma, I only need three or four days."

"Why endanger yourself even more?"

"Because, they're all involved in their different ways to get rid of us. So, to settle a score with one lot means to settle it with all. And as for Garcia, he'll hound us for ever, he's Mafia, Emma and we have his money."

"OK, you win. I'll go along with that," Emma conceded, after some thought.

"One more thing. What are we going to do about the money? We can't very well continue to work for Garcia. It's too dangerous. And at the same time if we don't launder his money, he'll be out to gun us down."

"Correct, Emma, that's why I want you to go back home. This is not going to be easy for me. And with you here, in this dangerous situation, it will only make things more difficult for me. Be reasonable, go home," Julian stated, trying again to make her see some sense.

"We've already discussed that, and the answer is definitely, no."

Julian shook his head in frustration; he knew what Emma was like, obstinate to the point of stupidity. He could do no more; he would do his best to protect her.

"Well, it's going to be a long, old, weary day. What about a fry-up for your old man, before he leaves," Julian requested, changing the subject and simultaneously giving her a whack across the butt, as he kissed her on the cheek.

"Ouch, Julian, that was painful," Emma faked, thankful that all this hadn't completely destroyed his appetite for nonsense.

"Sorry, darling, just a tiny bit over zealous," he said with a mischievous look in his eye.

"Good, I'm glad your humour didn't die with the men," was Emma's parting shot as she went to the kitchen to prepare his meal.

She cooked bacon, eggs, tomatoes, mushrooms and fried bread and he wolfed it down like a pig. He had just about finished when they heard movement coming from above.

"That'll be Maria stirring," Julian announced, "I'm off before an explanation is required."

They stood up and went out to the porch, both of them now showing visible signs of tension.

"I'll call you later, stay cool and don't worry," was all that he said, as he left by the rear gate.

"Did I hear voices?" Maria asked, announcing her arrival in the kitchen.

"No, perhaps you heard the radio," Emma answered, casually.

"What you doing today?" Maria asked light-heartedly.

"Oh, I thought I'd take a cab downtown and do a bit of shopping," Emma replied, indifferently.

"Yes, many fine shops here. But you need plenty bolivares."

After an acceptable time, for Emma was anxious to be going, she excused herself and took a shower and dressed. Then taking one of her larger bags, into which she stuffed an overnight change of underwear and some cosmetics. When she was ready, she went back down to the kitchen to where Maria was busy, called through the open door, "See you later, Maria, my cab's waiting." And was off.

Emma knew exactly what she was about to do. They would be on the lookout for her in Maracaibo, but they wouldn't be expecting her in Bogota.

"Where to, Senora?" the driver asked, as she got into the car.

"To the airport."

Emma stared straight ahead with the same determination that had got her to the top of her field, in Glasgow. 'No, I will not wait for the British Consulate to come up with some cock and bull story, and neither will I sit twiddling my thumbs at Maria's,' she resolved.

Julian barged his way straight into Sam Young's office in the Caloil Corporation Building. He was raging. Sam looked up, shocked, at seeing who had entered.

"What the fuck's going on?" Julian demanded, as he marched right up to his desk.

"What do you mean? You're supposed to be............." he stammered.

"Never mind that," Julian said, angrily, "You know what I mean. Spill the beans."

Sam, totally taken off guard at Julian's sudden entrance, stood up slowly.

"Now, take it easy Julian, I appreciate you've had a rough time out there, but you can't barge in here and make demands."

"Oh, can't I.....a rough time you say......I'll show you a rough time," Julian stormed, as he grabbed Sam by the collar and shoved him back in his seat.

"Now, out with it, you know what I'm fucking talking about," Julian said, as he menacingly towered over him.

"I don't know what you're on about.....you're crazy," Sam spluttered.

"Well, will I tell you!!!!!?.....and correct me if I'm wrong. Yes, there was a fault with the telemetry system, but you suspected that there was something more afoot out there in the oil field, and don't tell me that you thought it was a mechanical malfunction. Somebody was tampering with the settings, to disrupt the oil flow...Sam...And will I tell you who it was? It was an antigovernment faction working to bring down this Government.....Sam. Does it take four dead men before you can be honest? And I say only four dead, because the two missing are part of the guerrillas here in Venezuela."

"We didn't know for sure. It's a touchy subject. We're here by the grace of the Venezuelan Government. We can't rock the boat."

"Good God, Sam, you're here to produce oil, not to get caught up in some internal conspiracy. The Government doesn't want this to leak out, so you get me in quietly to sort it out. But you didn't tell me the truth. You didn't tell me what you suspected. You sat there on your fat ass, while I went through the tests.....I found the fault....Sam...Me and my men, only they didn't live to reap the accolades. They died out there. It was sabotage...Sam....sabotage."

"Calm down, Julian, there's nothing you can do. The Government won't acknowledge the fact that there's a faction here in Venezuela trying to bring them down. They want world wide recognition in trading and they don't want to be branded like Colombia as an unsafe country."

"So, it's a cover up, another white wash," Julian spat out in disgust.

"Julian, stop now and think about it. You ferreted out the problem; you'll be well paid for that. There's nothing else you can do," Sam pleaded.

"We'll see about that. Had I been aware of the full facts, I would have resolved the fault and at the same time saved the men, got it Sam.....got it."

By this time, Julian had worked himself into anger and grabbed Sam by the collar ready to punch him, but in disgust threw him back on his seat.

"Was I supposed to be a victim too, Sam?"

"Oh, for Christ sake, no, Julian. No. We only suspected some kind of disruption, but couldn't prove anything."

"If I thought for one moment you were involved, I'd take your life myself But you're not worth it, you're weak. You're typical of all the top brass... results....money....keep the costs down and to hell with the men....they're expendable. Well this time your judgement was up the fucking creek......you've now to rebuild a bloody platform. How are you going to explain this one.....malfunction? I think not. It's sabotage here and it's sabotage anywhere else."

"Now, look here, Julian, you can't go shooting your mouth off."

"Can't I, watch me. I don't need to live by your hypocritical rules, I've got some of my own; honesty, fair play, you know, all that old-fashioned crap your old man knocked into you. Well, Sam, I still believe in it. You're one sad son of a bitch. You make me fucking sick."

"Where, eh....eh......are you going," Sam spluttered.

"Fuck you, Sam."

Slamming the door behind him, Julian left the Caloil Building feeling a lot better than when he had entered; but he knew that nothing would ever bring back the four dead engineers.

CHAPTER 15

Earlier that day, Emma arrived in Bogota. Because her length of stay was indeterminate, one of the first things she did, and using her maiden name, Wilson, was to book herself into a hotel; a hotel she would class as second rate. Before leaving the airport, she had bought a map of the city, together with an index of street names. Sitting now in the hotel room, she flicked through the directory, jotting down all mortuaries and hospitals. First of all, those within the city, and then those in the suburbs and outer city limits.

Next, she phoned Chas Forsyth's office, and was informed by a secretary that he was out of town for a few days and no, she didn't know when he would be returning.

"Well, that's that then, who said it was going to be easy," she said, to herself.

She then went to the city mortuary, where she asked to see all male Caucasians that had been admitted during the last five days. The expression on the attendant's face told her that this was not going to be easy. But not to be daunted, she persevered and insisted on seeing all white males who had not been identified.

He reluctantly told her to follow him along the clinical corridor, still and dead smelling, to the room where the corpses lay. The atmosphere around her was thick with sinister silence. It clawed at her oesophagus and tightened her throat, evoking a sense of dread. There were only two white unidentified males, but for some perverted notion in her, she insisted that they looked at all the corpses. Drawer by drawer was pulled out, and each time, being unaccustomed to this undertaking, she felt she was going to black out, more from the suffocating stale odour that pervaded the room, even to the very fibres of her clothing, than at the sight of sculptured, expressionless flesh. Some, she noticed, had been badly disfigured and stitched together, while others had obviously died of natural causes. Regardless of the cause of their demise or their mutilated appearance, she stood in awe in this unfamiliar place, with her hand tightly wound around the strap of her bag, clinging to the only comforting thing she had.

As she watched the attendant open and close each drawer, she prayed to God that David would not be in one of them. It took them forty minutes and, at the end of which, Emma was relieved that David was not there. By now, feeling nauseous and light headed, she couldn't wait to vacate the mortuary, and, once out in the fresh air, began to feel better; the colour that had drained from her face, now blushed her cheeks.

Greatly relieved at not finding him there, she did realise, however, that it did not eliminate his possible death. He could be lying dead or dying somewhere, remote and hidden. But she didn't dwell on that probability, she had to keep on going with a positive attitude. Taking out her list, she selected three hospitals that seemed to be the nearest, and set off to check them out. Should this prove negative, she would leave the remaining ones for the following day.

The bedroom was nothing luxurious by any standards, but it was a place to rest her weary bones after a long day traipsing the wards of three hospitals. She had given each hospital a brief explanation regarding David's disappearance. With his description, they had been only too pleased to have her escorted round the casualty, intensive care, and all male wards. Legs and feet aching she collapsed on top of the bed. Disappointment and despondency with her day of fruitless effort had exhausted her more than she realised. But her physical exhaustion was nothing compared to her mental anguish. She needed someone to talk to, to give her some strength and encouragement to be able to carry on the following day. All thought of her own imminent danger had gone, and her only objective was to discover what had happened to David.

There was no warmth in the room which, to Emma, looked hostile with its well trodden carpet and rough dull furniture upon which cigarette burns had defaced the surfaces, making little black craters on what would have been, originally, an equally cheerless brown veneer. Looking around, she saw fear on the walls where the light from outside played grotesque shadows of imaginary monsters on the dark surfaces; and the dark corridors of the mind took charge, making the imaginary pictures real.

Emma thought she heard something moving outside her door, and the hostility that was in the room took over, entering her body, vibrating through her like waves of electric shocks, shaking her in terror so much that you could have used her body as a pneumatic drill. The phone screamed out suddenly, and somehow her jellied legs carried her to the small table where the telephone lay.

"No thanks," she heard herself say, "I won't be requiring my bed turned down."

Placing the phone down, she went to the mini-bar and poured herself a stiff vodka. She took half of it in one gulp and immediately began to regain some kind of composure. Emma thought that she was going mad to get herself into such a state, and the only thing she thought that could have caused it, was the reaction to all the corpses at the mortuary.

She rested for a short while to sort out her tangled thoughts and later, when she felt she could act normally again, picked up the phone to contact Maria, whom she assured all was well, no, don't worry, no, she wouldn't be back that night, but would make contact the following day. She then called Julian, who was not at all pleased with her, but did understand that she just had to get out herself and do something about finding David. Reassuring him that she was fine and safe; convincing him that nobody would be looking for her in Colombia, she hung up, promising to contact him the following evening.

It was two-thirty in the afternoon as two of the nursing staff were taking their tea break when the phone rang.

"Ward 2A, Nurse Callas speaking," Sonya answered, picking up the phone.

The voice on the other end said, they were sending up a young woman who was looking for a missing person.

"OK, show her up," Nurse Callas replied and hung up the receiver.

A few minutes later, a striking woman appeared at the office door, introducing herself as Senora Findlay, and that she was searching for her ex-husband, who had been missing for five days; and could she please have a look at the patients.

"Certainly, Senora, follow me," Nurse Callas offered, courteously.

There were twenty bed bays in ward 2A and, as they went from bed to bed, Emma could only repeat solemnly, "No, it's not him." By the time they got to the last two, Emma broke out in a sweat, despairing that this was the last hospital on her list, and what would she do now if he wasn't here. She was on the point of dismissing the patient in bay two. But, when she neared the bed, she couldn't quite believe that after two days of hunting she had found him at last. She had to look again to make sure, because his face was partially covered with bandages, but there was enough of his features showing to identify him.

Nurse Callas, who had been praying for someone to come forward and identify her patient, could only stare at Emma with eyes wide open, too fearful to ask the question before Emma rested her hand on the nurse's shoulder and nodded, "Yes, that's the person I've been looking for, that's him, that's my ex-husband, David Findlay."

The staff in the intensive care unit had kept a vigilant watch over the man in ward 2A, room 2. They had monitored his vital signs, heart rate and respiration, around the clock, and had changed the dressings on his wounds. Since his arrival he had been on oxygen to ease his breathing. They didn't know who he was, and nobody had claimed knowledge of him or had made any enquiries.

It was now into the fifth day since he had been admitted and, up until now, had given no signs of coming out of the coma. They willed him to regain consciousness so that they might be able to contact a friend or family. But apart from the policemen who had brought him in and who were waiting to take a statement should he make a recovery, nobody had visited him. His wounds were extensive but were beginning to heal slowly; however, his mind was not responding.

Emma had to hold on to the side of the bed to steady herself.

"What happened to him?" she heard herself ask.

"We've no idea, he hasn't regained consciousness."

"You mean he's in a coma and has been like that for five days," Emma said, incredulously.

"Yes, Senora. Come, you've had a bit of a shock, I'll fetch you a cup of tea and then tell you what we know," Nurse Callas said encouragingly, taking Emma by the arm.

She helped Emma to the staff office where she sat her down and gave her a hot cup of tea. Then she began.

"Your Mr. Findlay was brought in, late in the evening five days ago, by the police who found him lying, left for dead, on a deserted street in one of the worst areas here in Bogota. He had two bullet wounds, one to his head and one to his stomach, right leg fracture and had severe head injuries. He had been beaten unconscious and was barely alive when he was admitted. The surgeons worked on him for hours, doing the best they could. We, of course, have been monitoring his progress and he's made a slight improvement; and I repeat, slight, meaning that his pulse is a little stronger today."

"When will he come out of the coma?" Emma asked.

"That, we don't know. Under these circumstances, some do regain consciousness while others don't ever come out of the coma. With the head injuries he has sustained and the loss of blood, he wasn't expected to live. All I can say, for the moment, is he's just holding on."

"What about his bullet wounds?"

"They're serious of course, but he should recover from them in time, that is, if there are no further complications. But it all depends on how much brain damage was done at the time of his beating."

Emma put her face in her hands and began to sob. She hadn't cried in years and she just let the tears stream down her face. She couldn't hold them back any longer. It was as if a dam had burst and nothing was capable of controlling the flood water. She didn't know if the tears were out of relief at finding David alive, or out of guilty fear that he might never regain consciousness, and never again would he be able to enjoy the life that he once knew.

Nurse Callas supported Emma through her emotion and, after a while, spoke to Emma in a soft voice.

"Senora, you must be strong now. He's in good hands and he will need you if and when he comes round."

"Will he have any permanent brain damage?"

"Again, that all depends on the severity of his head injuries. Only time will tell, Senora. We must wait and see what happens."

Emma went back to David's room and could only stand and look at him with all the self recriminations that any one person could feel. She went over to where he lay and took his lifeless hand in hers. She stroked the back of it, trying to will some warmth and feeling back into it. She began to talk to him about things from her past, when she was a child, things she hadn't recalled in years. She jumped from one era to the next. There was no sense or connection in her babble.

Nurse Callas reassured her that hearing is the last sense to go, so talking to him was therapeutic. She spoke of the events that had taken place during the last week and voiced her concern for Julian. She begged him to hear her and to come back from wherever he was.

She dozed off from time to time, and only the jolt of almost falling off the seat woke her up, bringing her to a light-headed consciousness. She sat with him all evening and refused to leave his side even when the nurses were tending him. They brought her a coffee and some dry biscuits before dimming the lights for the night, begging her to lie down and take a nap. Eventually, she must have fallen asleep with her head resting on the covers, and the early morning bustle of hospital routine woke her from a nightmarish slumber.

Shaking the drowsiness from her head, she sat upright and found she was still holding on to his hand. Gently putting his hand on top of the covers, she walked to the window to stretch the cramped ache out of her tired body. With hands on her hips, she stretched backwards to relieve the pain then, returning to his bedside, pleadingly said to him.

"David, you must hear me. You know I could never live with myself if anything happened to you here. You must recover, you must."

She knew he could hear somewhere in that grey void, but it did not make her feel any better. She would coax him into responding; she would bully him; she would try anything and everything she could possibly think of. She couldn't possibly lose him now; not after finding him. There would be no purpose to that, no purpose at all. The nursing staff talked her into freshening up and going down to the hospital canteen for something to eat. There was nothing she could do. She could only wait and see what developed.

Forty-five minutes later she returned to David's room, where the nurses were just finishing changing his dressings. They had moved him slightly, but the expressionless look on his face hadn't altered. He appeared to be as far away as ever. She wondered if he could sense anything at all or could feel them working with him. Again she felt so helpless and riddled with blame. She smoothed the bedcover with her hands, erasing all the creases and it looked so perfect again, but as soon as she removed her hands the imperfections returned. She wasn't aware of what she was doing, she just kept on smoothing the sheets. Then a spark of light, of hope, an idea was beginning to form. Addressing the nurse on duty, Emma said that she was leaving the hospital, but would return in a short while.

Emma instructed the cab driver to take her to the nearest shopping mall and to wait for her. Dashing to the entrance, she disappeared into the milling crowd of shoppers. A short time later she returned carrying a parcel, and asked the driver to take her back to the hospital. Full of enthusiasm now, she ran along the hospital corridors and breathlessly up the stairs, taking two at a time, bursting into room 2, with her mind racing at fifty miles an hour. Then, unwrapping the parcel, she took out a tape recorder and inserted the cassette she had bought at the store; plugged it into the mains and turned on the volume. She sat the recorder beside his bed.

"Let's see what you think of this, my dear, as 'Let's Face the Music and Dance' sang out."

Emma played the cassette for David, over and over again.

It's gentle soft tone had an encouraging magnetism. It was one of David's favourite tunes and he used to play it, over and over again, after a hard day at the office. She liked its silky enchantment and always imagined herself in the arms of a lover, swaying to its romantic rhythm and wearing a long satin gown. She imagined her lover in a black evening suit with a white silk scarf round his neck and his hand placed firmly on her back, holding her close to him and keeping step to the music. Her thoughts drifted to a time when she and David had danced like that, when they had been a lot younger and in love. They had both been utterly in love.

How long she sat there she had no idea. Her mind drifted and it was only when the nurses were doing their rounds and administering the daily dose of pills that she became aware of her surroundings once more.

She glanced towards David, willing him to hear her music, but there was still nothing cognisant in his expression. Taking his hand in hers, she began to remind him of times and events from the past. Only those intimate happenings about which only the two of them had any knowledge. With a cold, damp cloth she cooled his forehead, and all the time the melody softly filled the room. Perhaps it was because she was so painfully tired and hadn't had a proper sleep, during the last two days, that she was melancholic and nostalgic. She had had no regrets after she and David split up, all those years ago. So why did she feel like this now? It just wasn't good enough, she reprimanded herself, weakening at a time like this. She would need to pull herself together and think straight.

"Yes, he will dance again," she spoke to herself, "if I have anything to do with it; he will dance again."

With her anxiety over David, Emma had completely forgotten to contact Julian. She quickly dialled his number and let it ring for some time, but there was no response. She then called Maria.

"Hello, Maria, have you heard from Mr. Julian?"

"No, Miss Emma, I have not."

"Should he call, please tell him I'm well and safe, and I'll contact him later."

"Where are you, Miss Emma?"

"I'm with some friends and I'll see you in a few days," Emma responded, hanging up the phone.

Maria turned round to face the two men standing in her sitting room.

"Where was she phoning from?" one of them asked.

"She didn't say. Just that she's with some friends and would see me in a few days."

The other one asked, "Do you know any of her friends?"

"No," Maria answered truthfully.

They had been instructed to keep Emma under surveillance, but over the last few days she hadn't shown up at the Delago Hotel, and now they were stepping up their surveillance, without much success. They had been tipped off by the taxi company, who had been easily bribed, and confirmed that a woman answering to Emma's description had taken one of their cabs to this address. It was a long shot, they knew, but it was the only lead they had.

Politely thanking Maria for her help and not wishing to arouse any undue suspicions, they left. Maria didn't pay too much heed to their inquiries, as they seemed real nice people and she assumed them to be business associates. She didn't even think it strange when they indicated that she should be silent about their presence in the room, while Emma was on the telephone.

CHAPTER 16

Julian had waited until darkness fell before approaching the tender that would take him back to the main platform. He had seen the auxiliary boat leave for the field, carrying the 'back to back' shift to work, and was grateful that it was Barco's boat that would be returning from the oil field, arriving here within the hour. He had grabbed a sandwich from a kiosk before getting into a cab, and now sat in the tall grass behind the marina, eating and keeping watch at the same time. His car, which was parked in the same position between himself and the main building, looked abandoned and undisturbed.

The loss of the men still weighed heavily on his conscience like a sinking brick, and, although the full facts had not been made available to him, it did not placate him or lighten his capacity of anguish. Had he remained on the platform, somehow, he might have detected something unusual, and thus preventing the diabolical disaster. There was no way that he would have any peace of mind until he returned to the platform and found proof of what had happened that night. He considered this was his sole duty to the men who had perished through no fault of their own. His fundamental nature and sanity cried out for it. Somebody would be held responsible for this; someone would have to pay this debt. He even considered contacting Interpol, but the three of them had become so deeply involved with the drug barons that it would take more than a simple explanation to keep them from going to prison.

As dusk was falling, he heard the faint drone of engines and, looking out to the lake, saw the only too familiar streak of foam, flamingo pink from the rays of the setting sun, as Barco's boat cut through the pale grey water, heading towards the marina. Julian waited until the day shift had left in their cars before creeping across the car park and along the pontoon. Barco and Antonio had gone immediately into the building to collect more supplies for the platform.

Glancing quickly around him, first, Julian leapt on board and hid behind the wheel house. He saw Barco and Antonio now approaching the boat, both carrying heavy boxes.

"Sit them down there," he heard Barco tell Antonio, "and go back for the rest."

Barco proceeded to load the boxes on board and stacked them at the rear. Julian waited until they had cast off and well out before he announced his presence.

"Mr. Julian, you give me quite a start," Barco gasped, not expecting to see another person on board, especially Julian. "What you doing here?" he continued.

"I want you to take me to the main platform."

"OK Mr. Julian," Barco answered slowly, showing signs of curiosity, but knew better than to query it.

"Have you spoken to anyone about me or has anybody been asking questions."

"No, I just tell them what you say. Say nothing about you," Barco replied.

"Barco, you still have not seen me. I simply slipped on board without your seeing me. I don't want to incriminate you any further. Do you understand?"

Barco nodded his assent and continued navigating.

"Things are in a fine mess out there Mr. Julian," Barco then went on to inform Julian.

"I can imagine Barco, I'm going out to help, but I want as few people as possible to know, especially the insurance investigators."

They sailed out in silence, each to their own thoughts; Julian planning his movements and the course he was about to undertake, while Barco was wondering what in God's name Mr. Julian was really up to. He trusted Julian completely, and that was the reason he was willing to overlook company procedure and abide by Julian's wishes.

It was well dark when the boat tied up at the main platform, and thanking Barco, Julian proceeded to scale the metal stairs. He knew that his arrival would not go unnoticed, but he made as little of his presence as possible. Most of the men were hard at work and there was nobody hanging about, making it easier for him to reach Bert Ross's cabin, on the accommodation vessel, relatively unseen. Knocking quietly on the door, he heard Bert from the inside mutter,

"What do you want?" the installation manager asked, a bit short of good temper at being disturbed after an eighteen hour shift.

"Open the door, let me in, it's me."

"Who the hell is me?" Bert barked from behind the door, which opened immediately, allowing Julian to squeeze his way in before Bert had a chance to recognise him.

Inside, Julian took off his cap and Bert let out a gasp of surprise.

"What the hell?" he exclaimed, "You're reported missing after the explosion."

"I know, Bert, it's a long story, sit down."

Julian was smart enough to realise that, although Bert was an old mate and had worked on many fields with him, it was imperative to be open and frank if he wanted Bert's support and co-operation.

Keeping to the events pertinent to the oil field, he filled him in on everything leading up to and after the explosion. Julian told him he had gone back to the satellite platform to have a look around, but the heat had been too intense to get close to certain areas. But, he told Bert, he had seen enough to arouse his suspicions.

"Head office suspected that there was something else going on out here other than malfunction of equipment. They didn't say a thing, the bastards. I could have saved those men, Bert."

"You're saying you suspect foul play and it was not an accident?" Bert questioned, in disbelief.

"Yes, and the only way this antigovernment faction could achieve a result, was by planting two men in the inside."

Bert could hardly believe his ears, but knew Julian to be a man that did not jump to wild conclusions.

"Bert, trust me on this one. I need to go back over to the platform to make sure before the insurance guys start messing around, and there're some things I want you to do. One, I need the names of the two missing men who were working on the remote platform at the time of the explosion. Two, I need a work boat to get back over to the platform. I've got to be sure. Three, tell nobody that you've seen me."

"Right, on one condition, that any information you find, let me know right away."

"Agreed."

"Wait here, I'll get the names and a boat organised."

Bert headed to the office room, where it would be a simple matter to find out the names of the two missing men. He knew that a t/card system was in operation logging the location of all those on board, and when leaving a platform the t/card was moved to the required position. At given times a head count was taken showing their exact whereabouts. Bert went straight to the records room where he found the names of the two missing men who had were presumed dead. Quickly scribbling down their names on a piece of paper, he picked up the telephone and called for a work boat, telling them to tie it up at the bottom of the main steps, and that he would be down in a few minutes, but not to wait. Returning to his cabin he handed Julian the names, and told him the work boat was tied up below.

"Thanks, Bert and don't say a word to anybody, including head office. I'll call you right away with anything I find."

Julian, as surreptitiously as he came, crossed the main deck and down the metal stairs to the work boat. There was nobody around as he jumped on board. He started up the engines and headed outwards to the burnt out wreckage that was, until two days ago, a working platform. He saw the dark outline of bent metal as he approached, and although he was not sure which of the safety devices had triggered the down hole safety valves closing in the wells, it had obviously happened at sometime, because he noticed the wellheads had stopped burning, allowing him to mount the platform and start his investigation.

The control room was decimated, but the damage appeared to be outward judging from the outward bend of the steel. Julian noted that the twisted, blackened metal that once was the control panels, appeared to be blown out from inside; and outside the control room it looked as if the flare gas header pipe had been ruptured, possibly by a section of steel from the control room. He surmised that the resultant jet fire from the flair gas pipe had, in turn, ignited the aviation fuel tank on the helicopter deck. When this blew, burning aviation fuel would have cascaded down to the oil and gas separation area, and in turn created its own havoc. All these factors confirmed Julian's earlier suspicions that there was in fact an explosion in the control room.

Again, going through everything in his head, it made absolutely no sense whatsoever, because he knew that the control room was designed to be the safest place on the platform, where there was positive air pressure to keep out any gas, and, on such a confined installation, it was also positioned as far away as possible from any hydrocarbons. In conclusion, he knew it was not feasible for an explosion to occur in the control room without outside influence. He now knew, without a shadow of a doubt, that an explosive device had been imported and placed by someone who had access to the area. He was now fully convinced that it was sabotage and wondered, 'what pearls of wisdom the insurance investigators would report.'

There was no short cut; it would be a process of elimination by which Julian would obtain the addresses of the two men whom he suspected had been responsible for the explosion. He had sought out the main staff agencies who supplied labour to the oil fields, and here, now sitting in line in the Para Recruitment Agency, the sixth he had visited, waiting for an interview with the recruitment officer, he had a moment for the first time to think about Emma.

He hoped to hell that she knew what she was about, as she could be stupidly impulsive at times, and was capable of going off at a tangent. Although he had had no contact with her since she had phoned when first she had arrived in Bogota, he realised, as did she, it would be just as safe in Bogota as it would be in Maracaibo, in the short term.

He had abandoned the work boat earlier at the marina and, like the previous time, had to walk a fair distance before he had managed to hitch a lift into Maracaibo, where he found himself a hotel. Alone with his thoughts, going over everything until his head felt like bursting like an overripe mango, he had eventually fallen into a disturbed and semi-conscious sleep.

"Mr. Burton, Mr. Valero will see you now," the female receptionist announced, interrupting Julian's thought process.

Julian was shown into a fairly bright and cheery office, which showed the right balance between success and cost effectiveness.

"Please, take a seat," Mr. Valero said, indicating the one nearest to his tidy desk.

"Now, could I have some personal details and job description," Mr. Valero continued as he went for a pre-printed form, "and then we can think about getting some interviews lined up."

Julian cleared his throat.

"Mr. Valero," he began, "I'm not in fact seeking employment myself. But I believe your company placed two engineers, local men, four weeks ago with Caloil, and we are anxious to have them on board again. I want to speak to them personally, but I don't have their addresses. Your firm would get the normal commission, should we reinstate them."

"I was not aware that their contract had ceased, but I'm sure you'll have all the paperwork, together with time sheets".

"Yes, we have at head office," Julian lied.

"In that case there should be no problem. Let me see, when did you say they started?"

"Four weeks ago," Julian repeated, handing Mr. Valero the slip of paper with their names.

Valero punched in some details and hit some buttons on his computer.

"Yes, we did in fact recruit them."

Julian almost shouted out with glee, but restrained himself.

Valero scribbled down the addresses and handed them to Julian.

"If I can be of any more assistance, Mr. Burton, please don't hesitate to contact me. It's always a pleasure to do business with Caloil," Valero said, fawningly, as he rose from behind his desk to shake Julian's hand.

Julian was elated with his achievement, and with the addresses in hand almost skipped out of Valero's office, but it wasn't until he was out in the street that he relaxed his face into a smug grin.

It was three in the afternoon now and there would be a good few hours of daylight left. He would attempt a surprise visit to his suspect saboteurs, after dark.

Hunger was now gnawing at the pit of his stomach, but before he could relax and eat, he had one more errand to do. Any shopping mall would serve well his purpose, and after walking a few blocks he found one. Heading for a department store, he approached the section selling cassette tape recorders, and he chose a small, slim, pocket sized type, that could easily be concealed in his clothing.

Nothing else demanding his energy for a while, Julian sought out a cafe where he could get some food and relax for a time until he took up his new role as a self appointed private detective. The transition from engineer to investigator had been automatic. The murders and crime, that seemed to have become part of his life, had forced him into this other role. He was not aware of that change. His behaviour was as instinctive as a hunter stalking his prey; and when found, he would be judge and hangman.

Apart from a quick visit to the ladies, Emma stayed with David all that morning. The nurses came and went in their daily routine, checking on his progress, and were pleased to tell her that his pulse was getting a little stronger. Nurse Callas was back on duty and not only did she seem concerned about Emma's lack of sleep and nourishment, but appeared to be taking a more than professional interest in David's recovery. She had told Emma that on many occasions the patients, at no predicted time, came out of their long sleep, and also assured her that, on more cases than not, they, through time, made a full recovery.

A couple of times Emma thought that there was a slight change in David's breathing, but on each occasion when she went over to his bedside his position had not altered. Her brain was tired and she had exhausted herself mentally and physically with all the worry about David. Due to a lack in concentration, she was not even capable of reading. She began walking the floor, and only jumbled insane thoughts came crashing in, blocking out all sense and reason; and an overriding feeling of anxiety and panic took possession.

Sometime towards one o'clock in the afternoon David stirred. Emma didn't see the movement, but something made her turn away from the window and look towards the bed. She walked over to check on him, lifting his hand as she always did when she spoke to him. While she was encouraging him to hear her, she felt a slightest pressure holding her hand, and then nothing. Still holding his hand she watched him and again, ever so slightly, there was the faintest hint of movement in his hand. Staring at him in disbelief and at the same time continuing to talk, she saw that there was still no sign of movement in the body of his face. But there it was again; and this time, reaching above his bed, she pressed the bell to summon a nurse. Within seconds Nurse Callas appeared.

"He's gripping my hand, see for yourself," she said excitedly, passing his hand to the nurse.

Nurse Callas took his hand, and within minutes her eyes lit up with a broad grin on her face.

"I think he's responding. I think he's coming out of the coma."

Both women sat anxiously excited.

"You're safe David, it's Emma. Squeeze my hand if you can hear me."

They waited, and in a few seconds there was movement in his hand.

Nurse Callas raced off to fetch a doctor and shortly both returned. In turn they took his pulse, heart beat, lifted his eyelids and checked reflexes. Appearing to be fairly satisfied, the doctor then turned towards Emma, and guiding her away from the bedside, spoke softly.

"There does appear to be a slight change, but I don't want you to get too excited. He has a long way to recovery. He could regain consciousness at any time with a full memory, or he could have some brain damage," he informed Emma, showing no emotion as he left the room.

The doctor's negative manner deflated her somewhat, but on turning back towards David and Nurse Callas, Emma noticed a quiet confidence on the young face of Nurse Callas that gave her the strength she needed; and her mind now focused on David's full recovery.

David lay motionless. Somewhere in the distance he heard faint voices and he was trying hard to make sense of it. His vague mind would not work and the wheels in his head would not turn; they were stuck in a spiral rut and his brain could only focus on the distant voices and the soft music that seemed familiar. His brain would not move on; it was stuck like a needle in a groove playing the same notes over and over again; the faint voices and the soft melody continued to tickle the dark recesses of his memory. He lay still, in limbo with no memory.

Somewhere in the space of time his eyes involuntarily opened. He was not aware that his eyes had opened; all around was dark. Instinctively, he wanted to move but something was holding him down, something was restraining him. Gradually the darkness became lighter, and in front of him there was lightness and darkness. He was so tired now, his eyes shut and he fell into a deep sleep.

The next time David opened his eyes he was able to see shapes and shadows, but his vision was still blurred. And then came the excruciating pain that was his head.

"David, don't try and remember anything, you're alive and safe," he heard a voice.

What happened to him, he could not remember. He saw a blurred shape close to him and felt his body being transported and shifted. There was prodding and poking and he had no strength either to assist or resist. The movement stopped and he could make no sense of where he was. The pain in his head was so severe that it made him close his eyes. He could hear voices and a melody was playing.

"What is that tune?" he asked himself but was unable to recall it.

A blurred face appeared in front of him.

"David, it's Emma. Do you know who you are and do you know who I am?"

What was the stupid cow saying? "Of course I know who I am," he tried to tell her, but nothing came out. Somebody wet his lips and mouth. He tried croaking an answer, but could not speak the words; and all he could do was move his head upwards and downwards in the affirmative.

The shapes and shadows began to form into people; his eyes started to focus and his vision was coming back. His head was raised and some more water was dabbed on his lips, giving slight relief to his dry throat as he tried to swallow.

"You're in hospital, David. You've been very ill, but now you're getting better," Emma assured him.

This time he was able to croak a grunt. Slowly, he could see more clearly and understand what they were saying. With his sight returning so did his memory begin recalling events; eventually to the point when he shot upright in bed with terror as his last few conscious moments flooded his brain.

"Take it easy, David," Emma said holding him close, and then slowly lowering his shoulders onto the bed.

He was trembling all over, but now with his eyes wide opened he saw clearly, for the first time, the faces of Emma and Nurse Callas, and he smiled.

The puzzled expression on his face was asking the obvious question, and Emma, sitting on the bed beside him, began recounting the circumstances in which he had been found and his subsequent state of unconsciousness for the last seven days.

She missed out, for the moment, everything that had occurred in Maracaibo; that, she decided, could wait until later when he was stronger and could cope. When she had finished he lay quietly for some time, absorbing the information.

"Did you contact Chas Forsythe?" he asked after a bit.

"As a matter of fact I did, but his office informed me that he was out of town for a while," Emma replied.

David struggled to think clearly.

"Emma, if they knew I was prying into their affairs, then they most definitely knew that Chas was also in on it," he slowly made the conclusion.

"We've got to get out of here. If Garcia has any idea that

I'm still around and not dead, he will most definitely succeed the next time."

Emma was already aware of the urgency to leave Bogota as soon as David was able to travel, and she had already made a decision to move him. She was also certain that if the police, who were still hovering around to take some sort of statement, ever got to fill in a report, it would get back to Sanchez or Garcia sooner than later. She had asked Nurse Callas not to mention David's recovery to the police, in the meantime. Saying nothing to David, who had lapsed into a light sleep, she headed for the staff room. Luckily Nurse Callas was still on duty and Emma asked her if they could have a private talk somewhere.

"We can talk here, Senora."

"I'm going to be open and frank with you. We both know that David's condition is still serious, but it's imperative that we move him, you see, he's in grave danger, life threatening, indeed both of us are. But I want to assure you that neither of us have done anything wrong."

"You don't need to have committed any crime here, Senora," Nurse Callas interrupted, "to end up like Senor Findlay."

"He's got to be moved quietly and secretly and I can't do that without your help. Let me ask you a personal question. How much do you earn here? No, don't answer that, it is of no consequence. We'll make it worth your while, financially. I can't move David on my own; I need your help. What I'm asking, can you give up your job here, for a short while, and help me take care of David until he's well again?"

Nurse Callas remained thoughtful for a moment.

"It's not the money you understand, but I'd be glad to help you and take care of David ...eh Mr. Findlay."

"Can you do it?"

"I don't know. But I'm due annual leave; so if I can get somebody to fill in for me at such short notice, it's possible. Give me a couple of hours and I'll get back to you." Nurse Callas replied.

"Good, as soon as you can confirm it, I'll book flights, and we're out of here."

"Where to Senora?"

"I don't know yet; anywhere safer than here. Arrangements have to be made. So while I'm out, please keep an eye on David. Shouldn't be too long," she said to Sonya Callas, as she made for the door.

After Sonya confirmed that she was able to take leave at such short notice, Emma booked flights for the following morning, early, before the sun would light the sky. She arranged, with the help of a fistful of dollars, for an ambulance to be waiting at the rear hospital exit. Finally she went to the British Embassy, explaining the circumstances, whereupon a temporary passport was issued in David Findlay's name.

Shortly after 3.30 in the morning, when the officer had gone for his tea break, three people, one on a stretcher, quietly made their way along the now deserted corridors to the rear exit of the hospital where the ambulance was waiting. Pain killers and a light sedative had already been administered to make David's journey as comfortable as was possible under the circumstances. Emma understood that moving him at this time was taking a big chance, but the alternative, remaining in Bogota, looked equally bleak and grim.

David was hoisted in, followed by Emma and Sonya Callas. The driver was given instructions to take them to the airport, and it was not until they went through the gates, crossing the tarmac to the Cubana plane, that Emma revealed their destination.

"Now I can tell you that we're flying to Havana, Cuba."

Immigration was standing by to check passports, but seeing the severity of David's injuries they asked only the standard questions and left the ambulance. Carefully, he was lifted on board and laid on the three front seats. He didn't complain at all, but Emma could see from the strained, whitewashed look on his face that he was in dreadful agony. And as she continued to look at him, she shook her head in sadness, and couldn't help but wonder why man was never at a loss to inflict anguish, mental and physical, on his fellow creature.

A phone rang out in a dilapidated house in one of the poorer suburbs of Maracaibo. A big- faced man rose from a chair and walked lazily across the room to answer it.

"Yes, I understand, I'll take care of that right away," and replaced the receiver.

Walking back to where he had been sitting he addressed the other man by the window.

"The hit's on, we've to attend to it right away."

The big-faced man didn't tell the voice on the line that they had temporarily lost their quarry.

"Oh shit, what are we going to do?" the man by the window asked.

"Well, we can go back to the bungalow and rough up the woman for information, but I don't think she knows anything anyway, and also, if the Findlay woman got wind of it, our little bird won't come back to roost. What we can do, for the time being, is keep an around the clock watch on the house," the fat faced man answered, "and hope she shows up soon. We'll do it in six hour shifts."

CHAPTER 17

House, No. 13, was half way along an untidy street where empty cans and cigarette packets lay strewn and discarded, some on the pavement and others kept company with tufts of half withered weeds. Julian, concealed by an overgrown bougainvillaea bush that spread itself onto the pavement at number eleven, kept surveillance. From his position, he saw clearly into the well lit room of the house at number thirteen. So far he'd seen no movement from within, and his first impulse was to walk straight up to the door, and, under some pretext or other, talk his way inside. But that would be sheer folly.

He checked that the gun he was carrying was secure in his belt and a pat at his jacket pocket assured him that the recorder was still there. He had been keeping watch for half an hour, when a beat-up convertible rattled its way along the street and drove into the overgrown driveway of number thirteen. Out jumped a woman who went to the door and, on turning the handle, disappeared inside. She went into the well lit room and a man who had obviously been sitting on a low seat, stood up. After a five minute conversation the woman came out again, went into the car and drove away.

Julian remained hidden for a while longer, watching the house, but saw no further signs of anybody moving around. He then slipped into the darkness of number eleven and fought his way through some bushes, arriving at the rear garden of number thirteen. Here he saw another room that looked like a kitchen, also lit up, but again, after watching for sometime, found nobody moving about inside. Returning once more to his original position, Julian watched the man in the inside close the drapes.

At this hour, the only sound to be heard was the nightly chorus of barking dogs roaming the deserted streets in search of some scraps from the garbage bins. From his observations, Julian had to assume that there was only one person in the house, and, on leaving his position and keeping close to the shrubs, he approached the front door. With the gun in one hand he did exactly what the woman had done, opened the door, which led into a narrow hall. Taking a few steps he reached the door of the brightly lit room and, pausing for a moment to compose himself, he opened the door and entered

"Is that you, Josef?" he heard the man on the seat ask.

Julian grunted an incomprehensible reply but before the man on the seat had time to turn his head, Julian had sprung across the room, and with his gun pressed into the back of the man's neck he told him not to move.

"Keep perfectly still, don't make a move," Julian cautioned.

With the gun still directed at the man, Julian walked round the furniture to face him. Immediately, he recognised him to be one of the six he had left on the satellite platform to complete the fault and, in the same instance, the man, Pedro Rodregas, knew who was standing in front of him.

"Surprised that I'm not at the bottom of the lake?"

Pedro Rodregas, having had a moment to recover from the vision before him, put on an air of innocence.

"Mr. Julian I don't understand why you're pointing a gun at me."

"Listen, you piece of shit, I want some information," Julian continued, completely disregarding Rodregas's faked pretence, "and whether you're willing or not, you're going to tell me."

Rodregas shrugged his shoulders as in a gesture of indifference, but his eyes, like a cat's, watched Julian's every movement. The anger in Julian as his mind now began to recall the tragedy swept through his very being, and for a split second he lost his concentration. That's all it took for Rodregas to seize his opportunity and kick the gun from Julian's hand. However, before Julian could retrieve it, Rodregas was at his back, punching and kicking. Julian was able to ride some of the blows but some of them hit their mark. Miraculously, Julian, having regained his position, took a quick step forward with his right leg, then replaced his weight on his back leg, and with a lightening pivot swung his right foot which he slammed into Rodregas's testicles. He, Rodregas, was unable to move for a moment - he was motionless with pain - giving Julian the opportunity to follow it with an uppercut to his chin. He fell like a ton of bricks, crashing to the floor, making a sickening thud from the impact. Then Julian picked up the gun and went over to where Rodregas lay. He gave him a kick in the ribs. On getting no response, Julian then cautiously turned him over only to find blood oozing from the side of his head.

Still getting no reaction from the man on the floor, he gingerly bent down to feel for a pulse, but there was none. It took Julian a second or two to grasp the fact that Pedro Rodregas was indeed dead, and somehow had struck his temple on the stone brick jutting from the ornamental fireplace.

"Bloody hell," Julian spoke to himself, "just my luck that the creep dies before I get to the truth."

Now that his first lead had taken himself out of the equation, Julian considered his next move. Checking again that Rodregas was definitely in a state of no recovery, he made to leave the property, when he thought he heard a noise. Jumping behind the door he eared the silence and was certain that there was faint movement coming from the hall beyond.

The door noiselessly opened and a figure came into view. Julian seized his opportunity, and, like a butcher's cleaver, brought the butt of the gun down on the man's head, felling him. He wrestled with the dead weight, dragging him onto a seat; there he got a clear look at him and indeed recognised him as the other missing man.

Julian was taking no chances this time and, undoing the man's belt, strapped it around his ankles. Then, he took off his own belt and tied it tightly round the unconscious man's wrists. Sitting himself in front of the man, Julian threw a glass of beer over his face and waited for his reaction. It wasn't long before the man opened his vacant eyes, and with his head rolling from side to side, tried to rid himself of the dizziness and drowsiness. He was so dazed and disoriented that he began to blabber.

"You're supposed to be dead."

Julian quickly turned on the recorder.

"Why am I supposed to be dead?"

"They want you dead."

"Who wants me dead?"

"Us."

"Tell me, who you are?"

"We are the antigovernment group in Venezuela."

"Who else wants rid of me?"

"The Revolutionary Armed Forces of Colombia, drugs," the man muttered shaking his head.

"What's your name?"

"Josef Serna."

"Who was responsible for the explosive device on the platform?"

The man hesitated.

Julian stuck the gun in the man's face.

"Who?" Julian demanded harshly.

"We, the AGG, here."

"Did you put the explosive device in the control room?"

Serna, now becoming more 'compos mentis' began to hesitate.

"Answer."

"Yes," the man yelled.

Julian switched off the recorder.

The man, looking around for the first time since he came into the room, noticed the bundle on the floor.

"You killed Pedro," he accused.

"No, I didn't kill Pedro. That pleasure was snatched from me, he killed himself."

"What are you going to do to me?" Serna asked.

"I should probably shoot you, but I won't. Your 'compadres' will do it for me when they discover that I'm still alive."

Julian saw the fear in his eyes.

"That is, if you ever have the guts to tell them," Julian goaded.

Now that Julian got what he came for, he wanted to leave this house as quickly as possible He had no desire now to inflict any more pain. Life would execute its own terror. This man Serna would live in fear for the rest of his life. He, Josef Serna, would get his due deserts.

Walking at ease along the street away from the house, with the warm air caressing his skin, Julian was pretty sure that he and Emma would have no trouble, at least for a while, from the guerrillas in Colombia or the AGG in Venezuela. But they had still Garcia and Sanchez to think about, and they could be the most dangerous of all. Strange that he felt no guilt over the death of Pedro Rodregas; albeit he had been instrumental in the fall that killed him. He knew it was the man's destiny. In the case of the other two, that was a different story. If it hadn't been for his intervention, sooner or later, they would have been successful in killing Emma. He justified these killings as unfortunate but necessary. He had no bad conscience about any of it. Somehow he thought he would feel differently or things would have changed; but the killings hadn't altered a thing. He felt the same as he always did and still considered himself a good person.

Julian rationalised the deaths differently and was thankful at the outcome. Rodregas had planted a device that had killed four other engineers, and for that, Julian reckoned, Pedro Rodregas had earned and deserved the fate that had befallen him.

No authority here would pay much heed to another corpse, because this was a city where drugs, related crime and killings were rampant - a pandemic disease that spreads throughout the cities. Nobody cared; only perhaps, some lonely mother whose son or daughter hadn't been heard of for ages.

Because of existing poverty in rural areas, a large migration of the youth flock to the big cities in search of a better life; that golden dream. The reality of it is, they are no better off here than they were at home and, just to get by, many of them are forced to resort to crime, prostitution, begging and drugs; to take from those that have, and give to those, themselves, that have not. In due course, they are transformed from innocent young people into hardened criminals, and, as time goes by, become drug addicts. This state of affairs disturbed Julian, because the way he saw it the youth were not the real criminals.

Julian could be labelled an uncommon man, who possessed the qualities of tender heartedness and compassion for others, and in contrast the ruthlessness of a trained killer. He was capable of destroying the enemy and showing no signs of remorse.

He was totally opposed to the illegal use of drugs and those in power, the drug barons who, on setting up their cartels, not only controlled and suppressed the competition in this illicit market, but made millions of dollars from the misery of others, by distributing cocaine, heroin and the like, through fear, torture and brutal murder staged by the Mafia drug barons. They were responsible for the deaths of thousands of innocent young addicts. This was what Garcia and Sanchez were about. Emma, David and he were now tools in rapacity and treachery, and, Julian, although opposed to the illegal use of drugs and all that it involved, had been prepared to go ahead with laundering the money.

David's condition had worsened during the course of the flight, giving cause for concern. His pulse had weakened, and due to laboured breathing, Sonya Callas had administered oxygen. Thankfully it had not been a long journey; the very reason why Emma had chosen Cuba as their destination, but when they had him settled in the hotel room, there seemed to be a marked improvement. He had been fed intravenously during his stay in hospital. Now, more than a week along the road to recovery, his facial injuries had time to heal to the extent that he was able to take food orally. Emma had left Sonya with her charge and was now on her way to Matanzas to keep an appointment with an estate agent.

"I'm looking to rent a furnished villa, quiet and secluded, by the sea if possible," Emma informed the agent.

He went to a filing cabinet and on pulling out a folder began to leaf through its contents.

"We have some houses on our books, but I don't think they're exactly what you have in mind," he said, as he continued paging through the folder.

Then handing Emma some to study, he went on.

"Most of the properties have been neglected over the past thirty years, and only recently when the outside world began to recognise Cuba again, has any interest been shown."

Looking at each brochure in turn, Emma was disappointed that she could find nothing worth her consideration. Some were merely shacks in dreadful states of disrepair, while others were situated on busy thoroughfares.

"Have you nothing else to show me?" Emma pleaded in desperation.

"Well, we have one other, some way out, good outlook, but there again it requires some maintenance."

"May I have a look at the details?"

He pulled out yet another folder and handed it to her.

"This one," he went on, "belonged to an American actor, but it was abandoned after the Bay of Pigs. From time to time over the years we've had a let or two, mainly to high ranking Russians, but that too is all history now."

Emma studied the details and true enough it did need some redecoration and attention, but since there was nothing else suitable, she said she would view it. The agent handed her a local map with written instructions and she was on her way. Taking a cab she gave the driver instructions to head towards Cardenas and would give him further directions nearer the town.

The road wound its way sometimes over hilly and mountainous areas and at other times through flat and rolling terrain. In places where the route neared the sea, Emma could see that the coastline was indented by beautiful bays and gulfs, nestling at the foot of the cliffs. Approaching Cardenas, Emma gave further instructions to the driver, and the route led them over a hilly rise before dipping downwards to the sea. Half way along this road she asked him to make a right and a kilometre further make a left, arriving at what was once a handsome, colonial type dwelling, still showing signs of its dignity.

Emma went through the pillared archway and up to the house, in front of which stood two majestic palms, swaying and rustling as the light tropical breeze touched their leaves. The surrounding lawns, now totally overgrown, were home to subtropical shrubs such as oleander, canna lilies, hibiscus and many varieties of palms. Walking by way of a well neglected path to the front entrance, she came to the covered veranda which extended all around the house. The colonial effect was further enhanced by marbled structured pillars, supporting the upper balcony.

Inside, Emma found an elegant sitting room, leading to a dining room with windows opening out to the terrace. At the rear there were the usual kitchen and domestic offices with views of the garden as it slipped towards the beach. Upstairs, four bedrooms, each with their own balconies, offered splendid views of the gardens and the sea. Yes indeed, it did require some work, but a quick glance around was enough to convince her that this would be most suitable and exactly the right situation for David. Outside again, she found two more palm trees on the beach side of the house, and what impressed her more than anything else, was its open aspect to the sea.

Full of enthusiasm, she couldn't wait to return to the hotel and tell David and Sonya that she had found the ideal place. She described the layout in great detail together with all its advantages. Even if they were opposed to it, they didn't have the heart to tell her. Her enthusiasm was so overwhelming that they could not burst her bubble.

The estate agent agreed to have all renovations, including a fresh coat of paint, completed within two days, and on that premiss, Emma contracted to lease the Villa Verdi. David, by that time, should have recovered fully from the journey, and Emma noticed he was already brighter and livelier. She arranged for a gardener, domestic help and for the supermarket to make a delivery of victuals, necessary for a month.

"I think that's everything taken care of," Emma reflected, and then she remembered, "Oh, money. I knew there was something else."

She phoned her secretary, Maggie, in the Glasgow office, for a money transfer. She was also pleased to hear that all was well and no unsolicited mail had been received. Sonya then went on to suggest that David should begin moving some muscles and with the help from the two women, he managed, for the first time, to walk round the bedroom and into the bathroom. But when they got him back to the chair by the bed, he was totally exhausted and light headed from the little bit of exertion.

"It's progress, just a little more each day and you'll soon be back to normal," he heard Sonya say, encouragingly.

"Yes, you're possibly right," David concurred, but showing signs of impatient disappointment.

"Sonya, your turn for a break. Take a walk or have a swim," Emma then suggested.

"Oh, good for some," David muttered from the chair, ostensibly regaining some of his old spirit.

"We'll even get you out tomorrow. I've arranged for a wheel chair to be sent up and, before you know it, you'll be up and running with the rest of us," Emma said, letting out her secret.

David merely grumbled at that, showing a healthy intolerance.

"I think I'll take you up on that offer," Sonya announced, "I could do with some fresh air."

"Take your time and don't hurry back," Emma called as Sonya left the room.

"Good idea of yours to bring the nurse along," David admitted, for the first time, after Sonya had left the room, "from a medical point, I mean," trying to explain away his last comment.

"Do you think so?" Emma teased, raising an eyebrow. "I can see you're making vast improvements already."

"I'm feeling a little drowsy," David said, quickly changing the subject, "you know you don't have to stay all the time."

"Well, in that case if you're sure I'll go to my room. If you need me, the room number is 409."

Emma saw him back into bed and told him that she would return in half an hour. Quietly closing the door behind her, Emma made for her own room and decided to take this opportunity to get in touch with Julian.

CHAPTER 18

With the cassette in hand, Julian once more barged into Sam Young's office, unannounced, with a very excitable secretary at his heels. Sam shot out of his seat at the sight of Julian striding towards his desk.

"There's your evidence," Julian said, throwing the tape across the surface. Without saying a word Sam picked it up and played it. Julian had mellowed somewhat since the last confrontation; his ire had abated by the confirmation of his suspicions. He stood silent now, waiting for a reaction.

"All right, you've got the proof, but I assure you that we at Caloil didn't believe it would come to this, otherwise, we would not have sent you in and let four men die at the hands of these fanatics, fighting for something they haven't a chance in hell of winning. But nothing's changed; our hands are tied, and even should we challenge the Government, they'll deny that any movement like this exists and, at the same time, throw us out of the country."

Julian attempted to speak, but Sam continued.

"No, let me finish. Caloil has invested millions here; this is big business and, although four of your men have lost their lives, they won't jeopardise their interest here. The families will receive a handsome settlement. As for the Government, they're not interested in the deaths of four men. Look around you; people die here every day, innocent people, for no good reason at all. There's nothing you or I can do, not even Caloil. It's a 'fait accompli'."

"So what you're really saying is that the explosion was an accident, due to malfunction of equipment and everyone goes home, happy ever after."

"Yes, that's exactly what I'm saying: that's what the accident report will say: that's exactly what the insurance investigators will come up with: and you can do nothing as an individual. If you persist along this line of thought, the company will give you a free ticket home and you'll never work in this country again."

Julian didn't like it one bit, not one bit at all. But he did accept that as unethical and crooked as it was, Sam was right.

"And the insurance company pays out for the reinstallation of the platform," Julian said, shaking his head in disgust, "and up against these boys the ordinary man in the street has no chance at all."

It made Julian sick in his stomach at the injustices that life dished out. Resigned to the fact that nothing more could be gained, he made a move to leave.

"Now that I'm finished here and found your problem, send my money to the usual bank account."

"You'll be well paid for this one," Sam beamed.

Julian turned back.

"Just give me what I'm due," and he turned towards the door.

"One last thing," Sam said, smugly, "after you've had the usual rest, say two weeks, we need you out in Russia."

Disgusted with the whole bloody affair, Julian now needed a drink. He was too sober; he couldn't think straight; he had no idea what his next move would be. He walked into the first bar he came to, not far from the Caloil Building, and ordered up a beer, then made for the pay phone.

"Bert, Julian here, it's what we suspected, found the two missing and one talked. Sam Young's got the proof."

"What are they going to do about it?"

"Nothing, Bert, nothing. Caloil's hands are tied tightly, they can't do a damned thing, won't rock the boat. You'll receive a full report from Sam, showing the explosion to be accidental malfunction of equipment."

"Fucking hell," Bert exploded, "they can't get away with that."

"They can and they will, so forget it Bert."

"For fuck sake, and we stand around and take the blame. One massive cover-up."

"Something like that."

"What are you going to do now?" Bert asked.

"Don't know yet, but in the short term, get drunk."

"Where are you?"

"In some bar or other, close to the Caloil Building," Julian informed him.

"I think I know it. I'll see you later. I'm due to wrap up here."

Julian hung up the phone and went over to the bar.

That's what I need, Julian said to himself, taking a mouthful. He swallowed the rest in rapid quick time and ordered another.

"Work around here?" the bartender asked as he put the pint in front of Julian.

"Off and on."

"In the oil business?" the man asked again.

"Yeah," Julian replied, wishing to hell the barman would go away and leave him alone with his thoughts.

It was not to be.

"With Caloil?"

Julian nodded.

"Great company, that one. Brother-in-law works out there. You might know him, Pedro Rodregas."

Not any longer, Julian said to himself.

"No, can't say that I do," Julian said aloud, showing no interest.

"Jaime, can we get a drink over here?" somebody called from the other side of the bar.

Thank the Lord, Julian thought with relief, when the barman left. He was in no mood to carry on a conversation with the barman, especially one concerning Caloil, the very subject he was trying to forget.

The bar had become busier now, and a bit further along from him stood a group of expatriates with loud voices and jolly laughter, making the usual noises regarding the 'pros and cons' about life and work in Venezuela. From their conversation, Julian deduced they were mainly oil people out for a good time. Now they were singing the praises of their particular football team. They had no ear for the other man's opinion, because at this stage in the revelling the only voice they wanted to hear was their own. The more they consumed, the louder they became, and their loud raucous laughter escalated and erupted throughout the bar. Sitting on his stool, Julian overheard parts of the nonsensical blather around him, and, after four pints, he felt cheerier and revitalised to the degree that he now desired to be part of a lively group. He was just considering going over and striking up a conversation, when Bert appeared.

"Over here," Julian called out, glad for company. "What's your poison?"

Bert thought for a second, smacking his lips in a peculiar idiosyncratic manner as if his decision would change from his usual.

"I'll take a beer."

Julian summoned the barman.

"When you're ready, two beers over here."

The man brought the drinks and bumped them down.

"Cheers," Bert said, taking a mouthful.

"I see you're in better spirits," Bert continued.

"Yeah," Julian responded with a roughness in his voice.

"Have you had anything to eat yet?"

"Yes," Julian answered, "I'm drinking it."

Bert and Julian had often worked on the same contracts, and through the years had spent many an hour in similar circumstances, sorting out to no avail the world's problems in a bar room haze.

"Bad business, this," Bert said, referring to Caloil.

"I'm not through with them, yet," Julian asserted, "but for the moment I haven't a clue what's to be done. The answer will come to me, you'll see".

By the time the afternoon was well spent, Bert and Julian had sunk a good few, and at that point in time when alcohol slips down like honey, Julian thought it a good idea to order tequilas.

Sometime later when he began slurring his words, Julian knew it was time to call it a day. Bert managed to get him back to his two star hotel where he poured him into bed, and thinking at the same time, someone was going to have a bad head in the morning.

At first, Julian did not know what was causing the ringing. He tried to recall where the hell he was. The ringing persisted. He opened his eyes and quickly closed them again. His head ached and his mouth tasted like a badger's ass. Then he remembered yesterday. That ringing, oh blast, it's the phone. He grabbed it as fast as his reflexes would allow.

"Julian?" he heard Emma's voice.

"Hello da........." he croaked, not able to finish. "Hold on a mo......"

He swallowed a glass of water and tried clearing his throat.

"Hello, Emma," managing to complete his greeting this time.

"How are things?"

"Had a skinful last night and you know the rest. Where are you?"

"Good news. Hadn't time to call earlier. I found David in a hospital in Bogota, badly beaten up and two bullet holes in him."

"My God, Emma," he exclaimed, coming round slightly.

"Anyway, he's on the mend and we managed to get him to Cuba," she continued.

"Cuba," he repeated, in disbelief, "why Cuba?"

"We had to get him out of the country as quickly as possible, and this was the best option at such short notice."

"Why not the UK?"

"Too far; he's not fit to travel that distance. To fly him to Cuba was even a risk."

Julian's head began to clear slightly.

"Did you say 'we'. Who's we?"

"Nurse Callas, whom I've hired to take care of David until he's fit to travel home."

"That sounds sensible, I suppose. You have been busy. Look, I'll join you there as soon as I can. I've some unfinished business here."

"What sort of business?"

"I'll fill you in when I see you."

"No, that's not good enough. I'm returning to Maracaibo. Most of my things are still at Maria's."

"I don't think that's a very good idea," Julian said, his head still thumping.

"I'll call you as soon as I arrive," Emma insisted.

Not feeling up to arguing with her, at that particular moment, he reluctantly gave her the name of the hotel.

"Need to dash, Julian, I'll see you soon," she ended and the line went dead.

As soon as Emma had hung up, he fell back on top of the bed. What I need is a beer, the hair of the dog and, going over to the not too clean looking mini-bar, he took out two cans. Drinking them down in quick succession, he began to feel a bit more normal. Never again he reproached himself as he went in to take a shower. The effects from the beer together with a cold shower began to make him feel almost human again. Now dressed and ready for whatever the day had in store, he left his two star bedroom and took a cab to Barco's house to collect Emma's belongings.

At the far end of the street from Barco's house, he noticed a stationary car. It wasn't so much that it was parked, but the model seemed incongruous with the surroundings. On passing, he saw there was a man sitting in the driver's seat and instinct told him not to stop. He asked the cab driver to continue, and, as soon as he was well out of sight, he paid the fare and got out. He had a hunch that Barco's house was being watched, so rather than walk right up to the house he made a decision to use his mobile. Maria was delighted to hear from him and he informed her he would make a visit sometime soon. Yes, Emma was fine and with some friends, Julian told her.

Just as he was about to end the call he heard her say.

"Mr. Julian, I don't know if it is important, but a few days past, two men were here asking for Miss Emma."

"What did you tell them?" Julian asked.

"I tell them I don't know where she is and they just leave."

"What were they like?" he asked her.

"Very nice gentlemen, very polite and then they just leave."

"That was it?"

"Yes, Mr. Julian."

His instincts, again, had been spot on, and as he suspected, Garcia had sent his rooks. Although Julian had taken a few pieces, he and Emma, King and Queen, were still in check. Up until now, he had made no decision about what he should do, if anything, regarding the deaths of four of his men. Now, with this latest piece of information as well as the attempted murder of David, Julian knew in order to stay alive some sort of action on his part was necessary. He could only surmise that the presence of Garcia's men, if indeed they were Garcia's, was to keep check on Emma and the money.

A plan began to formulate in his brain and he could only see one way to ensure their future safety. And now at last it came to him; the situation could only be resolved in one way and that would require his going to Caracas. Emma's few possessions, still in Maria's house, could wait until another time. It wasn't worth the risk to collect them at this point.

Deep in a remote part of the forests of Eastern Guaviare, Colombia, hidden by the overhanging canopy and shielding it from the sky, lay one of Garcia's illegal drugs laboratories, located in the basement of what appeared to be a residential dwelling. This area was hazardous and difficult to reach, because parts of this province were still unexplored and almost impenetrable - due to the tangled subtropical plants and trees. It was a perfect place for Garcia's operations.

A shipment of illegal precursor chemicals used in the treatment of the coca leaf from its natural form into the white crystalline powder sold on the streets had arrived a few days earlier, and, although, Garcia had secured the expertise and presence of Burmese and Thai chemists, his attendance was necessary to oversee the clockwork running of his lab. The process was a lengthy one, and over forty different chemicals were used to render the coca leaf, first into a paste, after which it was further refined into cocaine. He left nothing to chance. He trusted no one. He felt that nothing would make him more satisfied than to find that his suspicions were not just based on something twisted inside him, in his make-up, in his genes or his paranoia, but on factual deceit. It was as if he willed betrayal.

Garcia and his manager were doing the rounds of the processing plant as was their usual routine whenever Garcia made his visits. They walked in silence through the laboratory where chemists, with their faces half covered with masks and heads bent over their equipment, were too intent in their work to notice the presence of the two intruders. Garcia stopped from time to time to ask a question from the white coated figures and with a satisfactory reply moved on to another process. There was an aura of foreboding and unease about the place and only the hum of the machinery and clink of instruments were audible. The laboratory was working in silence. Their inspection completed for the time being, they returned to a room, at the rear of the building, which was used as the office.

"Everything seems to be going well," Garcia opened as they drew up seats.

"Yes, I'm pleased with this batch," the manager replied.

"How many kilos of coca leaf are being processed?" asked Garcia.

"One thousand."

"That should give us three kilos of cocaine," Garcia calculated.

"I'm expecting another delivery of seven hundred kilos of coca leaf the day after tomorrow and four kilos of paste," the manager informed Garcia.

"Keep it flowing. Any problem with the supplies?" asked Garcia.

"None so far, the supply is never ending. As soon as the anti-narcotics police eradicate one field of coca leaf by aerial spraying with herbicides, the peasant producers move further into the jungle of the northern Amazon to start new fields."

"Any more trouble from the narco-guerrillas?"

"No, I paid out one hundred thousand dollars in protection money last week, so we should have no more problems," the manager answered.

"That will be all for the time being," Garcia announced as he began to flick through the paperwork.

"In that case, I'll leave you to go over the books. I've some things to attend to and I'll see you before you go."

Left on his own, Garcia meticulously went over the records, jotting down figures and calculating his net income.

"This will be the best batch so far," he said to himself.

All he saw were dollar bills flashing in front of him. He had no sympathy for the plight of the peasant producers, who could not be classed as traffickers. They were merely trying to carve a modest living from the only thing they knew how, grow the coca leaf. He gave no thought to the coca pickers whose hands were stained yellow from the leaf and whose feet were green from stomping the coca leaves soaked in potassium carbonate, water and kerosene to free the alkaloids. Nor had he any care about the destiny of the user. His only concern was for himself. His was a motivation of avarice and power. This would be the best batch and he saw the dollars mounting and with it the power.

Sure, he thought to himself, this batch of cocaine would still contain impurities such as solvents; ether, acetone, carbon tetrachloride, and caustics; sulphuric acid, lye and hydrochloric acid, all of which were used in the processing. But this would be the best. And he saw the street value increasing. With his new outlet, the Findlay woman, nothing could go wrong.

It all hinged on the woman. Even if she were having second thoughts about carrying the money to The Dominican Republic; it would make no difference. Once his men had finished with her she would be only too pleased to co-operate and fulfil her side of the deal. He had not come this far to be thwarted by a woman. His plan would not fail.

The helicopter swooped over the jungle and dropped down in a clearing, some distance from the processing laboratory. Garcia and three others emerged from their concealed position in the dense undergrowth and, within minutes, they were airborne on their way to safety, away from the dangerous existence of the government anti-narcotics police. Before he took his final leave, Garcia had instructed his manager on the time schedule and details of transportation of the next batch of cocaine.

"With the protection of the narco-guerrillas whom we pay handsomely, the cocaine will be brought to this clearing in the jungle marked here with an X," he said, pointing to a cross on the map.

"Then, from point X it will be taken by helicopter to point Y, here, where it will connect with the shipment of coffee beans, destination the warehouse in Bogota. Now have you got that? These are the time schedules that you must adhere to, there's no room for error. It's up to you to get there on time. Is that clear? The helicopter will not wait. It is too dangerous."

"Yes, Senor Garcia, everything is clear," the other confirmed.

Since his manager was confident that all would go according to plan, there was no other reason for Garcia to tarry any longer at the laboratory. So, he and his bodyguards had fought their way through the dense forest and had arrived at the clearing ten minutes earlier. Now on his way back to the safety of his other life with his family, he was thankful to be out of the jungle, which he considered most hostile and awesome, but he was wrong. It would be a beautiful place of natural habitat, a hidden paradise, if it was not so scarred by the conflicts and deaths, caused, within its boundaries, by its drugs trade.

CHAPTER 19

Later that day Julian called Barco before boarding the flight to Caracas.

"Yes, I'm well, Barco. Listen, I want you to give a message to Senora Emma should she be in contact. Let her know that I have gone to Caracas and I will be at the Continental as usual."

"Is that all, Mr. Julian?"

"Yes, remember to give her the message yourself," and hung up.

He thought he was being a bit dramatic with his cryptic clues, but he was not willing to take a chance should any of those thugs question Maria and Barco or even worse kill them, for information concerning Emma and him. This way Maria and Barco had nothing to hide. Also, he knew that Emma was a determined person and, sooner or later, would make contact with Maria, but he was happy in the knowledge that she would not simply walk up to the front door and ring the bell. She was more astute than that and would take stock of the situation before making a move. She could handle herself well, perhaps not so much physically, but she possessed a shrewd brain.

He was still trying to formulate plans for his next move; his head was buzzing. There were too many different approaches flashing through his brain all at the one time and he could not get a positive thought on any of them.

He deliberately held back as the plane was boarding, watching the passengers filter through, watching for anyone suspicious. However, most of them appeared to be family groups and oil workers. He boarded last, and got himself comfortable. As the thrust of the engines dragged the plane into the air, Julian began to sort things out in his mind.

So, he had succeeded, for the moment, in taking out the Venezuelan assassins, and that being the case the trail would go cold, giving him a few days before they were back on their tails. That left the Colombian guerrillas, The Revolutionary Armed Forces, who could, with a bit of luck, change tactics and go straight for Garcia. Their main motive was to stop the flow of the drugs revenue into the Government's coffers.

Now, there was Garcia himself, who would stop at nothing in his endeavour to launder money and enforce this deal with Emma. He had too much to lose; his sole motivation was based on rapacity and power. In that case he would try to beat Emma into submission, to an inch of her life, or worse still, kill her. Neither was acceptable.

So, what could he do? There were two immediate forces to contend with, the Colombians and Garcia. The Venezuelan Government would not be overjoyed if it became public knowledge that Colombian guerrillas had infiltrated into the country and were operating from within its boundaries. On the other hand, since the Venezuelans were trying to clean up their own drugs trafficking, they would not welcome added problems from their Colombian neighbours such as Garcia.

How to eliminate the danger surrounding Emma and him was his constant thought. He sat for a time in quiet reflection, and he could almost smell some sort of plan formulating.

"Can I get you something from the bar, Sir?" His thoughts interrupted by the flight attendant.

"Umm... yes... tea," he voiced.

He had to keep his head clear.

"Very good, Sir", and she proceeded to attend to his request.

As he was waiting for her to hand him the tea, he couldn't help but notice that even under the formal blouse she was wearing, she possessed a pair of boobs that a blind man would notice, and a smile broke out across his face.

"Down boy," he reproached.

How could he be thinking of that when all this shit was flying around? He was imagining holding those two beautiful 'babies' in his hands as the stewardess, sporting a knowledgeable smile, reached over and handed him his tea.

'In his hands' as his thoughts returned to the impending dangers. 'In his hands', the words kept repeating themselves. For a moment his brain went blank. Then, in a flash, he saw all too clearly what his next step would be. The solution had been there all the time. It had been in his hands. Pleased as could be with his new found answer, he almost jumped up and grabbed those two beautiful 'things', but his better judgement somehow kicked into play and he simply sipped his tea.

They had been in the air for a couple of hours when the Captain began the plane's descent. With his mind not so troubled and in a more calm state, he started to take notice of the mountainous contours and the landmarks below. From above,

Caracas presented a serene and peaceful appearance, with its buildings creeping up the hillsides and its houses nestling warmly into the cleavages. The sun was three quarters of the way along its daily path, casting shadows on the slopes and adding a depth in colour to the picture below. From here it looked at peace, unlike the real Caracas where muggings and robberies were a daily occurrence, a concern for the authorities and a business for others. Caracas was more orderly than most of the South American cities and, like everywhere else in the world, to know one's way around was a ticket to safety.

As Julian alighted, he passed the stewardess with the 'big boobies', who gave him a come on smile. But alas! In a way he regretted his licentious leer, but thanked her for all her help..... More than she would ever know.

He checked in at his usual hotel which, at this time of the year, was overflowing with tourists, not to mention the ex-pat business men who were accompanied by beautiful Latin girls, well dressed in designer clothes and dripping with gold and diamonds. The foyer was a place for promenading and, it seemed to Julian, that the entire hotel was on the move, strutting to and fro, in a constant motion, displaying their fine clothes and attractive bodies as if at a Parisian haute-couture fashion house.

Earlier, Julian had made up his mind that he would set the wheels in motion, the following morning, and that being so, he too strolled through the foyer on his way to the cool air-conditioned cocktail bar outside of which the well maintained gardens became an extension of inside, like a mural or a still life. And only when the automatic doors glided open with the approach of promenaders, did the frangipani shrubs and the palm trees take on a real and vibrant identity of their own.

His attention was now drawn to a commotion that had erupted at one of the other tables and a young woman hastily stood up and left. As she passed, he noticed that it was the same flight attendant and found it a strange coincidence that, twice in the one day, he was aware of this young lady. He was too long in the tooth to interfere or pacify her distress and his gaze returned to the man still sitting at the table, now attempting to mop up the red wine that had obviously been tipped over him. Well, well, he thought, a lovers tiff.

After he had finished eating, Julian made his way back to his room and, before switching off the lights, wedged a chair underneath the door handle, just as a precaution against anyone that managed to get past security and attempt to mug him. He knew it to happen to many business men in these parts, when muggers had in fact managed to get through the very tight security and into the bedrooms; he was taking no chances.

The following morning, Julian, after having a light breakfast, took a cab to the cafe bar, El Nogal, which his investigations had revealed was frequented by businessmen; the well to do, the elitist of Caracas. While he had been breakfasting, his mind kept drifting back to the stewardess. The very fact that he had brought it to mind again, gave him the strangest vibes and sensed there was something odd about it all. However, since there was no sign of either of them that morning he had dismissed it and put it out of his mind.

The traffic was slow moving due to the volume of motorists all heading to their morning destinations, causing traffic jams at intersections. Horns were blasting and impatient drivers were shouting obscenities at their fellow travellers.

Julian had never been in this particular cafe and, on arriving, was shown to a table by the window with a good view of the rest of the restaurant. Most of the patrons that morning were men who had stopped by for a coffee and breakfast before beginning their working day. Taking a newspaper from the stand and ordering a coffee himself, he settled down to observe the happenings within the cafe.

An hour later, when he had read most of his paper, he noted that, while most of those that had ordered had left within twenty minutes; the few that were still remaining were conducting their business over the mobile phone. Not wishing to attract too much attention to himself but, at the same time, still wanting to remain in the cafe for a little while longer, he ordered another coffee. By the time he had finished, most of the men had left and a few women were now drifting in. He saw everything that he wanted to see for the moment, and it was unlikely that there would be anybody of any interest visiting the cafe until later. Deciding to return later in the afternoon, and with a lax gait he left the cafe.

To give himself an air of authenticity and that of a typical tourist, Julian had the cab driver drop him off at a shopping mall where he would purchase some designer clothes for himself, not forgetting something for Emma. Only tourists went around laden with carrier bags, and to make it more real, what better than a few designer labels flapping about.

He bought himself two pairs of Armani pants and three Ralph Lauren polo shirts. After that, he visited the Escada boutique and found the perfect cocktail dress for Emma, in silver grey crepe, embossed with a silver pattern. He was just on the verge of leaving the shop when the assistant brought out the matching shoes and handbag, and needless to say he was talked into buying them also.

'What a small fortune it's costing, just to look like a tourist,' he mused. But he knew that no price could be put on Emma's life or his own. His shopping expedition had taken longer than he anticipated. However, he certainly would look the part when he returned to El Nogel laden with his purchases.

"Had a successful shopping trip, I see, Senor," the waiter commented as he sauntered back into the cafe, sometime later. "And something for the lady; we can't forget the ladies."

"Yes, indeed," replied Julian, pleased that his pretence was working.

The time on his watch told him that a cocktail was the order of the day and, placing his goods on the stool next to him at the bar, ordered a tequila sunrise. Two places to his right sat one man who was talking louder than the rest, and Julian made up his mind to strike up a conversation with 'loud mouth', in a few moments.

"Does the bar get any busier?" Julian asked of the bartender.

"In about half an hour this place will be crowded."

He was just on the point of starting a conversation when loud mouth turned towards Julian.

"I see you've been busy. Staying here long?" he opened.

"Only for a few days," Julian answered. "Out purchasing a few items and a little something for the good lady," Julian boasted patting his designer bags, "cost me a small fortune, it did."

And trying to keep the conversation on a trivial level, Julian continued.

"And I'm not finished yet. She wants an Ebel gold watch, studded with diamonds. Got my orders, you know. Must please the good lady."

Julian waited for the right moment and then asked in a half bored manner.

"What line of business are you in, then?"

"Government secretary.......name's Sanmarco... Philippe Sanmarco," the loud mouthed man replied, extending his hand.

"Julian Burton, scrap, scrap dealer back in the UK," he volunteered.

"Your little lady, where is she?"

"Where else but the beauty salon. In fact, must dash. Picking her up you see."

"I'm here most afternoons. Might bump into you tomorrow," Sanmarco said, invitingly.

"Yes, might do," Julian answered, as he gathered his shopping together.

Julian left the cafe bar elated with his first contact, and not wanting to appear interested in anything but his designer clothes and 'his good lady', he felt it appropriate to leave any further questions until the following day.

After Julian had left the cafe, Sanmarco immediately turned his attention to another man standing near him and started up a conversation, giving no further thought to Julian.

CHAPTER 20

This was the second time that Emma had driven over the hilly rise and along the narrow winding road leading to the Villa Verde; only this time she had David and Sonya Callas for company. The previous time she had not noticed there were a few villas dotted here and there along the road, nestling into the hillsides. Then, she had been too excited to take note of the surrounding area. Most of these dwellings were in a state of disrepair, and their flaking paint work, which had been scattered over the fields for years, left them looking shabby and forlorn. But to her, they seemed to be well presented and happily positioned in their pitiful state, with their windows and doors wide open to the sun, like happy smiling faces.

Nobody had spoken very much during the journey. Before leaving earlier that morning, they had wheeled David out for a stroll in the grounds of the hotel, the result of which, he was now sound asleep in the back seat from his exertions. Sonya, who had been sitting quietly beside Emma, straightened herself up and began to take notice as they approached the pillared archway leading to the grounds of the villa.

Emma had rented a four by four vehicle, and as she drove slowly up the driveway she was pleasantly surprised - the lawns and the gardens had been transformed from the wilderness that it was, two days earlier, into beautiful manicured grounds.

"Well, what do you think, folks?" Emma asked, unable to hide the enthusiasm in her voice.

Sonya turned her head towards David, who had been aroused from his slumbers by the four by four coming to a stop.

"This is unbelievable....it's fantastic Emma....how on earth did you find this place?" David responded, genuinely delighted and surprised at the view in front of him.

"Sonya?" Emma questioned.

"Yes, I agree with David, this is an amazing place. It's just great and what a wonderful outlook. You know, Emma, your description didn't do it justice, it's just the right place to recuperate," Sonya acknowledged, which made Emma more pleased than ever.

"Come on, let's go over to the beach side," Emma coaxed, anxious to show them around.

It took them a few minutes to get David organised and lift his wheelchair out from the rear door.

"Leave the rest of that luggage. We can get it later," Emma instructed, as they made for the pathway leading to the beach.

"This is really magnificent," David enthused, when they stopped at the bottom of the garden.

"David, I shouldn't go any further if I were you. You'll get the wheels stuck in the sand," Sonya chastised, lightly.

"I shouldn't think that would be too much of a problem, after all, I've got two strong women to dig me out," David jested.

"Come on you two, let's get back to the villa," Emma suggested and turned David's wheelchair around.

The domestic help and the gardener had already arrived and were standing in line by the front entrance to greet them. After all introductions were made, the domestic, Eva, went inside, and the gardener, Juan, helped to fetch their belongings from the vehicle. The grocery order had arrived and had been put away in the kitchen cupboards. Eva had already set the dining room table upon which a selection of various salads, chicken and cheeses were on offer.

"You can't begin to imagine the transformation of this entire place," Emma went on excitedly, as she went from room to room. "They have done wonders not only outside but inside too, restoring the rooms and the furnishings to their almost original appearance. The drapes, carpets and curtains have all been cleaned and I'm delighted with the overall results."

"This must be costing a mint," David commented in his usual accountant's way.

"Yes, it is, but don't worry about that for the time being," Emma answered sharply, in an attempt to kill the conversation on money.

"Emma!" David challenged, suspiciously. "You've already got the money in your possession, haven't you? Don't deny it. Be sensible for once; look what happened to me and you'll be the next one to get hurt!"

"I know, I know! But I don't want you to worry about anything. I know what I'm doing; nothing's going to happen to me. There was a change of plans, and the money was delivered to me at the hotel Delago. It surprised me just as much as it does you," Emma replied, trying to reassure David, but not feeling too confident about any of it. Keeping her reservations to herself, she simply said they would decide about the money in a few days.

"Enough of this anyway. There's a wonderful buffet waiting for us, so let's sample Eva's dishes. After that, I think we could all do with a nap. In the meantime, until David is fit enough to negotiate the stairs, Sonya, you could perhaps have a bed made up in the room next to the study."

With lunch over, Emma had allowed Sonya to attend to David's needs and headed for her own room in the hope of having a nap. She had been lying for half an hour but with so much going on in her mind she couldn't induce sleep. Now, with towel in hand, she headed for the beach. She was fairly happy with David's progress and knew him to be in the capable hands of nurse Callas. The two servants seemed extremely good and reliable and would present no trouble at all for David and Sonya, should she want to leave.

As she lay there on the sand, she made up her mind that she would talk to both of them at dinner this evening, and let them know of her wish to return to Julian in Maracaibo. She was well aware of the dangers that awaited her there, but, after all, this had not been Julian's problem either. Because of her, he had become involved. How long she had been lying there she couldn't tell and had obviously fallen asleep. Then she felt someone giving her a gentle shake.

"We wondered where you had gone," she heard Sonya saying, as she slowly sat up.

"I couldn't sleep and came here for a swim."

"Well let's go then," Sonya egged her on.

Emma didn't need much encouragement and the two of them sprinted to the water and plunged in.

"My, it feels good. I try to swim as often as I can," Sonya called over the noise of the sea.

"Me too," Emma called back.

They swam around for sometime and Emma was the first to come out and dry herself. Sonya came out of the water shortly afterwards and, since they had rarely been on their own without David, Emma took this opportunity to ask Sonya about David's progress.

"So, you think David's making a reasonable recovery, Sonya?"

"I would say better than reasonable. He's recovering quicker than I thought he would. At the beginning, when he was admitted to the hospital, he was not given much of a chance. We didn't think he would live. But now it seems like a miracle. Look at him. In a few days he'll be able to walk with the help of crutches and soon on his own. All he has to do is build up his strength, and with the help of physiotherapy he'll make a full recovery. It's more than I expected."

Emma was indeed pleased with Sonya's progress report and assessment on David's recovery, so much so, that it positively confirmed her decision to leave in the morning, and relieved in the knowledge that time and rest was the best solution for David. Not a particularly demonstrative person, but quite overcome with happiness, Emma threw her arms round Sonya.

"Thank you for being here and taking care of David so well; I couldn't have done it on my own. You know, it means so much to me to see David getting back to his old self again, and should I need to return to Venezuela I wouldn't worry so much about leaving him."

Sonya was also equally happy with David's improvement but said nothing more. She felt a little disturbed by Emma's last remark, and all she could do was turn her back on Emma and walk away.

At dinner that evening, Emma announced her intention to return to Maracaibo and Julian.

"Look David, everything will be fine. You mustn't concern yourself about me if you're to make a quick recovery."

"Look, we're talking about real danger here. Have you any idea what those people are capable of?" David exclaimed, not willing to accept Emma's impulsive notion.

"Yes, I do know how dangerous all of this is. But I can't allow Julian to fight my battles on his own. Can you understand that? The same way I couldn't just leave you to your fate."

Making this point, although he did not agree with her, he had to concede that if it was what she had to do, then he would have to go along with it; and, at the same time, he had to admit that she had been more than instrumental in his progress.

"I'll be back here before you know it, you'll see," Emma concluded, putting on a light, cheery inflection in her voice.

The dinner passed pleasantly and amicably enough under the circumstances. They laughed and joked about David's lack of agility these days, but there were underlying tensions, because neither Sonya nor David was too happy about Emma's decision to return to the framework of the jungle; though, in Sonya's case, there was a slight element of elation at the prospect of having David to herself for a few days.

"You know, Emma Findlay, you've got me at a disadvantage. I would physically restrain you from going on this mad mission had I the ability. You're nothing but foolhardy and stubborn."

To Emma's relief, Eva came in to clear away the dishes, interrupting any further discussion on the matter.

"Could I have tomorrow's menus," Eva asked, taking from her tray a notepad and pen.

"I think we'll let David and Sonya decide on that," Emma quickly interjected.

"What about a light breakfast, croissants and juice and, let me think....cold lobster and salads for lunch. How does that appeal to you, David?" asked Sonya.

"Sounds good to me."

"And for dinner... I think you should decide on that," Sonya continued, turning to David.

"Well, let's see....it's Sunday tomorrow.....what about roast beef and Yorkshire pudding with roasted parsnips, carrots and potatoes?"

"Senor, what is Yorkshire pudding?" Eva asked, obviously quite confused

"You don't know what Yorkshire pudding is?" David asked, fully amazed.

"No, Senor, I do not," Eva returned, emphatically.

"In that case, if you allow me into the kitchen, tomorrow, I'll show you how it's done."

The expression on Eva's face at the idea of Senor David in her kitchen said it all, and she left the dining room stunned as if someone had just hit her with a sledge hammer. When she had closed the door behind her the three of them, not able to suppress their laughter any longer, burst out in loud guffaws. This seemed to break the ice and any lecturing that David intended for Emma was completely forgotten.

"Shall we see you at breakfast?" Sonya asked Emma, as they were retiring for the night.

"Yes, I don't leave until mid morning," Emma answered.

"That's great. See you at breakfast then," David called back, as Sonya guided his wheelchair towards his make shift bedroom.

Emma felt bad about the lie, but she couldn't bear any painful goodbyes. So, early that following morning she slipped out of the villa, leaving a note in front of David's place at the table.

Earlier that day, Emma had arrived in Maracaibo but waited until dusk before making any attempt to enter Maria and Barco Serrano's house. She had driven along the street, well hidden behind the coloured sun reflective glass of the taxi. There had been a number of cars parked outside various houses and one in particular attracted her attention. It was a fairly old Mercedes. However, it wasn't for that reason alone but more because the man sitting in the driver's seat had something familiar looking about him, and it appeared to her that he was especially watching the Serrano house. Taking a quick note of the model and number plate and, so as not to arouse any unnecessary suspicions, she had instructed the driver to take her to the nearest shopping mall. After a reasonable amount of time had passed, she had another cab take her back.

Standing now at the far end of the street, she saw the same car that had been parked earlier with the driver still in the driver's seat, still in the same position. She knew full well that it was Garcia's man that was in the car, searching and looking. Her problem, now, was to find a way past the car and speak to Maria and Barco without being spotted.

On her arrival, earlier that day in Maracaibo, she had gone straight to Julian's hotel only to be informed that he had checked out two days before. Her only contact to his whereabouts was the Serrano family, and it became imperative to speak to them.

Now, continuing her way to the next street which ran parallel, she recalled the time when Julian had used a back entrance to the Serrano house, and keeping her fingers crossed nobody was lurking around, she headed in that direction. But before she reached it, she came upon what looked like a service lane, well overgrown with tall grass and wild bushes, running in between these two streets.

Darkness was creeping along the lane like a predatory monster and she hesitated momentarily before turning into the shadows. Her presence was concealed by the tall grass and bushes, towering over her head. She gingerly moved along the lane. Some of the houses were lit up, while others were in total darkness and Emma was confused as to which one was the Serrano house. She recalled it to be well towards the far end but was unsure of the number.

It took her ten minutes to pick her way to the other end. She turned around and started back along the lane once more. It was deadly quiet and pitch dark. Only the lights from the odd house gave her any indication as to where she was. She stumbled her way back to number four, frequently getting entangled in the bushes as she went. She stopped there and while she was pondering, she looked towards number five.

"Which bloody one is it?" she impatiently asked herself.

Number four had no light burning, whereas number five had. Damn it, the decision was made for her; she would try number five first. She fumbled for a while for an opening in the fence and after a bit, found a section that appeared to be the gate. Reaching over the top, Emma ran her hand down one side and then the other, eventually finding a bolt device which, with a bit of effort and pressure on her part, moved and the metal gate creaked open. With a sigh of relief she was inside; and keeping to the shadows she approached the back porch. This could be the right house, it has a porch, but there again probably all the houses in this street have porches. Quietly turning the door handle she found it unlocked and quickly stepped inside. Moving now to the connecting door to the kitchen area, she did the same but this time found it to be locked.

"Blast and damnation," she muttered.

All she could do now was to wait until somebody entered the kitchen.

Maria had noticed that, for the last two days, a Mercedes had been parked across the street and the driver had just sat in the car, making no attempt to get out. It was still there today but not in the same position, which led her to believe that it had been driven off and returned some time later.

She mentioned this to Barco when he arrived home from work.

"There's something strange going on here, Barco. First, two men call enquiring about Miss Emma; secondly, that car across the street has been there for the last two days and the driver just sits in it. Nothing like this has ever happened before. If you ask me it has something to do with Miss Emma or Mr. Julian," she told him straight.

Barco had suspected something similar but had said nothing to his wife. However, after Mr. Julian's last message he had known something was afoot.

"Well, it's probably nothing. But tomorrow, I want you to leave at the usual time but instead of taking the children to school, go to you mother's," Barco said. "It's probably nothing as I said," he added, when he saw the look in her eyes. "And to be on the safe side stay at your mother's for a few days."

"What'll you do?" she asked.

"Oh... me? I'll stay offshore. I've got accommodation out there."

Maria now felt quite uneasy. She was a woman of simple habits. Her concern was only for her family, her husband and now she felt threatened.

"Well, I don't like the sound of it all. Do you think Miss Emma and Mr. Julian are mixed up in something.....in some sort of trouble.....I mean, she took off very suddenly without any warning?"

"Look, Maria, I don't know anything. Just do as I say. Go about your business as normal and another thing, don't take any clothes."

She is a good woman, Barco was thinking, but she could drive a man crazy with all her questions.

Maria was still feeling uneasy about everything and wanted to ask more questions but thought better of it and, instead, went to the kitchen to make a pot of coffee. In the kitchen she had a strange feeling that she was being watched and, looking out to the porch, she instinctively put her hand to her mouth to stifle the scream that was about to erupt at the sight of Miss

Emma's face at the kitchen door. Emma put a finger to her lips indicating silence and, Maria, moving quickly, unlocked the door letting Emma crawl past her to sit on the floor under the level of the brightly lit window.

"Maria, when you finish making the coffee, leave the kitchen, switching off the light as you go. Casually close the curtains in the other room if not already drawn; and act as normally as you can."

Maria, too much in shock to question Emma's motives did as she was told, went back to the front room and closed the curtains. When Emma thought it save to move, she stood up and followed Maria to the other room.

"Miss Emma, you gave me quite a fright, appearing at the porch door, just like that," Maria exclaimed.

"What's this all about?" demanded Barco in a louder voice than normal.

Emma walked towards a chair and sat down.

"Let me explain, but first of all, are the children in the house?"

"Yes, they're finishing homework for school tomorrow," Maria replied.

"Good, and don't let them out tonight. You're aware of a car parked across the street."

Maria and Barco nodded simultaneously.

Emma continued. "For your own safety and for that of your family I'll explain only that much which is safe for you to know. The least you know the safer you'll be. Very briefly; I came to Venezuela to negotiate a business arrangement with, how would you say, a business man. After the usual practise of making enquiries and investigations, I decided to decline their offer. And that's why they're looking for me; to put a little pressure on me to accept the deal. As I have already mentioned, your house is being watched but it's simply me they want. I'm not going to take any chances nor do I want to involve you, but should they fail to find me, it is possible they may question you and that is the reason why I am going to ask you to leave in the morning, as usual, but instead of taking the children to school, go somewhere safe"

Maria now turning to Barco, who hadn't uttered a word, stated firmly, "I knew something odd was going on."

"Hush, woman, let Miss Emma finish."

"I'll be leaving shortly. However, for your own safety you won't know where. I promise you, I have committed no crime or anything illegal. I would not have risked coming here had I known Julian's whereabouts. You see, earlier today, I went to his hotel only to be informed that he checked out two days ago."

At that Barco interrupted, remembering Julian's last phone call.

"He gave me a message for you."

"So you've seen him then?" Emma interjected.

"No, not exactly. He called and asked me to give you this message. He was flying to Caracas and you could contact him at his usual hotel, The Continental, the one he always stays at."

"In Caracas?" Emma questioned in surprise.

"Yes, that's what he said. Continental, the one he always uses."

Emma was slightly confused but, for the moment, there were more important issues to deal with and she would sort that out later. At least she knew where he was.

"The people in the Mercedes, what do they want?"

"They're looking for me, Barco, to put a little pressure on me to accept the business deal."

"And you're not accepting?"

"No Barco, I'm not. It's a non viable proposition."

Emma, for very obvious reasons, had missed out any reference to drugs, and also the attempted murders by person's unknown on the lives of David, Julian and herself. For their own safety she would refrain from revealing any of it. Neither did she mention the Colombian guerrillas nor the antigovernment faction here in their own country. It would be all too much for them to comprehend. She couldn't quite grasp it herself but for the mere fact she had witnessed some of it herself. David and Julian had been dragged into this murderous and dangerous situation because of her greed.

Her driving ambitions held no bounds. Due to a quick brain and a sharp wit, she had achieved great success in her field. She was accepted by 'the club' of accountants, an almost male dominated profession that hadn't quite come to terms with women's equality. She was not interested in the women's rights and equal pay; she was doing all right 'Jack'. However, due to her success she had been invited to speak at various universities and seminars on the subject of 'Women in Business' and, in spite of her own feelings, she had given talks.

With a galloping lack of perception she had plunged the lot of them into an impossible situation and now, with a tinge of conscience, she was going to do something about it. Even as far back as Cuba she felt certain that Juan and Jesus had been murdered, by whom she did not know, but it was all part of this wild, harrowing scheme to intimidate her.

Emma helped herself to coffee and taking a sip she continued.

"You'll be in no danger as long as all of you go somewhere safe for a few days. Sooner or later, when they can't find me, they'll possibly question you and they may get a bit rough. Should that happen, tell them everything you know, everything that I've related to you tonight. Even if it's necessary, tell them that I'm in Caracas. Do you understand? But hopefully it won't come to that, and I'm sorry that I've brought this upon you. We'll make it up to you, somehow."

"Don't worry about that. As long as we're all safe, that's all that counts," Barco assured her.

Barco wanted to ask her about the explosion on the oil platform, but his better judgement for the sake of his family told him to leave well alone. Miss Emma was right; the least he knew the better for all of them.

With her few belongings in hand, Emma left by the same route she had arrived; by the back porch, out through the now dark garden and along the even darker lane, until she was far enough away from the house to hail a taxi and head to the airport. She hoped that Maria and Barco would be safe and get away in time, before Garcia's men became suspicious and edgy. Time was running out. She was also aware that they would stop at nothing, even murder, to extract any information that would lead to her whereabouts. Please God let nothing happen to them!

After she had gone, Maria and Barco sat in silence, stunned by the recent revelations. Both of them were only too familiar with the violence that existed in the cities, where people simply disappeared off the face of the earth, never to be heard of again. The authorities could not cope with the crime rate and they certainly would not be interested in a suspicious car that seemed to have been parked in the street for a few days.

No, the best thing they could do was to take Emma's advice. So, early the following morning, Barco left for the oil field and Maria, as was her custom, left with the children. But instead of going to the school, she headed for her parents village, deep in the farming lands of the Llanos.

CHAPTER 21

El Nogal, the following day, was more crowded than it had been the day before. The waiters were a friendly lot and immediately recognised Julian. They asked how he was enjoying his visit to Caracas and did he like their country? People really were basically the same no matter where you went in the world. They had to be reassured that you liked their country and that you would return again some day.

Julian answered that he was enjoying his visit to Venezuela very much, and talked about taking a trip to Angel Falls, which threw them into great depths of description and explanation that they thought he should know. How to get there and what to do when he did arrive for which Julian thanked them, still pretending to be a pretty naive tourist.

"Mind you," one of them said, "the hotel, because it's the only one at the falls and has got the monopoly, is expensive."

"It's the highest uninterrupted cataract in the world, dropping over 3200 ft. from the mesa of Auyantepui in the rain-forest-covered Guiana Highlands," the other waiter, called Andrea, proudly informed him, eager to sell his country.

"Yes, and do you know why it's called Angel falls? Well, I'll tell you," Andrea continued eagerly, at Julian's blank expression "It was discovered by an American aviator and adventurer named James C. Angel back in 1935. Isn't that something?"

The first waiter butted in, "Yes, isn't that something," to which Julian had to show an expression of wonder and amazement.

Finally, the need to serve the other patrons in the cafe, thankfully, took the waiters off to the other side of the bar, leaving Julian alone with his thoughts.

Earlier that morning, after breakfast, Julian had made his own line of inquiries for information that was prerequisite before he put his plan to the test. He had also gone to the library and dug out old newspapers whose reports, which were now history, revealed, nevertheless, the names of some high ranking officials and the present General Director of the National Police, who headed the anti-narcotics Police.

He had now been in the cafe for twenty minutes, cluttered with some shopping bags, once again, when he noticed Philippe Sanmarco enter. Sanmarco looked around for a moment and when he spotted Julian, made straight for him.

"Well, well, so we meet again," Philippe enthusiastically greeted him.

"What's your poison?" he continued, taking up the seat beside Julian.

"I'll have a beer, thanks," Julian replied.

"I see you've been at it again," Philippe went on, pointing to Julian's purchases. "When do we get to see the lucky lady?" he added.

At this point in time, Julian seriously wished Emma was here with him to authenticate and reinforce his guise.

"Soon," Julian answered, not wanting to commit himself. The least said at this stage the better.

"Had a bad day in the office," Philippe volunteered, "one of those days where nothing goes smoothly. I had the big boss on my tail all morning. He had me researching into our Constitutions."

"That sounds like interesting work," Julian encouraged.

"Yes, it would be in itself, but a new Constitution at this point in time would not solve our problems. I find the work a waste of time."

"How's that then?" Julian asked, hoping he would continue.

"It's like this. The idea that the constitution-forming power or any similar proposal will solve many problems originates largely from the desperation provoked by the chaotic situation in which we find ourselves together with the collapse of the government management. What we really want to do, is embark on a path of monetary stability, low inflation, economic growth, less crime (including narcotics) and more law and order. This is the universal desire. But we are being sold the idea that a reformulation of the Constitution will be our salvation: a miraculous way, don't you think," Sanmarco explained, with a tone of sarcasm, "to transport us almost instantaneously from this quagmire of incompetence to the firm ground of prosperity."

Julian, knowing a little about the instability in Venezuela, interrupted.

"Yes, but your current Constitution needs to be brought up to date, surely. It is a socialist Constitution, written during the euphoria that accompanied the return to democracy, and now resembles a letter to Santa Claus: full of good intentions, unkeepable promises and faith in an all powerful and all knowing government. The bottom line is that it's inappropriate and so it should be amended to bring it into line with your current requirements."

"Yes, I agree with you, but that is just one thing - one that can wait. Quite another is the needs of our people that must be met. Do you think that after promulgating a new Constitution, the hospitals would improve; schools and education or the wide variety of services the state is obliged to provide would change for the better? No, they would not. Let's not be naive. Neither would inflation disappear nor much less would we have a strong Bolivar. The solutions to our crisis are known by all. They lie in the free market economy, in the fight against inflation, in monetary stability and in the opening of the economy. But above all else, they lie in the possibility of the public administration operating competently. No, my friend, our problem is not one of laws; our problem is one of men."

Julian was struck, for the first time, by the emotion that this man showed for his country and for his beliefs. He had considered him not exactly a buffoon but more of a whimsical and jestful character.

"I can see where you're coming from and I have to agree with you," Julian happily conceded, his only intention being to encourage Sanmarco to open up and talk about the government.

"I enjoyed our discussion," Philippe admitted, "you seem to know a little about our country."

"Not much, just what I read in the newspapers," Julian lied, "anyway, the same again?"

"No, I'll have gin and tonic, this time," Philippe said, "and by the way, should you be interested, some of our Senate's Deputies use this watering hole. One or two might be along later and they would be interested in meeting someone like you, someone who takes an interest in things."

"Cheers," Julian said, raising his glass and dismissing any further conversation about politics.

"Salute," Sanmarco replied.

This was all going according to plan, Julian thought, and with some luck there was now a strong possibility of an introduction to the man he was seeking.

It wasn't until after the flight for Caracas had departed that Emma had begun to think about the hotel and Julian's message. The Continental? She had queried... The Continental as usual. She had never known him to stay at a hotel called the Continental. And it was not until she was aimlessly paging through the in-flight magazine at the map of the world that it had dawned on her. The Continent of Europe...the Continent...Europe. Then she had it. He was at the Eurobuilding. That was his usual hotel. Why on earth had he thrown her a cryptic clue? Why not be straight forward? Not unless he was expecting further trouble; not unless he was expecting to be followed. Was this an attempt to protect himself, the Serrano's and her? At this point she looked around anxiously, but to her mind an impossible task. Any one of these passengers could be the threat. She couldn't watch all of them.

Just to be on the safe side, she had told the cab driver to take her to the Continental, but as soon as she had alighted and the cab was out of sight, she had hailed another and asked to be taken to the Eurobuilding.

After checking in, she enquired about Julian and had been informed that a guest by that name was in room 3012. But after having rung his room and getting no response, she assumed Julian had gone out. What to do until he turned up, she had wondered, now sitting in her room. Not knowing how long she would have had to wait, her decision to visit a shopping mall to pass the time and then perhaps a snack, had seemed to be her best bet. She purchased a few silver bangles and, before leaving the mall, had asked one of the nice assistants to recommend a restaurant.

"There's a very popular place nearby, about two blocks from here," the girl had replied, writing down the address.

Emma had thanked her and, with her gaggle of bangles on her wrist, left the mall. It was not far at all and now she was standing in the El Nogal looking around for a suitable table.

Julian had to look twice and hoped that Philippe did not notice his surprise.

"Oh, my wife has just arrived," Julian said out loud, addressing Philippe, "excuse me for a moment," and, like a blind man at rush hour, bumped his way through the clientele towards Emma before she had time to select a place. Julian was at her side. Emma opened her mouth to vent delight.

"Don't look surprised, I've no time to explain, but follow my lead, I've got company," he eared a whisper as he kissed her, stifling any sound that was about to be expelled from her lips.

"So, this is the little lady you've been hiding," Philippe declared as Julian made the introductions.

They shook hands; Emma smiled sweetly and demurely, wondering if this was the right act.

"I was just saying to your husband, you're a lucky lady. This is the second day he's been laden down with gifts for you."

Emma took a quick glance at the carrier bags by Julian's side and cottoned on straight away.

"Yes, you're right, he's an extremely generous man and I love him," Emma gushed over enthusiastically, making a production out of kissing him.

"Your usual, darling?" Julian addressed her, still with one arm draped over her shoulder.

Not wanting to risk leaving the two of them alone, he beckoned the waiter.

"Vodka soda and the same again."

Turning his attention back to Emma and Philippe in an attempt to put her more in the picture, he said. "We're thinking about making a visit to Angel Falls while on holiday here, are we not, darling?"

"Yes, it would be too bad if we came all this way and didn't see them," Emma concurred.

"Have you seen the Falls?" Emma continued, turning to Philippe.

"Strange you should ask. No I haven't. But I suppose it's the same the whole world over. We don't appreciate those things that are right on our doorstep. But also, I've been concentrating on my career of late and my boss keeps me truly busy. You see I'm secretary to the Minister of Internal Affairs, Senor Gabriel Carreras, here in our Senate," Sanmarco spoke out boastfully and Emma could almost see his feathers fluff out.

“Must be an interesting career,” Emma remarked.

“Yes, very interesting and I must say demanding,” and he was just about to recap on his day’s trials and tribulations, because he liked to blow his own trumpet - that was the type he portrayed - when a group of men walked in to the bar area.

“Excuse me, Julian, I must have a word with Gabriel Carreras about tomorrow’s business,” he said as he scurried off, timely, leaving Emma and Julian alone for a few moments.

“What’s going on?” Emma whispered when he was out of earshot.

Julian, grabbing his opportunity, began.

“I’ll explain in detail later, but I’ve told him we’re tourists and on vacation for a few days. Back in the UK I’m a scrap dealer and acting like a typical tourist.”

“Why a scrap dealer?” Emma asked, quite amused.

“It was the only thing that I could think of at the time, that would give the impression of loads of cash, and not a lot of interest in anything else but squandering it. You know the ‘nouveau riche’ set.”

“What about a professor? You could have been a professor. I don’t like being a scrap dealer’s wife,” Emma teased.

“Don’t be silly, a professor doesn’t have much money ...well, not the kind that I’m talking about. This scrap dealer husband of yours has spent a fortune on you,” Julian laughed. “And if I had been a professor I wouldn’t have been able to buy anything.”

They joked with one another in good humour until Julian spotted Sanmarco returning.

“Here he comes, we’ll talk later.”

"Like you to meet the man who controls my life, Gabriel Carreras.... Julian and Emma... what is...your....?"

"Burton, Emma and Julian Burton."

They made polite conversation, Julian acting jolly and in good spirits, making it obvious that he was impressed at meeting a Deputy of the Venezuelan Senate.

"This is surely the most important day of my life, to meet an important person such as you, isn't it, honey?"

"You flatter me," Carreras replied, but noticeably enjoying the compliment.

Emma played her part too, beaming at the man as one would, when first coming into contact with a dignitary.

Senor Gabriel Carreras, Minister for Internal Affairs, was a small round man with a shot of black hair, now greying at the temples. His clothes were expensive and he was dressed immaculately in an Italian suit, and like all well dressed men his shirt and tie blended perfectly. He had the aura of importance and, although diminutive in stature, he exuded largeness. He seemed a pleasant enough man, Julian thought, but got the distinct impression that the real man could be a lot different. Julian suspected that he could turn on the charm when it was not a threat to him.

The other two men were given no introductions, and when Julian scrutinised them a bit closer, realised they were his aides, his body guards. They didn't crack a smile. One looked continually around the room while the other kept his gaze fixed on Carreras, whose smug authority was ever present.

"Good to hear you're enjoying your visit to our country and hopefully we'll be able to meet again before you leave,"

Carreras concluded as he wheeled around and left, followed by his two stooges.

Philippe Sanmarco finished his drink, told them he had further business with Carreras and would probably see them tomorrow if they were still here.

"What an unpleasant arrogant little man," Emma whispered, "I wouldn't care to get on his wrong side."

"Yes, I got that impression too, but he's one of the men I've got to deal with."

"What do you mean?" Emma asked.

"I'll put you in the picture back at the hotel. For the moment we've to act out our parts here. I also want to watch them for a while. So, let's be real tourists, have some drinks and get a little merry."

While Emma and Julian held their vigilance, conducting light hearted conversation, nothing deep or too engrossed that would distract their attention, Carreras and Sanmarco, it appeared, were going over the following day's schedule of appointments, the most important of which was Carreras' meeting with the Judiciary, The Supreme Court, the topic being New Constitution and the Supreme Court's support for the all-powerful Constituent Assembly, both of which were already controversial issues within Congress.

Sanmarco would accompany the Interior Deputy as usual.

"You have completed everything and carried out a full research?" Carreras asked, pleasantly. He never attempted to bully Philippe or raise his voice to him

"Yes, all the paperwork has been finished and in a safe place overnight."

"Good man, now we can relax. I don't know what I would do without you, Philippe," Carreras said, softly, touching Philippe's arm.

"Oh... you would soon find another secretary, Gabriel," Philippe joked, but knew full well that Carreras was so demanding that nobody would work for him for long.

It only suited Sanmarco's purposes to stay in his employment, even when he distinctly disagreed with his policies.

"There's something going on between those two," Emma announced, interrupting Julian's hilarious account about Fanny Craddock's doughnuts.

"Where?" Julian asked.

"Over there by the window, the attractive blonde and the Latino."

When Julian looked in the direction that Emma was indicating, to his surprise, he saw that it was the flight attendant with the big boobs and the man that had been in the restaurant with her.

"You seemed surprised," Emma voiced.

"No...not...really...but I've seen her before. She was the stewardess on my flight from Maracaibo, that's all."

"Well, I've been watching them and they don't act as if they know one another, although that's the impression they're trying to portray," Emma said, somewhat indignant.

In fact, Julian was slightly concerned that she had turned up again, but as he looked over she did not seem to recognise him...... and why should she? With the number of passengers she would see every day. For the moment he decided not to mention the scene at the hotel but, at the same time, he was not sure why he was keeping this information from Emma.

They had now been sitting in the bar for an hour and Julian had watched the movements of the two body guards. Whenever Carreras moved around the room to talk to fellow members, they watched him like a hawk but didn't infringe upon his privacy when in conversation with others, but kept him well covered all the same. To Julian's eye, they were professionals.

"I think, Emma, we've stayed long enough. What do you say?"

"Yes, you're right. We don't want overkill, and anyway, I'm dying to see what goodies you've bought, albeit in the 'line of duty'," Emma teased.

"Oh Julian, how beautiful, I love it," holding the grey dress against her. "In fact, I love all of it. Thank you, darling," Emma exclaimed as she gave him a familiar kiss on the cheek.

"Is that all I get?" and held her closer to him. As she looked up into his face, his mouth found her lips and the longing feeling surged through both of them. They stood in each other's embrace until Julian gently pushed her away.

"In the 'line of duty', my ass. I could have picked up designer-label bags and stuffed them with tissue paper, 'in the line of duty', I'll be damned."

They both laughed as Julian continued to tease her.

"To show my appreciation I'll wear the dress tonight, just for you."

Emma, for the moment, had forgotten about the dangers that still menaced around, until Julian reminded her that they were not out of the forest yet.

She began, first of all, to enlighten him about David's progress and how well and quickly he was recovering. She described the old colonial house, with its panoramic view out to the Caribbean. Then she began filling him in on the more unpleasant; the car that had been stationed near the Serranos: and as far as she was concerned, she told him, it was there at Garcia's instructions, and how she had successfully slipped in through the back entrance, unnoticed. No, she couldn't be hundred percent sure that she was not followed here.

"Maria and Barco will be in danger now."

"We thought about that. Barco is staying on the platform while Maria and the children will be with her own mother in the country," she assured him.

"As soon as they realise that the trail has gone cold, Garcia will contact the airlines and it will only be a matter of time before it's discovered that you're here in Caracas. He'll need to pull some strings, mind you; the airlines are strict about divulging that kind of information, so hopefully we'll get a few days grace."

Julian then brought Emma up to date on recent events and gave her a detailed outline of his plan to get them to safety. Emma sat quietly listening, not interrupting him until he had finished.

He looked at her.

"Well, what do you think?"

"It's a long shot, Julian, but I think there's a chance we could pull it off."

"We've got nothing to lose; otherwise, we'll be running for the rest of our lives."

"Or dead," Emma added, now outraged by the impossible situation they were in.

Later, they had come together, their bodies erupting with a passion that took them to the apex of frenzied ecstasy. Never before had Julian felt this overwhelming desire. He thrust between her legs and she opened herself fully to him. Her cries of delirium with every orgasm her body gave up were of an animal kind. With Julian still by her side, she rested peacefully, until the sun went down.

Enjoying a lavish dinner in resplendent luxury, sometime later, Emma's anxieties and fears evaporated into the friendly atmosphere of the restaurant. She was madly, passionately, completely in love with this man and it was great. Looking as stunning as ever in her grey cocktail number with platinum accessories, Julian was completely besotted and, for such a hard man, every time she was close to him he became as soft as silk.

Just short of midnight, they decided to call it a day. Tomorrow was another challenge, and, for once, things might fall into place for them.

"Yes, we've got a lot ahead of us," Julian agreed, rising from the table.

"Darling, you go on up to your room, I'll join you in a few minutes. I just want to pick up my belongings so that I can cancel my room in the morning. We don't need two rooms," Julian announced to Emma just as they were entering the elevator.

Julian got out at his floor while Emma continued to level eight. The corridor was silent and the lighting dimmed at this time in the evening. As he turned the corner, to his astonishment, there stood the flight attendant. Thinking there may be something wrong he stopped as he approached her.

"So, we meet again," she smiled at him, moving up close, "I saw the way you looked at me during the flight and I want you, too."

She pushed herself into him and to his further amazement put her arms round his neck and then began to stroke his thighs.

"You're insane," he could only whimper, in disbelief.

Taken completely by surprise, it took him a second or two before he realised that thing's were not all right in these 'woods'. He sensed shivers going up and down his spine and the hair rising at the back of his head. In one quick movement, he wheeled them both around just as something exploded in front of him. For a moment he hadn't a clue what it was, not until she began slipping from his grasp. And there standing before him was the Latino with a gun in his hand.

They stared at each other for a split second before the Latino turned and fled. Julian took a quick look at the girl who now lay crumpled on the floor before he gave chase. He had only taken a few steps in hot pursuit and stopped. It suddenly occurred to him he was being foolish, he had no weapon with which he could defend himself, and, also, there was a great urgency to get as far away from the scene before the girl was found.

He glanced back and his stomach turned at the sight of the body lying there with half a head missing. He made for the stairs at the end of the corridor and flew up the three flights to

Emma's floor. When Emma opened the door, he flung himself into the room almost knocking her over.

Emma began to speak, but before she got any words out.

"Pour me a stiff brandy."

"What?" but she didn't complete her question. The state that Julian was in with blood all over his clothes was more than enough to tell her something most awful had happened. She handed him the drink and he threw it down his neck. Without saying a word he handed her the empty glass. She poured him a second glass.

"I can't believe what's just happened..... I can't get my head around it.....I can't take it in."

"What, Julian....what....can't you...?"

"That...that...woman...the one in the restaurant, today....the stewardess..."

"What happened, Julian?" Emma almost screamed.

Julian started to pace up and down the room, while Emma could only stand there in helpless stupefaction. She had never seen him like this. She thought he was just about to have a heart attack.

After his second brandy he felt a bit better.

"Tell me what happened."

He took in a deep breath and started to speak slowly and precisely.

"It's like something out of the Hammer House of Horrors. She was waiting for me when I got out of the elevator...the stewardess. She came on strong and, at that moment, I got the feeling that something was not right. I turned round quickly pulling her round with me and he shot her through the head."

"Who shot her, Julian?"

"The Latino, the one she was with in the bar. Shot her through the head.....dead."

"Oh my God," Emma exclaimed, now beginning to shake.

"Emma, that bullet had my name on it ....it was intended for me. He got such a shock that he fled...took off. I was about to give chase but, thankfully, decided against it."

"We've got to get out of this hotel," was the only thing Emma could say.

"We'll be found anywhere we go. No, this hotel will be overrun with security guards and police, soon. It'll be the safest place in Caracas. He won't attempt it here. It's out there we've to worry about."

CHAPTER 22

Sonya was more than surprised at the progress David had made in such a short time. In all her experience as a nurse, she had never witnessed such rapid recovery in one so badly injured. Each day had shown a marked improvement and, simultaneously, his impatience and frustration escalated. She had kept him to his programme, not allowing him to peak too soon, but it had been difficult to curb his restlessness. He wanted to be doing more and inevitably feelings of resentment and tension grew between them. Each day she had allowed him to do something more for himself, but that had not been enough. He had wanted to do everything for himself.

Yesterday, when they had taken a picnic to the beach for the first time, David had insisted on leaving his wheelchair behind. With the aid of crutches and his dogged determination, he had painfully shuffled down the garden path, to the delight of both of them. This new achievement, momentarily, seemed to arrest the strain between them. But it was an uneasy and short lived peace.

Juan had carried the hamper which Eva had filled with cold meats, salads, freshly baked bread and cheeses, not forgetting a bottle of chilled 'vin du pays'. The sea had been still and calm that day and, with Sonya's help, David had struggled through the heavy sand to the water's edge from where he dragged himself further out until he was waist high and was able to float.

With Sonya standing by, he had managed to swim ever so gently at first, and after a few minutes, with his renewed confidence, his strokes became stronger and more vigorous. They were both delighted with David's first swim, but Sonya had to discourage him from going too far out.

"Where's your sense of adventure?" he had challenged.

"When you're fit enough I'll leave you to the sharks. Is that adventurous enough for you?" she answered, tersely, not knowing why she was being so curt with him.

But soon they were laughing and splashing again, and he even managed to duck her a couple of times, which he thought hilarious. Her instinct was to reciprocate but thought better of it.

"My time will come, David Findlay, when you're a bit stronger and then we'll see what happens?" she had muttered to herself.

The hour they spent in the water turned out to be tremendous therapy for David, mentally and physically, and, as time went on, he appeared to be much brighter in himself with a lightness of spirit returning, vanquishing the quiet hostility that had crept between them, earlier. Sonya was a strong swimmer but, on this occasion, had kept to the shallow water thus minimising any attempt on David's part to overdo things in his impetuosity.

"How's about some lunch, pretty senorita," David had chirped up, some time later.

He's in a better frame of mind, now, Sonya had noted. Sometimes he withdrew into himself, consumed by a black mood and under those circumstances, not wanting to pry, she had normally left him alone with his dark thoughts.

"Where are you Sonya, what's it to be?" he had spoken again, interrupting her thoughts.

Turning her round towards him he had waited for her reply, but all she had done was nod her agreement. At that point their eyes had met and Sonya noticed a strange expression pass over his face. She had then helped him slowly back up the beach to where the hamper lay and, on reaching it, they had thrown themselves on top of the towels, exhausted from the struggle.

"I think you've had enough exercise for today; if you haven't, I certainly have," Sonya had reproached him, putting on an authoritative voice.

"Spoilsport.... you're nothing but a domineering old woman," he cheeked back.

Those words had both irritated and hurt her but she had let it go. She didn't know why she was behaving so badly and childishly. It was not like her to become upset so easily. They had enjoyed their picnic together with the most welcomed of chilled wine. Afterwards, fully sated, they lay back on the sand and soaked up the sun. Lying there, Sonya's thoughts once more had returned to David. She silently reprimanded herself for being so silly.

"This is just another job.... Soon he will be well and leave..." she had told herself.

Oh, she so wanted him not to get better; that way he would stay with her. But she knew he would be well again. It was no use......she knew she had fallen in love with him and each day was becoming more of a strain and more difficult to get through. She must pull herself together and get on with the job for which Emma had hired her.

He only saw her as his nurse and never seemed to notice she was a woman, too. Oh, how could it be otherwise? She despaired. After all, she was convinced he was still in love with Emma, and, because she had taken a great liking to Emma, she couldn't find it in her heart to hate this woman who still seemed to have a tremendous hold over him.

Sonya had washed and bathed David throughout his illness; during the coma and later when he was recovering, and, until yesterday, she had been helping him off and on with his clothes. Earlier on in his recuperation, he had seemed so grateful and even welcomed her help. But now, it appeared, he shied away from her assistance and was making a needless effort to do things for himself. He seemed to be shutting her out and she was sure it was because he really wanted rid of her as soon as he could manage on his own.

He'll never notice me she had thought sadly. I'll need to forget him, and when he's well enough he'll give me a grateful pat on the back, send me on my way and that will be that. He's right; I'm wrong, she chastised herself. She must encourage him to make every effort for a full recovery and put all personal thoughts for herself out of her mind.

Last night they had made a decision to take a trip, the following morning, into the interior and perhaps get as far as Sierra de Trinidad on the south of the island. That morning before breakfast, she deliberately did not approach his room until she knew he would be up and dressed.

Knocking on his door she called out, "Are you decent?"

"What's this all about, come over all shy, have we?" David teased.

She would never understand him.

"No, not really. Just for the record, I thought it high time you did more for yourself now, without my fussing around," she replied, just as mischievously.

"After breakfast," she continued, "I think we'll make a start, if that's all right by you? I've mapped out our route and we could stop somewhere for lunch."

"Yes, sounds good to me," giving her a friendly pat as she bent to pick up his discarded towels.

They had been on the road for an hour before the flat rolling terrain gave way to more hilly surfaces as they headed south for Santa Clara. They passed through a wide variety of subtropical vegetation, much of which was unknown to Sonya and David. But they did recognise some of the palms that Cuba, David informed her, had more than thirty different types. Among some of the other plants they identified sugar-cane, tobacco plant, citrus and walnut trees. Passing through the verdant and flourishing countryside was like a garden route of tranquillity and peace, and with every bend and twist in the road another amazing panorama came into view.

"Look, over there in that field," Sonya declared, indicating in the direction of the oxen pulling wooden carts, which were laden with sugarcane, and following on behind them was an old, out of date harvesting machine.

"Yes, and look at that old man throwing the cane into the cart. It's like being in a time warp."

Little brooks wandered and twisted in and out of rock formations as they made their way through fields of green and summer days, learning their lesson as they grew into rivers and ended their days as they finally crashed against distant shores.

On the road, most of the trucks, old and pitted with rust, belched out fumes as they struggled with their load to the top of the rises, and looked out of place in this rural setting.

When Sonya and David arrived at Santa Clara, they found an outside cafe under the shade of citrus trees, where the tables were old and sat unsteady on the uneven ground beneath them; where the tumblers were made of the thickest glass possible like gargoyles' eyes, and where the red and white checked tablecloth was frayed at the edges. But all this did not detract from the surroundings; it merely added to the authenticity of the place. This was Cuba at its most natural.

The sun had left its wizened mark on the faces of the old men who sat around other tables, passing their time playing dominoes. From time to time they silently sipped coffee from small round glassware and only the movement of their hands indicated that they were not asleep. There was no sense of urgency here; it was as if time was standing still.

Sonya and David idled away their day in this peaceful but surreal setting. Their conversation was easy and it drifted naturally from one topic to another. To his surprise he found himself liking this tranquillity. Never had he been a man of solitude, but had spent most of his time in the hub and bustle of the financial world where the motto was 'dog eat dog'. That life to him now seemed so far away.

He talked a little about his past and the high-pressure life he had led, but his voice lacked the excited ambition that it once held, not that long ago. She talked excitedly about her very ordinary life style, about her siblings, about her parents and her love for nursing and helping those in need.

He listened to her; completely transfixed with everything she was relating and he hung on to her every word. She told him about the poverty in Colombia, where the peasant boys were forced to leave home in search of employment in the cities but found nothing. In the end, the only thing left open to them was to resort to violence and become street criminals, mugging the rich for money to survive. In the rural areas the youth of Colombia had three alternatives. They could join the guerrillas, join the paramilitaries or become raspachines (coca pickers), not forgetting prostitution.

The government, she said, was not doing enough for the people who were badly in need of more schools, hospitals and a higher standard of living. The mortality rate in infants was at 27% and, up until now, very little was being done to turn the situation around.

They prattled on like this, right through lunch, neither of them wanting the day to end. It was their first outing together and both were savouring every moment of it. In the end it was Sonya who took up the initiative.

"It's now getting on and I think it's time we headed back."

"I suppose you're right, as usual, Nurse," David sighed. "I've had a great time and don't want the day to end."

"Well, we can always do it again, what do you say?"

"Good idea. Now help me to my feet, Nurse, I've gone a bit stiff sitting this length of time."

The day's outing, for David, had been mentally stimulating. At last he was capable of doing something. Ever since he had regained consciousness in the hospital at Bogota, he had been less than enthusiastic about his surroundings, and only when it had been expected of him did he show any interest, especially in Sonya's company. She had gone to such lengths to make his recovery complete and, for this alone, he could never show her anything less than absolute gratitude.

On the journey back he had been genuinely excited, taking notice of the vibrant colours of the flora, the billowing silk cotton trees, the butterfly jasmine with its white flower and the rainbow of hues of the bougainvillaea and hibiscus. And he noticed for the first time the bird life, especially the tocororo, dubbed Cuba's national bird due to the red, white and blue plumage, the colours of the Cuban flag. From time to time they passed groups of men under the shade of palm trees, strumming guitars and playing bongo drums in rhythmic salsas and cha-cha-chas. All this intoxicated them, and neither of them could find a reason to end the allusion.

After a rest, David had soaked in his bath for half an hour, and was now feeling pretty rejuvenated and invigorated as he dressed for dinner. And as usual, at this time, Sonya came into his room to administer the necessary injections and medication. As she busied herself collecting the soiled towels, he wondered if she had enjoyed her day as much as he had. Had it been the same for her?

She fascinated him. There were those dark laughing eyes set in a face so beautiful and full of mischief, but she could also be sensible and serious when the occasion called; and he could talk to her forever. She didn't realise the depth of her own beauty: it was something she never thought about. Her hair was dark brown, laced with wisps of blonde where the sun had touched, framing an oval face. She gave the appearance of one who was delicate and fragile, but, at the same time, there was power and resilience in her bearing.

He watched her for a while as she sorted out his clothes.

"Come, sit down for a moment, Sonya, I want to talk to you," taking her hand and drawing her towards the chair.

"Sonya, I'm so grateful to you and I don't know quite how to say this, but without your help I wouldn't have made such progress."

Here it comes, a bit earlier than expected, she thought, the grateful pat on the back and goodbye, Sonya. She hated having these cynical thoughts. What was the matter with her?

"I'm now well on the way to a full recovery," he continued, "and I want..........."

He got no further. She didn't want to hear the rest, not now... later perhaps. And keeping all emotion out of her voice, she quickly interjected.

"Yes, David, I'm so pleased for you and you have made a marvellous recovery. You've done so wonderfully well, and when Emma sees you she'll be as high as a kite."

Sonya tried to read his eyes at the mention of Emma's name, but could detect nothing. He's a good actor, she thought to herself. David never managed to finish his sentence because the house phone rang with Eva enquiring as to the time dinner should be served.

"Yes, Eva, that will be fine, the usual time," Sonya answered, and as she replaced the receiver, turned to David.

"I must rush. I've still to shower and dress. See you at

dinner," and she darted from the room before David had a chance to call her back.

Why was she running away from him when all she really wanted was to be with him? She was behaving like a bloody fool, like a teenager who had the 'hots' for her teacher. She felt she should leave as soon as possible, tomorrow, but she had committed herself to nurse him until he was fit. She couldn't shirk her duty; she had given her word and it wasn't within the bounds of her nature to give up. She was struck by a profound yearning for the time when things had been so simple between them, uncomplicated, when she was merely the nurse and he was her patient. She was happy then, now she felt so miserable and confused.

When she went down to dinner, she found David sitting comfortably on the veranda watching the sunset slip over the garden and slowly sink into the sea; the silence audible as she studied him for a brief moment.

"Can I mix you a cocktail before dinner?" she asked, light-heartedly, interrupting his thoughts.

"How about two margaritas?" he suggested, knowing that Sonya was more than partial to this particular imbibition.

Sonya went back inside and took the crushed ice that Eva had already placed in the ice bucket, poured two measures of tequila and then added lime and triple Sec. They toasted one another; and made reference to a great excursion; and they must do it again very soon. Just as they were finishing Eva announced that dinner was now ready to be served, and they made their way into the dinning room. Eva had prepared a typical Cuban meal of chick-pea soup and 'picadillo', minced beef and rice, which was most enjoyable, and washed down as usual with white wine.

To finish off the evening they had a night-cap on the veranda while listening to a tape of Cuba's popular music, the 'son', developed in the hills of the Oriente, and the evening song of the crickets gave air to an acceptable harmony; sounds of a tropical night.

The following morning, with the sun streaming in her window, Sonya woke with a start. She had spent a restless night tossing and turning, and not until dawn was breaking did she fall into a deep sleep. That night her mind would not shut down. She wanted David so badly, but, as far as she was concerned, he only saw her as his nurse. She knew that he still loved Emma and she could not do a thing about it.

She had had many boyfriends, but none of them had made her feel the way that David did. At twenty-one she had even been engaged to a young doctor, but in the end had been unable to go through with the marriage. It had been a bit of a shock to her parents, at the time. He had a promising career ahead of him and had worked in the same hospital as her father, who had subsequently retired. She knew her decision not to marry had upset her parents and had told them she wasn't in love.

Love will come later, they had told her; you will learn to love him, but she hadn't believed them. He had subsequently found someone else and had married. But she had never met anyone that she would follow to the ends of the earth, that is, not until now.

She had tried to convince herself that it was pity she felt for David, and even the knowledge that he loved someone else could not dispel her passion. Nothing could change the physical desire or the love she felt for this man, whom she had nursed back to life, from a crippled, battered and maimed wreck to a mended whole being.

While he had been unable to do things for himself, she had bathed his broken body, dressed his wounds and wiped his fevered brow. There was no part of him that she hadn't touched. She was familiar with every scar, every blemish, every muscle and every contour of his body. Eventually, mentally exhausted by all the conflicting thoughts, she had fallen asleep.

Now fully awake she glanced at her watch. How could she allow this to happen? It was already 9.30. She scrambled out of bed and, throwing on her negligee, half stumbled to her patient's room. Getting no response to her knock, she quietly opened the bedroom door and saw that he had already risen. Then she became aware of running water coming from the bathroom. Taking a few steps towards the door, she called out over the noise of the shower.

"Are you all right, David?"

"No, Sonya, I need your assistance."

Thinking something dreadful had happened she opened the door immediately and went directly to the shower, which, when she slid the door opened, found David facing her. He extended his hand towards her and without hesitation gave him hers. He gently pulled her into the shower and now with the water running down her hair and over her body he bent towards her.

"I love you Sonya, I need you and I want you," he whispered, barely audible through a thick voice.

She felt his hands slip her negligee from her shoulders, and, when she looked up to him, she saw a soft, loving expression on his face. He put his mouth to her breasts and gently caressed her body, his hands moved over her soft belly to her thighs. When he was ready he slipped himself inside her and all the passion she had tried to conceal exploded within her.

Afterwards, they soaped and cleaned each other, touching and kissing and rubbing their bodies against one another. Then they stepped out from the shower and dried each other, simultaneously. It wasn't until they were completely dry and had stepped back into the bedroom that they both realised what had happened.

David took her hand.

"I meant what I said, I love you and I want you. I've wanted to do that for a long time...."

"But," Sonya got no further.

"No buts. I wanted to tell you that, yesterday, but you seemed preoccupied."

"But...but, you are in love with Emma," she spluttered out.

"Where did you get that silly idea from? I love her as a friend and as a business associate. I would do anything for her, but I don't love her like that, I love you.... I'm in love with you."

"Oh David, I thought you didn't notice me. I tried to tell myself I was being stupid. But I love you, too. I've wanted you, too. I've been so miserable recently, and, when I realised how I felt about you and thought you were still in love with Emma, all I wanted to do was run away, out of your life, but I couldn't and I felt so trapped...oh... and now...I can't quite believe you feel the same way."

"Well, I do, and there's nothing you can do about it. It just happened and it's the greatest feeling in the world."

"Good gracious, look at the time!!!!!" Sonya exclaimed, "the breakfast will be ruined and Eva will be furious."

"Damn Eva, it's not every day that you tell a girl you love her. But I suppose you're right; we had better get to the dinning room."

They weren't at all surprised when they lifted the lids from the heated trays to find the eggs and the bacon dried up, the sausages beyond recognition and the toast hard. But they didn't care about that.

Eva came in, not too amused.

"The breakfast is ruined," she complained, "I suppose you want me to prepare more."

"No," they cooed in unison, "it's quite all right, Eva," and they giggled like children.

"What's come over you two this morning?" she questioned, taking a closer look at the both of them. "Ah, I see," she sang out, her voice softening now, "I wondered how long it would take you both to realise you're in love." And without another word she hummed her way back into the kitchen, leaving Sonya and David astonished by her last remark. But it only sent them into another fit of laughter.

All that day they laughed and giggled. They went to the beach and swam. When they were exhausted, they lay down and let the sun kiss their bodies. Juan had brought down the hamper, and when they had an elegant sufficiency of food and wine, fell asleep in each other's arm, under the shade of the umbrella.

They woke up and made love again; they couldn't get enough of each other; they had both been starved of the passion of love for so long. He never wanted to be without her, she fascinated him. She was twenty years his junior but that didn't matter to either of them. For her years she acted older. Perhaps that was something to do with the duties and responsibilities she had to endure as a nurse. And he was like a teenager again. He wanted no more of the burden that the financial world thrust upon him. He never wanted these days to end.

She was so much in control, yet demanded nothing for herself, just happy to be giving, especially now, to this man, whom she loved.

He felt so lucky to have found her. He felt he did not deserve this, this wonderful feeling of being born again. He was frightened he would wake up and it would all have been a dream or something would come along and take it all away. He couldn't get rid of the nagging, foreboding feeling that it would end, all too soon. He was obsessed in his love for her, happy and scared at the same time.

But when he sat up and looked at her innocently lying beside him, so peaceful, the feelings of impending dread dissipated; and he made love to her again, selfishly this time, taking all that he could, as if he was making love to her for the very last time.

Her longing and need for him was every bit as strong. He fulfilled all her needs and the thought of his being with her, made her want him more. They remained on the beach all day, and it was not until the sun went down over a calm sea that they gathered their belongings together, and went back to the villa.

CHAPTER 23

It was immaterial for whom the Latino was working. Whether it was Garcia, Colombian guerrillas or the Venezuelan antigovernment faction; it was of no consequence now. What was important was that they required protection from all of them. It had become too dangerous and complicated to work out. They were caught up in the crossfire, and some of them or all of them badly wanted Emma and Julian dead. That night they had barricaded themselves in Emma's room, placing every piece of moveable furniture against the door; they were taking no more unforeseen chances.

The Euro Building sat high, and as they looked out over the brightly lit city, nestling in the fertile valley between the hills, peaceful in its appearance, they were unable to grasp the happenings of the last few weeks. It all seemed bizarre and incredible. But what they were aware of was their lives were in real danger and they were beginning to doubt if either of them would ever get out of this predicament alive. They were trapped, and these people were capable of following them anywhere they went.

Julian had formulated a plan; it was a long shot; but it was the best he could propose other than simply flee the country. However, he had very quickly dismissed the last option since he wasn't prepared to look over his shoulders for the remainder of his life. They had talked long into the night outlining in detail Julian's line of approach and recapping on what was required from each of them. For both or even one of them to survive, it was essential and safer that they worked individually. There was too much to accomplish and so little time in which to do it.

For some reason or other Emma was not scared. During the night she had faced the worst scenario and, accepting that she had everything to gain, had cemented her mind firmly on a determination to win and survive.

Julian on the other hand had no fears for himself. He had faced death before, in recent years, on unsafe working installations, in the jungles of Colombia and as a younger man in the service of his Queen and country. But he did have fears and trepidation for Emma's safety. Would she be equipped to carry out her assignments without getting herself killed in the process? That was his main concern.

He had then gone on to give her times and places of contact, with their final rendezvous in three days time. Emma was in no doubt about the improbability of their success, but she would not think about that. If their survival was dependant on a positive attitude, she certainly had plenty of that. And to see her face set in a resolute determination had given Julian a glimmer of hope. He could only but admire her courage. They had waited for the morning hustle and bustle of hotel life to be well underway before leaving their room. This, they felt, would ensure their departure to be less conspicuous.

Now, sitting alone in a busy cafe, Emma went over the plan step by step. Before destroying her notes, she made sure that she knew every move she and Julian would have to make.

Julian had left her when they were well shot of the hotel, with instructions to pick up a card for her mobile, but cautioned her not to call out with the given times and likewise, not to answer; excepting of course, in any real emergency, whereupon Julian's contingency plan would come into play; two rings—switch off—three rings—switch off and he would know to get back to her.

To sustain her energy levels she was now sipping an orange juice and biting into a corned beef sandwich. She glanced at her watch. "Any minute now," she muttered to herself. Within a few seconds when her mobile gave out the old familiar few notes of 'London Bridge is falling....' she answered

"Everything OK at your end?" she heard Julian ask.

"Yes, fine."

"Where are you?"

"Having a bit of sustenance."

"Trust you, Emma, to be thinking about your stomach as usual. You'll never change," he said laughingly. "Now," he went on in a more serious tone, "you're quite sure what you have to do?"

"Yes, I've just gone over everything again for the last time."

"Good, everything seems to be working. Take care, love you, be in touch," and he switched off.

For a moment she wanted to burst out laughing. It seemed so ridiculously amusing and funny, and she was unable to suppress the smile that broke across her face. However, the seriousness of her situation, all too soon, came galloping back to wipe out any thoughts of the ludicrous. Emma had a couple of hours to kill before her first assignment and, this being the case, took a cab to the famous Plaza Bolivar, one of the squares and gardens in Caracas, where she would try to forget, for the moment, her plight.

There were many people milling about, and from the babble of many different tongues, she deduced they were mainly tourists. A few sat on benches enjoying their lunch 'al fresco' and threw crumbs to the many birds that cautiously approached the tiny titbits.

The bronze equestrian statue of Simon Bolivar, the South American revolutionary and statesman born in Caracas, stood tall and gallant in the dancing sunlight. From there she walked a short distance, still anxiously watching the crowds, to the impressive gilt-domed capital building, now the Central University of Venezuela and the National Parthenon, where Bolivar was buried.

Emma, wherever she visited, always took an avid interest in the country's history. And this was no exception even although other things occupied her mind. She found the past fascinating, and always tried to imagine how and what the people of bygone days, whose feet had trod the very ground upon which she now stood, were like. She tried to get a mental picture of their lifestyles, their hopes, their desires and the family structure. The traders; were they too rich and powerful to notice the poor? And the poor; were their lives so full of misery that each day was a constant struggle against disease and poverty?

From her historical knowledge Emma was familiar with the fact that Francis Drake, the English navigator, in 1595 had landed here, and she wondered if his only thoughts were that of loot and plunder of this captured city, or had he thought to its future well after he was dead and gone.

She snapped herself out of her imaginary world to find that she had been wandering for over an hour. She anxiously checked her watch. She had a strict time plan to observe. Time to make a move, and left her thoughts of history in the Plaza Bolivar as her eyes, once again, questioningly scanned the crowds.

A cab drew up in front of the restaurant El Nogal and Julian jumped out. He looked around casually and, noticing nothing untoward, walked into the bar. Inside, he took a moment to glance around and decide where he should sit. Over in a corner a young dark haired man took up his attention and briefly held his gaze. To be less obtrusive he chose to sit at a table where the shadows fell; then nodded to the bartender and his usual drink was brought over to him.

"Buenos dias, senor, como esta?"

"Very well, thanks," Julian replied, happy to be accepted, for the time being, as a regular customer.

Carreras and Sanmarco had already arrived and were in deep conversation over by the bar. Julian made no attempt to join them. He was banking on their noticing him. He didn't have to wait very long and on hearing Carreras's voice, he raised his eyes from the newspaper.

"Ah, Julian, good afternoon. May I join you?"

"Be my guest," Julian replied in a hospitable voice.

"All alone today, I see."

"Yes, and you? Is Sanmarco with you?" Julian asked, pretending he had not noticed them earlier.

"He's gone off on an errand. He'll return later," Julian heard Carreras reply.

Julian noted that Carreras was as pompous and arrogant as ever. He liked to be in control and was in his element when holding court. Julian thoughtfully wondered how Carreras would fare once the cards were on the table. The topic of conversation drifted to government affairs about which Julian was only too delighted.

"There is corruption among the members of the assembly of which you're one," Julian tested.

"Corruption is all around us, my friend," Carreras replied, patronisingly.

Julian continued.

"A few days ago the supreme court voted 8 to 6 to recognise the Assembly's right to intervene in Government, making it an all powerful Constituent and at the same time to prohibit Congress from passing laws. In three days from now the Assembly takes a vote to change the constitutions, making Gonzales, in turn, secure in his authority. What would happen," Julian went on, "if it became public knowledge that, contrary to what the President and his supporters claim, there is still ongoing mass corruption not only within the Assembly members but also within the Supreme Court itself?"

Carreras was just about to expound.

"No, I'll tell you, Senor Carreras. There would be mass demonstrations in the streets of Venezuela, defending democracy. The opposition is already aware and accusing Gonzales of preparing for authoritarian rule, but his claim is he is merely cleaning up some of the worst political corruption in the world. Ha!! Bullshit!! Gonzales can't afford this knowledge to leak before the Assembly takes a vote on a new Constitution. As I said, it would lead to mass demonstrations and even beyond, to a coup. There is a strong antigovernment faction, of that I'm sure you are aware, and if they get a foothold with the support of the people you and Gonzales can say goodbye to your fine sinecures within the Assembly."

"What are you driving at?" Carreras sneered.

"This is what I'm driving at. I know that you, Carreras, bribed members of the Supreme Court to support the Assembly. Is that not corruption? I ask you, what would happen if this became public?"

Carreras's face turned ashen.

"None of this is true. Where did you get this slanderous information?" Carreras flared up, almost rising from his seat.

"I've got my sources," was all Julian said, not wishing to reveal that his source of information was partially conjecture based on what he had read in the newspapers together with a few short hours of detective work.

"Who are you?"

"All in good time," Julian smilingly answered, now beginning to enjoy the pain he was inflicting on Carreras. "But first let me tell you, all this information and proof is lodged with my lawyer, just in case you get any bad ideas about my welfare."

"What do you want, money?" Carreras hissed, unable now to conceal the man inside.

Julian ignored the last statement and he now knew that he was right about Carreras.

"I have evidence that, one; there is a strong antigovernment faction operating here in Venezuela and that they planted an explosive device killing six men at an oil field in Maracaibo. Reason; to disrupt the flow of oil and a contributory factor to bring down your present Government."

"Two. I have proof that Colombian drug traffickers, Roberto Garcia and Luis Sanchez, to name but two, are now operating in Venezuela, and, if known, would neither please your people or the DEA."

"Three. I have proof there is corruption within the members of the New All Powerful Assembly."

"Four. I have proof that you, Carreras, on behalf of that New All Powerful Assembly, bribed the Supreme Court."

"Five. I have proof that the Revolutionary Armed Forces of Colombia are supplying and supporting the AGF here in Venezuela, with drugs and drugs money to help their cause. Need I go any further?"

Carreras remained silent for a moment.

"You can't prove any of this," he stated, "you're lying", was the best Carreras could say.

"I can assure you I can; and a quick whisper in the ear of the media will blow your little game plan with Gonzales and your new constitutions, sky high. Gonzales will be forced to resign and his career in politics finished for good."

Carreras scowled. He could not be sure whether this man was bluffing or not. He could not take that chance. They were too close to winning. The stakes were too high.

"What is it that you want?"

"Now you're beginning to see it my way," Julian replied with an oleaginous smile.

Julian spelt out his demands and with each one Carreras's face went through violent muscular spasms.

"I'm not in a position to do any of that."

"Au Contraire, I think you are. You will demand that the Colombian government picks up Garcia and Sanchez; you will persuade the AGF to get off our case; you will arrange for a forty-eight hour protection, and finally, you will have a boat waiting at Guaira port at midnight tomorrow. Otherwise, I'll release this information to the media before the Assembly takes a vote in three days, and Gonzales will not get the support he requires for authoritarian rule. I'll be here at the same time tomorrow for your answer."

Julian watched as Carreras, now literally frothing from the mouth, stood up and staggered out of the bistro.

Shortly after Carreras left, Julian went over to the bar, wondering if he had scared Carreras enough into complying with his demands or had he added one more to his list of enemies. That was the calculated chance he had to take if there was any hope of their getting out of this alive.

While he was mulling over all the possibilities in his mind, Sanmarco appeared, and, noticing Julian at the bar, bellied up to him at the same time looking around for Carreras.

"Seen Gabriel?" he asked on approaching Julian.

"He left a short while ago."

"Strange, I was supposed to meet him back here. No matter."

Julian waited until Sanmarco got a drink up before he began.

"What do you know about the antigovernment faction here?"

"Why do you ask? Not much. I know they exist in a small way. Not much support."

"Your boss, Gabriel Carreras, is Gonzales's man and you are his secretary. Is this not true?"

"Yes, that is so."

Julian feigned an irritation in his throat to give himself a moment as how to word the next statement.

"What would happen if I had to tell him, that you are in fact an AGF supporter and indeed a very important one at that? You have been placed in the government as a spy."

Julian saw the fear settle on Sanmarco's face for a moment then fade, and immediately knew that his suspicions were warranted. Sanmarco made no attempt either to confirm or deny the allegations and allowed Julian to continue. He's shrewder than I thought, Julian reflected.

"The AGF placed an explosive device on an oil platform at Lake Maracaibo killing four of my men. And you personally put the Latino on to me at the Euro Building. You will call off your henchmen, all of them; otherwise I'll blow your cover."

Sanmarco, unlike Carreras, remained cool and it was difficult to read his mind. Julian admired him in a way. He was a good agent, giving the outward impression of an over talkative, loud buffoon, when in actual fact he was a killer and gave nothing away that was of any significance.

"How can I trust you?" was all he said.

"I leave here in two days and should anything happen either to myself or Senora Findlay, an attorney has instructions to open a letter and divulge its contents to the press. Do I make myself clear?"

At that point, Julian became aware of his mobile, which had been switched to silent mode, vibrating. Two rings, then off, followed by three rings. Great, that's Emma, he thought. Meanwhile, Sanmarco seemed to be deep in thought, and Julian took the opportunity to casually look around him. He noticed the approach of two muscle-bound men, wearing their suits like a second skin.

"Join us for a drink?" he invited them and, before they could respond, called the barman. Julian moved slightly to one side allowing all three to face him. Then addressing Sanmarco he said, "Shall we say 2.30 tomorrow afternoon?"

Julian wasted no time in their company nor did he wait for Sanmarco's response. He simply, with a slight nod of his head, left the bar.

Outside he grabbed a cab and as it drove away looked back in the direction of El Nogal to determine if he were being followed. But the only person that appeared was the dark haired man who had been sitting in the corner of the restaurant.

Checking the time, Julian took out his mobile phone and called Emma.

"Yes, everything's fine, I'm on my way to the Director General of Police."

"So far so good. I'll see you later," and Julian switched off.

Emma didn't have an appointment, but after ten minutes of pleading she was shown into the Director's office. She explained her position and told him that she was concerned about information she had received regarding a Colombian drugs trafficking organisation now operating through

Venezuela and, if something was not done about it, she, as an anti-drugs campaigner, would approach the press and the DEA. Before leaving she handed the Director General of Police the names of Garcia and Sanchez and informed him she would be in contact the following day.

The Director General, in recent months, had scored some major victories against the drug traffickers of Venezuela, and in no way did he want added problems from the Colombians. He had worked closely with the United States DEA, who, not only thought highly of him, but also had given him all the assistance necessary in the combat against narcotics. So, as soon as Emma had left his office he picked up the phone and called the Minister of the Interior.

"This is outwith my jurisdiction; this is on a Government level. You deal with it, now," he shouted down the phone at Carreras. "My job is difficult enough with the drug dealers of our own country without the infiltration of the Colombians," he continued to blast.

"What can you do?" he yelled down the phone at Carreras's lack of direction. "For one you can contact Colonel Jose Gallego, director of the anti-narcotics police in Bogota and have him handle it, this very minute," and banged down the phone.

Carreras, after the phone had gone dead, sat with his head in his hands. He knew Gonzales well enough; he was ruthless and ambitious; he would allow nothing to jeopardise the successful transformation to authoritarian rule. Should any hint of this reach the ears of Gonzales, Carreras would immediately be removed from his position in the Assembly. His decision to comply, not only with the Director General of

Police but also with the demands that Julian Burton had made, did not come easily. But aware of the consequences and the ensuing results, it left little doubt in his mind what action to take.

Damn that blasted Burton man, he fumed inwardly. The malevolent streak in him would not allow Burton to get away with it. He held too much information that, not only today but in the future, if released, could topple and bring down the present Government. He had to be stopped and Carreras would at all costs do just that.

CHAPTER 24

The following day, Emma and Julian went their separate ways again, each on their own mission. Emma didn't know for how long she had been followed, but it had begun with a feeling that somebody was staring at the back of her neck, giving her a dose of the shivers, making her feel cold in the warm sunshine. She had stopped once or twice to look in the shop windows and, casually glancing back along the street, found nothing to substantiate her gut feeling. Nobody had hesitated abruptly or suddenly changed direction; but still the uneasy feeling persisted, and she couldn't shake the notion out of her head, that everyone around was a potential threat. Was she imagining this?

She decided to leave nothing to chance. This was a game of survival, not the national lottery. To give it one more test while strolling along, she let the street map which she was holding in her hand, fall to the ground. She quickly bent down to retrieve it, and as she looked backwards at the many pairs of legs coming towards her, one pair came to a halt in double quick time, turning inwards towards a shop window. From her bent position she could not see the full torso, but the owner of the legs was wearing pale blue pants and training shoes.

Her first instinct was to quicken her steps and shake off blue legs, but any obvious change would only indicate that she had become aware of her pursuer; so she simply continued on her way as if nothing was afoot, but all the while thinking how she could get rid of him. What's my best tactic here? Where can I go? The questions burst into her head. Instinctively she wanted to run and hide, somewhere, anywhere.

It was eleven o'clock, now, as she was passing the Museum of Fine Arts, and, as logic told her, at this time of the day there would be many tourists and perhaps she could lose her unwanted company. Inside, a special exhibition of Dutch and Flemish painters was attracting greater interest than usual, with throngs of people milling around. Joining one large group, into the centre of which she slowly edged her way, giving her enough concealment, she idly looked around.

People around her were expressing their appreciation of the art and Emma turned towards the woman next to her, giving her own impressions of Van Gogh's, The Drawbridge 1883, an oil on canvas. The rest of the group wove its way towards the next Van Gogh, which was The Field of Poppies 1889, leaving her companion and herself slightly apart from the main body and giving Emma a better all over view.

Over by the group that was standing by Rembrandt's collection, she spotted a tall man with black curly hair sporting a white polo shirt, pale blue pants and white training shoes. It had to be the same guy; she never believed in coincidences.

Emma and the woman now caught up with the main group and as they were passing an exit door, she, without hesitation and in a split second, darted through. On the other side she found stairs, and hoping he would not notice her absence, just yet, clattered her high heels down, coming to a metal door at the bottom. She stopped, just for a moment, listening for following footsteps, but heard none.

Pushing down the lever handle, the door creaked open into the basement car park, and, wasting no time, she ran past seven cars before stopping to crouch down behind one. For what seemed like hours she stayed put. Certain that if indeed he were following her, he, on noticing her disappearance, would do exactly as she had done and appear through the door.

Only the street traffic outside broke the silence; inside it was deadly quiet and the dark shadows, where the inadequate lighting didn't penetrate, made the basement look scary and creepy. But the dim lighting could also work to her advantage. There was the inevitable toxic smell of exhaust fumes that gave her a smarting sensation at the base of her nostrils and a sneeze was beginning to develop. Oh, not now, please don't let me sneeze.

Suppressing her sneeze, she was just about to rise from her position when the creek of the metal door made her freeze. No footsteps could be heard, but after a short time she did hear the squeak of rubber soles against the hard concrete flooring, coming closer. She was unable to breathe now, she was scared, a fit of nervousness overtook her; a shudder vibrated through her body making her jerk and twitch as if some unknown element had taken control and the fear was so strong that she began to feel faint and life itself was being sucked out of her. He must be very close now, she thought, and then the squeaking sound ceased.

"No, don't come any closer, I can't take any more of this shit," her terrified brain screamed.

Now she imagined him looking around and then the squeaking trainers, once again, moved across the concrete.

This practice, she counted, was repeated five times, before it stopped completely. Where was he now? He must have gone over to the other row of parked cars.

After what seemed a lifetime, she slowly eased herself up just to take a cautious look, and to her horror she found herself gazing at the back of the same man that had been in the Museum. He was looking around him and bending down to look underneath the parked vehicles. She froze but continued to watch him. After what seemed an interminable time, he either made up his mind that she was no longer in the basement and had taken some other exit or he just plain gave up because he started to walk back to the metal door and, with a backward glance, he, his pale blue pants and trainers disappeared. The spasmodic convulsion that had entered her body at the outset of this caper slackened its grip and her breathing became more normal.

For a further ten minutes she held her position until she was satisfied that this was not some sort of trick and he would suddenly appear back through the door. When she decided she had given it long enough and without the reappearance of the pursuer, she made her way along the rows of vehicles, her heart racing, and finally into the daylight at the exit gate of the car park. With caution and a vigilant eye, she walked along the side of the Museum, hugging its shady walls, until she spotted a cab coming in her direction. She stepped out to the kerb side of the pavement and quickly jumped inside.

The cab dropped her outside the Police Headquarters, and the Director General was only too pleased to see her immediately.

"I was rather shocked, yesterday, with the information you gave me," he opened, "but now I've had time to reflect, and we, the anti-narcotics police in this struggle, are forever in your debt. This problem, to let you understand, is slightly out of my jurisdiction, government level you know, but I have put the wheels in motion and we should see some results soon."

Emma was extremely pleased, and indeed, what she was hearing was no more or no less than she and Julian had anticipated.

"I'm simply doing my duty as a citizen, and one who finds the unnecessary deaths of the young from drugs, appalling in every way. We will never keep the streets of our cities free from narcotics until those that profit by it are wiped out and brought to task," Emma told him, sincerely.

"I can reveal to you, at this present moment, Colonel Jose Gallego, Director of the anti-narcotics police in Bogota has been advised of this situation, and, in the past, has fought many front-line battles against the armies that protect the drug laboratories and traffickers. Like his superior General Jose Serrano, Director of the National Police, who took and smashed Colombia's biggest drugs cartel in Cali and Medellin, and who is now No. 1 on every hit list in Colombia. These are the dedicated men who risk their lives daily in the fight against narcotics. So you see, Senora Findlay, how grateful we are for your information. Without the help of the general public and people like you, who in most cases are too scared to come forward, our task would be more difficult.

The Director General then made his apologies that he must conclude their discussion as he had a further appointment to keep. Standing up he shook her hand and once again expressed his gratitude. It was a satisfying feeling to encounter an honest and incorruptible man like The General Director, who wouldn't be bribed. It was rare to find this quality in someone in his position, and Emma wondered how long it would be before his name appeared on that hit list, if it wasn't already there.

After his meetings with Garcia and Sanchez, Julian had returned to the hotel, sometime before Emma was due back, and had gone straight to the bedroom, where he first of all bundled their few belongings into a holdall. If everything went according to plan, they would be on their way tonight at midnight and hopefully out of immediate danger. But he had kept his reservations about that to himself. It was too much to hope for; he would simply take care of each stage as it developed.

When he had checked in with Emma, as prearranged, an hour ago, and without going into any details, she had appeared positive and cheerful about the way things had progressed at her end. A quick glance at his watch told him she would be arriving back just about now, and he had stressed that under no condition should she venture to the room on her own. The reported muggings that were happening all over Caracas were real and not to be taken lightly. Even at this very exclusive hotel, visitors had their wallets stolen and even worse on some occasions had been tied and trussed up in their very own rooms, where they were found in the morning by the chambermaid. He too, on entering the suite, had been extra cautious and had checked every room before relaxing.

Taking a last look around, satisfying himself that he had not left anything of importance, he vacated the room. As he walked towards the elevator he noticed that the security guards, who had been posted along the corridors since the discovery of the flight attendant's body, were still there. To Julian this meant very little, because he knew there was also massive corruption even within the walls of the police force and the security companies. Here, trust was merely an empty word.

The transient business population, who, after their day's toil, had crowded into the pool bar in their droves, and with lively chatter, were relaxing and enjoying their favourite sundowners. Emma had not arrived as yet, but Julian went ahead and ordered a beer and settled down at a table.

His meeting with Sanmarco had gone well enough and he had assured him that there would be no further trouble from the AGF; not now, since Emma and he were taking nothing to do with Garcia & Co. The AGF was satisfied for the moment that Garcia's 'laundering business' from drugs money had taken a backward step, and this would be sufficient for AGF's collaborators, the Colombian guerrillas, to back off.

Sanmarco had asked him again and again the same question, "But how can we be sure?"

"You can't, you can only take my word for it, and as I've said to you previously, we're not involved with Garcia and neither will we be involved with Garcia in the future."

Julian made no reference to the unfortunate brutalisation of David or the case holding Garcia's money. That was other business and could be dealt with later. But he hadn't made up his mind what to do. Should he try and return it or keep it. Returning it could lead to their deaths and keeping it was a criminal offence carrying a prison sentence. In the beginning, it all seemed so simple; make a few trips to Dominique Republic, open bank accounts for Garcia, and collect their share, amounting to millions.

Julian's mind drifted away from the 'illicit booty' and came back to Sanmarco, whom he believed was being honest and truthful. He felt the AGF was convinced that he and Emma were no longer a threat to their cause. He left Sanmarco feeling confident that, although he and Emma were still in danger from other sources, the AGF were no longer an impending threat.

On the other hand, Gabriel Carreras was an entirely different issue; he didn't trust the man one iota. His eyes hardly ever focused on Julian's; they were shifty, and whenever Julian, on the very odd occasion, did happen to make eye contact, Carreras's eyes revealed all. They were full of malevolence and hatred; a window of the mind.

Carreras had confirmed that Julian's demands had been addressed; that Emma and he would suffer full protection until they left Venezuelan soil; a boat would be at berth seven Guaira docks as requested; and that the Colombian Narcotics Police had been informed and everything possible was being done to find Garcia, Sanchez and the location of their drugs laboratories. This should have been sufficient to erase Julian's sense of foreboding, but it wasn't. Julian had watched Carreras's expression as he spoke, and, although he could not put his finger on it, he knew Carreras was holding back something. Perhaps Julian had only complicated matters and Carreras' henchmen were on to them at this very moment. His thoughts were interrupted when Emma gently rested her hand on the back of his shoulder and bent forward to kiss him on the cheek.

"Hello, darling," she wearily sighed, as she sat down beside him.

"How did your day go? Did you meet with them?" she went on.

He recounted the events of the day, giving a detailed account of his conversations with Sanmarco and Carreras, but admitted that, although he was fairly satisfied that Sanmarco and the AGF would be of no further threat to them, he was not at all happy with Carreras, even although Julian had been assured that all his demands were being met.

"I just don't trust that bastard, and, for our own sakes, we must continue to assume that not only are Garcia's guerrillas out there, somewhere, ready to pick us off, but also the possibility that Carreras has added his henchmen to our list of enemies. However, we don't have much of a choice, Emma; we've got to go along with it all, for the time being, but with our eyes wide open and our fingers crossed."

It wasn't until Emma had finished describing her earlier experiences at the museum that Julian was now fully convinced Garcia was still after them.

"It could only have been Garcia's man," Julian concluded.

"Why are you so sure?" Emma replied. "It could also have been Carreras, we just don't know. The Director General assured me that everything possible was being done and it would only be a matter of time before they caught up with Garcia and Sanchez and, that being the case, the threat from Garcia's men would vanish."

"I believe what you're saying, Emma, but we just don't have time on our side, that's what we don't have, time."

The waiter brought Emma her cocktail and when he was out of earshot they continued their discussion, going over their plans, at the end of which, Julian suggested, "We should have something to eat here at the hotel, it's safer than anywhere else with all those security guards buzzing about. And around about ten thirty make our way to the waiting boat."

"Yes, that sounds reasonable enough to me," Emma agreed.

They went over again and again the possibilities and the probabilities of danger and even failure, until they exhausted themselves with the 'what ifs and ands'; then they dropped the subject completely with Emma's concluding statement, "What a bloody mess!!!!!"

They had a light dinner since neither of them was hungry enough to do justice to a full meal, and towards 10.30 they prepared to leave the hotel. They didn't hear the news bulletin from the television located in the TV lounge that, to quote a statement just issued by the Director General of the Anti-Narcotics Police. 'Late this afternoon the anti-narcotics police successfully located and burst a drugs cartel in the Medellin and Cali areas of Colombia, and among the men now in custody are congress man, Luis Sanchez, and prominent businessman, Roberto Garcia, who was seriously wounded resisting arrest'.

La Guaira, the seaport town in the Federal District of Venezuela, lies about three quarters of an hour's drive from Caracas, on the other side of El Avila N.P. Cruise liners, tankers and container ships have all graced her docks. At this section of the docks, tankers and container ships sit high in the water, with crude lighting to show the way up the gangplanks and along the steel passageways. Their dark, colourless shapes are daunting and ghostlike as they sit in the water as black as pitch. As in any other seaport, crates and containers stand in neat rows ready to be shipped to distant shores.

There are few people about at this time in the evening; all work has ceased for the day. Only the night watchmen keep their vigilance. A soft rain is falling and where the sun has warmed the tarmac, a light and flimsy vapour rises.

There is an uneasy silence as a man and a woman walk along the dock, passing along the rows of stacked containers that tower above them in threatening impatience, as if they are about to fall over at any moment and crush them. They stop from time to time to look at this boat or another. They walk on in no particular haste, unaware of their surroundings; they laugh easily and appear only to see each other.

Further along, where the large tankers and container ships give way to smaller freight carriers, tugboats and pleasure boats, they stop to admire a Moody 33, whose slim streamline hull caresses the water as the gentle ripple laps against her sides.

They don't see the eyes and forms that keep a constant watch. They are not aware of the silent shapes that move in the eerie moonlight. They don't notice the pack of men dogs that follow their steps, moving between the containers now half hidden in the dark shadows of the night. The sky is colourless except for the new moon's cradle, painted yellow on a black canvas, which appears from behind the rain clouds.

The shapes that silently follow come from a different world, a world of violence and extortion, a world of hatred and deceit, and a world of kill or be killed. The black shapes follow like hyenas, whose courage is evident only in numbers. A night watchman, who has just completed his round, steps into his Portakabin and turns up the volume of his transistor. He neither sees the couple nor the men dogs that creep up on them. His only thought is to catch a few hours stolen sleep before the next round of duty.

The men dogs are now getting into position as the couple approach berth seven. There they stop at the Fairline 46 with her impressive three-helm seat flying bridge and her interior ablaze, lighting up her cream and mahogany salon. She sits majestically in the water inviting her admirers on board. They are oblivious to the dangers that skulk furtively around them, for theirs is a time of happiness that blocks out all that can't be seen.

The men dogs lift the stock of their rifles to their shoulders, pulling them in tightly, and look through the telescopic sights. As the woman turns to speak to her companion, her words are lost as the silent fire, raining down, mows them to the ground. They feel no pain, their demise is instantaneous, they die with the same loving smile on their faces; they were in love.

The men dogs slip quietly away in the night, and only the lapping of the water against the Fairline's perfect hull breaks the silence.

CHAPTER 25

A week had gone past without any news from either Emma or Julian, and David's concern had grown daily, causing him further stress. Sonya had noticed his anxiety mounting as the days increased their numbers and she tried to dispel his worst fears. Inside she felt a similar angst, but when she spoke to him, she made sure her face remained expressionless and revealed none of her inner apprehensions.

"You know, David, that old clichè, 'no news is good news' and I think you're worrying unnecessarily. Emma is an exceptionally capable and astute woman with the heart of a lioness and when it comes down to trouble she's a survivor. And she's also got Julian who's more than streetwise. She'll be fine, just wait and see; nothing's ever got to her yet."

"They're not dealing with your normal run of the mill people; these are criminals, gangsters and Mafia. Need I go on? They are not equipped to fight these people because they don't have the necessary knowledge. These thugs can wipe out Emma and Julian, just like that. Sonya, you can't begin to imagine the power they can wield and the pressure they can bring to bear. They're power is omnipotent, it's in their wealth and they've bags of it. They're capable of preventing Emma and Julian from leaving the country by controlling the availability of seats; hotels for inexplicable reasons are fully booked or something mysterious has happened to their credit at the bank, and so on and so on."

As much as she tried, Sonya could not convince David that he was overreacting, and this whole affair was making him overwrought, which was the last thing she wanted, especially now that he had almost made a full recovery from his own unfortunate scrape with the very people he had been talking about. A setback at this stage would be disastrous.

She supposed it was something to do with her childhood and her training that had blessed her with this endless optimism and faith. She had a buoyant cheerful personality and she constantly encouraged her patients back to good health, teaching them to believe in themselves, which was part of the therapy. There was nothing pessimistic, negative or misanthropic about her and in general she trusted people easily.

"They're up against a whole army of corruption and I have this impending feeling of doom that I can't seem to shake off. If we don't hear from them by tomorrow, I'm going to call the Euro Building, which Julian always uses when in Caracas, even although Emma left strict instructions, for our own safety, not to make any calls to Venezuela."

David was so adamant that she reluctantly agreed to a compromise and made no further efforts to discourage him. After making up his mind to call the hotel the following day, David had brightened up a bit and put his worries and concerns to rest for the present.

The time they had spent together over the past two weeks had been flawless, full of fun and laughter. David's fast recovery had been mainly down to Sonya's encouraging determination and faith in him. She was besotted by him and every time he looked at her, he couldn't believe his good fortune to have happened upon and fallen in love with this wonderful beautiful creature. Petite in stature with fine bone structure, she exuded an aura of serenity which had captivated David instantly. From her honey coloured face, framed by rich brown hair, danced her sparkling green eyes that twinkled when she laughed, reminding David of a warm autumn day; and she was totally oblivious to the sensuality that the curve of her lips produced as she smiled. With her shiny scrubbed face, she looked much younger than her years. It was only when she wanted to appear older and sophisticated that she applied make-up.

Their lovemaking was erotic and demanding, and now that David had regained his strength, he had great difficulty in restraining himself whenever she was close to him. With a passion of uncontrolled joy and ecstasy they explored each other's body. When she looked into his eyes she saw the hunger that was there, and unconditionally responded to this man whom she knew loved her completely.

Almost every day they had gone to the beach, except on those occasions when they explored the island, sharing first time experiences. One of the most interesting trips they took was to Bayamo, the capital of Granma province, the country's most southern point, which, due to its position, sees very few tourists; one of the reasons for going there.

They had set out early that particular morning, directly after breakfast. Their journey once more had taken them past fields of sugarcane, coffee, and tobacco and through the fertile flatlands where cattle grazed lazily. Different species of palm trees sprung up everywhere, interspersed with the sacred silk-cotton tree and the mariposa, the white butterfly jasmine, Cuba's national flower. Apart from a bullock driven cart and the odd 50s and 60s American automobile, their route had been undisturbed by modern technology. On the southern coast the environment changed to mangrove swamps where, in the silence of their surroundings, flocks of birds were seen flying and swarming above the marshlands.

The journey to Bayamo, being a fair distance from the Villa Verdi, had taken them longer than anticipated, and their first stop on arriving was to head straight for a bodequita, where they had enjoyed good wine and local fish, all set in a pleasant and relaxed atmosphere.

Afterwards they had visited the national park, Gran Parque Nacional Sierra Maestra and the Ayuntamiento, where Cespedes in 1868 proclaimed independence for Cuba. According to history, the Creole planter Carlos Manuel de Cespedes freed his slaves, formed a militia and overran the eastern end of the island. And in more recent times, Castro and 81 rebels landed at Cabo Cruz aboard the Granma in 1956.

The following afternoon, Sonya noticed that David, when he still had received no communications from Emma and Julian, had gone quiet and began pacing up and down the veranda.

"David, you're doing yourself no good, getting in a state like this. Sit down and relax. You're driving me crazy with all that shuffling back and forth."

"I know, I know, but something must have happened to them to be out of contact for all this time."

Without saying another word, he went inside and picked up the telephone. After a few minutes, she heard him asking for a Mrs. Emma Findlay and Mr. Julian Burton; and then, a short time later, she heard the hand piece going down on the cradle.

He came back out to the veranda.

"Seemingly they checked out of the hotel two days ago," David said, slowly, as he churned over the information. "Two days ago," David continued reflectively, while Sonya sat in silence.

"That means at least they were still alive on Tuesday. Something must have happened to them since then."

"We don't know that, yet," Sonya opened but becoming a bit alarmed herself. "It narrows it down a bit, doesn't it? We could contact the authorities and find out if any tourists have gone missing or any bodies have been found," Sonya suggested.

David thought for a moment.

"No, I don't think that would be a good idea. We can't give their names nor can we draw any attention to them. To phone the hotel is one thing, but to alert the police is a different matter. In any case, that was the one thing that Emma specifically asked me not to do, under any circumstances. We can only sit and wait this one out for another while."

"Well, we've got to be more positive otherwise we'll go mad with worry," Sonya advised.

"Yes, you're right."

But try as they might to lift their spirits and get through the next few days, their thoughts kept returning to their missing friends.

Later that evening, while they were relaxing after dinner, Sonya happened to be glancing through the newspaper that Eva had delivered, when something caught her eye and reading on intently she let burst loudly.

"David, look at this!!!" she exclaimed, as she began translating the section.

"War against drugs in Colombia. Look here David," as she drew her finger along the line of print.

"Roberto Garcia and Luis Sanchez, Minister of Education, both arrested, by the anti narcotics police, for drugs trafficking, and laboratories in Cali and Medellin destroyed. This is a great breakthrough in the war..." Sonya stopped reading and looked at David unable to believe what was in front of her eyes. She reread the section for a second time, to make doubly sure of the facts.

"I can't believe it, it's too good to be true," David cried out, excitedly. "Are you sure?"

But he knew, even before he read for himself in his limited knowledge of Spanish that the report in the paper was right. Throwing the paper in the air he whooped for joy.

"This is the greatest, good news and I wonder if Emma and Julian had something to do with it."

"They most probably did have; it's too much of a coincidence and do you know what, this means...you're safe and free from them, David, and I hope it's not too late for Emma and Julian. And if they are still alive at the moment, they're home and dry."

They could hardly contain themselves, dancing around the room, throwing cushions in the air. The din was such that it brought Eva to the room, wearing a disapproving frown on her face.

"It's all right, Eva, just received the best news ever," Sonya tried to explain, unable to pay much attention to Eva's questioning look, as David danced her around the floor.

"On you go now, back to the kitchen with you," David laughingly chastised as Eva left them, muttering to herself, "Children, nothing but children."

"This calls for a celebration. What do you think?" And before Sonya had time to reply, he had danced his crutches to the drinks cabinet.

"Here's to us and here's to that great man whose name is Emma, to quote a phrase from Voltaire, referring to Catherine the Great," David offered, never shy of showing off his knowledge.

"Oh, you're safe now, David, and I hope it's not too late for Emma and Julian."

A radiant sun enriched an incredibly blue sky as the motor yacht glided over the calm aquamarine sea. The Island of Margarita's distant coastline stretched in front as Emma sat in the fly bridge.

Julian had kept watch all night allowing Emma to rest. And when the sun had risen above the horizon, the sea was coloured in a shifting palette of blues and greens. He had then given her a few navigational instructions, leaving her to it, while he went below to grab a few hours' kip. Emma had never taken the helm but, since the sea was still and the distant fishing boats were well out, there was no need for panic. Julian had been confident with her ability to handle the boat while he napped.

They had been at sea for the best part of seventeen hours since leaving Marqieta marina, the day before. Julian had made an arrangement with a local charter company after his final meeting with Carreras, which left him in no doubt that the contingency plan should now be put to the test.

"That man," he had confided in Emma, "can't be trusted. He's hiding something." At the eleventh hour Julian realised he couldn't trust the swine and was not prepared to take unnecessary risks. Julian had then visited two charter boat companies and finally selected a motor cruiser from the Marqieta marina.

However, he was certain that in order to win Carreras into a false sense of security, and to be seen to be happy with all arrangements, he allowed Carreras to believe that he and Emma would be at Guaira as arranged. Carreras, he was sure, would definitely have a boat berthed at Guaira for them, but Julian suspected, so too would hired killers be waiting for them there. Carreras, in Julian's opinion, had too much to lose to let them live, and the threat of an attorney holding a letter of proof was weak. He had forcibly been made to comply with Julian's orders, and, apart from that, they knew too much about the pervasive corruption within the Assembly that was impoverishing Venezuela, to be merely forgotten about and allowed to go free.

But if Julian had calculated correctly, Garcia, Sanchez, the left-wing guerrillas and the local AGF would either be eliminated or instructed to back off. So instead of making their way that evening to Guaira, he and Emma had taken a cab to Marqieta marina and had quietly slipped out to sea.

Now, from the fly bridge Emma had a panoramic view of the Caribbean Sea around her, and far into the distant horizon the coastline of Margarita, hardly visible to the naked eye, lay sleeping in the early morning sun. She had a good idea of the distance from Julian's rough navigational drawings, which she had been following for the last two hours, and, as there was nothing stirring out there in the vast expanse of water, she had no reason to rouse him.

Being in control with her hands to the helm, so to speak, made her feel exhilarated and her thoughts drifted to a future life at sea, while cruising the warm waters of the Caribbean and visiting the many romantic islands. From time to time, she saw fins coast smoothly by, but in her ignorance of the living creatures of the seas, she couldn't tell whether they were dolphin, marlin or shark. Whatever they were, they didn't come too close and Emma was quite happy with their indifferent distance.

Overhead a small aircraft droned on its route to the airport at Porlamar, on Margarita Island, and, with that exception, only the noises of the engines broke the audible stillness of the sea. In a little while, she thought, when we draw nearer to the coast I'll waken Julian, but for the moment she was completely at one with herself and the sea. Her thoughts drifted to the Hemingway character, Santiago, from the Old Man and the Sea, whose relentless struggle with the giant marlin ended in failure. She compared it to her own ongoing struggle with her adversaries, and flinched from the thought that she too might loose the battle in the end.

So deep in thought was she that she didn't hear Julian's approach, and his presence was announced when he put his mouth to the back of her neck and kissed her.

"You can't be doing that to the Captain, be off with you Mr. Hawkins," she jested flippantly, brushing him away.

"Captain, I'll be damned, below Jim lad and rustle up breakfast," was Captain Julian Silver's reply, as he gave her an affectionate shove.

"Aye, aye Captain, Jim lad at your service."

Sometime later the announcement, "Breakfast is served," was music to Julian's ears as she returned with a mass of fried eggs, mash and fried beans.

"Thanks, darling," he responded and hungrily took possession of his plate.

"What are those two land masses?" Emma asked, pointing ahead.

"Those, my dear, are Aubuga and Coche, Margarita's sister islands. And after we pass them, the south side of Margarita should come into view," Julian replied, munching through his feast.

"How long will it take?"

"I should think about another hour and we'll be in Porlamar."

That hour passed quickly enough, and after finding a suitable berth and tying up the boat, they took a cab to Playa El Agua, on the east side, where they found an acceptable hotel, without too much trouble; their intention being to remain there for the next forty-eight hours until they felt it was safe to head for Cuba.

"The bloody fools," Carreras rasped into the other man's face, throwing the photographs at him. "They've killed the wrong people; these are not the bodies of Emma Findlay and Julian Burton."

The man stood quietly not uttering a sound, fearful of Carreras's temper.

"They've escaped!!! Find them and kill them!!!!" he ranted.

"But where?" the other man asked.

"Where you ask? Get your men on to it, now. That's what you're paid for."

"The airport?"

"Don't be so bloody stupid. If they decided to fly, they've gone by now. Do you think for one moment they're hanging around an airport, like sitting ducks, just waiting for you lot to turn up? No, they've taken a boat somewhere. Check out the nearest islands and don't go by names, they'll be using false identities."

A faint glimmer of comprehension appeared on the other man's dim-witted face as it began to register.

"Try Margarita, Aubuga and Coche. They'll be keeping a low profile for a few days. And don't screw this one up. Send a couple of your men to each island and if you lose them your head will roll."

With that, Carreras wheeled around and leaving the other man speechless, he stomped along the dark alley back to his office, in a foul temper. Life was becoming too complicated now and it was imperative that Findlay and Burton were eliminated before their trail went cold, and before they did some real damage.

He spent the remainder of the evening hours sorting through paperwork for tomorrow, when the Assembly was scheduled to take a vote on the most important issue to change the constitutions.

"Now where's that damned secretary, Sanmarco, he's never here when he's required," Carreras hissed out loudly.

Most people had left the building at this time in the evening and Carreras was just on the point of taking the documents to Sanmarco's desk, when an explosion ripped through the office, bursting into flames, destroying everything in its path. A nearby fire alarm was heard to peel out, but Carreras was incapable of hearing it. Carreras was no more.

Emma and Julian had spent the previous day by the hotel swimming pool, listening to the Latin American music as it drifted their way. Jaime, the hotel entertainer, had fooled around as usual with some of the younger guests, who had been mightily impressed as he swayed his tanned body and moved his tight buttocks to the rhythm of the salsa. On this, their first day of relaxing since the trouble had started, they had imbibed in cocktails, a little more than normal and both of them had become a little squiffy. But it had been good fun and all thoughts of the following day's travel had vanished. The pool had been inviting and they plunged in to cool off, in between idle chitchat and sips of cocktails. The day had pleasantly idled away.

In the evening, they had taken a stroll along the sand covered track to the beach restaurants, and shops that displayed the only too familiar souvenirs. Brightly lit bars and restaurants stretched for two and a half miles along Playa El Agua, and, wherever they had turned, Caribbean music sang out. Couples meandered, without purpose, enraptured in the romantic fantasy of this sultry evening and intoxicated with the erotic rhythm.

Down on the beach a disco had been in full swing attracting the young at heart. Emma and Julian had selected a table near the water's edge where it was quieter, and had sat, sometimes in the silence and sometimes in laughter, enjoying the ambience of their surroundings. They had, from time to time, joined the dancers, and Julian had noticed that Emma could still command a lecherous look from the males and envious glare from their partners, as she moved her body to the beat of the music, sending a pang of jealousy through him.

Eventually they had called it a day and Julian, for the first time, had felt a sensation of male dominance as he led her through the revellers, and mildly chuffed that this beautiful woman by his side, was his woman and she belonged to him.

"Are you all ready and packed?" Julian called to her from the bathroom, gathering together the last minute toiletry items before they vacated the bedroom.

"Yes, I've managed to squeeze everything in."

She was gazing out the window hoping that the following twelve hours would pass without incidents as they made their last bid for safety. For comfort she had selected cream pants and cream silk top, and as she stood with her back to him, he found that even wearing these simple garments, she was capable of arousing him. She turned round and smiled as he came up to her, hoping to hide any signs of strain that the last few days had caused her. The tension permeated through the room and they were more than aware that they weren't out of the woods yet, and their lives were still in the balance.

Because of the distance, they had dismissed the idea of chartering another boat and sailing to Cuba. There was no direct flight between Margarita and Havana, and so they were unfortunately obliged to return to Caracas for the only available connection to Cuba. The hotel minibus was already waiting and, after dumping their luggage at the rear, Emma and Julian climbed inside. There were two other passengers on the bus and with the usual greetings Emma and Julian settled themselves down towards the middle.

Sanmarco's men had been tailing Emma and Julian ever since they had checked out of the Euro Building. Their instructions, for the time being, had been to follow and observe, but not to approach. After Emma and Julian had picked up the charter boat at Marqieta, they had let a reasonable time lapse before following suit.

The men had kept a comfortable distance as the two boats headed for Margarita, where they continued their surveillance. They checked into the same hotel, but, for the most part, had kept a low profile, staying to their room, and only one of them at any given time had ventured out to watch Emma and Julian. Now sitting at the rear of the minibus, they attracted no undue attention and neither Emma nor Julian gave them a second thought.

The driver followed the coast road on the north side of the island, through mountainous formations and twisting roads. Here the landscape was lush with vegetation, and, as the road wound its way, bending and twisting, Emma caught sight of the spectacular bays lying far below.

Twenty minutes into their journey, Julian sensed a change in the vehicle's velocity, and as he averted his eyes from the picturesque scenery to look ahead, he saw that the driver was slowing down due to a car that appeared to have stalled half way up the hill in front of them. He felt a tension creeping over him and subconsciously reached for his gun. Noticing his movement, Emma's senses became alerted, also. Julian's body became rigid and motionless like an animal's before the fateful attack. There was no movement from within the coach as the driver brought it to a standstill. The silence was startling.

Two men appeared from the stalled car and casually walked towards the minibus as Sanmarco's men noiselessly withdrew their firearms. Emma sat motionless as the two men advanced. The driver slowly raised himself from the seat as he reached for the door handle. The advancing men were now at the passenger door, which had now been opened by the driver. Their smiles were lethal as their hands produced pieces of metal.

"This can't be the end!!!! Not here!!!!" Emma's brain cried out.

She was numb with fear as the guns slowly took up their position. Julian hadn't made a move, not a muscle; he waited, like the king of the jungle for the right moment; the right moment to strike.

Now!! Julian's brain screamed, as he pushed Emma down, and then from behind something exploded at the back of his head, rendering him senseless.

Something heavy landed on top of her and with her face squished deep into the seat, she, at first, hadn't a clue what it was. She struggled to free herself from the weight and, with her freed arms, was able to push the heaviness until it rolled off and fell onto the aisle.

"My God, it's Julian," she cried out, in horror, while her brain was trying to fit the pieces together.

She was struggling to move towards his now motionless body, when she became aware of the chaos around her. There were gunshots coming from all directions. She ducked back down on the seat, lying perfectly still, trying to comprehend the confusion. She recalled Julian pushing her downwards as the two advancing men produced their weapons, and for a moment must have been stunned with the impact of being suddenly forced down.

Now that she was fully 'compos mentis' she realised that they were still under fire. Bullets were flying in all directions and she lay there too scared to lift her head, her heart pounding and racing like a spring-driven clock, out of control. The windows were bursting above her head and she felt the shattered glass falling all around her as the gunfire continued. Now, edging herself off the seat and onto the floor of the coach, she was able to see, further along towards the front, a crouching figure of a man. Hardly able to breath from frantic terror and paralysed from fear, she could do nothing else but lie on the floor. Then she remembered the gun. She recalled that Julian had gone for it just as he had hauled her downwards.

"Where's that gun?" she whispered, wildly looked around.

She turned her head towards Julian and edged a few inches towards him.

"It can only be under his body, but how to move him?" she contemplated, now beginning to think clearly.

Everything around her was happening so fast and she seemed to be operating in slow motion. She felt frustrated because she couldn't move at the speed of the bullets whizzing overhead in mechanical precision. With one arm extended she tried to get under his twisted body, but from her position it was impossible to reach. She moved on to the floor and extending her arm as far as she could reach, she was able to get underneath him. Then her fingers came in contact with the metal and slowly she began to ease it towards her, taking great care not to touch the trigger device. After struggling with it, for what seemed ages, the gun was freed.

She was so engrossed in her effort to retrieve the gun that she hadn't noticed the firing had ceased and silence triumphed like a bad omen. She furtively glanced to the front of the coach and the crouching figure was beginning to stand up.

"Where were the other two passengers and the driver?" she questioned, now recalling the others that were in the bus.

She didn't know whether she should remain still and pretend dead or defend herself using the gun. Julian was still motionless and couldn't help. She silently manoeuvred herself into a kneeling position between the two seats, and with the gun now firmly in her hand, waited for the next move. If anything unexpected happened she had made up her mind to use the weapon in her defence. She knelt on the floor of the bus for what seemed like ages. Then she heard the silent noise of someone moving around. Anxiously alert, she waited. She was sure the person was now at the next seat, and she was just on the point of readying her attack when something cold was placed on the side of her head.

"I'll take that, if you don't mind," and a hand reached over the back of the seat, wrenching the gun from her grasp.

With Julian lying in a crumpled heap and shattered glass all around, it took her some moments before she became aware that she was now on her own, the reality of which hit like a mallet. She was prepared to defend herself to the bitter end and, on quick reflection, had been lucky to escape the ordeal, unscathed so far. All fear had vanished and her reaction to her situation was instinctive.

Without any kind of weapon and feeling extremely vulnerable, she gradually stood up. She took one look at the scene and was filled with horror at the devastation around her. There was broken glass everywhere; the man lying at the front of the coach, she presumed, was the driver; two men were lying outside on the road, oozing of blood, and Julian was still motionless on the floor of the bus. There was a further two men on the inside, one of whom was standing close to her and the other walking towards her. She couldn't quite grasp why one of the passengers was now pointing a gun at her.

Up until now, she had been too preoccupied with her own safety to think of Julian, but it suddenly occurred to her that he might be fatally injured. She immediately bent down to examine him. Thank God he was still breathing. She then turned her venom on the man next to her, demanding what had happened. Smashing the gun from the man, she gave vent to a viperous tongue-lashing.

"Look you," the man yelled in fury, now having retrieved the gun, "it wouldn't take much to put a hole through your head," and gave her a rough knock at the same time.

"Why don't you, you bloody bastard, why stop now," she spat at him.

"Now listen you stupid bitch. We haven't harmed your precious Julian," he rasped, giving her arm an extra twist that she called out in pain "You're a spitting wild cat."

Emma stood still for a moment, not saying a word.

Now having her full attention, they explained that Sanmarco had ordered them, against their wishes, to follow Julian and herself and, when needs be, to protect them until they were safely off Venezuelan soil. They had been watching them, so she was informed, from the moment they had picked up the boat at Marqieta. They told her that Sanmarco was adamant that nothing should happen to them and so they had reluctantly gone along with his orders. They were given no explanation as to the changed instructions, and, quickly added, that they did not agree with it. And when she looked out at the two men lying on the road, they merely stated in unemotional voices.

"We believe them to be Carreras's men. They picked up your trail two days ago."

One of the men then went over to where Julian was still lying and gave him a nudge.

"I had to give him a tap on the head," he gloated, "he was getting in our way."

The airport at Porlamar was quiet at this time of the day, with only a few people waiting for the Avensa flight to Caracas. Emma sat between the two men, still shaken and dazed from the horrifying event that had interrupted their journey, and was still unable to grasp the full significance of it all.

She was sitting between the two men who had saved them from a certain death but, at the same time, wanted rid of Julian and her as quickly as possible. Although her anger had now abated, she was still somewhat traumatised by it all. Julian had fully recovered, but was suffering from a pounding headache and a giant size lump on his head. He had gone off to check their flights, leaving her in their protected custody.

She began to feel more animated when Julian returned with the good news that the flight to Caracas would leave on time from gate two, only to be deflated again when informed that they would have the pleasure of their protectors all the way to their connecting flight at Caracas airport. Unlike Emma, Julian understood the sense in it, because they were still not out of danger from Carreras, even in Marqieta airport or Caracas.

Earlier, he had been prepared to use the gun in their defence. Not a violent person but he knew for sure that he would have fired the gun. In a way, he was relieved that the decision had been taken out of his hands and, on reflection, to have escaped with only a bump on his head was good enough for him. He bore Sanmarco's men no grudges and was forever grateful that they had been there. He was certain that, while he may have got one of the attackers, the odds of hitting the second man were poor indeed.

It had amused him on learning of Emma's violent attack on their saviours and had laughed at her courage. She was certainly no shrinking violet, he mused, and she had real guts, one of the qualities that endeared him to her. She was the most feminine of women he had ever encountered, sensual and erotic in her movements and totally unaware of the sex appeal that she exuded. But at the same time, possessed a quiet independence interlaced with logical reasoning, never giving of herself fully and only when they made love, melting into his embrace, did she surrender completely to him.

CHAPTER 26

The day began with the sun streaming through the slit in the curtains, bringing David to a peaceful and contented awaking. Glancing over to where Sonya lay asleep, he recalled the many hours of loving and happiness she had given him. He warmed to her angelic face, tranquil in its repose and to the little puffs of air that, from time to time, escaped her lips. Her kitten-like body was half covered with a white cotton sheet under which the shape of her figure was sculptured. Her legs rested slightly parted with one bent underneath the other.

Tracing her sleeping outline, his eyes feasted on his imagination and he let them wander slowly up those shapely limbs to her firm thighs. They came to rest on that curvaceous hollow in her thighs as it blends into her bulge, waiting for his touch, inviting him to caress gently and lovingly, teasing her to arousal. His eyes soaked in the softness of her abdomen and her breasts, full and round, nestling in the crumpled cotton, enticing him to kiss their brown tips.

He wanted to reach out to her, his male member hardening in anticipation. He could no longer control his need for her; it was insatiable; he could wait no longer. Turning now to her, he gently cupped her full breasts, and as he eased his hand under the cotton sheet to the warmth between her legs, he heard her moan in ecstasy. Searching wildly, teasing, he heard the soft purrs becoming louder as he brought her to a dreamy arousal. As he slipped himself into the softness he felt her hips moving, and they moved together in an ethereal dance until they erupted in unison, completely fulfilled.

She rested quietly in his arms, neither one of them speaking. No words could express the feeling that lay between them. Words were superfluous. Her perfect happiness was so great that it was frightening. How could anyone deserve this amount of serene joy?

David had come to mean so much to her during the last few weeks. She had given everything to him and the possibility that he would leave soon, scared the hell out of her. How would she survive living without him? She would never meet anyone again that felt so right for her, who made her laugh so easily, who could make her feel a complete woman. In the few weeks they had been together she had come to understand his moods, his hopes, his desires, his fears and those small things that could bring an instant smile to his face. She knew he was happy when he was with her and wanted to stay with her, forever; but that gnawing and underlying feeling that one day soon, they would be going their own different way, he, to Scotland and his work, and she to Colombia. She didn't care to think about that, not yet. It was all so unfair, she thought, as soon as you found what you were looking for, it was snatched away all too quickly, and it made you wonder if it ever existed in the first place.

David was the first to rouse, and without saying a word to Sonya headed to the shower, heavy of heart with his own thoughts. He loved her, he was in no doubt about that, but had mixed feelings about spending the rest of his life with her. He didn't want to be tied to someone again; he was not ready for that. In fact if he were honest with himself it scared him.

He would tell her soon and let her down gently. But how could he let her down gently? Somehow he would find a way and the guts to do it, still leaving her with some of her pride. She would hurt for a while, he realised, but she was still young and would find someone else to love, in time, someone of her own age, whom she could love and to whom she could have children.

Stepping out of the shower now, refreshed and ready for the day, he had other things on his mind, the most taxing and demanding of which was the whereabouts of Emma and Julian. Were they still alive? If so, where were they?

The last information he had, was when they checked out of their hotel in Caracas four days prior. Surely Emma would have the sense to contact him if she were alive. She would know how extremely worried and concerned he would be after such a long lapse in time. He needed to clear his head; he didn't want to dwell on the probability of their demise. No longer could he justify remaining here, wallowing in sunshine and bliss, while they could be in trouble somewhere.

Towelling himself dry, he made up his mind that, after breakfast and a full stomach, he would come to a decision about his next move. By the time he had returned to the bedroom, Sonya was also up and showered. Trying to make light of the despondent thoughts that were shooting through his head, he cheerily broke out, "All set for another of Eva's hearty breakfasts? And afterwards you choose what we should do today."

He was no longer enthusiastic about romantic picnics on the beach or taking in another sightseeing trip. His heart was no longer in it. His concern for Emma and Julian was so great that it overshadowed everything and took control, even his own happiness. He would let Sonya decide what they should do today, and in that way he would feel less guilty about enjoying himself while Emma and Julian were still not accounted for.

And then a thought occurred to him. He would let Sonya believe he was going off to find Emma and Julian and when he did, he would simply continue on his way to Scotland, eventually dropping a note explaining himself. That would be easy. But he was not that kind of man. He couldn't run away, not from her, not without facing her with the truth. But later; Emma and Julian were first priority and Sonya could wait. This would buy him time to think it all out and, at the same time, delay the dastardly deed that would have to be addressed.

He waited until breakfast was over before he gave Emma and Julian any further thought. While Sonya was organising the following day's menu with Eva, he took himself into the solitude of the garden where he could calmly consider the alternatives. He understood that he could no longer remain here with any peace of mind, while the well being of Emma and Julian was uncertain. But what could he do? Where to begin?

As he saw it, the only option open to him was to return to Caracas and pick up their trail from the last known place, the Euro Building. He pondered over making contact with the police, but dismissed it as a bad move.

The sun began to warm up the early morning air, but he felt cold, cold with a dreadful fear that something awful had gone wrong and still he didn't want to think about it. But think about it he must. He had to find out exactly what had happened.

Deep in thought, he sat on the garden seat which overlooked the great expanse of blue water, with a gentle zephyr blowing in from the sea. The stillness around him had a calming effect and he began to mull over in his mind, the various reasons that could explain Emma's unprecedented silence. It was so out of character that, with each scenario he imagined, the conclusion was always the same.

It was not too warm yet and the birds were having their early morning playtime, chirping and tweeting in their song as they hopped amongst the delicate twigs. They scratched and scraped at the dry soil and with their wings outstretched, as if in flight, disturbed the arid sand around them, puffing up their feathers simultaneously. David watched their performance with keen eyes and wondered at the significance of their behaviour. He heard the snapping of small dried up twigs lying beneath the flowering shrubs as the birds continued performing their ritual, hopping, scratching and agitating the sandy soil.

Completely absorbed with the antics of the bird life, he didn't hear Sonya's approach until she had rested a comforting hand on his shoulder. She knew what was bothering him as she stood looking at him for a few moments but was powerless to give him any help.

"They are so happy and free with only their inherent instincts to guide them."

David looked up at her.

"Yes, you're right. I wish we could be more like that and follow our instincts without the confusion of reasoning. We humans are so sophisticated in logical science that we have forgotten how to use our inborn gut feelings that lie deep within us," he reflected.

There was silence for a moment before David continued and then it came to him slowly.

"I believe you've given me the answer to my dilemma, Sonya."

"What do you mean?"

"Instincts, Sonya, natural instincts. I must follow my instincts, what I feel. Not what Emma or Julian would have me do. Not with logical equations, between this course of action or that course of action, but instinctively, the gut feeling way. You know what I'm talking about, Sonya, don't you?"

"Yes, I do know what you're talking about, but what's your basic instincts telling you?" Sonya countered.

"I feel they're still not out of trouble; I can't fathom it out or put my finger on it. I have a feeling that something ominous lurks, hidden, and my mathematical brain can't get to the root of it, not yet. However, for me to return to Caracas at this stage would be pointless, it would take me some time to pick up their trail. I believe they are alive still, but at the same time something is disturbing me to the degree that I'm still extremely concerned about their well-being."

Relieved that he had changed his mind about haring back to Caracas, for the time being, anyway, she expressed her approval. Even if he had decided to look for them, she could have done nothing about it; she would not take the responsibility or become party to deterring him from the course he felt he had to follow.

"I'll go along with that and I think you've made a wise decision under the circumstances. I know it can't be easy for you, just to sit here and wait for word, but I would leave it for now and address this problem in a few days."

"And," she continued, "I suggest that we take a trip to Cardenas, sit by the harbour and watch the fishing boats, while we imbibe in a light refreshment."

"That sounds like a good idea, my sweet," David concurred, now feeling a bit more cheerful at the removal of some of the anxiety that had been plaguing his mind for some time.

CHAPTER 27

It was with a great sense of joy that Emma stepped from the plane at Varadero and placed her feet on safe ground. All the tensions and fears of the past weeks evaporated and vanished from her body, and she was enjoying a new found feeling of euphoria. Their minders had finally abandoned them in the departure lounge at Marqieta airport and Emma was not at all sad to see the back of them, even although they had been responsible for saving Julian's and her life.

After collecting the luggage Emma and Julian got a cab destined for Villa Verde. In the course of their travels, they had discussed but dismissed the idea of contacting David because they felt too much time had elapsed, and it would be better to arrive, fit and well.

"There was no way we could risk contacting them from Caracas while we were trying to save our skins. Telephones have ears, you know," Emma said, suffering from pangs of self recriminations, now that things had begun to calm down.

"Apart from that, there was always the danger of alerting Garcia to the fact that David had survived," Julian added, kindly, making her feel a little bit better.

"Well, we'll soon be there and we can all celebrate a wonderful reunion; not to mention our survival," Emma volunteered, feeling less guilty, but knowing full well that David would be worried sick by this time.

As the cab neared Villa Verde, Julian saw that the house sat below the approaching road, in a hollow surrounded by palms and fruit trees. And when they drove through the arch pillars into the grounds, he was more than pleasantly surprised with Emma's choice.

"This is indeed wonderful. How on earth did you manage to dig up such a peaceful setting in such a limited time? You never fail to amaze me," giving her a tender squeeze.

Like Emma, the lush gardens with their rolling lawns reaching all the way down to the sea, made him stop in his tracks, soaking in the sight and admiring the magnificent views.

"And the villa too with its colonial flair; it's tremendous." Julian voiced, as he walked round the sun terraces, which were dotted with garden seats and umbrellas from a past era, adding to the authenticity of its character and former residents.

After the initial excitement, they went inside to find David and Sonya. They looked in all the rooms but nobody was in the house; and even Eva had gone out.

"It would appear they've gone for the day, and the only one here is Juan, happily working at the other side of the garden," Emma announced as she bounced back into the bedroom.

"What I suggest is, we take a dip in the sea," Julian said as he donned his trunks, not waiting for a reply.

"Why not," Emma returned, "the others could be away for the full day. Oh, and while you're at it, darling, grab some soft drinks and a bottle of wine. I think this calls for a celebration."

"Too damned right it does," he called back, half way to the kitchen.

Emma lay afloat on her back and let the water caress her body, making soft lapping sounds as it gently lifted her in its ebb tide. There were no disturbing thoughts in her head, only the soft whisper of the tactile sea, touching her, rocking her to a calm tranquillity. Nothing that the last few weeks had thrown at her, nor the thought of future strife, could take away the over-powering peace she found here, alone and at one with nature.

It was beautiful; the world was a beautiful place again; this was a beautiful place and Julian was beautiful. All was perfect as she floated and bobbed like a cork, to where - to her dreams - to her immortal soul. The dreadful past was gone, the future didn't exist, and only here and now, the present, was all that mattered.

How long she lay there in the motion of the sea, she had no idea. She felt herself drifting; drifting to a wonderland of soft pink bubbles and candyfloss, vanilla ice cream and strawberries.

The shrieking call of a gull that had swooped down and settled on the water close by, released her from her day-dreaming and brought her back to reality. Slowly and lazily she turned over to discover she had been carried out quite a distance by the current. She started to swim slowly back, reluctant to leave her perfect peace, this beautiful and wonderful serenity.

As she approached the shore, she heard Julian calling out to her, raising the bottle of champagne to entice her back. Giving him a wave of acknowledgement, she lashed out with more defined strokes, and felt her body glide effortlessly through the water in buoyant motions as if some unknown force was holding her up.

Julian came out to meet her as she reached the shallows, sporting a happy grin. He caught her and kissed her wet hair, running his mouth along her shoulders, sending shivers through her.

"You went too far out, darling, be careful, there are sharks around these waters."

"I know, Julian, but it was all so peaceful and still out there, all alone with the lonely sea and the blue sky. I can't explain it, but it was just such a wonderful feeling."

"Well, next time, not so far," and with that he ducked her.

"Bastard," she spluttered, through mouthfuls of salt water, "I'll get you for that," she threatened.

"No, you won't, I'm off for a light libation."

The champagne and the glasses were still chilled: Julian lifted them from the cool box. The cork flew off with a loud pop and he poured the sparkling liquid into the glasses, while Emma cried out in delight as some of the champagne ran along her arm.

"Too good to waste," Emma called out, licking the champagne from her salty arm.

"To us and to our continued safety, you're wonderful, Emma, love you to bits," Julian toasted, raising his glass in gesture.

"To you, Julian, I'm glad you're you and not someone else. You're beautiful," she countered, as she put the glass to her lips and champagne bubbles burst in her nostrils.

"Steady on, old girl, I'll go weak at the knees with any more of that flattery."

"Less of, the old girl, bit," she retorted, lashing out with a kick, which he was relieved to note, missed its mark.

They laughed and joked and ran along the thick sand, still holding on to the champagne, just like a couple of teenagers. The relief that at last they were safe was so potent that, even before the bubbling effervescence had taken effect, they became a little tipsy.

"Did I hear voices coming from the beach?" Sonya called to David, as they parked the four-wheel.

"I didn't hear anything. You must have bells in your ears."

"Yes, there it is again. I wonder who is using our beach, nobody comes here," she went on.

She listened for a second.

"I'm going down to take a look."

As she strode off, she thought she heard English voices and began to walk faster, calling back to David to join her. Down the path through the garden, faster and faster, running now until she reached the beach.

"David, Oh David, come quickly, she called out, breathlessly running on.

"Emma, Emma," she yelled, ploughing through the heavy sand, half stumbling as she went.

They were in one another's arms, shrieking and shouting, hugging and kissing, dancing and twirling, falling down and eating the sand.

"Oh, let me look at you, you're alive," touching Emma to make sure she was real and the merriment started all over again.

Even after David arrived on the beach the din and the revelry continued; shouting, hugging, pushing and dancing. Inevitably as things would have it, David and Sonya ended up in the water fully clothed. When, eventually, exhaustion took over and they had calmed down, Julian and Sonya were formally introduced. They sat down still covered from head to foot in sand.

"Tell me all about it, what happened, where did you go, what detained you?" David asked, all in the one breath, anxious to know the details.

"Let's not spoil the fun; that can wait until tomorrow. We're grateful to be alive and we're here safe at last."

"Yes," David said," you're both alive and well, and that's all that matters."

But he had still the nagging feeling that something bad was about to happen. He chastised himself for being such a pessimist. As he looked at their happy faces, he wondered why his thoughts were still despondent. Perhaps he was just being neurotic after what had happened to him, and, immediately, dismissed all misgivings.

"OK, you win for the moment, but it was extremely inconsiderate of you not to keep in touch, we were worried useless."

"David, why don't you fetch some more champagne, we'll have a beach party," Julian stated, changing the subject, "and while you're at it, tell Eva it's barbecue on the beach, tonight."

"Oh, that'll put her in a great mood, now that she'll have prepared dinner," Sonya joked.

None of them gave a sod; they were too deliriously happy and intoxicated with glee.

The following morning, breakfast which consisted of a hearty sufficiency of bacon and eggs, was a jolly affair. The celebratory reunion on the beach had continued well into the wee small hours and everyone had a fair share of champagne.

David and Sonya became deadly quiet as Julian began to relate the dreadful events after David's departure from Maracaibo, and everything leading up to yesterday when they finally left Caracas.

They were speechless as they listened to the frightening experiences in the jungle area on the River Limon; the explosion on the oil field killing the engineers; Julian's brush with the Colombians at the apartment; the underhand negotiations with Carreras and Sanmarco, and the final instalment on Margarita, where two of Carreras's men held up the coach and subsequently died in the shoot out.

"You're both lucky to be alive and that Sanmarco's men were on the bus," David contemplated.

"Don't we know it? We took our chances. Also, Sanmarco seemed to be a fair and honest enough man. You see, he isn't motivated by greed and money. He has a conception of a better Venezuela under a more democratic Government. He argues that the present one is running too near the wind of a Dictatorship and is totally corrupt. Anyway, enough of this, we're well away from it now, and thank God he was able to persuade his men to change tack and give protection rather than elimination. But what I would really like to know, Garcia and Sanchez, are they still operating their drugs business, or have they been found?"

"Then you didn't hear the news bulletin some days ago", David cut in excitedly. "It is alleged that Garcia and Sanchez were arrested and the Narcotics Police burst their drugs cartel, warehouses and laboratories."

"Great news. It gets better by the minute."

"That would only leave Carreras, an evil man, in play, and he would travel anywhere to settle a score," Emma spoke out, for the first time.

"What did you say his name was?" David enquired.

"Carreras, Gabriel Carreras, a deputy in the Venezuelan Government."

"Well, if my memory serves me correctly, there was a report in one of the newspapers the other day that an office used by this man, Carreras, was blown up and Carreras with it. But we can check it out."

"If that's the case, then all the chess pieces have fallen and we've won, Julian, we're truly safe at last," Emma said.

"That's right, Garcia and Sanchez with their merry men, arrested, Carreras dead. That leaves Sanmarco, who it would appear has no further interest in us."

"Can we be certain?" Emma asked.

"I would be inclined to say, yes; as certain as we can be under the circumstances."

"Look, if you're all satisfied, I would like a change of subject. It was a dreadful experience. We came through a lot; didn't know if we were going to make it or not and I, for one, am tired talking about it," Emma announced, abruptly, indicating that the matter was closed for now.

"I think we all deserve a few days to recuperate, so I suggest we stay on here for a further week, and then we can all decide where our next port of call will be," Julian, sensing Emma's tension, moved the conversation on to a lighter subject.

"I will second that," David affirmed.

"OK, if we're staying on here for a few days, I would like to go into Cardenas and pick up a few casual things, shorts etc. and I may as well get it over with this morning," Emma decided.

"Want anybody to accompany you?" Sonya offered.

"If you've nothing else to do, I don't mind, but I'll only be a couple of hours anyway."

"Well, I have been neglecting David's medical report and I should really bring it up to date, so I should really get stuck into it this morning, if that's all right with you."

"Sure, then I'll nip into town quickly and I'll see you all in a couple of hours. Don't worry guys, I won't put you two through the agony of trailing around ladies boutiques," Emma joked, rising from the table.

"Do you mind while you're there, picking up some snorkelling equipment, Emma, please," Julian called, over his shoulder.

As she was leaving, Emma was amused to hear the two of them eagerly discussing the repair to an old boat that David had discovered in the boathouse, smiling to herself that they had found a hobby to occupy themselves, and never thinking for one minute that it could ever be seaworthy.

"Go on, man, show me where she is," Julian commanded, nudging David into action.

The Boston Whaler was a sad looking boat, leaning pathetically to one side in the dark, gloomy boathouse. It had a fibreglass hull, which appeared to have been cleaned recently.

"I say, old chap, somebody's been here recently," Julian muttered.

"Only person I can think of is Juan, the gardener," David replied.

"Get him down here."

When Juan appeared, he explained he had started to clean her up a bit, but hadn't got round to checking out the engines.

"What sort of condition is she in?"

"Last time in the water, Boss, three years ago and was in good nick then."

"Know anything about boats, Juan?"

"Should do, sailed all my life until I got too stiff, fishing boats, used to catch big marlin. Took rich Americans out, ah, I miss those times," he said, remembering his past adventures.

"Those times may be returning, old man of the sea. We've got work to do, forget about the garden," and turning to David, "are you up to it, I mean, after your injuries?"

"Are you kidding, I'm as good as new."

They opened up a hatch and went below to the engine room.

"In not bad condition," the old man diagnosed, after he had a look at the twin 340hp diesel inboards.

All morning they worked on the engines, oiling, overhauling and between the three of them, gave her a thorough service. Juan was then sent in his beaten up old van for enough diesel to get her started, and all they had to do then was to wait for high tide to slip her into the water. Julian and David, covered in oil and grime, stood back to admire their efforts. They were over the moon with the results and for the first time in weeks had something happy to look forward to; the prospect of some deep-sea fishing with Juan's guidance. They had never been as chummy as this before. In the past, they had kept at a healthy distance from each other. The traumas of the last few weeks had brought them a bit closer. There was no sign of the underlying rivalry and jealousy that had been apparent in past trivial conversations. Their catty remarks and sniping at one another had ceased.

"She's a beauty, what a discovery!" David enthused, strutting around her beam.

They were like two small boys with a new toy, eager and impatient to get her afloat. Not to incur Eva's wrath, they had to leave her, the Sea Lady, and, reluctantly, they made their way back to the villa for lunch, prompt at one; instructions from the head cook.

It hadn't taken too long to choose the few bits and pieces, shorts, tops and a couple of bikinis. Thanking the sales assistant for her help, Emma returned to the parked four-wheel, laden with her purchases, which she threw into the back seat. Jumping in herself, she was just on the point of driving off when she remembered the snorkelling equipment for Julian.

"Blast and be damned," she muttered, to herself. "Now I'll need to find a chandler and hopped back out.

Impatient to be finished and get back to the villa, she set off at a brisk pace towards the harbour area, where she was certain to find what she was looking for. The streets were crowded with lots of people going about their daily business before lunchtime, and she had to jostle her way in and out in her haste, as the other pedestrians slowly meandered along in the heat of the day.

Her attention was drawn to a man walking towards her. Her first impression was that he looked so out of place in a black suit and white shirt. As he came nearer, he seemed familiar to her, his build, his strut, his movements and as he approached, his face. But she could not recall where. She shivered and a feeling of dread passed through her.

They were on the point of passing one another when she heard a thick voice.

"Ah, Senora Findlay, we meet again."

She stopped and turned towards the voice, alert and wary. The face, yes, she had seen it somewhere before, it was familiar, but for the life of her she still could not remember.

"I see you don't recognise me," the voice continued, noticing the puzzled expression on Emma's face.

She hesitated for only a moment.

"No, I don't, should I?" she curtly responded.

"Carlos Lopez, at your service. We met some time ago here in Varadero," offering his hand.

Now it all fell into place, Garcia's man, the negotiator, she recalled.

"Yes?" was all she said, ignoring his extended hand.

"You don't seem very pleased to see me," he smirked.

"What do you want?"

"My dear Ms. Findlay, nothing more than a friendly chat over a cup of coffee."

"Look, I've got nothing to say to you, now let me pass."

"Not so fast, senora, I merely want to discuss and explain something of interest to you."

She couldn't think that anything he had to say would be of interest to her, but as he was blocking her path, she merely informed him.

"Say what you want to say, here."

"I can assure you, you're safe, nothing will happen to you, if that is your concern."

"As I said, I have no wish to talk to you," she repeated, angrily, attempting to push by him.

"On the contrary, I think you will," now gripping her arm.

"Take your hands off me," she fumed indignantly, struggling to free herself, but his grasp was too tight.

"All I want is a chat, and if you come peacefully, nothing will happen to your friends at the Villa Verde," he smiled, relaxing his hold.

How did he find out about the Villa? She really didn't believe his idle threat, but there again was unwilling to take that chance. What could happen to her here anyway: there were too many people milling about. All she needed to do was scream. She didn't feel happy about going along with him, but she had to find out what he wanted. She couldn't let anything happen to them, not now, not after all they had come through; and very reluctantly allowed him to lead her to the boat, berthed half way along the pontoon.

"Please, have a seat. Coffee?" he offered, smiling as he proceeded to make coffee.

"I don't wish coffee and I haven't come here for a social visit, now what do you want?"

"As you wish," taking a seat opposite her.

"You may recall, sometime ago, a sum of money was given to you by Garcia," he said, slowly, giving her time to digest the words.

She was somewhat astonished that he was aware of the money, but, there again, as Garcia's chief soldier, he would be party to that kind of information.

"And so?" she interjected.

"I want it Ms. Findlay, I want it, the million."

"That has nothing to do with you, it doesn't belong to you, and it's Garcia's."

"Belong, Ms. Findlay, belong? Garcia, as you may know, is in prison and he won't see the light of day for years, if at all. Now, what I want you to do," he gloated, now standing up and towering over her, "is to transfer the money into my account. I will let you leave here, unharmed, as soon as the million is safely deposited into my account. Now, there is the radiophone, this is an account no., please call Burton," he crowed with malicious pleasure.

"You can't hold me here. You're crazy; I'll do no such thing. I'm out of here," and she made towards the upper deck

"Not so fast," he said, pushing her back down.

"Now listen carefully, if you don't do as I say, I will kill your friends, one by one, and feed you to the sharks. I will get that money one way or the other," he hissed, his voice thick with cruelty.

"You wouldn't, you wouldn't get away with it," she shouted, in disbelief that she had walked straight into a trap.

"I'm going to be kind to you and give you some time to think it over and in the meantime you are my guest and I suggest a rest in the cabin below."

He would have been surprised if she had made the call straight away, and he had planned for that. He would take the boat out, away from the harbour, out to sea, where he could torture her into complying.

"You can't do this to me, you bastard," lunging at him. She fought him with her fists, but to no avail as he grabbed her and lifting her off her feet, bundled her into the cabin below. Still kicking and fighting against his hold, she was thrown on top of the bed.

"I do like a woman with some spirit," he jeered as he left, locking the door behind him.

She lay there trying to mentally absorb what had just happened. What the hell had she got herself into? She then heard the radio being turned up to such a pitch that it would drown out any cries for help. After a few moments she rose and tried the door. It was securely locked from the outside. She tried banging it but it was firmly shut. The windows, she thought, and ran over to the porthole. Moving the flimsy curtain, she saw to her anguish that it was also stuck, sealed from the outside This is hopeless, she thought. 'Perhaps I could break my way out' and ran around the cabin and the bathroom looking for some object heavy enough to use, but found nothing.

In desperation she threw herself back on the bed. What could she do? There must be a way out. Perhaps Julian will come to my rescue, but sadly he wouldn't know where to find her. Her aggression now depleted, she began to feel frightened. She was a prisoner on this boat, she had been stupid enough to walk into this trap and she could do nothing about it, she was totally helpless.

Whether she handed over the money or not, she knew he would kill her; and not only her but the others too. The money was no longer important, she really didn't want it, she had forgotten about it. It had caused too much grief. But she knew even to hand it over would not save their lives. They would all die. She couldn't let that happen, not now, not after all they had endured, and to be thwarted by a creep like him, an evil and avarice gangster.

She tried to think on some solution, but nothing came to her tired and fuddled brain. She lay on top of the bed tossing and turning trying to find an answer and, eventually, drifted off to sleep. How long she had been sleeping she couldn't tell. The noise of the engines suddenly woke her up, and realised immediately that the boat was moving. Oh God, where is he taking me? Julian will never find me now.

What time is it? Her watch told her 5 o'clock, in the morning or afternoon? She looked out the porthole; it was still daylight, afternoon she decided. She could see nothing but water. This is crazy. I must not panic, she told herself. Keep calm, something must turn up to her advantage, be positive. But out here, at sea, all alone with this animal, didn't look too encouraging to her.

Later, Lopez appeared at the cabin door with coffee and sandwiches.

"Eat," he said.

But before she had time to ask him where they were heading, he closed the door, locking it again behind him.

Sonya, too, had been hard at it all morning, recording David's daily progress sheets and overall she was very pleased with his remarkable recovery, but it would take some months before he regained full mobility in his legs. A quick glance at her watch told her it was lunch time and quickly tidying away her paperwork, she hastily went down to the dining room, just as David and Julian were entering by the French windows, covered from head to foot in 'she didn't know what'.

"Taking a quick shower," they chorused and disappeared to their respective rooms.

"Everyone ready for lunch?" Eva asked, bursting in from the kitchen.

"Five minutes, Eva, they've gone for a shower," Sonya replied and strolled onto the veranda for a bit of fresh air.

"What have you two been doing?" she asked, now joining Julian and David at the table a few minutes later, "you look very pleased with yourselves."

"Well, you know that boat we discovered, it appears that it is in a better condition than we originally thought and we worked on it all morning, with the result that, The Sea Lady is ready to be launched, that is, as soon as Juan returns with the diesel."

"Good going," Sonya encouraged, "just the two of you?"

"No, we had Juan's help; he's good, used to do some fishing in his younger days."

"Where's Emma?" Julian suddenly remembered. "She's not returned yet?"

"She can't have. I haven't seen her."

"I thought she said she would only be a couple of hours," David queried.

"Uh, huh, she did, but you know what she's like, probably got herself involved in some sightseeing or other. I'm sure she won't be long."

Anxious to get back to The Sea lady as quickly as possible, they finished lunch rather hurriedly and reminded Sonya that they would be putting the boat in the water.

"Coming down to watch?" David asked.

"Eh, no, what time is it? No I'll wait for Emma and we'll come down together."

"Right, see you in a bit."

By the time Julian and David got back to the boathouse, Juan was busy pouring the diesel into the tank. Earlier, they had cleared months of sand from the metal tracks leading from the boathouse into the sea. With Julian operating the winch, the Sea Lady graced her entry with a skirted splash of white foam, as she glided down the slipway, settling elegantly in the turquoise water. There were cheers of delighted success as she sat proudly in the water patiently awaiting her first assignment.

Juan dropped anchor and Julian and David waded out, chuffed with their achievement.

"We'll have some fun, now, fishing her."

"There's just one small matter that you may have overlooked."

"What would that be?" David retorted flippantly.

"The engines, old son, the engines."

"Don't worry, boss, she'll start as sweet as a peach," Juan assured them.

At that they heard Sonya.

"Ahoy, there", she called out, "I'm coming on board"

David gave her a hand up.

"You missed the launching."

"Eh, yes, I'm sorry about that," she answered, distractedly, "but I'm more concerned about Emma, she hasn't returned."

They stopped in surprise.

"She hasn't returned yet? That's strange," Julian queried, showing signs of alarm.

They had all been too engrossed with the boat, that none of them had given Emma a thought. Julian looked at his watch, "Four-thirty," he said, out loud.

"Something's wrong, she would not stay away all this time. I'll need to get to Cardenas."

"We've only got Juan's old van," David said.

"We've got this, it'll be quicker by sea, just round the bay a bit, and it can't be that far. Juan get her started," Julian ordered, all in the one breath.

After a few attempts and some adjustments in the engine room, The Sea Lady spluttered and coughed into action. There were no shouts of delight this time, only relief, as the four of them remained silent, deep in their own thoughts.

It was six o'clock as they rounded the last bay and sailed into the harbour at Cardenas, where they were directed to a berth. Juan eased her into the allotted space. Leaving Juan on board, the three of them set out for the town centre and after searching the streets and car parks, the four-wheel vehicle was eventually found.

"Look here," Sonya said, pointing in the window, "there are her parcels, she must have come back and then left again."

"Do you see snorkelling equipment, Sonya?"

"No, none."

"That's it, looks like she's gone to find the equipment. We'll check out all the chandlers."

They visited all the chandlers in the town, but nobody of that description had been seen in their shops that day.

"So, she didn't pick up the gear."

"Looks that way."

"See, over there, there's a cafe. I suggest we separate and ask around. Ask if anybody has seen her and meet back at the café, later," Julian stated, now becoming seriously concerned.

He admonished himself for being so lackadaisical and allowing her to go on her own in the first place. However, nothing could be done about that now, he thought, as he walked towards the harbour again. It was getting dark and after an hour of getting nowhere, he was just about to head back to the cafe, hoping that the others would have some good news, when he spotted an old sea dog repairing his nets.

"Yes, a lady fitting that description was here earlier today. She was with a business type, a man, black suit."

Julian's hopes rose and heart beat a little faster.

"Do you know where they went?"

"Yes, I know that as well. See a lot down here."

Julian waited for a moment and the old man continued.

"She went on to a boat - over there on the other pontoon."

"Which one? Show me," Julian asked, becoming hopeful and turning to look at the row of boats.

"Can't do that, they left about two hours ago, sailed out."

"Are you certain the lady was still on board?"

"Sailed out?" Julian repeated, in disbelief. "What was she bloody doing?"

"Yes, took off," the old man confirmed.

"What's the name of the boat, do you know it?"

"The Katiya."

"Who owns it?"

"Don't know that, she just arrived, new boat in the harbour."

"I'll be over in that café. If you see her returning come and tell me," handing the old man fifty bucks.

"Thanks, senor, will do."

Downcast, Julian entered the cafe to find the others, equally sad faced, waiting for him. He related the old man's story.

"Doesn't look good to me, she would never just take off with an apparent stranger," David said.

"Unless she knew him or was forced."

"You're right, Sonya, but the old man didn't say anything about that."

"If what the old man said is true, we'll have to go and find her. I don't see an alternative," David stated, firmly.

Julian had been silently thinking the same thing.

"It's now dark, and we don't know in which direction they went, we'll never find her," Sonya expressed in despair.

"Juan told us the Sea lady can take the open seas, so this is what we'll do. Sonya, fetch some provisions to last a couple of days and meet us back at the boat. Meanwhile we'll refuel and we'll head out as soon as we can."

Later that evening, The Sea Lady silently left her berth, disappearing into the pitch void, dark and threatening, and only the boat's lighting indicated her position.

Darkness lasted long that night and daylight seemed unwilling to be seen. They had worked shifts during the night, with Juan and David on first watch and Julian and Sonya on the second.

The last vestiges of the night's dark shadows were melting into a watery dawn, as the Sea Lady skimmed over the water. A translucent haze hung over the light swell and the ocean was dotted with soft whitecaps. Smell of bacon and eggs from the galley wafted its way on deck, only to be left behind in the light sea breeze that embraced the boat. Julian had been at the helm for the latter part of the night and with a new dawn a good feeling of expectation braved his heart.

"Anything showing on the radar screen?" David asked, coming from the forward cabin.

"Yes, there are three vessels in the area. This one here is heading westward and doing about twenty knots, so she's a fair size and I don't reckon she's the one. This one dead ahead was on the move until half an hour ago, and the other to the east has been sitting there since I picked up her position."

"What do you think?" David asked, giving Julian credit for his greater knowledge of the sea.

"This one's the nearest and if I can get twenty to twenty- five knots, we should get there in under three hours. And if that proves fruitless, we'll swing to the east and check out the other."

"Distance?"

"I'd say, sixty-five miles."

CHAPTER 28

She drifted in and out of sleep all night, tossing and turning, experiencing bizarre and frightening nightmares, terrifying dreams of drowning, lying at the bottom of the ocean, of grotesque sea creatures and wakening to a more horrifying nightmare, that of reality, then forcing sleep again into the nightmares of the subconscious.

Exhausted and wiped out, saturated in perspiration, she lay on top of the bed as daylight streamed through the small porthole, giving her a slight feeling of encouragement. Her thoughts turned to surviving. She couldn't physically win against this creature. All she had was the power of her brain but even that was shrinking into submission.

The motion of the waves gently rocked the boat, swaying her to and fro in a never-ending rhythm. Where did all the waters of the seas go? Did they remain a moving mass within themselves or did they travel always, never resting, never going anywhere? She thought that one day every drop of water in the seas would have their turn to gently caress land when calm, and thrash against distant shores, beating and eroding when angry and disturbed.

She didn't know if she were calm or angry now; she didn't know if she should caress the situation or beat it; she had given up hope and with it resigned herself to her fate. But something deep inside was urging her to fight, to stand up, to challenge. But how could she? It was all so hopeless. And on the other hand she couldn't just sit around and let him kill her without a struggle. No she wouldn't make it that easy.

Stripping off her clothes she took a shower, letting the water cleanse away the horror of her nightmares, the resignation and the defeatism. And after the cleansing, the revitalisation, the challenge, the desire, the grit, the feeling that a new day brings; the will to live returned. When she stepped out of the shower her resolution had returned, she would survive somehow.

He waited until the sun was up before putting his plan into action. Whether or not she handed over the money she would die, he had decided that. After all she was responsible for his jobless state. And she was the one who was the cause of the upheaval in his life. He had just escaped arrest himself when the anti-narcotics police burst the Garcia Cartel, and forced him out of a very lucrative sinecure. No, she would pay, she would pay dearly, and she would pay with her life.

In a way he was perversely sad because he did admire a woman with spirit and this woman, Findlay, possessed spirit. He even believed that, through time, he could make her love him, but sadly, he could not take that chance.

Nobody else knew about the money; only Garcia and himself, and Garcia wasn't in a position to do anything about it, now that he was securely locked up in prison awaiting trial for drugs trafficking. He didn't know where she had the money stashed, but he would certainly find out; she would break sooner or later. He didn't have much time to work on her because he wanted to step into Garcia's shoes before anyone else.

With the help of the million, he would start off where Garcia finished and become one of the biggest drug barons. After all, he had learnt all about the business from Garcia. He had done Garcia's dirty work; he knew the areas where he could begin again and had all the contacts. It would be so easy and he wouldn't let anything stand in his way. He was certain he would be able to terrorise her into submission and to hand over the money. Were women not weak? They didn't like violence.

He went to the fish boxes where kilos of raw meat had been stored and carried a good quantity to the deck area. Sharks had been swimming around all morning, about half a mile out, and to attract them nearer the boat he chucked large chunks overboard and waited. As soon as they scented blood they would come and this should make his message clear to the woman. He waited for a bit before he went for her, and to his surprise, she looked refreshed and exuded an air of confidence. Not what he would have expected from a woman who had been locked in a cabin for over twelve hours.

No matter, he thought, the sight of the sharks would be sure to weaken her resolve and soon he would have her pleading for her life. It was all so easy.

"Good night's sleep?" he inquired, with a charming smile.

"Yes, thank you, I did," Emma, answered, equally as politely.

He handed her a coffee and toasted bread, which she accepted with charm and grace. Two can play this game, she thought, recognising his affable disposition as a mere decoy to put her off guard.

There was a light swell running with only a few whitecaps dotted here and there. At least the weather appears to be kind today, she reflected. She looked towards the horizon. No land was in sight and too far out to make a swim for it. She would die of exhaustion if the sharks didn't get her first. Thinking about sharks reminded her of his threat. Then she became aware that he had started to throw pieces of the rotting red meat overboard. If that's meant to unnerve me he's certainly succeeding, she thought to herself.

He was watching her closely now, waiting for the fear, the panic to show on her face, but to his disappointment nothing was visible. Her mouth was dry and she took a sip of coffee, hoping that he would not recognise the symptoms of a nervous twitch breaking through. She felt she was outwardly shaking and suffering from an uncontrollable spasm of hysteria.

Now she saw the grey shark fins cutting through the water like steel blades as they approached their appetisers, just enough to whet their appetite and come back for more. Help, help; her inside screamed. Lopez moved from the rail and faced her now. She looked around the deck for some sort of weapon, but could see nothing. Only a coil of old rope lay on the deck and she certainly couldn't make use of that.

"Well, Ms. Findlay, what have you decided, the money or the sharks," he leered, showing signs of brutality.

"You make the call now from the radio phone and I promise to return you to your friends, safe and unharmed. But if you refuse, you will be the next offering to the sharks."

He was beginning to enjoy himself now. The sharks were now gliding around the boat, in frenzy, this way and that, confused and hungry all at the same time. She counted five of them; she shivered at thought of their snapping jaws tearing her body, ripping it apart; and when would death finally come? Would she pass out quickly with shock and feel no pain? Oh God, please, she almost cried out. Stall for time, think, and think, there must be a way.

"If I agree to your demands, how can I be certain you will return me to Cardenas, and not just throw me to the sharks?" she heard herself ask, but didn't recognise her petrified voice.

"You have my word."

"Of an honest man?" she questioned, now rising slowly and moving towards the rail.

"Do be careful, senora, we don't want you to fall overboard, before you have made the transfer," he jeered, enjoying the situation even more.

She could hide her aversion no longer.

"Look, you stupid lump of stinking shit, I have no intentions of handing over the money. I may die here, but you!! You won't see any of the money, not a dime," Emma retaliated, finding her voice. "You can go to hell."

He was stunned for a moment by her audacity. Why was she doing this? She should be on her knees begging for her life, the bitch. He had made his plans, he needed that money, and she could not do this to him. A mere woman, a bitch, would not foil him. He would not allow her to ruin everything; this was not how it was supposed to happen.

He felt himself losing control; his anger was taking over and the pain in his head had come back again. He wanted to smash her, hurt her. The mad pain grew stronger until he lost control of all reasoning. She was hurting him now with her defiance and she would pay. The only thought that entered his head was to hurt her back and strike out, hit her, smash her.

He leapt across the deck in a blinding rage, his face now contorted and twisted, his hands outstretched in front of him, ready to grab at her throat and squeeze the living breath out of the bitch's body.

Emma saw the twitching creature hurling himself towards her; she was terrified of the wild thing that was no longer human as it lurched out for her, ready to destroy her. All she could do at the last moment was to drop down onto the deck and curl up into a ball. She covered her head in her hands in an endeavour to save herself from the blows that were just about to rain down.

Staying in that position for a few seconds, she became aware that all had gone quiet. The blows weren't forthcoming, she couldn't bring herself either to move or open her eyes. But slowly she began to uncurl and opened her eyes, expecting him to be towering above. When her eyes were fully open she couldn't see him anywhere. Where had he gone? Cautiously standing up and looking about, she was amazed that he was nowhere around. She had a dreadful feeling that he would lurch out suddenly from some corner or other. But it wasn't until she heard agonising screams for help coming from the water that she realised what had happened. In his blind fury he must have tripped on the coil of rope and fallen overboard.

Quickly going to the railing, she cautiously looked over the side and there he was, splashing about in an uncontrolled and frantic seizure, kicking at the water and calling out for help. She couldn't move; she was frozen still in camera, a still photograph, as the realisation of what was happening flashed across her mind. The sharks were closing in now, charging at the wriggling, splashing human target, like torpedoes homing in on their predetermined course.

"Help me, help me!" the wild cries tolled out.

She was confused. Only a few seconds ago he had been determined to throw her to the sharks. So, how could she help him, now? But at the same time she couldn't just stand by and watch him as the sharks battered and ripped him to death. She, at least, had to do something for him. Then she remembered the rope. She grabbed it in her fumbling shaking hands, searching frantically for an end to throw. The shark made its first attacking manoeuvre, colliding with its quarry and carrying him through the water.

"Oh, Christ, my leg."

One after the other, they made their attack on the man, hitting their target with radar precision, dragging and bashing him around in the blood stained water. She was in the process of throwing the line to him when she saw the top half of his body being thrust upwards, high out of the water and far enough to show that the lower part of his torso was no longer there. It was a mass of bloody meat and then within seconds it disappeared into the blood red pool; she saw nothing but red, red, red all around where he had disappeared. She threw up as the horror of it all turned her stomach.

She rushed from one side of the boat to the other in futile search, but only a pink tinge remained where he had last been seen. She continued to stare at that spot as the sea lapped, diluting the blood red water to pale. She sat with her head in her hands, sobbing uncontrollably. Whether her emotional state was from witnessing the horrible death of a human being, torn apart, limb from limb or from relief that she wasn't the one to perish out there.

How long it took, she had no idea, before her senses returned and became aware that she was totally alone with the ocean, lost. She was also on a boat about which she had very little knowledge. But she couldn't just sit here in the middle of the Caribbean Sea and hope that some boat or other would happen by and come to her aid. Looking out to sea, now, she noted that the swell, if anything, was building up and there appeared to be more whitecaps dotted about, with a spray blowing from the top of the waves.

"Heavier weather approaching," Emma said out loud.

Yes, she decided somehow she would have to start the engines and make for Cardenas. Emma knew nothing about boats and with her ignorance came the fear of that knowledge.

"I hope this thing comes with an instruction manual," she tried a nervous joke as she headed to the cockpit.

However, on studying the control panel, to her relief, all the dials and switches had their function printed clearly underneath.

"This shouldn't be too difficult at all," she reflected, as she set about familiarising herself with the purpose of the instrumentation before attempting to fire the engines.

The sea had been calm all morning as they headed for what they had indeed discovered was a fishing vessel. And now setting the navigational instrumentation on course for the second boat to the east, they were under way again in their search for Emma and The Katiya.

Julian noticed, but said nothing to the others, that the wind's strength was increasing and the gentle swell was beginning to build higher. However, he reckoned that there would be plenty of time to check the other vessel out before the seas worsened, forcing them to abandon the search and head for a sheltered haven.

"We're about ten miles off now, and we'll be able to see her shortly," Juan announced from the fly bridge.

They were once again eagerly scanning the horizon for the first glimpse of what they hoped would be the Katiya. Sonya stood anxiously beside Juan and the other two were in the cockpit.

"That boat has started to move," Julian called out, from the cockpit. He had been studying the screen for sometime. "And it seems to be heading back to Cuba."

"Yes, I can see her now," Sonya called back, pointing in its direction.

"Change course," he called to Juan, who was still in control on the fly bridge, "we should catch up with her in half an hour, and she doesn't appear to be moving fast."

"OK Mr. Julian," and he gave her full throttle.

Emma was deeply engrossed in the technicalities of the radar and navigation screens in front of her as she sat on the cockpit chair, fascinated and eager to be under way. She had worked everything out systematically. She was now ready for action. Turning on the main power switch, which she located after a brief search of the cockpit area, she selected the right hand ignition key, and started up the right hand engine. It burst into action, humming beautifully in her ears and then she fired the second engine in the same way. The noise of both engines turning over sounded so good to her, lifting her heart to warrant a few notes of 'A life on the Ocean Wave'.

From the screens in front of her, she now knew her exact position and in which direction she should be heading. The Katiya had been bobbing in the swell and drifting in the current thus indicating to Emma, in her limited knowledge, that she did not have to weigh anchor. She was all set. Slipping the gear sticks into forward, the Katiya began to move. She eased her gently forward, gathering speed slowly until she was confident enough to give it more throttle.

She had a panoramic view of the sea all around her, and an incredulous and heady feeling of self-mastery came over her as she took up position at the helm of such a luxurious boat. Well under way and able to relax somewhat, she noticed the radar screen was indicating another vessel in the area, to her port side, and thanked God that now she was not totally alone at sea.

She kept an eye on the radar and noticed it was heading towards her and within a short space of time was able to distinguish a small speck on the horizon. A feeling of joy overcame her as the anxiety, at being alone out at sea, was removed by the sighting of this other vessel.

When, eventually, it came alongside Emma could scarcely contain her joy. After she cut the engines, Julian, followed by Sonya and David came on board.

"How many times must I tell you not to go off on these extravagant day excursions," Julian scolded, trying to keep a straight face.

Emma glared back, anger flashing from her eyes at the thought of the unbelievable ordeal she had just experienced. It took a moment for the three of them to understand the significance, and they all burst out in nervous laughter with Juan looking on from the Boston Whaler, slightly bewildered at the sudden change of mood.

"All alone?" David asked, looking around as if some monster were about to leap out any minute.

Emma sat down and her face became serious again as the memory of it all flooded back. She reiterated all that had taken place since leaving the villa, the previous day. In disbelief they listened. At first they were unable to absorb the reality and too stunned to speak.

It was David who spoke first.

"I think, now, we have come to the end of our troubles," he affirmed, reflectively, and the foreboding feeling that had remained with him for days, vanished.

CHAPTER 29

It was three days after the fateful experience at sea, which had left all of them emotionally drained and exhausted, like limp sails on a broken mast, when David was forced to address the situation between him and Sonya. He had been procrastinating now for days, and was more than aware that the matter would need to be broached immediately, but somehow could not find the courage. It was not so much that he was tired from the recent, strange events, but more because he was acting cowardly, and it prevented him from being honest, not only with Sonya but also him.

There was no doubt in his mind about the feelings they had for one another. She had captivated his heart in the most delightful and loving way that he wanted to stay bound to her forever, and he knew, without a shadow of a doubt, that theirs would be a future filled with caring and loving happiness. But, at the same time, he was afraid to commit himself to any long-term involvement. One part of him longed to walk along that golden path full of dancing sunflowers to where the heart feels safe; and throwing caution to the wind, while the other part told him that the road was covered in poison ivy that would sting and hurt and scar him for ever. He was in a quandary and was unable to do anything about it. The stress and anxiety of his predicament consumed him so much that he had no control over his mind. He knew eventually he would have to explain to Sonya, as best he could, his conflicting emotions, which he could not quite understand himself, and as difficult as it may be, it would need to be done.

Sonya, this particular morning, had made herself scarce. In the last few days she had sought out things to do that normally would not have been her concern; anything to stop her mind from dwelling on David. She had spent more time in the kitchen with Eva and had pottered in the garden behind Juan. She had also taken it upon herself to spend more time in the company of Emma, who had been having secondary reactions to the nightmare of the seas and who sat quietly in the garden in silent sorrow. Only when Emma dozed off into a troubled sleep had Sonya wandered off herself to sit solitary on the beach with her own thoughts.

David was obviously avoiding her, confirming that he was about to give her the 'big push'. This thought began to fester, like a cancerous sore, destroying all the good feelings and reducing those fond memories they had shared together, to nothing. His recent coolness towards her, at first, had upset her and she could not understand the change in him.

Sonya closed her eyes for a moment to clarify a dark picture. She saw scales heavily weighted on her side with boundless love, and on the other side, David's was full of emptiness. What she saw, she could not handle.

Her first reaction was to simply disappear in the night and return to Caracas. But there, it would never be the same again; she didn't want to return to her old world and leave David. It didn't seem right, somehow; it felt wrong to leave him. She would be a stranger in her own country and she couldn't envisage herself fitting in anymore. However, she had a job to finish and, no matter how difficult that might be now, with resolve and expediency she would see it through to the end.

"There you are, Sonya, I've been looking all over for you," Emma said, almost in a childlike voice, interrupting Sonya's agony.

"Just enjoying the tranquillity," was Sonya's reply.

Emma had been so affected by the manner in which Lopez had died that she had withdrawn into herself, and was unaware of the happenings around her. The reality of what had taken place out there in the Caribbean had affected her some hours later, stunning and traumatising, and sending her to a place where she felt no pain. She thought about nothing past or present; she just was; in an unconscious dimension of self-adjustment. She had been totally oblivious of the unspoken drama between Sonya and David, and had she been herself over the last few days, she would have immediately recognised the signs.

Unaware of the passing of time that she spent in this void, Emma strove to understand a change within her that had neither a beginning nor an ending. She had undergone some sort of transformation, a metamorphosis. Without being able to analyse this change, she felt lost.

There was nothing bright and colourful in her world. Her heart was unable to rise to the magical highs, where the breeze took you beyond the ordinary, where the sun shone even on a bad day, where there was music when there was none. She seemed to be moving in slow motion, creeping along in restricted darkness, overcome by exhaustion, and the slightest of effort was a major task.

"How are you feeling, today?" Sonya queried.

Emma looked at her in puzzlement. Without understanding the insinuation, she simply looked at Sonya in silence.

"Come, we'll walk back together," Sonya suggested, and led Emma, who meekly followed her along the path towards the villa.

It was not until they had finally anchored the Sea Lady off the beach at the Villa Verde, that day, that Julian noticed any change in Emma. On the journey back, she had been naturally subdued and looked drawn and tense. But later the tension disappeared from her face, only to be replaced by a look of vagueness, as if a fever had taken her, dulled her brain and left her face expressionless.

At first, he had tried coaxing her out of the torment she was suffering. He had spoken to her gently saying that it was quite normal, under the circumstances, to feel the way she did and she would be fine in a few days. Getting no response he had tried bullying and badgering her into some sort of reaction, even anger. He had spoken sternly and cruelly, and was shocked that he had felt some sort of pleasure from inflicting harsh and unjust words upon her. He had told himself, he was doing it for her, to save her, but the perverted enjoyment he had derived from such actions had disturbed him greatly, and he had to walk away from the situation. Nothing worked and he resigned himself to the fact that, sooner or later, she would emerge from this half conscious state as the colourful butterfly she had been.

He now watched the two of them, Sonya followed by Emma, as they made their way from the beach towards the villa. He waved kindly to them, with an encouraging smile on his face, which was indiscernible at that distance, but he felt he had to do it anyway. They acknowledged his greeting, but made no attempt to approach him. Sadly, he understood. They were both united in their own sorrows.

He and David had spent some hours fishing during the last few days. They hadn't taken the Sea Lady out too far, because they were reluctant to go too far from the villa for any length of time. Neither he nor David was totally enthusiastic, but they did have some moments of satisfaction, especially when they caught their first marlin.

A quick glance at his watch told him it was almost lunch and quickly gathering the fishing tackle, leaving it on the aft deck, he proceeded towards the villa.

"Ah, here comes Julian, now," David remarked, to Emma and Sonya, from his seat on the veranda.

"How's it going?" Julian greeted to no one in particular.

"Fine," they chorused almost in unison.

"I've been sorting out the fishing equipment. You know, it wouldn't be a bad idea if we all went for a fishing trip tomorrow. We don't have many more days left, and we could take Juan."

"I'm game," announced David. "What about you?"

"Yes, I'd like that," Sonya replied.

"And what about you, Emma, do you feel up to it?" Julian asked.

"What do you mean, up to it? Of course I'm up to it," Emma retorted, indignantly, showing signs of irritation which took Julian by surprise.

"That's settled then," was all Julian could say.

After lunch they were taken aback when Emma announced she would be going to Cardenas as she had some business to attend to. They were speechless for a moment; it was as if they had been smacked across the mouth with a kipper. Emma's tone of voice left none of them in any doubt that she had returned to them. Even if they had been willing to challenge the sense of it, they dared not. Emma's self determination had resurfaced.

"Well, I'm going back to work on the boat," Julian announced, and Emma and Julian went their separate ways, leaving David and Sonya alone.

CHAPTER 30

The memory of what Emma had been through, the scarred tissue would remain with her for the rest of her life. It had made her tired, devoid of enthusiasm, energy and left her emotionally barren. With no definite direction, she felt like a cork bobbing in the water to be carried hither and thither at the mercy of the seas. She understood that she would never again be the same person, nor would she see things in the same light; how to differentiate between right and wrong, good and evil. Yesterday, all those matters were so clear and obvious; today, they were confused and muddled. The idea that somehow she might have been involved in the illegal business of drugs had horrified her a few days ago, but now, there was not the same aversion attached to it.

For the most part, decency and honesty had been her war cry. Her ethics, her moral principles had been sound. She had strayed a bit in the past, but nothing too bad. With all the temptations that had fallen at her feet, ripe for the picking, she had never been enticed into wrongdoing in a major scale.

Now, she began to wonder what life was all about; was it worth the sacrifice? Stand by your principles and integrity and get hurt, or go with the flow, take what you could when you could and fuck the rest of humanity; she didn't know; she was confused.

To sort out this conflict within, she had to begin somewhere, anywhere. So, that afternoon, when lunch was over, she made her mind up to retrace her movements and drive back along the road to Cardenas, where somehow it had all gone wrong.

Her legs were unwilling to get into the vehicle; they were like robotic extensions, stiff and deliberate. Only when the correct code entered her brain did they begin to operate in jerky movements. To drive back along the route to Cardenas and walk the streets, once more, scared the hell out of her. But she had to do it if she were ever going to recover from the haunting nightmare. Everything around her was threatening. The trees, flowers and birds were grotesque evil shapes, and she saw nothing comforting or beautiful in Mother Nature's creations.

Driving along the winding road, Emma saw in the trees wicked faced monkeys with gargoyle features; snakelike reptiles with large bodies slithering along the branches, reaching out with large tentacles to claim the lives of pterodactyl flying creatures; the mop heads of the silk cotton trees were in full concert, with gaping mouths, rasping out their displeasure at the floor show and the crane lilies with jaws like alligators were spewing out yellow custard.

She shook her head to try and rid herself of the horror movie show and, with each twist in the road, she saw Lopez in the form of the devil, laughing as the flames from the burning bushes licked at his body, consuming him in a sea of bright red fire.

How she got to be sitting in a cafe, in Cardenas, opposite a stranger, she didn't know. She couldn't remember driving there or for what reason. She wondered if any of the others had accompanied her, but dismissed that as she began to recall getting into the vehicle at the villa.

"Time to head back," she said, to no one in particular, not that there was anybody paying attention to her anyway.

David explained, as best he could, why he would be returning to Glasgow, alone, and the more he searched for the correct words, the more tongue tied he became. He saw the hurt expression on Sonya's face, which only made matters worse, and he stuttered and stammered his way through pathetic insincerities, voicing only his reasons for his decision.

"I'm hurting myself as much as I'm hurting you," he said, trying to soften the blow and make it seem right.

"Is that supposed to make me feel good?" Sonya choked out, putting up her hand to halt any further discussions.

They sat in silence for a while and when Sonya was able to speak without bursting into tears, she coolly stated, "In that case since you seem to be well enough, I'll be leaving for Bogota, tomorrow." With that she went to her room to make preparations for her departure.

On arriving back at the villa, Emma went straight to the boathouse to find Julian, who was still tinkering around with the boat.

"Hello, darling," Emma called out, over the noise of the drill.

Julian switched off the power, and, as he approached her, was a little more than surprised when he saw that she appeared more like her old self. Her facial expression had brightness to it and the sparkle had returned to her eyes.

"Did you manage to complete your business?"

"Yes," she simply replied, "and what about you?"

"I think I'm finished here for the day."

"Great, how about a swim?"

Emma and Sonya stood patiently at the check-in counter, in Havana airport, for flight 1509 to Bogota. It had been the longest journey of Sonya's life. She had found no reason to say goodbye to David or, for that matter of it, to wish him all the best in the future. She simply, when the time had arrived, gathered her cases and got into the four by four. The fishing trip had been abandoned, that morning, due to the lack of interest and breakfast had been a laboured event. Sonya sulked in her room feigning a headache and David repeatedly tried to justify, to Emma and Julian, his weak reasons for non-commitment.

The queue moved slowly and, eventually, when tickets and passports had been checked, Emma and Sonya found no words that could express their feelings. They were rendered speechless. Just as they were nearing international departures, Sonya noticed a ball of commotion rolling its way towards them, like a fireball, and when it came to rest before them, out fell David, with his clothes and his hair in disarray.

"I couldn't go through with it, I couldn't let you go. All that stuff I said was wrong. I love you, Sonya; I want us to be together. Can you ever forgive me?"

Sonya too stunned at first, could merely gasp, "I don't believe it."

"I'm going with you to Bogota and then from there we're heading for Glasgow."

The three of them stared at one another unable to move as if their feet were somehow soldered to the tiled flooring.

It was Emma who recovered her senses first.

"Listen, you two, if you don't get a move on and quit moving with the fluidity of frozen treacle, you'll miss your flight." And she pushed the both of them through the cordon into international departures.

It was not until they were on the other side that it dawned on them what was happening and they turned round simultaneously and waved back at Emma, who, by this time, was finding it a bit difficult to suppress the tears that began to form in the corner of her eyes.

"Thank you, Emma, thank you for everything," she heard them call, over the heads of the crowd as they were carried along in the sea of humanity.

That night was a night to remember for Emma and Julian. They had lost one another somewhere in the course of the last few days, which made their rediscovery a sweet reunion. It was like finding each other for the first time. Their passionate lovemaking took them both to the very edge of the world and beyond, to the stars, to the celestial bodies.

Julian's feelings for Emma had never wavered and neither had Emma's. He was looking towards that day when they would share more of a life together; just another few assignments; a few more years; and then pleasant idleness, 'dolce far niente'.

Emma would savour this night forever.

"I love you, Julian," she said, quietly and he crushed her against him.

But those were merely words. Words could never express the way she felt. He meant more to her than life itself. His life meant more to her than her own. She would die for him, almost did and perhaps still would.

She could never tell him. He would never accept her decision. She thought it would be all over with the internment of Garcia and Sanchez, but sadly she was mistaken. People like that conducted their affairs from within the confines of prison, and as long as there was one remaining loyal lieutenant on the outside, it was business as usual. Garcia's web was universal and she was caught up in it. The stranger in the cafe at Cardenas was Garcia's man and he had made it blatantly obvious, that it was the deal or Julian's life. After all she had come through, she had no more energy left to fight back, not at the moment. Perhaps in time a solution could be found. She had traded her integrity for his life. They had bought her, not with money, but life itself. They, the drug Mafia had won; they had won this round.

This was their last night together and as she lay peacefully in his warm protective embrace. She knew she must leave him now and tears began to roll down her beautiful sad faceat what might have been.